Fire Scion II: The Flying Dead

By Kathe Todd

The events in this novel begin approximately one year after the end
of Fire Scion I: The Hidden City

Chapter 1: Arrival

It was midafternoon in early summer, and the weather was not unusual for this season in Waterdon: rain poured down out of skies thick with dark nimbus clouds. On the road below Drakespring Farm two figures suddenly shimmered into existence, unnoted by anyone on the deserted stretch of highway. They were clad nearly identically in fine fabric trousers, leather tunics, polished leather boots, and light cloaks; but one was head and shoulders taller than the other.

"Damn!" Andi Drakespring exclaimed, holding his hands over his head and crouching as he ran through the mud for the house. Whooping and laughing, he and his companion hurried inside to stand dripping on the polished wooden floor in the farmhouse's front room. The room did duty for kitchen, dining, and relaxing, and as they came in four faces looked up from around the table. Bernadette had been knitting, Riki reading a book as Erik and Sigi played their favorite card game.

Bernadette jumped to her feet, face wreathed in a smile, and went to greet the newcomers. "Andi, Mothris, you're finally back! How did it go in Mzalendtham?" Realizing they were soaked, she settled for squeezing their hands instead of giving hugs. That could wait for later.

"Pretty well," Andi replied, hanging up his dripping cloak as Mothris did the same. "Is there anything to eat?"

"Sure," she smiled at her son and the leukalfar boy who had become like another son to her. He had gotten released from his position as an acolyte of Apoldros at the Eparchy shortly after they'd all returned from their adventure in Mrzhgradfendz and its mirror city Mrzhandtham, late last summer. He'd been living with the Drakesprings since then, though he and Andi were often away on business. The two of them had become an outreach team, contacting leukalfar tribes across Iscandia and working with them in the effort to bring them into human society once again.

The boys sat at the table, where they were greeted and hugged by its other occupants. Riki liked Mothris and was glad he'd become part of their family. He was nice, respectful, and a little shy – though his personality and manners were beginning to loosen up a little after more than a year of hanging around with Andi.

For Erik and Sigi, so alike in spirit, it was "the more's the merrier." They were happy to have their loving family increase still more, and Andi's close companionship with the leukalfar boy helped to make up for the fact that he and Fjuri weren't able to spend as much time together these days. His best friend since earliest childhood had been sent right back to work on the construction crew, his parents more than a little miffed at him for running off with Andi on that harebrained quest – even if the ultimate result of it had been a new life of freedom for thousands of formerly enslaved leukalfar.

Bernadette hastily whipped up a platter of sandwiches and a bowl of potato crisps, along with a couple of tall glasses of milk. Mothris had never tried the stuff before coming here, but he'd acquired a taste for it. He was already a couple of inches taller than when they'd first met him, making Bernadette wonder just how long the alfar adolescent growth spurt might be.

She sat down and put her arm around her tall son, giving him a squeeze, as he seized a sandwich in both hands and practically inhaled it. He was well past his sixteenth birthday now and the constant hunger that had plagued him a year earlier was beginning to ebb; but they'd just fast-traveled a long distance, and he was still a very active young man.

When the boys had assuaged their hunger and nothing but crumbs remained on the tray, Mothris was the first to speak. "We've got Lambris installed there teaching Common, working with the sentries and foragers first, and Syendor is training in city living. I'm afraid there are going to be Deep leukalfar in the undercroft of that place for another generation at least, but the younger people are eager to embrace the new ideas we brought. Not to mention the trade goods!" he grinned.

Andi smiled, too. The bold plan heartily embraced by old Arctoris, when Bernadette and Andrion had proposed it to him during their first visit after the closing of the portal, had proven so far to be mostly a success – and he was proud of his part in it. Starting within Mrzhgradfendz, they had gotten Kziintke to conduct classes in the Common tongue until there was a core of people (both the original residents and their recently freed kin) with some proficiency in the language. Now teams were moving throughout Iscandia with maps provided by Andrion, contacting the leukalfar tribes that lived in or beneath nearly every dypalfar ruin in the province.

Not every tribe had welcomed the idea of occupying their cities in the way that the Mirskhrazana had theirs. Many cities were at least partially ruinous, their leukalfar residents camping inside them sheltered by yurts made of mandimant chitin. But the contact teams spoke their language, so were usually at least provided with hospitality and a hearing. Trade goods were the bait, and what they sought in every tribe was a foothold – people willing to learn the common tongue and begin trying to interact with the Sky People instead of just shooting them on sight.

The cities the leukalfar tribes had occupied for millennia, since the dypalfar who were once their masters had abandoned them, were in truth by the laws of the empire their property. But they had in a way forfeited their rights, falling prey to any adventurer able enough to kill the sentries and steal the treasures therein. What the Drakesprings were trying to do, working with many of the leaders of the Mirskhrazana, was to get the leukalfar race to rejoin human society, and claim their rights of ownership once more.

"Have you heard from Meri?" Mothris asked the room at large. Like Rezira, he'd finally adopted the Common convention of shortening people's full names into nicknames. Erik smiled his angelic smile, mirrored on the faces of Riki and Sigi.

"We got a letter from her just a couple of days ago," he rumbled, pride in his voice. "After they met the bigwigs at Odwyna and Undwin's party, there's been a flood of inquiries about their trade mission – including a couple of offers of quarters to rent. Looks like she and Liamdor will be setting up shop pretty soon. Oh," he added, eyes twinkling, "and she really hit it off with young Arnwin."

Arnwin, the son of Eorl Odwyna of Mountmarch and her second husband Undwin, was close to Sigi's age. Odwyna had long been friendly toward Bernadette and had attended her wedding (accompanying her first husband, the late Eorl Bergen), so it hadn't been hard to get her to agree to throwing a party for the elite of the march at which Meri and the plump Chanter of the Mirskhrazana had been the honored guests.

This was the other half of the outreach effort, bringing leukalfar presence to the cities of men and alfar. Once people got used to seeing leukalfar walking around dressed like them, speaking their language, and engaging in the same pursuits of daily life as themselves, they would be a lot less likely to assume they were fair game.

"That's great!" Andi remarked, wiping his mouth on his sleeve and getting a reproving look from his mother. "Say, is…"

"…Rezira around?" Riki finished for him with a knowing grin. Her brother's romance with the beautiful, exotic dypalfar girl was the source of some amusement for her, an opportunity to tease him – and the source of occasional sighs as she considered the utter barrenness of her own love life. So far, it seemed that the boys were mostly afraid to speak to a red-gold beauty standing five-foot-eight inches tall. And still growing.

Andy's expression told her that was exactly what he'd been going to ask. Riki relented. "She's right down the hall in the craft room, working with Papa Andrion, Gylabris, and Kziintke on some project. Why don't you…"

"Thanks, sis!" Andi exclaimed, and was out the door to the hallway before she could finish her sentence. The rest of the people gathered around the table exchanged grins.

Chapter 2: Research and Development

Andi hurried through the open door of the craft room, and took in the scene inside. Gylabris and Kziintke were working at something on a bench, while Rezira (dressed in supple leathers that fitted her slender but curvy form like a glove) stood to one side, guiding them in what they were doing. Papa Andrion was at a desk on the other side of the room with a stack of books, evidently researching something.

Rezira turned her head at his step and her tip-tilted violet eyes lit up at the sight of him – as did his on spying her. They met in the center of the room and he enfolded her in a deep hug. He was now looking his father in the eyes and might still have more growing to do –he had already overtopped his sweetheart by nearly a foot. "Oh, Andi! I've missed you!" she murmured into his chest. She was now fluent in Common as well as in leukalfar and dypalfar, but spoke it with a slight, lilting accent that only made her seem more desirable to him.

The dypalfar girl, the only person of her race now living in Agena so far as anyone knew, had been resident for the past several months at the Maiden with the family of the innkeeper Drelos Elendion. The alfar family, which included his wife Larissa and their daughter Sintra, were happy to have another "daughter" added to their household; and she and Sintra weren't too far apart in age.

As a result of spending time at the Maiden Rezira had met many males of the races of men and alfar alike who did not look anything like dypalfar; but in that time her feelings for Andi had gone much deeper than the sharp initial attraction that she'd felt on their first meeting. He was still the only one for her, and she for him.

After their embrace Andi put his arm around Rezira and they walked back to where the little leukalfar Keeper and his sentient automaton were working. "Gylabris, Kziintke, good to see you back!" he said. "What diabolical mischief are you up to now?" Learning the Common tongue seemed to have freed Gylabris from some of the stilted formality that was a hallmark of his race, and he smiled at his young friend without taking the remark amiss.

Andrion looked up from where he'd been searching for a particular passage and smiled. "Hi son, remember me?" he joked. He couldn't really blame the boy for failing to notice a mere father when there was a vision like Rezira in the room, though their young love gave him a bit of a pang. Man-alfar relationships were doomed by the two human species' different lifespans, but he and his marriage mates had agreed it was best not to point this out to the youngsters.

"We're making a magic-block collar like the one Szursta put on you, in fact," Andrion went on. Andi's face took on a look of alarm.

"Why?" he asked. He had found wearing that to be one of the most unsettling things he had experienced in his life, and he'd been in some pretty odd situations for a kid his age.

"It's a lifesaving device, if you think about it," his father replied. "How else can you neutralize a hostile mage long-term without killing him or her?"

Andrion got up and joined them at the workbench where Gylabris and Kziintke were finishing their delicate work. "Rezira already got it enchanted," he explained. "The technique they use in Remus will let you apply any spell you know to any weapon or wearable item that could take it. But the hardware has been a little bit trickier, setting it so that the spell only operates while the collar is locked and activated."

"I think that's it!" Gylabris said excitedly. He picked the device up off the workbench and held it out for inspection. It did look very much like the one Andi had least seen around the neck of Szursta Bagrum, Rezira's mom, before she went back through the portal to the dypalfar world – never to see her daughter or the rest of them again. To Andi's surprise, the little tinkerer clasped the collar around his own scrawny neck, pulling the ends together until there was an audible "click" and the jewel-like indicator glowed red.

"Oh my," Gylabris said, looking a bit surprised. "Oh, that does feel very odd!" Most leukalfar Keepers also possessed some magic, though few of the Mirskhrazana had ever used it for much. They'd been mostly without enemies for many generations, even those of the long-lived alfar. "You can take it off me now, Kziintke," the little Keeper requested with a touch of anxiety. The gleaming seven-foot robon held up a little key in the delicately-constructed fingertips he'd had fitted, and in moments the collar was open and Gylabris set it back down on the workbench with a sigh of relief.

He looked a little rueful as he said, "That was really very disconcerting. I could still sense my magical energy, but it was as if there was an invisible wall preventing me from using it." Andi grinned at him.

"Exactly right," he said. "Did I tell you I wore one of those things for a couple of days while I was held captive in Mrzhandtham?"

The group in the room broke up into a discussion of their success. Every guard cadre in every town and city in Iscandia, probably throughout the empire in fact, was going to want at least one of these on hand for restraining prisoners with magical abilities – and they would fetch a pretty penny. As the materials and the expertise were supplied by the dypalfar via the leukalfar, the proceeds would all go to help finance the leukalfar initiative to reclaim the cities they inhabited. Most would need massive amounts of repair work before they were livable again.

Rezira clasped hands with Gylabris, Andrion, and Kziintke. "I should be getting back to the Maiden," she said regretfully. "Drelos, Larissa, and Sintra are expecting me to join them for dinner." Andi put his arm around her again and they walked down the hall to the nursery, which was deserted at this hour. With Meri away in Sylvanian Sigi had the large room to himself, though Gylabris usually bunked here when he was visiting.

They proceeded to the room's eastern end, where a door gave out onto the veranda that ran across most of house's length facing the Brightwater and the mountains to the east. Stepping out onto the veranda, they found the rain was still coming down pretty hard. "Wait awhile, Zira," Andi said as he squeezed her tight to his side. "If it doesn't stop pretty soon I'll get us some cloaks and walk you down there." She smiled up at him, eyes shining. The pet name had come easily to his lips not long after they'd met, and she loved to hear it.

They sat side by side in the middle of the settee, feet on the low padded bench that did duty as a footstool, enjoying the cool breeze that came in and watching the rain fall on the slope before them. Good for the crops, Andi thought idly – though he'd been so busy this past year his concern for the farm and the chores it entailed had receded somewhat.

Andi squeezed Zira tight, and turned his head to her as she raised her face for a kiss. The painful confusion such contact would have inflicted on him a year ago had faded away, but being this close to the girl he loved still filled him with powerful feelings – feelings he didn't yet know how to deal with.

For his sixteenth birthday last winter, Mom had given him one of her "special" amulets, identical to the one she'd worn for as long as he could remember (other than that time when she first turned into a dragon, and had forgotten to put it back on right away when she was human again – about nine months before Sigi was born). When she gave it to him she'd looked him in the eye and said "This is for your protection, and the protection of those you love. Be responsible, and be kind."

Again, he had turned to Papa Erik for advice on the subject. Erik had smiled, a look of fond remembrance on his face, and said "I'd been wearing one of those for years before I met your mother. After we were together, I gave it away." He'd given him some details about how the amulet worked, but seemingly it was up to Andi to take his own education beyond that. And he wasn't sure he was ready to do so. Zira certainly didn't seem to be anxious to rush things, but sometimes after necking with her he ached – for what, he wasn't sure.

As they sat there snuggling close and kissing occasionally, the rain stopped and the clouds broke up – golden sunlight streaming in from the west to bathe the mountaintops in glory. It was so beautiful they just sat there awhile longer, before reluctantly getting to their feet. Then they picked their way down the slope to the road, and set off along it to the Bathing Maiden a quarter of a mile to the north.

Chapter 3: Riki Goes Shopping

The following day Riki shouldered her pack and stepped out the door, calling "Bye, Mom! See you after lunch!" Bernadette waved her tall daughter out the door and returned to her cheese-making. Outside, Riki paused to watch for a few moments as her two papas, dressed in full armor, sparred with wooden swords on a level patch of dirt off in the direction of the cistern tower.

Boy, they were something. Other than observing them on hunting trips Riki had had no real-life experience of the weapons prowess that was embodied in the two men she called "papa." But even if they *were* creaking on the edge of senescence (Erik now forty-three, Andrion fifty), they could still put on a hell of a show with those practice swords. Though Erik was three inches taller and considerably younger, Andrion still had grace and a turn of speed that made it hard for the bigger man to get through his guard. Riki thought, with a touch of pride, that her papas could probably still kick the asses of any four young adventurers hanging around the Flying Horseman up in Waterdon. And that was *without* using any magic.

They were engrossed in their exercise session and paid her no mind, so she soon turned and went down the walk to the road. Those leathers Rezira had on yesterday had looked so hot, Riki had decided to wear her current set of fitted leather armor for the trip to town – a change from her usual garb of workaday trousers or skirts, a blouse, and perhaps a vest. All the Drakesprings had their clothing custom crafted for them by old Gerde Snowhair, who'd begun sewing clothes for Riki's mom before she was born. Having never known anything else, she was completely unconscious of her family's wealth.

This latest set of finely crafted armor, made not by Gerde but by Mom, was nearly unworn. It wasn't as if Riki had a lot of occasions to be armored up and going into battle! She was more likely to fantasize about being a pampered princess, dressed in silks and velvets and being waited on hand and foot (*not* milking cows and mucking out paddocks!), than to envision herself as a warrior like her "cousin" Anja. But today she was going into Waterdon by herself with a long shopping list in hand, and she felt sort of martial. She'd even brought her bow along, just in case there were any shria or bandits lurking along the way.

Riki greeted the guards on either side of the main gates of Waterdon with a smile. "Good morning, Jurgen! How's it going, Rolf?"

"Morning, Miss Drakespring," Jurgen replied. He wasn't a great deal older than she was, maybe three or four years, and though all she could see of him was his eyes she sensed that she had made him intensely uncomfortable for some reason. Good.

Inside the gates Riki spied her friend Julia, working away at Valkyrie. The jolly times of childhood, when she and Julia and Sintra had been almost inseparable, seemed to have vanished just under a year ago. She'd always had some farm chores to do, of course, but now both Julia's and Sintra's parents had decided that it was time for their daughters to join the adult world. And that meant spending a large part of each day working.

Julia's mom Alessia was working at the forge while Julia was at the bench, improving a set of steel plate armor. Not wanting to get her friend in trouble, Riki stopped by just long enough to say hello. She greeted Alessia respectfully, sent her regards to Julia's father Wolaf (who usually manned the counter at the store inside), then continued on her way. Wow, she thought, Julia's catching up with me in height.

Wolaf was very nearly the size of Papa Erik, though dark of hair. His daughter was not exactly pretty, with her dark brown hair and medium blue eyes, nose perhaps a bit on the strong side; but she was young and healthy and what you might call a "strapping lass." Riki figured that Julia would have no trouble finding somebody to take her away from all this, assuming she didn't really want to take over the family business.

Feeling strong and independent and joyful on this beautiful summer morning (yesterday's rain long past), Riki continued up Waterdon's main street. She did not stop in to visit at Brightsgate Cottage. Fjuri and Bjorn would be working at the current job site, off where Waterdon was creeping ever westward across the plains. Lifa and Edla would be on their own, no doubt involved in some household chore or another. Riki spared a moment's regret for Edla, missing her friend Meri. At only about twelve years of age, Meri had been drafted into the effort to bring the leukalfar race back into human society – and it meant she was often away from home.

Reaching the bend in the road, Riki went into The Potent Potion. Adele, getting old, had sold her business and retired back in Remus a couple of years ago now. But the name had stayed, as the local people were familiar with it. In fact she had sold it to Bernadette, an investment that had paid off already.

Bernadette in turn had sold a quarter-interest to Lucia Bertolini, a young transplant from Remus who'd brought with her a quantity of gold to invest. Lucia stayed in the living quarters at the shop and dealt with the customers, while Bernadette reaped the lion's share of the profits and could obtain most of the chemial ingredients she needed without paying for them. Bernadette's skill in chemia was such that she rarely needed any potions she couldn't make herself.

Riki went into the shop and greeted Lucia, a pretty woman perhaps ten years her senior. She had the dark eyes and hair, and the olive skin, so common among the natives of her home province. Lucia smiled in genuine pleasure to greet the lovely daughter of her business partner. "Hello, Riki! What can I do for you?" Riki produced Mom's shopping list, and the older woman studied it.

"I'm afraid not all of these have come in," she said, "but I'll get you what I can. You should tell your mom to consider sending some foragers out." This was Waterdon's only chemia shop, and the city got many travelers. But even so, the rarer ingredients were frequently hard to obtain unless you had people out looking for them. Mom had told Riki that in her younger days she had collected every ingredient she could get her hands on, in the course of questing around the province. But she rarely had time for it these days.

Riki's pack was somewhat heavier as she left the shop. Now, for the market square. Even on a farm, you didn't always have every ingredient you might want for a meal growing outside the door. And Bernadette had provided her daughter with a list, along with the suggestion to buy anything that looked likely. She was trying to teach all her children to be cooks, seizing inspiration from whatever was to hand. So far, none of them had shown a lot of enthusiasm.

Riki strutted across the square head up, long red-gold hair streaming behind her. The armor made her feel competent and powerful somehow, not a simpering helpless girl but a woman to be reckoned with. With her height, and her still-slim but increasingly lush body lined with the muscles from years of farm labor, she was an awe-inspiring sight. No one in that square who didn't know her doubted for a moment that here was a young adventuress, a warrior woman who could leave you dead at her feet if the notion took her. People got out of her way.

One did not. Alfmund Thorenson, arrived from Coldstein only a week before and already accepted as a recruit at Ynglingar, took one look and his heart was swept away. "By Agnar!" he cried in his bluff Norse voice, "What goddess is this who walks the earth before me?" Torn from her zone of aloof power, Riki turned her head to see a friendly-looking face. Pale skin and gray eyes sat beneath a thatch of sandy hair, the nose somewhat broad and turned up. Overall, his expression warmed her to her core, though his words seemed a trifle… *dramatic*.

Still in her role as the devastating warrior woman, Riki sized the young man up. He didn't look to be more than a few years older than she was, as she inspected him more closely. He was wearing standard steel-and-leather-armor, and had a greatsword sheathed behind his back. Not bad, really… "You are speaking to Erika Drakespring," she said in a voice dripping hauteur. Oh, this was fun! "And you are?..."

Alfmund dropped to one knee, head bowed. "I am Alfmund son of Thoren, of the city of Coldstein, my lady Drakespring." He had not been in town long enough to have learned of the Drakesprings, she realized from his lack of reaction to her name. At this point Riki's script ran out. That had all been entertaining, but she had no idea what her next line was supposed to be.

"Um," she said, trying to maintain her composure, "well met. May I ask what brings you to Waterdon?" He clearly had not been around until recently.

Alfmund rose to his feet, and took a step closer to look down at her. He was close in height to Andi, Riki realized, though shorter than Fjuri. It was so nice to be looking *up* at a man! "I have just enrolled with the Brave Company, at Ynglingar!" he said, gesturing toward the handsome mead hall on the level above to their right. Riki glanced up briefly, then her gaze returned to Alfmund's gray eyes. They were lighter, cooler, than her mother's, yet still brimming with good cheer. His boyish face smiled down at her.

"Have you been long in Waterdon, Erika?" he asked. Before she could answer he went on, "The Brave Company are always looking for good fighters, valiant heroes to aid the cause of Right. Perhaps you might join us?" Riki stifled the urge to snort. The Brave Company were little more than an organized band of adventurers, who obtained a small living from commissions to kill bandits, recover stolen property, exterminate nuisance wildlife, or rescue kidnaped family members. Though their traditions were long, the time of their glory was far in the past. Or so she'd been told by Mom and Papa Andrion.

"Actually," she said coolly, "I am a native here. And I'm little inclined to be joining the Brave Company." Alfmund was taken aback at this rebuff, but it wasn't long before he had recovered.

"Ah," he said, his boyish smile undiminished, "perhaps then you might be willing to guide this poor traveler, teach me what I should know about Waterdon and its environs." What a tongue the boy had on him, Riki thought – and then thought, this guy is years older than me! Why am I thinking of him as a boy?

It was approaching noon, a little early for lunch; and Riki had still not done her grocery shopping. But she was captivated by this Alfmund. His interest in her was so palpable, and it made her feel so grown-up and powerful. "I could possibly," she said, maintaining her pose as a far older and more sophisticated woman, "be able to spare you some time. Might we take the midday meal together?"

The way his eyes lit up was something to see. By the gods, Riki thought, scarcely believing the morning's turn of events, I think this guy is in *love* with me! A pity she'd never seen that look from Fjuri. Alfmund clasped her hands, a rather familiar gesture but she let it pass. "Let's go to the Flying Horseman!" he said eagerly, "I'll buy!"

An hour later much had been revealed. Alfmund was eighteen, the younger son of a member of the Coldstein city guard. Well-trained in arms since childhood, Alfmund had yet not wished to follow in his father's footsteps – so he had come here seeking a career of honor with the Brave Company.

For her part, Riki had confessed that she was still living at home with her parents. She had even admitted that there were three of them along with a confusing collection of siblings, but had not actually spelled out that she was but fourteen years of age. Alfmund was charming, Alfmund was sweet, and he was clearly taken with her. How could she just turn him away? It was the most attention a boy (or man) had paid to her in her life, not counting the love and devotion she'd enjoyed from her two papas.

They parted outside the Horseman with an agreement: Alfmund would call on her this afternoon at her home, and (assuming parental permission had been granted) escort her for supper at the Bathing Maiden. Even her family's connection with the Maiden Riki had not admitted, and as she bade Alfmund farewell (receiving a kiss on the hand, no less!) and resumed her quest for groceries in the market square ahead, Riki's mind was churning with anxiety. She felt as if she were, somehow, operating under a false identity.

Chapter 4: Mordendaal

Ricard crept down the dimly-lit corridor, Ragnar at his back. He could hardly believe they were here, in this ancient Norse ruin that had likely not heard the footsteps of living men in thousands of years. His bow was at the ready, a fine elven arrow held to the string, all his senses alert. Living men may not have trod here since long before he was born, but he had no doubts they would discover plenty of the undead. This was just the sort of place to be crawling with aptrgangr, and lots of plunder to be taken as well.

It had been the merest chance that had put them onto it, as he and his questing companion had been trekking through the mountains in search of a cave where a group of bandits were supposedly holding some townsman hostage. They'd found the cave, and the bandits (who were now no longer in need of any of the loot they'd amassed, gods be praised). But if that withered corpse they'd found in a cell near the innermost reach of the cavern complex was who they feared it was, they would not be claiming the reward for the safe return of Goodman Ursteg.

It was while he and Ragnar were enjoying some of the spoils of their victory (a sizzling haunch of goat and a couple of bottles of superior wine) in the bandit chief's private quarters, that Ricard had discovered the chief's personal journal. Not all professional criminals were illiterate brutes, and this one (now lying in a heap with the rest of his band down one of the cave complex's corridors, stripped of their valuables) seemed to have been something of a scholar.

A page in the journal showed a map with the location of Mordendaal, which according to the late chief's notes was an ancient Norse ruin cut off from access to man since a landslide had buried the main entrance leading to it thousands of years before. Yet this bandit chief, it seemed, had learned of another possible way inside. From his wide (now two years long) experience of questing, Ricard knew that most ruins had multiple exits – though frequently only one entrance. The exits could not be opened from the outside, or in most cases even be seen until they'd been opened from within.

After he and Ragnar had sobered up Ricard had pocketed the journal and they'd traveled to the spot marked. To his surprise, they found the ancient carved stone door, half-covered in moss, exactly where the map had indicated. And some 30 paces away, also as indicated, had been the hidden switch to open it from the outside. The lever had been broken off in ages past, but by tying the handle of his war hammer to the stub with leather strips and using his full strength, Ragnar had gotten it to move.

The door had opened on a barren, dusty corridor – and ominously, had closed behind them as soon as they had stepped inside. At the end of the corridor a hallway led in both directions through a labyrinth of catacombs. Ricard declared they would go to the left, as he knew that the buried main entrance to the tomb complex was on their right.

Soon they found themselves fighting aptrgangr on every side. Usually no more than two or three out of ten corpses would arise at their approach, though; and the pair of seasoned warriors had no trouble defeating the stiff, recently-revived undead guardians. Most of those they returned to unmoving status were lightly armed with ancient Norse war axes or bows, arms scarcely worth carrying as their market value was negligible. But a few had items of jewelry, and some had been interred with pieces of gold.

After more than an hour of this, Ricard was getting impatient for the Big Payoff. Somewhere in this barrow complex they were going to find the chamber where the important people were buried, the ones with the valuable grave goods. The elven armor he was wearing now had been looted from just such a tomb – and he hoped that this one, possibly un-robbed since its original closing, might yield sablium.

At last they came to a portentous-looking set of carved double doors. "This is probably it," Ricard murmured to Ragnar. "Are you ready?" His Norse companion gave him an evil grin, longsword at the ready.

"Are they ready for *us*?" he replied. As they entered the room, the two bold adventurers slackened their pace. The chamber was… enormous. And on either side of a broad three-tiered dais, reaching back into the dimmest recesses of the room, the walls were lined with vertical sarcophagi like so many oblong tiles.

Crack! Crack! Crack! As the men stepped further into the room the covers shattered, releasing their occupants. Men and women, well-armored though sparsely fleshed, stepped forth to do their final duty in defense of this tomb. Ragnar, true Norseman that he was, went into a battle frenzy. "Victory or Asengard!" he bellowed, and swept out his steel longsword as he ran to meet the enemy.

The aptrgangr in his path fell swiftly at first, surprised by the sheer force of Ragnar's onslaught. But eventually he slowed, as more and more aptrgangr emerged from their tombs and gathered around him. Ricard leapt up atop a table on which treasure was strewn, and began picking their enemies off with his bow. He was a crack shot, and most he hit fell and did not get up again. But there were so many of them!

He saw Ragnar fall, knocked out by a blow that had sent his helmet flying. Now all the glowing eyes turned to him, and Ricard began firing faster. Could he stop them all before they reached him and tore him down from his perch? All of the sarcophagi around the room were empty now, their inhabitants having awoken and joined the battle. Once Ragnar was down they ignored him, and there were half a dozen now moving in their deliberate pace, clustered in a group and heading Ricard's way.

Ricard was Galise, and like all of his race he had a natural affinity for magic. It was the alfar blood, so they said; though he hadn't noticed it granting a longer lifespan. His own lifespan, which ought to have gone on for another fifty years or so, looked likely to be terminating in the next few minutes if he didn't do something fast.

Slinging his bow behind him for a moment, Ricard hurled a lightning spell. It had taken him years of practice with lesser battle spells to be able to cast this one. The clustered aptrgangr were hit hard, the bolt of lightning crashing into the one in the lead and then leaping from her to the next until all six of them had been struck. It didn't kill any of them, but knocked them back for a moment. He resumed his arrow barrage, bringing three of them down for good.

The remaining three were much closer now, and in desperation Ricard produced a magic scroll he'd been hoarding. Using a scroll in the heat of battle was always a bit of trick, but they could have powerful effects. He unleashed its fury squarely in the middle of the group, and the three aptrgangr found themselves on fire. The conflagration would burn for thirty seconds only, but he prayed to the gods it would be long enough.

Behind the burning aptrgangr, with a painful groan, Ragnar arose from where he'd been out cold on the stone floor and got to his feet. He had an unbelievable headache, and his vision was blurred. He had the presence of mind to reach for a healing potion, and moments later he found himself sharp and ready for action.

Just then the fire died, and the three aptrgangr standing between Ragnar and Ricard staggered onward. They were not what you might call canny adversaries, though they were certainly dogged. Ricard made eye contact with Ragnar, relief evident that his friend and partner was neither dead nor permanently disabled. Giving a piratical grin and not bothering to find his helmet, the Norse warrior charged his undead enemies with blade swinging.

Two of them went down, taken from behind and already close to being finished by the flames. The third was pierced in quick succession by two of Ricard's arrows. He had only a few left in his quiver, and was looking forward to retrieving some almost as much as he was looking forward to the treasures he expected this tomb would yield. The companions looked at each other across the fallen corpses of their enemies, grinning from ear to ear. Ricard was about to congratulate Ragnar on his timely revival when both of them heard a loud crack.

Inside his massive stone sarcophagus, Meiskomtot's eyes popped open in an instant. They were glowing red. His mind, sleeping these thousands of years, took a few moments to orient itself. He was lying in a stone box, he was… ah, now he remembered. He was dead. There had been an accident, a mishap… somehow he was entombed here, waiting for the moment to arise again. And the moment was *now*!

Ricard looked behind and up, toward the very top of the dais, where a magnificently-carved stone sarcophagus sat in a position of honor. The lid of that sarcophagus had been violently thrust aside, and a figure was rising from within it. This must be the Big Guy, the one whose mortal remains had occasioned the building of this entire barrow. The one with the good loot! He wasn't worried. He and

Ragnar had met overlords before. They were no match for his Galise skill and cunning combined with Ragnar's Norse muscle.

Ricard hopped down from atop the table, slapped his partner on the arm by way of congratulation for the job they'd just done, then stalked beside him as they approached the top level and the creature who had just climbed down out of his not-so-final resting place. Huh, he didn't look much like an overlord. Instead of the familiar elaborate helmet and sablium armor, this aptrgangr was clad in a suit of armor that seemed to be made up of overlapping bony plates. His face was obscured by a dully gleaming blue metal mask.

Ricard fired his last few arrows, but they appeared to have no effect – bouncing off of that scaly-looking armor. Realizing his quiver was empty the Galise decided to try a magical attack, instead. He fired lightning at their strange enemy, but again the attack seemed to slide away without touching him.

Ricard drew his blade, an elven short sword, as he and Ragnar closed the distance to their mysterious foe. The creature gave a raucous cry, and in an instant their weapons flew from their hands to lie on the floor of the room two tiers and some thirty feet below. The two hesitated, wondering what the hell to do next. With a glance at each other they turned as one and began a hasty retreat. The scale-clad figure followed them at a leisurely pace, and when they had nearly reached the room's exit he cried out once again – hurling them forcibly against the stone walls and knocking them cold.

Chapter 5: Meet the Family

By the time Riki returned home Erik was working in the forge and Andrion in the crafts room, while Bernadette was doing some laundry in the deeper side of their kitchen sink. She dropped off her groceries in the kitchen, putting a haunch of goat into the cold chest, then went down the hall to the crafts room to put away the chemial ingredients she'd bought.

Riki found Andrion, Gylabris, and Kziintke consulting on some project and greeted them briefly, before getting down the alphabetized, neatly labeled jars to replenish their contents. Bernadette's organized chemia lab made it easy for anyone to produce simple potions, a fact that had bitten her on the butt years ago. Andi had been able to produce the Potion of Dragon Transformation for himself when he was only a little past his sixth birthday.

Riki was still feeling pretty anxious about the planned visit from Alfmund this evening. Here she was fourteen years old, and she'd just sort-of picked up a man wandering around Waterdon's market square and invited him home. She'd better face the music and tell Mom and her papas about it before he showed up.

As she was still clad in her fitted leather armor, the sense of being a brave and powerful warrior woman had not entirely worn off. Riki gathered herself and decided to break the news to Erik first. If ever there was a man who on first glance might intimidate a suitor, it was Erik; but he was also the sweetest-natured and most easy-going of her three parents.

On her way back out to the forge though, Bernadette nabbed her. "Thanks for picking up those things, sweetie," she said over her shoulder, "Could you give me a hand with the wash, please?" After clothing had been washed and rinsed in the big double sink excess moisture was removed from it using a set of hand-cranked rollers mounted on the countertop.

Riki stifled a sigh, and went to stand beside her mother at the sink. She took the clean clothes out of the deeper tub and rinsed them in the shallower one, then handed each garment to Bernadette who ran it through the wringer before tossing it into a large laundry basket sitting on the floor. This household dirtied a lot of clothing and bed linens, and they usually did laundry almost any day the sun shone.

As they worked, Riki asked "Where are the boys?" Bernadette smiled up at her tall daughter.

"Sigi's down at the Maiden playing with Joqui," she said. "He's going to eat down there and have a sleepover, so we won't see him until tomorrow I guess." Riki started at this. So her little brother might be a spectator on her date with Alfmund, assuming she was even allowed to go out with him?

"Andi and Mothris went up to town to kibitz on Bjorn's construction project," her mom went on, blissfully unaware of Riki's thoughts. "They're going to bring Fjuri back here for supper." Worse and worse! Was everyone she knew going to be inspecting her new swain?

"What about Rezira?" she asked, wondering if she'd have to add the presence of that utterly gorgeous, petite and mysterious young woman to the already-embarrassing mix.

"So far as I know, she's not joining us," Bernadette said thoughtfully. "Though I hope she and Andi will get to spend a little more time together before he and Mothris are off again. They're picking up another team from Mrzhgradfendz and then going to Alfenstein to contact the leukalfar tribe there."

"I never thought I'd see him work so hard," Riki said thoughtfully. She half wished it were *her* gallivanting all over Iscandia with her very own magic map (Andi's birthday present from Papa Andrion), instead of here working her fingers to the bone with housework and farm chores every day.

When the last of the clothes were in the basket and the water drained, Riki asked "Want some help hanging it up?"

"No thanks," her mom replied, "I can take it from here."

"Okay, see you later!" she said, beating a hasty retreat out the front door. Across the yard, at their outdoor forge, Papa Erik was working shirtless with only a leather blacksmith's apron to protect him as he hammered up an order of elven short swords. While it was Bernadette's forgings that fetched top dollar at Valkyrie, there was a good market for lower- and mid-range arms and armor as well. Erik contributed around forty percent of what the Drakespring forge produced.

He looked up from his work to grin at his daughter as she came striding over, looking damn near martial in that getup. Riki was nowhere near as warlike as either of her parents, but he supposed she could do more than look the part if the need arose. She was long-limbed, strong from years of farm chores, good with a bow, and not completely useless with a sword. At the least, she ought to be able to protect herself from attack – even if she didn't go looking for trouble, the way he and Berni had done so often in their early days.

A closer inspection revealed that she hadn't just come out to watch him work or say hello – she had something on her mind. "What say you, dear daughter?" he asked, putting the sword he was working aside to cool. Time to spit it out. Riki hoped that starting on Erik would make talking about it to Mom and Papa Andrion easier, or maybe even unnecessary if she could get him to take up the subject with them himself.

"Um, Papa? I was up in Waterdon shopping…" He eyed her curiously. What was she so reluctant to tell him? She squirmed. "Anyhow! I was just walking across the market square and I ran into one of the Brave Company's new recruits, a nice Norse boy from Coldstein…"

"Boy?" he asked, cutting to the heart of the matter. "Are the Brave Company recruiting boys now?"

Riki flushed pink. The tendency to blush like a sunset was something she'd inherited from both her parents. "He's a man, really, I suppose – but he's only four years older than me. You're three years older than Mom, and Papa Andrion is *ten* years older. He *seems* like a boy, anyhow, really kind of sweet and friendly. He reminds me of *you* a little…"

Erik frowned. At the age of eighteen he'd been a hard-fighting, hard-loving, freebooting adventurer, into just about any kind of trouble you can imagine that wasn't technically against the law. He thought he knew what Riki meant, but it didn't exactly fill him with joy and relief. "So," he said slowly, hoping to draw her out, "why are you telling me about this?"

"He bought me lunch at the Flying Horseman and we talked a lot. I really kind of like him, and it's so cute how much he likes me. I told him he could come by later this afternoon and meet the family, and then if it's okay with you guys he's going to take me to dinner at the Maiden. Just down the road and back, no fooling around…"

Erik grinned again. "That should be all right," he told her and patted her hand. "If we don't like his looks we'll just send him packing. Hmm," he added nonchalantly, "maybe I should sharpen my axe…"

Riki grinned back at him. "Papa! Don't you dare! But, do you think maybe you could…"

"Mention this to Berni and Andrion?" he asked, almost laughing. "Sure, Rikita. In the meantime, shouldn't you be changing out of that armor and getting the weeding done?" She sighed, stepped close to give him a kiss, then headed around the front of the house to the stairs leading down into the basement.

Summer had turned her face from the rain that so often fell on Waterdon at this season, to heat and unrelenting sunshine. By the time Alfmund made his way down the road, looking to his left as instructed for a glimpse of Drakespring Farm, the entire family (and company, minus Sigi of course) were gathered on the veranda enjoying the shade and a hint of cool breeze coming up off the Brightwater to the east. His mouth fell open.

Riki had bathed after finishing her farm chores, and was dressed in a cap-sleeved dress of lightweight cotton that gathered beneath her growing bustline (it seemed she would likely equal her mother in that department, in another year or so – take *that* Rezira) and fell in creamy, nearly translucent ruffles to her ankles. Her freshly-washed red-gold locks curved in soft waves to her waist, and though her summer-blue eyes were sparkling, her face was pale and there was a hint of fixity in her smile. She was scared spitless.

Bernadette had greeted Erik's report with concern, followed by a sense of inevitability. They had made this child between them, she and Erik, and was it any surprise that she might be turning into a young woman with a keen interest in the opposite sex? Andrion had been taken by surprise, Riki still (despite all evidence to the contrary) appearing in his mind as the adorable little girl she had been a decade before. Their daughter was now dating men? How could that be?

Observing the crowd awaiting him on the veranda of the enormous farmhouse above him, Alfmund momentarily had the urge to flee. But he was a young warrior, was he not? And Erika Drakespring had struck him to his soul. Gathering his courage, he turned in at the path leading up to the house and then cut across the yard toward the steps leading up onto the veranda.

Riki rose to her feet, her heart in her mouth. What in all the hells was she doing, inviting this *man* to meet with her family? She barely knew anything about him, and he far less about her as she had omitted so many details about herself in their discussion a few hours ago. Yet somehow she found the courage to maintain her poise, stepping down to meet Alfmund before he had reached the veranda and smiling at him gracefully. "Alfmund," she said, her sweet voice perfectly modulated despite the anxiety that was threatening to constrict her throat until she could scarcely croak, "Welcome to Drakespring Farm." She was her mother's, *and* her father's, daughter.

Riki led Alfmund up the stairs, to the settee where all three of her parents had been sitting. They arose for the formal introductions, and then there was a general move from sitting to standing as the rest of the people gathered in chairs along the covered porch's long length rose to greet the visitor. Alfmund was dazzled.

"Hey, I'm Riki's brother Andi."

"Fjuri Steadfast, pleased to meet you." By the gods, were those a couple of *leukalfar* standing there next to Andi? And what was that thing that looked like a dypalfar robon?

"Nice to meet you. I'm Mothris of the Ankhrazana, Andi's roommate."

"How do you do, Alfmund? I am Gylabris of the Mirskhrazana, here working with Andrion on technical matters."

"Greetings, young Norseman. I am Kziintke."

It was beginning to occur to Alfmund that there were a few things Erika had not mentioned. He'd had enough of a hurdle getting over the idea that her mother was married to two men, but she hadn't said a word about leukalfar or talking automatons. What other secrets might this maddeningly beautiful young woman be hiding? He realized that he didn't actually care.

The young visitor was given a chair opposite the settee, where he could face Riki and all three of her parents, and the interrogation began. Erik was pleased to learn that Alfmund knew his sister's family. Though they'd had little enough contact over the years she was still his sister, and her younger son was friends with Alfmund's older brother.

Under the guise of casual conversation, the three Drakespring parents probed and assessed the young man, and reached the conclusion that Riki's reference to him as a "boy" was not far off. He was friendly, and benign, and without guile. "One last thing," Erik said, with the gravitas he could command at need – entirely due to his six-foot-five-inch height and two hundred fifty pounds of muscled frame – "Did Erika mention to you that she is but fourteen years of age?"

Alfmund nearly choked. No *wonder* her parents were all over him like an oversized suit of armor! Fourteen?! He could scarcely credit it. He had taken her for his age, or at most a year younger. Four years. Was it so much? From the look of Erika's parents, her mother was quite a bit younger than either of her "fathers." She scarcely looked a day over thirty, but must surely be older since Andi seemed to be around sixteen.

He exchanged glances with the girl in question, and she gave him a Look that left him reeling. She might only be fourteen, and that certainly changed some of his ideas about the likely course of their relationship in the immediate future. But she had captured his heart from the first moment he had seen her, and he realized he was willing to do whatever it took, wait as long as he had to, to claim her for his own.

"Of course," Alfmund said suavely, addressing Erik but also Bernadette and Andrion. "I understand that Erika is yet young. But I was merely proposing to take her to dinner at the nearby inn. I've only been in the Waterdon area for a little over a week, but I have already heard great things about the food there. It's just down the road, and I'll have her back here well before bedtime. I suppose you must have eaten there, since it's so close?"

This speech didn't produce quite the result Alfmund had expected. There was a ripple through several of the people seated before him, as of... stifled laughter? Andi abruptly spoke up "Dinner at the Maiden? Great idea! Fjuri and Mothris and I will join you!"

Chapter 6: Dinner at the Bathing Maiden

They were greeted at the door with great ceremony by Remy, who shepherded the party of five young people to the Owner's Table – frequently left vacant these days. The amazing wood inlays Arngeld had created before Andi was born still glowed, thanks to constant loving care on the part of the Maiden's staff.

Sigi and Joqui were running about the place, having eaten earlier (the staff generally fed themselves and their families before the evening rush), and stopped by the table long enough to greet Sigi's older brother and sister and be introduced to Alfmund. He was still reeling at the way in which his planned intimate dinner date with the beautiful Erika had been completely hijacked by her older brother and his friends. And here was yet another brother? Plus, why was their party being accorded VIP status?

Instead of dissolving into a wreck Riki had risen above it all. Getting past the parental inspection was one thing, and surviving the revelation of her age another. By the time Andi had neatly invited himself and his companions along as chaperones, she had realized that there was absolutely no hope for salvaging the evening. She wasn't even particularly crushed, finding herself actually comforted by the familiar presence of Andi, Mothris, and Fjuri.

Alfmund seemed to be holding his own, as well. After all, he was only a couple of years older than Andi and Fjuri, approximately the same age as Mothris – though the alfar races seemed younger at this time of life. Larissa brought their food to the table, smiling down at all of them. She looked no different than she had in Andi and Riki's earliest childhood memories, still appearing to be a lovely young woman though she must now be close to forty at least. She had been part-time nanny to the Drakespring children during quite a few of the years after her marriage to Drelos, longtime assistant innkeeper at the Maiden.

Soon all of them had plates of food in front of them and the young men had begun to dig in. Riki, like her mother, was a girl with a hearty appetite. But she felt constrained by the presence of Alfmund, who sat beside her. Weren't women supposed to eat delicately? As she picked at her plate of food, Alfmund asked her, "What's the story with your family and this inn, Erika?"

29

Riki put a napkin to her lips, though she'd eaten scarcely a bite. If not for her nervousness, that plate of food would have had her shoveling it in with both hands – it looked delicious! Oh hells, she thought. Time to cast deception aside. If what she had to tell left her sitting there with her brother and his friends while Alfmund ran screaming from the room, so be it. This was, after all, her maiden voyage into the business of courtship.

She smiled up at him, nearly rendered speechless by the way in which his gaze conveyed his desire for her. "My mom is The Fireblood," she started, realizing she had just opened herself up to spending the rest of the evening reciting stories. No help for it. "The Bathing Maiden was built by one who was fireblood hundreds of years ago. It's the property of whoever holds that position, so it belongs to our family for now. Andi is fireblood, but as long as Mom is alive he's not *the* fireblood. Someday, though, it will belong to him."

Alfmund was momentarily struck dumb. The Fireblood? The savior of all Terris from Tarragin, the Soul-Devourer? That had all happened when he was no more than a baby, but he'd heard the stories his whole life – and had even owned a copy of the book, which he'd read over and over again when he was a child. Why hadn't he made the connection? He had been speaking to The Fireblood not an hour past, and his only concern had been trying to charm this rather attractive older woman in hopes she would consent to let him date her daughter!

Emotions roiled within him as he considered all the shocks he'd been hit with since arriving at Drakespring Farm this afternoon. He took another bite of the food on his plate, which he realized was damn good. Then he shook off his paralysis. "Amazing!" he said, giving Riki the full effect of his boyish grin, "You must really have some family stories to tell." He dug into his supper with a will.

Rezira arrived at the table and squeezed in between Andi and Fjuri, greeting Andi with a deep kiss. She'd eaten earlier, but had enough appetite to steal morsels off his plate from time to time as he tried to eat. Under the table, her hand rested on his thigh – distracting him enough from his meal that her depredations went unnoticed.

Alfmund glanced up in surprise at the startlingly beautiful and exotic dark-haired, violet-eyed elf woman who'd inserted herself into their gathering. But between the food and the lushly beautiful maiden at his elbow, he soon paid her no further mind. Across the table, Fjuri glared furtively at the young Norseman. Sure, he was a couple of years older. But he was shorter and no more muscular than Fjuri. What did this Alfmund have that *he* didn't? And what made him think he could just step in and sweep Riki, *his* Riki, off her feet? As he polished off the last of the food on his plate, a horrifying realization came to him: he loved her!

Chapter 7: Courtship

After finishing their meal and enjoying some of the evening's entertainment they all walked back to Drakespring Farm together. Alfmund planted a chaste kiss on Riki's lips in front of the entire group before joining Fjuri on the walk back to Waterdon. The young Brave Company recruit, friendly as a puppy, tried to engage the tall youth in some conversation – but found him strangely unresponsive.

During the next couple of days Andi and Mothris spent some rare time just hanging around the place enjoying themselves. They even helped Riki and Sigi with the farm chores, old hat for Andi but different enough to seem enjoyable to the leukalfar boy. While his uncle worked as a farmer in the Ankhrazana's communal economy, he had never before had a chance to try milking a cow. They were a lot bigger than goats, that was for sure! Andi and Riki took pity and gave him old, placid Freydis as his subject, and he didn't do too badly.

Alfmund was away for the following day and the next on an assignment with the Brave Company, but on the third day he appeared at their door in mid-morning and invited Riki up to do some weapons practice at Ynglingar, then take the mid-day meal at the mead hall's capacious board. Bernadette warily granted permission, wondering where this was going. If that boy (and she, too, couldn't help but see him as a boy) thought he was going to get Riki to marry him any sooner than two years from now, he had another think coming.

Her own sister Marie, back in Auverne, had married at seventeen. Even that seemed awfully young to Bernadette. She loved her home and her husbands and her babies, but there was a lot more to life than that and she wanted Riki to have a chance at it before she got tied down. Riki put on her fitted leather armor for the excursion, getting Bernadette to braid her red-gold hair into a long queue down her back that made her look even more warlike. Bernadette gave a little sigh as she watched her daughter striding along beside the young Norseman, bow slung over her back. She'd always wished *she* might be a little taller.

Weapons practice might not seem like every girl's idea of a romantic date, but Riki was somewhat surprised to find that it suited her – and Alfmund – to a tee. They were both little more than kids, really, and vying against each other to hit the bull's-eye (here using real arrows, not the blunt-tipped target arrows Bernadette made for her children to practice with), then jumping around sparring with wooden practice swords, was good exercise and great fun.

After Riki got through his guard a second time Alfmund let his blade fall to point at the stones of the courtyard, panting and grinning. "Are you *sure* you don't want to join the Brave Company, Erika? I took you for a warrior woman the first time I saw you in the market square, but I had no idea!" Riki grinned back at him, exhilarated by the exercise and the challenge – and by the compliment as well. With her cheeks pink from exertion and her eyes sparkling, she looked so beautiful he just wanted to sweep her into his arms on the spot. Slowly, Alfmund, slowly…

By lunchtime they'd worked up a good appetite, and Riki was no longer in the least nervous in Alfmund's company. She felt as if she'd known him forever, as if he were one of Andi's childhood friends, and liked him immensely. They joined others of the Brave Company at Ynglingar's feasting table, which formed three sides of a rectangle in the center of the spacious hall. Most were little older than the two of them. Much like the Bathing Maiden, the Brave Company tended to draw young people who would stay there for a few years on their way to something else.

Digging into some roast venison with fresh bread rolls and grilled leeks on the side, Riki said "Thank you, Alfmund! That was so much fun!" He smiled at her. What had begun as a powerful attraction was beginning to turn into full-blown love, despite the barrier of her age. Could he wait that long to claim her? At this moment he couldn't imagine *not* waiting, if that was what it would take.

After chewing up a succulent mouthful of deer meat and washing it down with a swallow of (alas, room-temperature) ale, Riki went on, "You never said, what was the assignment that took you away the past couple of days?" She'd intended it as casual conversation and a chance to show her interest in him and his doings, but Alfmund's face clouded over.

Quietly, he said "Old Szaras told me to chase down an escaped prisoner from Eisenstag. He strongly implied that they didn't care if the prisoner was dead or alive, they just didn't want him running around loose. I had to go way up north, and when I found the prisoner it turned out to be an Afran woman about the same age as my mom."

Riki's face was white with shock, blue eyes wide. "What did you do?" she asked. "Did you capture her?" Alfmund's face fell.

"I had to kill her," he said quietly. Riki put a hand on his arm, squeezing through the armor to show that she cared.

"Oh, Alfmund! I'm so sorry!" He gave her a weak smile, thanking her for her sympathy, and resumed eating his lunch.

As Riki sat eating, she mused about the disconnect between her culture's glorification of weapons prowess and battle, and the real human consequences of killing. It was fun to dress up in armor, it made her feel competent and powerful. And this morning's session had reminded her that she really had been well-trained by her parents in the martial arts. Archery put food on their table at all seasons, and swordplay was good exercise (and more fun than mucking out paddocks). But would she really be able to kill someone if she had to?

Alfmund wanted to walk her home again after the meal, but Riki smilingly told him she was fine getting back by herself. She really wanted a chance to visit with Julia, even if it were only for a few minutes before she needed to return home and take up her burden of chores. They parted on the front porch of Ynglingar with a kiss that was considerably less chaste than the previous one had been.

Chapter 8: Meiskomtot

Meiskomtot took a moment to assess the two armored figures who'd been attacking him. They were dead, or at least no longer a threat. As he surveyed the chamber, memories came flooding back. It had been... such an unbelievably long time. He looked down at his body in its suit of dragonscale armor. All looked normal. But when he brought a hand up, he realized that it was skeletal – dry, mummified flesh barely covering the bones.

What had gone wrong? He was supposed to be immortal! That had been the promise, and the Reward given was to have ensured it. The dragons, rulers of Agena, would reign forever – and their priesthood, given the ability to assume dragon form, would rule with them when their human bodies could no longer sustain life. He had no actual memory of dying, though there was dim remembrance of energy passed from aptrgangr clustered around his tomb.

Ah, now he recalled – Great Tarragin had vanished, done away with somehow by the leaders of the Uprising. They had entombed the remains of the dragons that died in the war, in sure knowledge that someday Tarragin would return and they would be resurrected. Here Meiskomtot was in human form, so he must not have been dragon when he died. *Why* could he not remember?

Meiskomtot strode down from the top of the dais to the floor and prodded the bodies of his recent foes with a booted foot. They remained motionless. He took a tour of the room, but all of his aptrgangr guardians had been released from their tombs only to fall. Now he was awake, he supposed he no longer needed them. He heaved a crackling sigh, then headed for the back of the room beyond the dais.

The curve of a Spell Wall stood at one side, a testament to the power of the dragons. Priests in training would come here to learn. He walked behind the wall to a wooden door, plain and unadorned. Beyond it was an anteroom, with chests heaped with treasure standing on either side of it. He paid them no mind. He had his armor, his mask, and his staff – and that was enough. His dragon spells were always with him.

He pulled a chain on the wall, and a section of stone at the rear of the antechamber sank into the floor with a rumbling sound. The dypalfar might account themselves masters of machinery, but the ancient Norsemen, too, had built to last. The door he had opened led back into an area of the tomb and temple complex near the main entrance. He stepped through, and the stone door closed behind him.

In the main burial chamber, strewn with motionless bodies, all was silent for a time. Then slowly, Ricard rolled over and dragged himself into a sitting position. "Ragnar?" he asked hoarsely, looking around for his companion. The strapping young Norseman lay face down on the floor perhaps five paces away, crumpled against the wall on the far side of the room's entry door. "Unnnnhh," came the weak reply.

Alive, thank the gods! Ricard did a self-assessment and found that nothing was apparently broken, though he had a splitting headache and felt bruised and battered in every limb. He dragged himself to his feet and limped over to where Ragnar was starting to sit up. "By Marmira's massive tits," his companion growled profanely, "what in all the hells *was* that thing?" As he knelt rummaging through his pack for some health potions, Ricard replied wearily, "*That*, my friend – I believe – was a dragon priest."

Meiskomtot stalked across the circular chamber, which showed evidence of having been looted. Probably by those two fools he'd left behind him, he didn't doubt. After reaching the center of the room he turned left and climbed a long ramp going up to the double doors that led to the outside. The doors were there, but they seemed buckled slightly and refused to open.

The dragon priest stalked back down the corridor some fifty feet before turning to face the doors again. He was losing patience, but it was not wise to use the Staff of Rending at close range. He himself, though vastly more powerful and important than those lesser aptrgangr he'd left behind him, could also be deactivated or damaged to the point where he would be unable to walk. And healing spells didn't work on the undead.

He released a blast from the staff, a bolt of energy as thick as a man's leg that struck the doors with an actinic flash and a rumbling explosion. The doors flew away, smashed to splinters. But behind them was a mountain of piled rock. The roof of the outer portico must have come down! That might explain why it seemed to have been so long since anyone living had come here.

Cursing, the powerful aptrgangr bent to the task of clearing the way to the outside. He hauled away smaller rocks down the corridor, then blasted again with the staff. It pulverized larger rocks to make smaller ones, but until the blockage was completely cleared they had nowhere to go – so he had to remove them by hand. Meiskomtot's mood was getting fouler by the hour as this task dragged on.

Finally, with one last roar, the Staff of Rending blew the last of the stone blocking the entryway out and down the slope toward the river above which the ruin stood. Triumph warred with the undead priest's pique as he stepped out into gray mist and light rain. The blue metal mask he wore was also called Meiskomtot. The mask, the staff, the dragon scale armor, and the Reward had been his tokens of office at the ceremony in which he had been invested at the highest level of the dragon priesthood, and had taken his new name. He no longer remembered the one his mother had given him, nor anything about his former life before joining the priesthood – something that had happened when was just a boy.

Now he removed that mask to lift his head and feel the rain falling on his withered face. He took a deep breath of the cool, moist air with its hints of greenery. Breathing was not necessary to sustain the "life" that he now had – he could have sat at the bottom of that river down there for the rest of the day without any inconvenience. But it was necessary for speech and for dragon spells, and it felt good.

Meiskomtot felt joy to be standing upon the earth, feeling the rain and breathing the sweet air. And a bitter rage that he was doing it in this withered husk, this walking corpse, instead of soaring above the earth in the immortal dragon body that had been promised to him as his lot. He hoped there would be some chance to rectify this error. But first he must find out what was going on in the world. What year, what age was it? Had Tarragin returned? Was mankind once again in thrall to their dragon masters?

The undead priest replaced the mask on his face, once again granting him the power to completely resist magical attacks, and to cast dragon spells as often as he liked without scarcely any time spent waiting for the stones to recharge. Then he cried "Weit-Stos-Zet-Blik!" The mask, his armor, and the staff at his back all vanished, leaving his withered body standing naked at the top of the rise. It was not a pretty sight.

Unconcerned by his nudity, Meiskomtot reached within, sensing the mask that still enhanced his powers, the armor that still protected him though it could not be seen. This was all part of the Reward, a potion and four dragon spells that enabled a man to ascend to the ranks of the immortal dragons in whose priesthood he served. Now he cried "Mon-Drache-Ein-Korp!"

Where the naked aptrgangr had stood a moment before, an enormous undead dragon now occupied the hilltop – lifeless-looking gray scales, thin dry limbs and wings that hung ragged. I'm much bigger! Meiskomtot realized. The rule that one's dragon form grew in proportion to the years elapsed since one's birth as a human apparently applied even if you were undead. He'd half-hoped to find that though his human form was a walking corpse his dragon form might somehow still be immortal, still truly alive. But as long as it could still fly, he should be able to learn more. A plan was beginning to form in his mind, but it would depend on what he discovered.

He crawled laboriously a few yards down the slope, then spread his tattered wings and flapped them fiercely as the hard sinews of his withered hind legs launched him into the sky. Clawing at the air, he pulled himself higher and higher. Yes! Now to find others of his kind!

Chapter 9: Mission to Alfenstein

Andi and his party shimmered into existence just inside the tall and imposing front gates of Alfenstein, the Elven City. With him were Mothris, Gylabris, Kziintke, and the middle-aged leukalfar woman Umina, late a slave of the dypalfar in the city of Mrzhandtham. She had been one of the leaders of the slave revolt that had been simmering for thousands of years in that place; and now that she and her cohorts had finally achieved their goal she was not content to rest on her laurels. Andi and the others had left Drakespring Farm and collected her in Mrzhgradfendz, before coming here.

Andi smiled as he looked up at the city, appreciating the summer sunshine. From the look of the light, it was around midmorning. He was feeling tired and hungry from fast-traveling twice in the last day, but they needed to get to Dypendwelve and connect with the rest of their team while they could. Lunch, or whatever meal it was supposed to be, would have to wait.

Alfenstein was one of the first places he'd added to his personal map after acquiring it a few months before. The Drakespring Clan owned a fine house here, Eastview, and he had been here many times as a child. Old Miurlion's dypalfar museum was a favorite excursion for all of the Drakespring children, Mondi excepted. Their dragon brother had been excluded from many human places because of his size, since he was only a few years old.

Some old friends of Andi's parents now lived here, and had been working with the old elf mage Miurlion in his explorations of the extensive dypalfar ruins below Dypendwelve – finding and cataloging the artifacts therein and working to unravel the technology that had created them. They'd fallen out of touch with the Drakesprings, but the visit with Nerissa and her family at Castle Hordenhaal last year had brought them back into contact.

One of the first things that had happened after Andi, Fjuri, and Meri were back from their adventure was that a delegation of Drakesprings had gone to Alfenstein, using Bernadette's map, to reconnect with Georges and Diane – and Miurlion. The old elf had been working here since before any of the rest of them were born, and would likely be doing so long after they were dust; but they had an important message for him: stop going down into the ruined city below and killing the leukalfar sentries.

All of them were astonished, and horrified, to meet Meri and learn through her and Andi that the leukalfar were fully people – with all that implied. They had their own language, their own culture, their families and loved ones – and intruding into their territory in the interests of archaeological investigation was tantamount to an armed invasion.

That had been months ago, and since then Diane, Georges, and Miurlion had contented themselves with examining, categorizing, and tinkering with the artifacts already in their possession. The revelation that the dypalfar yet lived, though now lost forever in a plane of the Netherworld to which there was no further access, had been another stunner.

Andi wished he could have brought Zira with them. Miurlion and Diane were dying to meet her, but she was busy with so many things. Maybe in another few months… For now, they would have to be content with Gylabris and Kziintke, who he expected would likely provide them with enough excitement to last for years.

Andi and Mothris had been here before, but for the rest of the party it was their first visit and there was much exclamation as he led them along the winding stone pathways that zigzagged up, crisscrossing the river that flowed down through the center of town, toward the eorl's "palace." He took them through the forge of Dhyazh dan-Lugab, a long-time friend of Mom's from her earliest days in Iscandia. The verdalfar woman looked little changed from the first time Andi had met her, and she greeted him with her usual gruff demeanor. But her eyebrows rose at the sight of the three leukalfar accompanying him.

Over the months since the Leukalfar Initiative had been launched, the one factor that its architects had found most useful was costume. People throughout Iscandia were a hundred times more likely to accept a leukalfar as a fellow human if they were *dressed* like everyone else. The clothing also helped to cover up some of the leukalfar race's more obvious differences from the rest of humanity, and gave them a chance to demonstrate their lack of hostile intent – and command of the common tongue – before the other party started shooting. Thus all three of them were clad in trousers, tunics, vests and hats.

"Dhyazh, these are my friends Mothris, Gylabris, and Umina of the leukalfar race. We're here to contact their fellows below Dypendwelve." The typical uruk composure showed signs of cracking, but Dhyazh held her own.

"Well met, then," she said shortly. "I suspect we may find that another of the alfar races has its strongholds."

"Right you are, Dhyazh," Andi replied. "My mom told me to say hi, but we must be off now. See you again later."

With that he led the party up the hill past Magichemia, where Andi's mom had been trading in potions and chemial ingredients since before he was born, and on past the guarded doors of Dypendwelve. The guards blinked at them, more concerned by the gleaming, seven-foot dypalfar robon in their party than by the leukalfar. But they made no attempt to bar the way.

Surprisingly, Eorl Galdur Staerlin(brought to power by an imperial shakeup twenty years before, and now succeeded by his son) had eventually proven to be more proactive than any of the eorls of Alfenstein before him. He had not only done much to root out the Insurgents' opposition within his march, but had invested some of his extremely wealthy family's fortune in making improvements to Dypendwelve.

No longer did it look as if the ruler of Alfenstein had taken up residence like a rat in a ruined dwelling belonging to others. Fallen masonry had been cleared away, and there was now a stone-lined corridor running straight from the main doors of the keep up toward the throne room and the eorl's residential quarters. Side corridors, also finished and well-lit with ever-burning dypalfar lamps, led off to the guards' quarters, the entry to Miurlion's work area and the archaeological site, and Miurlion's dypalfar museum (site of several visits that Andi regarded as some of his fondest memories from childhood).

They turned to the left and headed down into another section of the keep, where Miurlion could often be found working. Instead of the old ljosalfar mage and scholar, they found a couple of his young apprentices. One, a Galise little older than Andi, recognized him from his last visit. "Andreas! Good to see you," he said – looking up from whatever he'd been doing at the enchanting table.

"Hi Demian," he replied with a smile. "Is Miurlion or Diane around?"

The young man nodded. "You'll find both of them, and Georges as well, down at the museum. I think they're expecting you to show up soon." He looked at the group standing behind Andi with a great deal of interest. He'd met Mothris a couple of times before and the idea of leukalfar dressed like "regular people" and speaking the common tongue was no longer alien to him. But what captured his attention was Kziintke. Could this be the fabulous talking dypalfar robon he'd heard about?

Following his gaze, Andi decided he'd better satisfy Demian's curiosity. "Kziintke," he said, gesturing toward the two apprentices, "this is Demian … uh sorry, I forgot your last name… and Turkan" – nodding to the young nachtalfar who was Miurlion's other trainee. "Kziintke is a fully autonomous robon and possibly unique in the modern world." The robon stepped forward with a clank and managed a passable bow.

Speaking in Common, he said "I am pleased to meet you. I would like to introduce my friend Gylabris, who restored me to life and thought."

The little leukalfar tinkerer stepped forward, twinkling. Since the arrival of Andi and his companions a year before, his horizons had expanded enormously – and he was loving every minute of it. He'd gone from being somewhat of a joke among his fellow Mirskhrazana Keepers to becoming one of the most important people on Terris for the future advancement of the leukalfar race. The discoveries he'd been making with help from Andrion and Rezira would help to fund a new era where the leukalfar could join the rest of human society and, finally, claim what was theirs.

Though he was now fluent in Common, the idioms of the leukalfar tongue still haunted his speech. "Greetings, young fellows. I'm delighted to be here, and look forward to meeting with your master." He turned to Andi and added, "Shall we go?" Andi grinned at him, waved to the apprentices, and took a sharp left – leading them up a long corridor to the dypalfar museum's main entrance.

Once they were inside it Andi's companions, especially Gylabris but also Umina and Kziintke himself, were distracted as they passed among a host of dypalfar automatons displayed on pedestals. The museum took up a surprisingly large amount of territory within Dypendwelve, including some labs and dypalfar living areas that were not open to the public.

Kziintke halted before a seven-foot robon standing motionless in an alcove up against one wall. "Gylabris!" he said with excitement in his voice. Without the brain chemicals that made up the human limbic system it was hard to understand how a mech like Kziintke could have emotions – but he did seem to possess them.

Gylabris approached, and stood beside Kziintke staring at the mech that had drawn the robon's attention. "By Apoldros, it looks just like you!" the little Keeper said, awe in his voice. "Do you think…?" Kziintke looked down at him.

"It is very possible that this is another of my kind. Though I don't specifically recall him, I somehow feel that there *were* others, long ago."

"Him?" Gylabris asked, gesturing. "Her, don't you think?" The rest of the party gathered around, and they realized that while the gleaming automaton before them and the one at Gylabris' side were nearly identical in shape, with the extra-large heads that marked them as more than just killing machines, the torso of the one that stood silent was molded in the shape of a woman's.

Now Kziintke as well stood silent, until they were beginning to wonder if he had short-circuited. The automatons' power, derived from the power cells that appeared to tap a constantly-renewed energy source from another dimension, never seemed to run out – sometimes outlasting the automatons themselves, if they were deactivated or destroyed.

The humans gathered around all seemed to be holding their breath, riveted by the discovery. Then finally Kziintke shifted slightly, his voice coming so quietly they almost missed it as he murmured, "Jerzha." He took a step closer, gazing fixedly at the mech before him. She appeared to be in perfect condition, untouched by the millennia – just as he had been. He spoke louder, and in

Dypalfar: "Jerzha, activate." With the faintest of whirs, the jewel-like eyes glowed blue.

Chapter 10: Below Dypendwelve

Jerzha stepped forward from the wall. "She" was the same height as Kziintke, but not only was her torso shaped with slight feminine curves, her voice proved to be in a higher register. Gylabris wondered what on earth had inspired the ancient dypalfar to give gender to an automaton that was, after all, just a construction of metal with a mind.

For a moment he had a whimsical vision of Kziintke and Jerzha getting together and manufacturing little two-foot robons. That was nonsense. Still, it was amazing that after he had agonized over bringing Kziintke back to life for so many decades, less than a year after he had finally done so here was another – and Kziintke himself had activated her!

The two automatons conversed back and forth in rapid-fire Dypalfar for a couple of minutes as their human companions stood around in shocked silence. Whether this was to make their conversation private, or because Dypalfar was in essence their "native" tongue, Gylabris didn't know. Finally Kziintke turned to his master to deliver his report.

"I have recovered a memory from long before I was deactivated the first time," he said. "Jerzha was created when I was, and there dozens more of us. We were intended to act as guards and interpreters for traders, and we traveled widely before the troubles. When the dypalfar became besieged in their cities, and the leukalfar were lured in to be enslaved, our usefulness was at an end. I believe that many may have been destroyed, though some – as I was, and Jerzha also – were merely deactivated."

"Well," the little Keeper told his pride and joy (Gylabris had never married nor had any children, and Kziintke was his greatest achievement), "I am pleased that you have found a friend, or a sister perhaps. But who is her master?"

"I am," Kziintke said thoughtfully. "We are programmed to obey the one that activates us, provided that they know our name. Shall I tell her to obey you instead?"

Gylabris looked surprised. "Hum, I suppose so…"

45

Kziintke spoke to Jerzha in Common now. Like him, she had the common, leukalfar, and dypalfar tongues at her command. "Jerzha, this is my master Gylabris. Please do as he says."

"Pleased to meet you, Gylabris," the gleaming automaton replied. "What are your instructions?"

"Well, erm… Follow me, I suppose… Andi, we're following *you* so where are we going, exactly?"

Andi started from his reverie. The events of the past few minutes had him flummoxed. He'd admired this robon many times in the past, thinking it was kind of cool that this one (unlike any others he'd seen) had breasts. No beard, either, of course. But he hadn't made the connection until now that she was of the same design as Kziintke.

"Right this way, people," he said. "We'll be going down into the workrooms on the floor below." He led the way through several turnings and through a pair of imposing doors, then down a ramp into the lower level of the museum. They found Miurlion standing at a workbench with Diane and Georges Baudin, and a medium sized boy of around twelve, with dark brown hair that had a reddish cast to it.

He looked up and squeaked "Andi! You're here!"

He ran to them and Andi put the boy in a headlock, mussing his hair. Edouard Baudin was a full-blooded Galise born in Iscandia just like him, and he idolized the older boy as the brother he'd never had – despite that this was only their fourth meeting. Meanwhile the adults had turned to look at the party approaching, and their mouths hung open in expressions of disbelief to see that the promised robon was accompanied by another – one they thought they recognized as belonging to the museum.

Introductions were made all around, and then Jerzha spoke up. She was as sentient and capable of autonomous action as Kziintke was, it seemed. Though he would obey orders from the one designated his "master," he didn't hesitate to think for himself. "Greetings, Miurlion, Diane, Georges, and Edouard. I am Jerzha, recently reactivated by my brother who is now known as Kziintke. He tells me that I have been standing in the museum where he found me for many ages. But I have no memories of that."

"This is astounding!" Miurlion said, fairly quivering with excitement. The old ljosalfar had been engaged in his dypalfar studies here in Dypendwelve for longer than any of the non-alfar among them had been alive, yet he had never realized what a treasure he had had – polished up and nicely displayed as if she were no more than an ornament.

After the excitement had died down, some half an hour later, Andi said "So the plan is that Miurlion and Diane are to accompany Mothris and Umina down into the ruined city?" Those mentioned all nodded, and Kziintke spoke up.

"Gylabris has told me something of the city below," he said. "I think it would be wise if either Jerzha or I were to accompany you. From the reports of others who have attempted the depths, there are many automatons still active. It would be far better to command them in Dypalfar to cease hostilities, rather than to fight them."

"Excellent point, Kziintke," Diane said. She'd been studying dypalfar technology for decades, and had trashed dozens of automatons just to save her life. How much better to leave them intact, and study them in working condition!

"I will be happy to accompany you," Jerzha said. "I think that if you wish to contact the leukalfar below as friends, two robons might be... an inducement for them to listen to what you have to say before they start shooting."

"That's set, then," Andi said with relief. The effects of fast-traveling here from Mrzhgradfendz were beginning to get to him, and he could only imagine that his companions were also suffering. "I think Mothris, Gylabris, Umina and I are all in need of a rest," he told them. "Why don't we go get something to eat at the Staerlin Inn and then go up to Eastview to sleep? We'll be back here bright and early tomorrow morning, and see off the expedition."

Assuming the ambassadors were successful in contacting the leukalfar tribe that lived below Dypendwelve, they intended to bring back a delegation from that tribe with them. Alfenstein was a special case, since unlike virtually every other dypalfar city in Iscandia it was (and had been, for many years) fully occupied by people other than the leukalfar. In most dypalfar ruins, it was only the odd group of bandits that sometimes set up housekeeping.

So they could not offer the leukalfar the chance to take up full ownership of the entire city, as had now been done in a dozen places with varying degrees of success. But the biggest part of the city far below Dypendwelve was deep and broad, connected with the upper levels only by narrow corridors. There was no reason the leukalfar therein couldn't set up some kind of a trading post within the keep itself, perhaps near what was now the entrance to the archaeological site.

"All right then," Miurlion said. "Will Kziintke and Jerzha stay here in the meantime? I am very eager to converse with them." "Certainly," Gylabris replied. "We will see you all in the morning."

Chapter 11: The Search

The ancient undead dragon flew slowly not far above the ground, searching for places out of distant memory. This undeath brought none of the joy Meiskomtot had experienced as a living man transformed into a living dragon after receiving the Reward. Flying was a chore, constantly flapping to stay aloft – and able to make only a fraction of the speed he had once possessed. At least, he found, he was able to keep flying thus for hours without being tormented by hunger.

As a living dragon he had been hot. Now he was cold, dead but animate. The magical force that motivated this mummified body did not require food for sustenance, which saved a lot of time and trouble hunting. In his years as an ascended dragon priest, Meiskomtot's dragon form had been fed with endless carcasses of beef, goats, and the occasional human – all provided as sacrifices by their subjects.

Meiskomtot spotted a familiar ring, one of the burial mounds where the dragon priesthood had interred the bodies of dragons killed in the wars – awaiting resurrection by Tarragin on his prophesied return. He remembered this mound, dimly – though the name of its occupant escaped him. There seemed no whiff of the lord's soul about, as he landed and inspected the soil within the ring.

Gone! This mound's occupant was gone, and some years ago it seemed. The earth had been flung aside, but many seasons of rain and snow had softened the contours once again. There were only two conclusions to be reached from this: either Tarragin had returned, and this dragon lord (for all dragons were lords, in the time of their rule) had been resurrected; or the humans, freed of their dragon masters, had systematically dug up the burial mounds and destroyed the corpses. Dragons were a great deal more fire-proof than most creatures, but it was not impossible to turn one to ashes in any fire hot enough to smelt iron.

Meiskomtot gave a mental shudder at that thought, as he took to the air once again. If that were the case, and all the dragons were now gone, he might well be the last one left. Then he might wish himself truly dead. He must continue his search, no matter how long it took, until he had learned what had really happened!

He was flying along the course of a river through a broad valley, with no human habitations but an outcropping of ruins standing high on a hill to the north, when he spotted some bones protruding from the water where it ran shallow near a ford. He landed with a splash, finding that the cold water felt good on his dusty hide. Experimentally Meiskomtot bent his head and took a drink, but found that the water came right back up again. Seemingly he was as dry and dusty inside as out, and no digestion was possible. He heaved a sigh.

As he'd thought, the bones were those of a dragon – a large one, from the size of the spine and rib cage. The skull was no longer present, and most of the smaller bones had been carried off – either by spring floods or human scavengers. Again, there was no whiff of a soul. The secret forms of necromancy practiced by the dragon worshipers, which accounted for the aptrgangr and Meiskomtot's own current status, would have told him immediately had the dead dragon's soul still been near.

He doubted whether any person now animate, present company excepted, could have had the power to cast the essence capture spell on a dying dragon. Likely those secrets had died with the dragon worshipers itself. But what other means could there have been to remove it? From the condition of the bones, this lord had died not much above fifteen years ago.

But wait, what of the prophesied Fireblood? The same prophecy that declared Tarragin's return and the resurrection of the dragons (leading to one last final age of dragon rule before the destruction of Terris and the birth of the world that would follow it), said that if one who was fireblood should arise at that time, that person *might* stop Tarragin.

And anyone with the fireblood, when present at the death of a dragon, would spontaneously absorb the dragon's mana and soul. It went not into a magical essence vial but into their innermost being – where it fortified their own mana, reducing the time required to recharge any spell stones within them.

The fireblood heritage had not been uncommon in the time when Meiskomtot was alive. It was firebloods who had the spark, who formed the upper echelons of the priesthood. But with the war and the persecution of his kind, how could the lineage have survived? The ability was usually passed only to the firstborn of one who was fireblood, though rarely a second child would also be gifted. Even when two firebloods mated, the odds were no higher. As almost all who were fireblood sought the priesthood, most likely all of them would have been wiped out when the mundane humans rose up and cast down their rulers.

It was a puzzle, and Meiskomtot still didn't have any answers – only speculation. He spoke the common tongue – it was his native language, after all, though knowledge of the dragon tongue had come to him through study and later, all at once, when he first transformed into a dragon using the Reward. If the language had not changed too much over time, he might be able to find some isolated person and interrogate him or her. Preferably, someone a little more knowledgeable than a cowherd.

Some hours and many miles later, Meiskomtot had still found no inhabited dragon mounds and no unaccompanied wandering mages or scholars. He felt as if he could continue flapping his ragged wings indefinitely, he was not physically tired; but the tedium and his urgent desire for answers were beginning to erode his patience.

Thus, as the last rays of the sun were fading from the western sky, and he spied two armed figures walking tiredly along the road below, he folded his wings and came in for a landing ahead of them. The two of them stared at him aghast, hardly believing what had just plopped itself down in their path with an earth-shaking thump.

"Augh! By Agnar, what *is* it?" Ragnar cried out in terror. Overall it hadn't been a good day. True, he and Ricard had found that tomb – and after they'd unaccountably survived running into that dragon priest, they'd come away with a heavy load of good loot. He was fully recovered from his earlier injuries, but he was also utterly exhausted, ready to throw his bedroll down and go to sleep in the middle of the road – and now this.

The two of them, staring in disbelief at the enormous, tattered figure before them, began stepping carefully backward. Their faces were white as sheets. "I think it's a dragon, but it's an *undead* one," Ricard murmured out of the side of his mouth – his eyes never leaving the hideous apparition.

Observing that the two of them were nearly wetting their armor in terror and were about to flee, Meiskomtot tried to speak softly: "Fear not, I will not harm you. I only wish to speak with you for a moment." It came out as a dull roar, and the two adventurers cowered back still more. Oh, this was ridiculous. Angrily the undead dragon cried "Drache-Mon-Zur-Heim!" and shrank to a wizened walking corpse shorter and far skinnier than either man. The dragon spell had nearly blown the companions off their feet, and as they regained their composure and realized that the incomprehensibly huge undead dragon had been replaced with what looked to be a perfectly ordinary (if oddly naked) aptrgangr, they relaxed.

Ricard was the brains of the operation, not that he was a great deal beyond his partner Ragnar in mental capacity. But the pair had a sort of natural aptitude for adventuring, and were quick to seize any advantage. They exchanged a glance in the fading light. Then, "Get 'im!" Ricard shouted, drawing his short sword as his burly Norse companion unsheathed the enormous sablium longsword that had been his pick of the loot from Mordendaal.

Clunk! Ragnar's blow, which should have cloven the slightly-built aptrgangr from shoulder to crotch, unaccountably bounced off. The aptrgangr glared at him with a look that seemed more annoyance than malevolence, and Ricard withheld his blow. He was getting a bad feeling about this. "Kraf-Luft-Struung-Wund!" Meiskomtot cried, sending the two tumbling down the road before him.

As the pair were just beginning to pick themselves up he cried "Yetz-Dies-Ruk-Shao!" Everything Meiskomtot had had with him or on him at the moment he had uttered the Send Within dragon spell before taking his dragon form, now became evident and useful. Apparel, such as armor or enchanted jewelry, would work fully though it was invisible. It meant that in his dragon form, with his dragon scale armor, he was doubly resistant to attack. And if he'd been wearing his mask, invulnerable to magical attacks as well. The Reward was sweet!

Weapons, however, were not usable until they had been restored with the Return spell. Of course, he had little enough need of them while he had his dragon spells and his magical abilities. He was somewhat surprised that these two were still conscious; but just as glad they were. Maybe *now* he could get some information!

Ricard was now climbing to his feet, preparing to draw his bow though he suspected it was a futile gesture. He looked at the dragon priest standing twenty feet away, and his face fell. "*You* again!" he breathed. Oh, they were so screwed.

"Relax," the priest told him, speaking in passable Common but with a curious accent, "I truly do not intend to harm you. I only wish some information. Then I will be on my way."

The two young adventurers had met and permanently disabled many, many aptrgangr over their two years of questing together. On occasion these had included upper-level aptrgangr with the ability to use dragon spells as did this priest before them. But other than those raucous, violent cries, they had never heard one speak. They now stood in silence, waiting for the ominous figure before them to say something more.

Sundown had occurred, and though they were far to the north dimness was clustering around them. "First, let's have a little light, shall we?" Meiskomtot cackled. Was I that old? He wondered. He seemed to recall having been… not young, but still in the full of his power – not some wizened old geezer. Surely he would have gone dragon and stayed that way, long before then. But he had no memories of the time leading up to his death. He flung a hand up in a gesture that sent a globe of magical light high above, illuminating a fifteen-foot circle over his head. "Step closer," he commanded, and his spellbound subjects obeyed.

"Now," he went on in a deeper voice, a voice of command. This walking corpse's body had vocal cords as dry and ruined as its other sinews, and it was an effort to speak in anything besides a spidery whisper. "What year is it?" Meiskomtot demanded. As he'd guessed, the young Galise was the spokesman of the group.

It was he who stammered, "Imperial Era, Year 2118. Uh, sir…"

Imperial Era? What nonsense was this? Why could not men sensibly number years from the beginning of time, instead of breaking it up into these meaningless "eras"? How was someone who'd been there at the beginning supposed to figure out how much time had passed, without enrolling in a history course first? "How long since the Uprising then, how long since Sigrandil's time?" he asked. Meiskomtot was *really* starting to feel old.

Ricard had actually had considerably more education than did Ragnar, but still that wasn't saying a lot. He cringed as he realized what would likely happen if he failed to deliver an answer this powerful being liked. "Um, that was roughly about six thousand years ago." So long! It was astonishing that they were able to communicate. The common tongue must hold some magic, that it had not transformed beyond recognition in all that time.

That was an almost *inconceivably* long time, Meiskomtot realized. His own memories, from his adolescent initiation into the priesthood until some point before the death that had evidently come to him, encompassed scarcely a century. Yet millennia had passed – and things here in Iscandia didn't look all that different from the way they had then. If anything, the region seemed somewhat depopulated. Clearly those dypalfar with their machines, their technological innovations, had not taken over the place as he recalled having half expected. He wondered what had happened to them.

Ricard and Ragnar stood slack-jawed, staring at Meiskomtot as he processed the information he'd received. It appeared he was not going to blast them on the spot – that was good, right? The ancient creature spoke again: "And what, young adventurers, can you tell me about dragons?"

Oh my, he'd struck a rich vein. The ancient dragon known as Tarragin, the Soul-Devourer, had appeared in Iscandia some seventeen years previously and had begun resurrecting dragons from burial mounds. And just as prophesied, a fireblood had arisen to oppose him. A young woman, apparently, who had won followers to her cause. Only a month or two after Tarragin's reappearance, she and they had tracked him to Asengard and there, with assistance from the embodied souls of the same ancient Norse heroes who had banished him the first time, brought that most ancient of dragons to his final end.

Meiskomtot's soul felt as ashen as his desiccated body on learning of this. Tarragin had been the hope of them all, a final chance for restoration of the power and prestige they had enjoyed when dragons ruled the continent. But there was more: Tarragin had been busy during the fairly brief time he had been active in this era, and he had raised many dragons.

But without the dragon priesthood to aid and guide them, they had become like enormous rogue predators – hunkering down at mountaintop altars waiting for heroes to do them battle, or flying in to flame the odd farmhouse, kill a few defenders, and make off with the cattle. That the lords had been reduced to such circumstances! It scarcely bore consideration.

"But the dragon situation isn't like that now, sir," Ricard was saying. So far, it seemed to have gone really well. This dragon priest, whoever he was, had remained silent and passive as he babbled everything he knew about the history of human-dragon interaction in Iscandia during his lifetime. He'd been not much more than five when The Fireblood had defeated Tarragin, but the story had captured a generation with its tale of valor.

"What do you mean?" Meiskomtot asked in a voice as cold as the breath of old tombs. "What is it like, *now*?"

"The Fireblood," Ricard went on in what he hoped was a cheerful and conciliatory tone, "she figured out how to turn into a dragon. And then she and this big dragon, must be one of the ones Tarragin raised, got together and had babies. There's a whole bunch of them, and they're all around eleven years old now. I've seen a couple of them, I think, though I haven't talked with any of 'em."

He went on, inattentive to his audience's reaction. "She told them they had to be friendly with humans, see, because humans have killed most of the old dragons Tarragin raised. I guess there's a few still around, but they're pretty heavily outnumbered if you see what I mean. Now people are starting to talk about how dragons are a help, how they're all right. Some will even trade 'em beef in exchange for killing off predators or bringing in game – even giving some people's kids sky rides."

Ricard finished this spate of information with a friendly grin. Well, his teeth were showing at any rate. He and Ragnar stood waiting, praying silently to all the gods that the dragon priest would be satisfied with what they'd told him and fulfill his promise to leave them unharmed.

Meiskomtot's mind was spinning. This fireblood had the Reward? How could that be possible? The potion and dragon spells that comprised the Reward had been the most closely guarded secret of the priesthood, unknown to anyone, not even their members, until they ascended to the highest ranks. It just made no sense! And what was this about young dragons being "helpful"? Dragons were intended to rule, not to cozen humans into exchanging favors!

He'd sought information, and he had found it – and it had given him no peace. "So," he said, "there are still a few dragons around who were raised by Tarragin?"

"Oh, a few I guess," Ricard replied. "Nobody's seen one around human settlements in a long time. They're supposed to be immortal, you know, but a few dozen bows and some longswords will put paid to them, sure enough. And I hear the ones the Fireblood kills can't ever come back. Of course with Tarragin dead, *none* of 'em can come back." As he realized he was speaking with a being who until very recently had been a resurrected undead dragon, it occurred to Ricard that now might be a good time for him to shut up.

Meiskomtot seized on the pronouncement. "This Fireblood, she did not kill all the dragons Tarragin raised herself?" "Gods, no!" Ricard replied. "She's only one woman, wasn't much older than I am now when she killed Tarragin. And not long after she did that, she married the guys that helped her with the quest and settled down. I doubt she's killed more than a dozen or two, all told. All the rest would've been killed by adventurers (like us, he almost said, and thought better of it), or townspeople who were being attacked."

Meiskomtot had heard enough. He knew what he had to do, and these "adventurers" had offended him for the last time. Glaring up at them (and was it not the last straw, that they towered above him?), he cried "Kraf-Luft-Struung-Wund!" and for the third time this day Ricard and Ragnar were thrown through the air, tumbling along the ground until they were some thirty feet away from their undead antagonist – lying stunned on the broken cobbles of the road. Then he wielded the Staff of Rending and blasted them for good measure, with a fiery explosion that tore a hole in the road and hurled the hapless companions to either side of it.

His ire temporarily sated, the undead priest spelled his weapons and apparel back into invisibility, residing somehow in a closely-knit parallel plane from which he could claim them at will. Another dragon spell, and the enormous undead dragon flapped its tattered wings heavily – taking to the air.

Chapter 12: The New Order

Schickhimseel (Beautiful Sky Spirit) flapped heavily through the air with the dead deer in her claws, as she headed in for a landing at Bendari Farm in the southeastern part of Remus. Her brothers Wissliiben and Tapferverd trod the air a few dozen yards above her as she glided down into the farmyard below.

The lean, dark-haired woman hoeing the cabbage patch, a few paces from where the lithe female dragon with her glistening red scales had touched down, looked up with a smile. "Schickhimseel!" she exclaimed, her eyes already sliding from the 22-foot young dragon to the freshly-killed deer she was carrying, "it is good to see you!"

"And you as well, Lucretia!" Schickhimseel said in flawless Common. She had been speaking it almost from birth, as much a native tongue as the dragon language that had been hard-wired into her brain. Her earliest memories were of Mama, in her dragon form as Schunmurte, teaching her and her eighteen brothers and sisters the tongue of her own birth.

"I happened upon this deer," Schickhimseel said casually, "and I had already killed it when I realized I was just too full to eat another bite. So I thought maybe you and your family might like to have it." Lucretia smiled at the polite deception. She hated to take charity, least of all from these strange scaly creatures that spoke like men, but what else was she to do? With Giovanni gone, killed by a lion while he was hunting just such game as Schickhimseel had brought, her family had few resources.

Their only cow had died two years before. They had a small flock of chickens, but they needed the eggs more than they needed the meat and feathers. And their little farm was isolated, far from any other human habitations where a helping hand might be found. So, what meat Schickhimseel and her brothers brought was usually all they had.

The young dragon helped Lucretia get the carcass hung up on the stand in the yard, where in years past Giovanni had bled and cleaned the deer he brought home. Meanwhile Wissliiben and Tapferverd circled down to land a little outside the rail fence that delineated the property.

Just then Lucretia's children, nine-year-old Julius and seven-year-old Gianna, emerged from the henhouse where they'd been cleaning and egg-collecting. "The dragons are here!" Julius said excitedly to his younger sister. "Quick, take the eggs in the house!" Her olive-skinned face glowing with excitement, Gianna hurried to do his bidding and returned in moments.

The young male dragons looked down at the children with pleasure. After the three of them had come to this territory a couple of years before, they had learned of the Bendari family's troubles and had more or less adopted them. Their mother's goal was that dragons would share the world with humankind, helping them with the skills only they had and benefitting from the advantages men and alfar had due to their agile, creative minds and marvelous opposable thumbs. They would not be rulers of men, or their bane, but partners.

At this point the Bendaris were not able to reciprocate, having nothing to offer the children of Schunmurte and Sneyagflug; but the young dragons' hearts had been touched by the family's plight – they were happy to help. They had all the time in the world to wait for repayment, if it ever came; and meanwhile they were rewarded just with the chance for some human interaction. Their mother was human most of the time, after all, and they actively enjoyed human company. Perhaps this would change after they'd lived for a few centuries, but right now they were scarcely older than Julius.

"Can Wissliiben and Tapferverd take us for a ride?" Julius asked of both the male dragons and his mother. He and Gianna had been allowed to ride the dragons a couple of times, and it was the favorite experience of their young lives. To soar high above the beauty of the province, seeing the land laid out beneath you like a carpet, the spires of Roma shining in the distance!

Lucretia smiled. That she trusted these young dragons – *dragons!* – with her children's lives seemed almost unbelievable to her if she thought about it. But she did. During the years after her family had lost its principle means of support, Schickhimseel and her brothers had shown them far more kindness than she'd had from her fellow humans. "It's all right with me if it's all right with you boys," she said to the dragons on the far side of the fence. Their personalities suggested they had minds similar to what you might find in a boy of sixteen, and she had truly come to think of them as such.

"Yay!" Julius cried, slithering between the rails of the fence and climbing up onto Wissliiben's head and thence to his shoulders just behind the neck. His sister, grinning from ear to ear, stepped up on Tapferverd's front leg as he crouched low to allow her to reach her seat.

"Not too long now," Lucretia admonished with a smile. "Those two still have chores to do!"

"Just a few minutes, I promise," Wissliiben replied as he carefully launched himself into the air with Julius clinging like a limpet to his back. Truth to tell, with the improvement the dragon siblings had made in the family's diet Julius was beginning to get a little heavy. After more than a few minutes the young dragon would be burning with hunger. Only the largest of mature dragons could carry much weight beyond their own.

Schickhimseel took to the air too, keeping her brothers company in the air. Lucretia had sharpened her butchering knife and cut the deer's throat, and looked up as her benefactress flew off. "I'll leave the entrails in the bucket for you, as usual," she said. "And thanks for everything." The young dragon made a graceful gesture like an airborne curtsy, then clawed skyward.

"It's our pleasure!" she said as she swiftly winged away.

Chapter 13: The Course of Love

Alfmund and Riki sat side by side on the veranda at Drakespring Farm, looking out over the Brightwater to the east and admiring the dramatic play of sun and shadow as the day that had begun with thunderstorms began to clear now that mid-afternoon was at hand. She'd joined him for lunch at Ynglingar after a late-morning session of weapons practice again, and this time she'd permitted him to accompany her home. There were yet chores Riki was expected to do, but for the moment she was free – and Bernadette had agreed that Alfmund could stay and join the family for supper.

Alfmund sat holding Riki's hand, aching to take her in his arms. He was not a virgin, not quite. There had been that incident with an older girl in Coldstein when he was sixteen, a passing fancy for her and an earth-shaking event for the young second son of a city guard. But clearly Riki was still a maiden – and as much as he longed for her, he could not see any honorable way to press her into a deeper relationship than the one they now had.

They had definitely become friends. The time spent at weapons play, and lunch at Ynglingar, was not only perfectly aligned with his budget (room and board was the bulk of the stipend afforded to young Brave Company recruits), but also something that Riki's parents were more than willing to allow – and that she enjoyed as much as he did. If only she weren't still so young! Why, oh why couldn't they have met in another three or four years, when he would be a commanding young man and she a grown woman free to choose her destiny?

Alfmund squeezed Riki's hand and sighed, which caused her look up at him. He was so sweet, so cute, so likeable. His ardent pursuit of her, despite the obstacles of her age and her parents' oversight, made her feel amazingly special and flattered. It reinforced her sense of self-worth, of being desirable, in a way that nothing else had since she'd first begun to notice the opposite sex as something more than "stinky boys."

Exactly what "desirable" meant in this context was something Riki had only a general idea about. It was akin, or so she believed, to what happened when Farmer Bendstrom came by with his bull once a year –planting calves in the wombs of their milk cows so that they'd continue to produce milk. Like the rooster treading the hens. But with loving, and care for one another thrown in – like with Mama and Riki's two papas.

The idea of Mama doing with Papa Erik and/or Papa Andrion what the bull had done with the cows was kind of hard (and a bit icky) to imagine, but it was clear they loved each other and supposedly that was what married people did – not just to get babies, as in the case of the bull and the cows, but as an expression of their love. Mama had given Andi one of her amulets when he turned sixteen, and he had completely refused to explain what it was for. So had Mama. It was all so mysterious and frustrating!

Alfmund's thoughts were running in similar paths to Riki's, though she knew it not. He disengaged his hand from hers and slipped his arm around her, pulling her close. Oh! Did she feel about Alfmund in a way that would make her want him as the cows wanted the bull? She wanted to feel that way, she felt she should – it was clear that he felt that way about *her*, and he had put so much effort into his courtship that she almost felt she owed him something. But when she thought about romantic passion, it was Fjuri who appeared in her mind's eye.

Recently, since Alfmund had become a presence in her life, Riki had caught Fjuri looking at her with an expression of tortured longing once or twice. He seemed incapable of friendly interaction with Alfmund, another sign – but then he appeared equally unable to interact with *her* – in any way whatsoever. They hadn't seen each other all that much recently, since he was Andi's friend and Andi had been spending a lot of time away from home on his missions for the Leukalfar Initiative. Riki was a bit proud of her big brother for that, but she missed him – and she missed the visits from Fjuri that usually happened when Andi was here.

Now it was Riki who sighed, and Alfmund looked down at her. "Penny for your thoughts," he said softly. She looked up at him, summer-blue eyes shining with innocence.

"I was just missing Andi," she said. "He's doing great things out there while I just spend my time doing chores." That was close to the truth. By the time Sigi was big enough to do the milking Riki would be of age and probably off doing whatever it was she was going to do in life. But it looked like she might very well be stuck as a farm hand until then – while her big brother, only two years older, was engaged in things that really mattered.

Alfmund looked down at her, gazing into those bottomless blue eyes, and spoke from the heart. "Ah, Riki! (He had eventually figured out that nobody called her by the birth name she'd given him on their meeting.) You are *so* beautiful!" He drew her to him in a deep kiss, and Riki closed her eyes and fell into his embrace. But behind those closed eyes, it was Fjuri Steadfast holding her, kissing her. Would he ever speak his mind?

Up along the main street of Waterdon, where a second story was being added to one of the town's small houses, Fjuri Steadfast wielded a hammer with fierce strokes. His powerful muscles drove the iron nails deep, as he struggled to contain his anger and frustration. An hour past, while he sat with his fellows finishing a late lunch, he had seen them walk past. Riki, holding hands with that Alfmund. That he was unable to condemn the young Norseman for anything beyond his persistent courting of the woman he loved, only added to his frustration.

I've known her since she was a baby… Bam! She's been like a sister to me… Bam! So why in all the hells can't I just tell her that I love her? Bam! Bam! Bam! His fellow construction workers eyed him askance. Fjuri now stood close to six-foot-four-inches and had the muscles to go along with his height, nor had the reports of the quest he'd completed with his best friend Andi Drakespring last year gone unnoticed. If he wanted to go on some kind of a rampage, the rest of the crew would just as soon keep their distance – even if he wasn't armed with anything deadlier than a carpenter's hammer.

Chapter 14: Return of the Lords

Meiskomtot flew high, very nearly enjoying himself, as he sought out one of Iscandia's mountaintop altars. Though he had been as deep into the mysteries of the dragon worshipers' magic as anyone, it was both delightful and perplexing that he was able to fly thus even in his undead state. The wings worked, though he had never taken on fuel to power them – nor was he capable of doing so. Where did the power come from? Was the energy of some star in a far-distant universe being plundered to keep him aloft?

He had to admit, reluctantly, that there were advantages to being undead. No need to stop and rest, no need to eat or drink, no need even to breathe. On the other hand he would have traded it in a heartbeat for the chance to truly live again. That didn't appear to be an option. As he approached the altar from the air he saw it was one with a Spell Wall. The central perch, which would have been occupied by a dragon in his time (receiving obeisance and tribute from pilgrims, and on the lookout for any who might arrive showing the spark that meant they were fireblood) was empty.

Dragons were few indeed in this modern world, if – despite the existence of a new generation and a remnant of elder dragons resurrected by Tarragin more than a decade past – this prime location had not been claimed. Tattered wings flapping, Meiskomtot came in for a landing atop the wall, facing outward to the altar's approach so he could survey the scene.

The steps and the hillside around them were strewn with bones. Some seemed to be those of mammoths, suggesting that a very big dragon indeed must once have held sway here. There were also the bones of cattle, and of men. Meiskomtot's memories of his life before awakening in that tomb were riddled with holes, and he could not recall which lord had claimed this perch, in the years before his presumed death.

One large skeleton far down the slope was of a dragon, but the undead shape-shifter felt no echo of a soul within it. This must be the remains of one of Tarragin's resurrected dragons, later killed by The Fireblood. The idea of there being only one fireblood in the world was so odd – it made Meiskomtot feel like a member of a nearly-extinct species, a relic of a forgotten time. He was both.

His glowing eyes continued to cast about, searching for clues. Then he spotted it – a contour of the snow-covered ground that looked unnatural. And he sensed a soul there, calling to him. It was one he knew: Schlangsachflom, serpent-inferno-strike, one of the most skilled with Holocaust of the dragons who had ruled during Meiskomtot's lifetime. Yet he had been brought down by ordinary men with ordinary weapons, lacking even the power of dragon spells!

Creaking, the undead dragon launched himself from his perch, gliding downslope to the spot where the corpse of Schlangsachflom lay covered in snow. "Fjur-Bruns-Zon-Ens!" he shouted, flames shooting from his mouth and melting away the snow cover. The corpse was mummified – but in far better condition than his own, he saw. Dead fewer than ten years, he judged. Only Tarragin had possessed the ability to return a dead dragon to full life, but Meiskomtot had a power of resurrection – of a sort – at his command. He used it.

As the withered, frozen heap of leather and bone that was once the mighty Schlangsachflom came to life, Meiskomtot uttered the spell that would command his aid: "SCHLANG-SACH-FLOM, I bind you! Follow me and obey my commands, until the moment of my fall!" For a natural-born dragon who had died thousands of years in the past, been resurrected for a few years, and then died again at the hands of mortal men and their puny but sadly effective weapons, Schlangsachflom was surprisingly quick to assess the situation.

"Meiskomtot!" he croaked in dragon tongue, the first word spoken since his most recent death, "What happened to you?" At that, he glanced down at his withered body and added, "What happened to *me*?"

"I have but recently awakened from a very long sleep," Meiskomtot said stiffly. His situation was a sore point, and he didn't need any crap from recently dead dragons – lords or not.

For the next several minutes, the undead dragon priest-turned-undead-dragon brought his recently-revived undead minion up to speed on the current state of affairs. Schlangsachflom was not any more delighted to learn of it than Meiskomtot had been. "What now, Master?" the undead dragon asked.

Natural-born dragons grew for as long as they were alive, and stopped growing at death. Schlangsachflom had continued to grow after Tarragin had resurrected him, but had enjoyed less than a decade of life before being killed again. He was now far smaller than the transformed dragon priest who had revived him, whose dragon form had somehow continued to increase in size during the millennia he had been in stasis in his human form.

Aside from that, the spell Meiskomtot had used bound Schlangsachflom to him – making *him* the lord instead of the natural-born dragon. "Now," Meiskomtot said in a rasping voice of doom, "we remind the mortals who their masters are. If Tarragin is truly gone we may never live again – but there is no reason we cannot *rule* forever! Follow me!" The two undead dragons took to the air.

The village of Wolf Crossing was little more than a small inn and a couple of cottages that had arisen where two of Iscandia's half-ruined roads met. The Wolf's Head Inn barely scraped by on the sparse trade from travelers, and the cottagers kept kitchen gardens and some livestock to support themselves – as well as obtaining a slight income from the sale of produce and handicrafts to the inn and its customers. There were four adult men and three adult woman in the settlement who were capable of wielding weapons, and they all had something – a bow they also used for hunting, a rusty sword brought back by an ancestor from some forgotten war. There was no need for such things, as who would threaten a place with so little to offer?

The two undead dragons, one of them huge beyond belief and so tattered it scarcely seemed possible it could fly, came in the middle of the afternoon with fire and destruction. There had been only two travelers staying at the inn, a messenger armed with nothing but a dagger and a young adventurer with a longsword. Neither of them were much use.

Meiskomtot perched on the inn's roof tree, only to have its beams collapse beneath his weight. Though there was little flesh on his bones, he was so large that no building in the tiny settlement could support his weight. The occupants fled, even as he set fire to the roof. Schlangsachflom, still getting used to being animate again after years of immobility, came down to the ground at the crossroads and attempted to engage the desperate defenders.

Considering how poorly armed they were, the villagers and the two inn visitors put up a surprisingly fierce fight. One woman who'd emerged from the larger of the two cottages (the roof of which was now aflame, thanks to Meiskomtot's Holocaust spell) proved to be an adept archer with a bow and arrows of quality far beyond what you might expect for a backwater like this.

Schlangsachflom was taken by surprise, as she darted around to his side and began firing those arrows at close range into the area where the left foreleg met the body. With a stab of agony, the undead dragon discovered that his heart had been pierced, and he fell. Damn fool! Meiskomtot though angrily. Was it not possible to get good help? He repeated the ritual, and the triply-dead Schlangsachflom became animate once again. As long as Meiskomtot himself lived, those he reanimated could rise over and over again – unless their souls were taken by essence capture or The Fireblood.

The smaller undead dragon returned to the fight seriously angry, whirling on the woman archer and seizing her with his jaws. He shook her like a terrier with a rat, breaking her spine, then flung her aside. Another of the villagers strove to pick up her bow, but was knocked down by a wing and raked from collarbone to pelvis with the long claw at its joint.

Meiskomtot rose again from the conflagration that was the inn before it should catch his own somewhat-flammable body on fire. Now that would be ironic, were he to perish in his own flames. He blasted the roof of the remaining cottage, sending it up in a pillar of fire, then amused himself by toasting individual villagers with neatly focused bursts of flame as they struggled from the wreckage and attempted to flee.

In a few minutes Wolf Crossing was only a trio of bonfires, scorched bodies littering the landscape and mounded at the crossroads. One last living resident, a boy of around twelve, attempted to flee from the rear of the second cottage to burn and Schlangsachflom was eager to go after him. They could not eat these people or their livestock, but there was a great vengeful satisfaction in destroying them and everything they had wrought.

As the smaller undead dragon rose from the ground to go after the fleeing boy, Meiskomtot bellowed "Hold! Let him go free!" Hovering in midair, Schlangsachflom turned to look at his master.

"Tender feelings, Meiskomtot?" he asked in tones of scorn. Though the spell – and the shape-changing priest's vastly larger size – bound him to obey, it was not a situation he happily accepted.

"No, you fool," the larger undead dragon rasped. "We need someone to spread the word. The people of Iscandia must know that their lords have returned."

Chapter 15: The Word is Spread

Bernadette was at her forge, putting the finishing touches on a fine sablium sword. When it was finished, it would be enchanted – though she hadn't yet decided which enchantments to use. She'd been fascinated by Rezira's revelation of techniques that would allow you to cast any known spell that would be applicable, such as magic wards on armor, or lightning storm on a blade.

The day was warm and she was working with the eastern side of the forge open, able to see the road and the view of the river beyond it. Erik had taken Sigi and his friend Joqui down there this morning for a fishing expedition, hoping to bring back some salmon for dinner. Bernadette usually just slipped into the water after the large fish and tickled them into her hands before flinging them up onto the bank, but they could be caught on hook and line as well.

Andrion had been gone the past two days on a trip to Sylvanian, visiting with Meri and the pudgy little Mirskhrazana Chanter, Liamdor. The leukalfar trade mission in that city was going well. They had rented a space near the market square, and goods were beginning to flow in. Householders loved the beautiful dypalfar artifacts the leukalfar offered for sale, and there was a market as well for the many things they made with chitin.

Putting the sword to the grindstone to sharpen it, Bernadette sighed. She missed her girl! Last year they had been apart for months while she and Andi were studying at the Eparchy. After their return from their remarkable quest through the dypalfar portal, the kids had gone back to their studies for a few more weeks. And now it seemed like they were hardly ever home any more. At least Andi should be back from Alfenstein soon.

"Hello the house!" came a shout from the road, and Bernadette shook herself out of her reverie and looked to see who was calling her. She recognized the tall, lean nachtalfar woman dressed in full steel armor and called back, "Miralis! Come up!" The elf warrior had changed scarcely at all in the years since Bernadette had first met her, only a few days after her arrival in Iscandia. She had rarely seen her outside of Wyrmshalla, for that matter. Miralis was body servant to Waterdon's elderly Eorl Ormund, and his constant companion.

Bernadette hung the sword in a rack to work on later, and hastily banked the forge fire. Then she walked down to meet her visitor. There was no one else here, as Riki was up in town at weapons practice with that young swain of hers. Another occasion for sighing. At this point in their lives, that four-year age gap between Riki and Alfmund was nearly insurmountable. Bernadette did not foresee a happy outcome for that relationship, though it was Alfmund's feelings more than Riki's she worried about.

The two women approached each other and stood on the walk halfway between the road and the front door of the farmhouse. "Fireblood," Miralis said, "I am glad to find you at home." Her face looked rather grim, causing Bernadette a spasm of concern. What was wrong?

"Is something amiss, Miralis?" she asked. "Is Eorl Ormund all right?"

Surprisingly Miralis cracked a smile at that, an expression seldom seen on her dark, stern countenance. "Oh, aye. That old warhorse will probably outlive us both." Her face resumed its seriousness. "But a messenger has just arrived with some distressing news, and Ormund is very anxious to consult with you about it. Can you accompany me now to Wyrmshalla?"

Huh! What was *that* about? Better get to it, though. "Please bear with me for just a couple of minutes while I lock up and get a few things," Bernadette told the body servant. "And then I can speed things up by fast-traveling us up there with my map." Since Andrion had unraveled the making of magic maps, less than two years after assuming the Magister-ship of the Academy at Eisenstag, he'd made them for an ever-widening circle of family and friends. Andi now had his own, as did Meri, and several of the leukalfar working closely with the Initiative had also been given them – though it would take quite a bit of ordinary travel before these new maps were well-populated with locations to which they would transport their owners.

Yet Bernadette still had her original map, the one she had innocently bought from a gatti trader shortly after arriving in Iscandia from Auverne. She had scarcely charged her anything for it (which was just as well since the young recent immigrant been nearly penniless at the time), and in later years she'd decided it must have been stolen. Or perhaps the trader had been motivated by her "doom-driven" status to give it away!

After closing up the forge and hastily changing into a more suitable outfit for calling on the eorl Bernadette tucked both her original map and the one that included the entire continent of Agena into her pouch, then accompanied Miralis out onto the front stoop and locked the door. In another few seconds, the two of them were standing at the approach to Wyrmshalla. The guards seemed startled to see them appear, as if they were on edge. "Welcome, Fireblood," one said respectfully. The current crop of guards seemed to be getting younger and younger, she mused as they swept through the doors up the long hall toward the dais at its far end.

The old man, his once-golden beard now white, looked profoundly relieved as he saw them approaching. Surprisingly, he went so far as to stand and come down the steps to greet her. They were old friends, and had been through a lot together. It had been a long time, though, since she had seen him looking so troubled. "Bernadette!" he said, clasping her hands. They'd gotten onto a first-name basis more than a decade before. "Thank you for coming – I have dire news."

"Please Ormund, don't stand for me," she replied. He had to be in his seventies now, and though he certainly was not frail it made her uncomfortable to see him standing.

"Let us *all* sit," he suggested, gesturing toward the long dining table that ran down the center of the hall. At this hour no one was sitting there. The eorl and his body servant sat on one side, Bernadette facing them, and he began.

"I received a messenger from Forestville not an hour ago," he explained gravely. "A young boy came staggering into town scorched and half-dead, and was taken up by the gate guards who carried him to the inn. After they got some food and water into him he had a horrifying tale to tell. He was from Wolf Crossing. You know it?"

Bernadette nodded. It was really just a wide spot in the road, similar to Bohrsstead or a dozen other little places where a few people gathered at a crossroads and decided it was a village. "I've been there," she told the eorl.

"But you will not find it there again," Ormund said grimly. "The entire village has been razed – burned to the ground and all the inhabitants save this one boy brutally slaughtered."

Bernadette's face paled, showing her shock. In Iscandia these days, who would do such a thing? Bandits didn't want to kill villagers or burn towns, as that would stop the flow of loot past their lairs. In answer to her questioning look, Ormund went on. "It was destroyed by dragons."

Chapter 16: Gathering

Bernadette walked down from Wyrmshalla, relief and worry swirling in her mind. The dragons that destroyed Wolf Crossing were none she knew. Some few of the remaining dragons raised by Tarragin had been swayed by Sneyagflug's arguments and had begun to interact in a more friendly fashion with humans. Far more of them had simply taken themselves away from human settlements entirely. Though the province's population was growing, there were still many square miles of empty space.

But the dragons involved in this attack had been undead. The boy had been very clear on that point, had even witnessed the larger, more ruinous-looking one reanimating the smaller one with some kind of spell. It had killed his mother, and that was when he had run for his life. But he had stayed long enough to see that the dragons did not eat anyone – or anything.

Her feet moved faster down the many steps to Ynglingar as questions roiled. Tarragin was long dead, beyond a shadow of a doubt. And she had witnessed him resurrecting a dragon down in Delvewood. That dragon had been completely fleshed and fully alive – before she, Andrion, and Giselle had killed it again. What could create a dragon *zombie*?

She trotted up the front steps and went into Ynglingar. The handsome hall reminded her of the Maiden, architecturally. Lunchtime was approaching, but she didn't see Riki and Alfmund sitting at table – so she continued on out the back doors to the practice yard. Sure enough, there was her girl. Her heart skipped a beat as she saw how beautiful Riki was in action. Tall, graceful, strong, and lightning-quick. She was sparring with Alfmund, laughing and happy, and giving as good as she got.

Bernadette hated to break up the party, but this was an emergency and she needed to round up the troops. As she approached the pair, Riki spotted her and her sword point fell. "Mom! What's the matter?" Was it that obvious? She supposed it must be.

"Hello, Alfmund," she said. "Riki, I'm sorry but something has come up and I need you home for a family conference – now."

Alfmund's face took on a look of disappointment coupled with concern. "Is there anything I can do, Mistress Drakespring?" Bernadette considered for a moment.

"I hope this problem won't be spreading, but if it does there's a chance the Brave Company's aid might be needed. For right now, though, I need to take Riki home with me."

"All right," he said softly. Then he stepped forward to give Riki a hug and a brief kiss, adding "Let me know when you can what's going on, Riki."

When the two got home, Bernadette once again using her map, they found Sigi and Joqui happily cleaning fish in the kitchen, while Erik sat at the dining table drinking a chilled ale. As soon as he saw them come in he knew something was wrong, and rose to his feet. He put his hands on Bernadette's shoulders and looked into her face, searching for clues. She jumped up and kissed him, then hopped down again and said "Relax, Erik! Finish your ale. In fact, I'd like one too."

The boys finished cleaning the fish. There were six of them, good-sized salmon, and Sigi put three into the Drakespring family's cold chest while the other three were wrapped in waxed paper and given to Joqui to take home. They might end up as the Caron family's lunch. After Joqui had left Sigi joined them at the table and Bernadette spilled the beans.

"Eorl Ormund called me up to Wyrmshalla to tell me that a village was wiped out by dragons," she explained briefly. Looks of shock appeared on the faces around her. "It wasn't any of the dragons we know," Bernadette went on. "At least none we've known recently – these dragons were undead."

There was a moment's silence, then Riki asked "Why did he call on *you*, Mom? We don't have anything to do with undead dragons."

"Because I'm The Fireblood, Riki. As long as the dead dragons that are being raised by this necromancer dragon or whatever it is have their souls, they can be brought back to life time and time again. Even if we killed the dragon that's raising them, somebody else with those powers might be out there too, and it could start again. I think that I may need to absorb the souls of *all* of the dragons that are now dead, in order to stop this."

Riki looked stricken. There were dozens, maybe hundreds out there! Then she had a thought. "It's a good thing we have Andi, then," she said. "He can absorb dragon souls too, right?"

"Good point, Riki. We need to get him back here, and Andrion too. If anybody knows what kind of magic might be able to raise undead dragons, it's probably him."

"What about Sneyagflug?" Erik put in. "He was alive back in the days of the dragons' power, one of the dragons that Tarragin brought back to life." Bernadette jumped to her feet. Lunchtime had come and gone, and she was getting hungry; but this situation had her so troubled she didn't want to wait any longer to start dealing with it.

"Good idea, Erik!" she called as she made for the door. The rest of the family trailed her out into the yard as she stood and cried, "SNE-YAG-FLUG!" They had to wait a couple of minutes before they saw the big red dragon winging in from the north. He had promised Bernadette he would always come to her call, even before she had become his Schunmurte, and he was as good as his word.

There'd been no rain for a couple of days, and dust swirled as he came in for a landing. Seeing her in her human form with some of her human family around her, he said, "Bernadette, it is good to see you. To what do I owe the pleasure?" They'd seen each other only rarely over the eleven years since their babies had been born, most recently last year when she and Andi had called him and the entire dragon brood to help at the Battle of Mrzhgradfendz.

"I'm afraid it's trouble, Red. Trouble that might be putting a big dent in all of our public relations efforts." He looked at her quizzically. So far as Bernadette knew her former consort was the second-biggest dragon living in the modern age – assuming old Ehrgeizig was still alive. His head was nearly as long as her body, his glowing red eyes bigger than her fist.

"A few days ago," Bernadette explained, "a tiny village in Waterdon march was completely destroyed by a pair of dragons. The witness said that one of them was huge beyond belief, the other smaller but still large. And they were both undead." Sneyagflug rumbled deep in his throat, a sound like a small avalanche, as he pondered what she'd said. Finally he spoke.

"This is ill news indeed," he said in his deep voice. "It must surely be an undead dragon priest who has stirred from his slumbers. You know of the potion and the dragon spells that allowed you and your human son to become shape-shifters, of course. This was what the dragon priests called the 'Reward,' being enabled to become as one of us when they had achieved the highest rank in their priesthood."

"Does that mean that both dragons were priests in dragon form?" Bernadette asked.

"I doubt it," the huge red dragon replied. "More likely, the larger was a dragon priest and the smaller a dead dragon that he raised to serve him." He went on, trying to explain. "Even we, who were supposedly the object of their church's worship, were not party to all of their secrets. They were deep into the necromantic arts, interring the dragons killed in the war with rituals that would let them be restored to full life when Tarragin came again. And they created all those aptrgangr to serve as guardians of their tombs and temples. If this dragon priest has broken out of his tomb and is raising dead dragons – as seems likely –he may well be planning to wreak havoc on Iscandia, to bring mankind under the thrall of the dragon worshipers once again."

Bernadette considered this, as the rest of the family stood looking stricken. They had spoken in Common for the sake of Erik, Riki, and Sigi, none of whom were fluent in the dragon tongue though they all had a few words of it. "I guess we need to find him and stop him before he raises many more dead dragons or causes any more destruction," Bernadette said at last. "But how *can* we find him? By the time word of him reaches us, he could have flown hundreds of miles away."

"I think," Sneyagflug rumbled, "that it's time for another family reunion."

Her agile mind quickly followed his thought, and she cried "DRACH-MON-DIEN!"

Sneyagflug joined her, Shouting "SCHICK-E-MAAD!" They took turns, working their way through the nineteen names of the children they had together, as one by one the young dragons winged in from wherever they had been when Called.

There was scarcely room for them all in the area of the road between the Maiden and the farm, and lest locals get freaked out by the sight of this many dragons in one place, they relocated their gathering across the road – to the land that ran between it and the Brightwater. Drachmondien, their Mondi, was the first to arrive – and he was greeted warmly by everyone in the family. They missed him, their little brother who had grown into a giant flying monster all too quickly.

When everyone had greeted one another and the commotion had died down, it was their father who addressed them. Still in Common, though, for the young dragons spoke it as fluently as any man or elf in Agena. "We believe that an undead dragon priest, one with the gift of taking dragon form, has escaped his tomb and is seeking vengeance on the descendants of those who defeated the dragon worshipers in ages past. He has reanimated at least one of the dragons that were killed after Tarragin resurrected them, and they are out there in Iscandia wreaking havoc. We need to find and stop them!"

"I think what we need to do," Bernadette put in, "is have everyone go out in parties of two. If your party spots any undead dragons, Call a member of the group nearest to here. If you're in that group and your teammate is Called, wait five minutes and then Call them back. Then the team nearest here will get word to the strike team, and we'll go there and stop them."

What a pity, Bernadette thought, that the Joining used by the dypalfar to communicate mind to mind across vast distances could not be used by anyone but the dypalfar. Using the power of the Calling spell to bring news of undead dragon attacks was going to be a complicated, time-consuming nightmare. But it was the only thing she could think of that stood a chance of pinpointing their enemies' location and striking at them.

"Sneyagflug, I imagine you can look out for yourself if you meet this dragon priest and any of his flying zombies. But you kids, I do *not* want you trying to fight him yourselves. If he killed you, he might be able to resurrect you under his command, and then you'd be fighting your own people and eroding everything we've worked for since you were born. And I don't want you killed, in any case!"

There was a chorus of "Yes, Mama" around the scaly circle. They might be many times her size while she was in her human form, but she had always commanded their respect. Erik, Riki, and Sigi were standing near the road, close enough to hear the conference without being in the way. Sigi happened to be glancing back toward the house, thinking fondly of lunch, when he spied a shimmering in the air a few paces away and his older brother (the human one) suddenly appeared.

Andi spotted Sigi and waved, then did a double-take as he realized that his view to the east was full of dragons. What were Sneyagflug and Andi's nineteen dragon siblings doing here, and why was Mom standing down there in the midst of them delivering a lecture of some kind? Like his younger brother (the human one), food was on his mind. But this seemed like it might be important enough to make him wait.

Andi turned and walked down the slope, hugging his human family members as he arrived. Mom was just saying, "You all work out what teams you're going to form and which area each team will search in. I need to go get Andrion and bring him back to join the strike team." Sneyagflug rumbled, "Bernadette, I believe it would we wise if we could locate Ehrgeizig to consult on this issue. He may have some information, may know who this dragon priest might be."

Bernadette had been about to wind her way through the crowd of her dragon offspring toward the house, thinking that lunch would be a good idea before fast-traveling to Sylvanian. That stopped her, though. "Just let me get something to eat," she told him. "Then we'll figure out how to do that."

When she got to the other side of the dragon herd she discovered Andi, and rushed to embrace him. "I'm so glad you're here!" she said. "This is perfect timing." Then looking around her she said "I suppose everyone here would like to eat?" There was a chorus of assent, and they made their way up to the house. Andi went downstairs to drop off his pack and gear in his room. By the time he'd returned to the kitchen, a big platter of sandwiches and a bowl of potato crisps were sitting in the middle of the table. They all dug in.

"So you're here by yourself?" Andi's mom wanted to know. He smiled. "We found another mech like Kziintke in Miurlion's dypalfar museum, and Kziintke activated her."

"Her?" she asked.

"She's molded to look like a woman, and I think that her magical essence vial contains a woman's soul," he explained. "Anyhow, she was really helpful getting the leukalfar down below Dypendwelve to listen to reason, and they're working on setting up a trade mission."

Andi went on, "Miurlion was a bit taken aback, but now he's really excited about the project. He and Kziintke and Jerzha, that's the new mech, are working with Gylabris to go through all of the mechs in his museum. It turns out a lot of them are in operational condition, and just needed to be activated."

"And Mothris?" Bernadette asked. She'd almost come to think of the leukalfar boy as another of her sons, over the year he'd been living with them.

"Uh, it turns out that the chief of the leukalfar beneath Dypendwelve has a daughter…" Oh dear. Bernadette supposed it was bound to happen sooner or later. She just hoped he would come to his senses soon, as his efforts were an important part of the Leukalfar Initiative.

Now that they'd been brought up to date on events in Alfenstein, Bernadette filled Andi in on the situation here – which was grim indeed. They thought it likely it wouldn't take too many villages razed by dragons before some vigilante fool would get it into his head that undead dragons and live ones were all pretty much the same, and the young dragons would be at risk. And they had been doing so well in their campaign to encourage the two sentient species to coexist in harmony!

"So, you're going fetch Papa Andrion and team up with him to track down these undead dragons?" Andi asked around a mouthful of chips.

"Right, we'll form nine teams of two dragons each to search for them," his mom replied. She explained her scheme for semi-rapid communication using the Calling spell.

"Why don't I go dragon and hook up with Mondi to make a tenth team?" Andi suggested. "We could search for Ehrgeizig while everybody else is looking for undead dragons."

Wiping her mouth with a napkin, Bernadette looked thoughtful. "That's not a bad idea," she said after a moment. "But there's one problem. You don't have a dragon name, so I can't use the spell to Call you." Andi grinned cheerfully. "You're right, I guess you got Schunmurte from Sneyagflug, but nobody ever thought to give *me* a dragon name. Why don't *you*?"

When Schunmurte and Sneyagflug had named their brood, they had given each dragonling his or her name in a sort of ceremony that turned that name into a dragon spell. The spell was referred to as Calling, but it was specific to the individual so named. In recorded history, no two dragons had lived at the same time bearing the same name. They were never a numerous race.

"I'm not sure how it works," she replied, "but I suspect *you* at least need to be a dragon when I name you. Maybe *I* don't, though… we'll see."

Erik spoke up, "If you're going after Andrion, Berni, I want to come along." She considered, then turned to her daughter. Though she was only fourteen, she had been fulfilling her responsibilities on the farm for a long time now. And with her height, it was hard to think of her as other than an adult.

"Riki, are you up for being the lady of the house while we're gone? This is a big responsibility, and it'll mean you won't be able to go around with Alfmund while we're gone." Andi's eyebrows went up. So, Riki's boyfriend was still hanging around. He'd thought the guy would cut and run when he found out how young she was, but it must be True Love. Just like him and Zira, he realized. Or was it?

Riki flushed. She was so frustrated, so tired of being treated like a child. And now she was being given the opportunity to step up and act like an adult. How could she refuse, even if it meant she couldn't go places with Alfmund for a while? Besides, Mom hadn't said *he* couldn't come *here*. That opened up a whole new, scary train of thought but she firmly stifled it. "No problem, Mom," she said with what she hoped was an air of mature equanimity. "It's just Sigi to look after, and the usual farm chores. And the Maiden's right down the road if I need to call for assistance."

Bernadette nodded, and met Erik's gaze to make sure they were on the same page. He smiled at her, his usual look of unruffled happiness backed by strength beyond steel. "All right then, Riki," she said. You'll be looking after the place and Sigi until we're able to come back. It'll probably be a couple of days at least."

The meal was finished, and Riki took it on herself to clear the dishes and begin washing up – a demonstration of her mature, responsible attitude. She half wished, after all of the weapons play lately, that she was being called on to join the strike team and go out there slaying undead dragons. But she lacked the inborn ferocity of her "cousin" Anja, and a part of her was just as glad to be staying here keeping the home fires burning and her baby brother safe.

Bernadette looked around at Erik and Andi. "We'd better get geared up for this," she told them. "Andi, you should put whatever you might be going to need in your flying pack. We'll meet outside in ten minutes, and see whether I can give you a dragon name that will work for the Calling spell." He nodded to her and went out the front door, going down the outside steps to his room again. He was a good enough mage that he didn't need to bring along a ton of armament, but he really wanted his bow. For the hundredth time he wished there was a way to transform to dragon without having to remove all his clothes and gear first.

Erik grinned at Bernadette, and stepped close to put an arm around her as they walked down the corridor to their rooms. The three of them most often slept together in the house's master bedroom with its enormous bed, but Erik kept most of his armor and weaponry in his own space next door. His summer-blue eyes were dancing with excitement. It had been a long time since he'd been called on to practice his skills in combat, and he was looking forward to fighting with Berni and Andrion at his side.

A few minutes later all of them had assembled on the walk between the front door and the road. Down the hill, the dragons were still working out their team assignments. Andi came up the stairs wearing a robe and carrying his specially-designed pack, heavy with his armor, bow and quiver of arrows, and various supplies. He left it sitting on the ground near where his family was gathered and excused himself to walk around to the west side of the house. There, only people standing on the walls of Waterdon far above had a view of him as he hung up his robe, stepped naked to the center of a clear space between the house and the cistern tower, and took his dragon form.

Next, Andi hopped into the air to clear the house and came down in a swirling of wind near where Mom, Papa Erik, Riki, and Sigi awaited him. "I hope this works," Bernadette said. Then she went into the ritual, in the dragon tongue: "Young dragon, thy name is GULDEKIIND. Henceforth, when one with the power of dragon spells speaks your name, you will hear it and have the power to go to them if you desire."

Andi felt a sensation as though an impossibly thin silken cloak had fallen over him, floating down from top to bottom to envelope him completely. Golden Child, he thought. Odd. Riki was Mom's truly golden child, but then "golden" didn't necessarily have to be about looks. It was kind of flattering, he supposed. "I think it worked, Mom," he said, "but I suppose we'd better test it. Let me fly up the road a bit and see if you can Call me back."

His mom beamed at him, and he took to the air. He flew north for a couple of minutes and then landed, finding the Maiden as well as their farm lost beyond the southern horizon. A young dragon could fly fast, when he wanted to. Suddenly he heard it: "GULD-E-KIIND!" (though surely he was far beyond normal earshot) and he knew who was calling him and from where. He leapt up into the sky. And somehow, just by willing it, he found himself suddenly within sight of the person who had called and was winging toward her. Wow, what an amazing spell!

They reunited, and Andi dipped his head so his flying pack could be hung around his neck. Then they went down to rejoin the dragons in the field to the east. Mondi was quick to speak up as they came, "Mama, I want to team with Andi and go to look for Ehrgeizig." Two minds with but a single thought, it seemed.

"Good," she said, "that was his idea too. And everybody, your older brother now has a dragon name: Guldekiind." A cacophony of chatter erupted as the young dragons commented on the name and eventually decided it was good.

Finally Bernadette was ready to send them on their way. "Erik, Andrion, and I will be back here within two days and ready to mobilize if the undead dragons are sighted. In the meantime, who has the area closest to here?"

"That would be us," Purpurflug and her brother Wissliiben spoke up. "We're going to cover from here to Coldstein."

"Everybody got that?" Bernadette asked. "If you spot any undead dragons, Call Purpurflug or Wissliiben. Whichever one was not called, you'll call your partner back in five minutes to get the information. Then both of you will fly here to report."

They all acknowledged her instructions, then in twos they took to the air and flew off in nine different directions. Some of them would have many hours of flight ahead of them before they reached the territory they'd been assigned; but they'd be keeping their eyes open on the way. Bernadette heaved a sigh, half relief and half anxiety, as she watched her children fly away. Andi/Guldekiind remained, along with Mondi and Sneyagflug.

"Do you have any idea where we might look for Ehrgeizig?" Andi asked the big red dragon. "I have not seen him since that time on Muuterhorn after the fall of Tarragin," Sneyagflug rumbled. "It may be that some of the dragons from that time who still remain may know of his whereabouts. I have been… busy with other things."

"I know somebody we can talk to," Mondi said. Since he'd gotten too big to live at home, he had traveled widely and knew of several elder dragons who'd either become more friendly to humans or removed themselves from human contact.

"I'm relying on you, little bro," Andi said. He knew Mondi the best of his numerous scaly siblings, and had not had nearly as much experience with the "dragon community." "Okay, let's go then," he went on. It occurred to him that he was probably in need of a rest, after fast-travelling in from Alfenstein. But he was so excited by the situation, and the opportunity to go on a flying quest with his much-missed younger brother, that he felt ready to fly for hours. "'Bye," he said, encompassing his human family and Mondi's enormous father as well. The two young dragons, larger bronze and smaller red one, took to the air and had soon winged out of sight.

"What are you going to do, Red?" Bernadette asked Sneyagflug.

"I think I will just cruise around, looking for undead dragons and keeping an eye on the kids," he said. "If I find any, I'm going to need you or the boy to be there for the kill so their souls can be taken out of play."

She nodded tensely. "We'll be in touch then," she said. "Safe travels."

After the last of the dragons had flown off Bernadette surveyed the field. The green grass was trampled in a huge circle. She joined the rest of the family and they went back to the house. Then she and Erik, both fully armed and armored, kissed and hugged their daughter and son before shimmering out of view, on their way to Sylvanian.

Chapter 17: The Search for Ehrgeizig

Andi, aka Guldekiind, flew side-by-side with his brother Drachmondien. They'd been constant companions from the time Andi was five until around five years later; when the young dragon had gotten too big to fit inside the house, too hungry to be fed at home. He'd hooked up with two of his dragon siblings then, hunting and roosting in the mountains to the east of Waterdon, and the family he'd grown up with only saw him a few times a year after that – but they all loved him.

They'd climbed to an altitude where an air current was blowing in the right direction, and didn't have to exert much effort in flying, so they were able to converse as they flew. They hadn't seen each other in months, as Andi had been so busy with the Leukalfar Initiative. He'd scarcely gone dragon half a dozen times in the past year, though he loved being able to soar.

"So what have you been up to, Mondi?" he asked as they glided along.

"I've been doing the Grand Tour," his brother replied. "Visiting with everyone. I was at home twice in the past year, but you weren't there. Missed Meri, too."

"Yeah," Andi replied. "She's been as busy as I have, working with the other half of the Leukalfar Initiative. Mothris and I have been visiting the various tribes and trying to get them with the program, start teaching them Common so they can communicate with the rest of humanity in Iscandia. She and Liamdor, and a few others with good Common, have been getting men and the other alfar races used to the idea of leukalfar among them. She's been in Sylvanian the past couple of months, setting up a trading post for leukalfar goods."

"So what's next," the younger dragon asked facetiously, "snow troll outreach?" Andi chuckled, a peculiar sound coming from a dragon.

"I wish," he said. "Ghrztum and I have discussed it, but I don't think there's any way for us to communicate with his fellow snow trolls. They must have a language and some kind of culture, or he wouldn't have turned out to be the person he is. Maybe after we're finished getting the empire to accept leukalfar and dragons, we can capture a wild snow troll and hog-tie him or her until it can learn to speak Common. I'm not sure what good it would do, though – it's not like snow trolls make anything that humans want. But maybe if they could speak with us, there'd be fewer killed when the two species meet."

"Well," Mondi replied, "good job. I'm glad to see our family involved in such good works." He really had been indoctrinated by his mother, more so than the rest of his siblings though they were scaly angels by comparison with the dragons from ages past.

"So who are we going to see?" Andi asked.

"A dragon by the name of Zuumerzohn," his brother replied. "I met him four years ago, after he'd taken up a hunting territory near the northwest coast of Iscandia." Drat, Andi thought – it was going to be a *long* flight.

Mondi went on, "He hadn't had that much contact with humans since being resurrected. He wasn't too happy about getting killed in the Uprising. And he's one of the few of the elder dragons who were willing to listen to what we had to say about staying out of trouble. To most of them, we're just a bunch of upstart brats. We usually only got respect from most of those old-time dragons if Father was along. Anyhow, he knew Ehrgeizig, and had seen him a few times since Tarragin was killed. I'm hoping he might have some idea where the old fellow is hanging out these days."

They didn't make the trip all at once. Spotting a small herd of elk down below, the two young dragons decided it was suppertime and stooped silently (or as silently as possible for a scaly creature with leathery wings – owls they were not) on the prey. Each of them successfully bowled over one of the large deer with Gale before pouncing to snap their necks.

Mondi had been raised as a human (within the limits of his size and shape) for the first few years of his life, and his culinary preferences were much like those of Andi in dragon form. They both liked their meat free of hair, crispy outside and hot/juicy inside. How convenient that they carried their own stoves within. As they were devouring the hapless elk, Andi remarked "wouldn't this be great with some of Mom's wine and mushroom sauce?" Mondi managed a fair approximation of a smile, jaws half open and tongue lolling out, red eyes glittering. He took another bite.

It was getting dark, and they decided to curl up and sleep for the night. They were in the wilderness, and there were no creatures near here (except possibly a rogue dragon they didn't know about) that would be likely to disturb them. As soon as the sky was light they were on their way again, the first rays of the morning sun glistening on the scales of their backs.

They flew far north of Alfenstein, moving along toward the coast. Andi could have reverted to human and used the map to take him and Mondi to one of the landmarks in this part of Iscandia, but it would have been awkward appearing out of thin air accompanied by a largish dragon. Even more awkward to then strip naked and go dragon to continue the journey, if there were any people around (which was likely, since such landmarks were usually the work of man). Besides, just as much or more time would have elapsed – and this way he and his brother had the chance to spend some time together.

As they neared the coast their sharp draconic vision picked up a dragon circling in the air above it, roaring as the elder dragons so often did. The new wave dragons, that is to say Mondi and his siblings, were much more sociable and not nearly as territorial – and they'd found that circling silently was a better strategy for catching game.

As they drew within speaking distance, Mondi called out "Hail, Zuumerzohn! Drachmondien greets you!" The green dragon, who was far larger than either of them though considerably smaller than Sneyagflug, ceased his circling and hovered in midair.

"Young Drachmondien!" he said, "It is long since we met. How fare you and your kin?"

"We're all well, Zuumerzohn," the much-smaller dragon replied. "This is my Fjurblut brother Guldekiind, who was born human. Might we land? We have something to discuss with you."

The larger dragon nodded, and the three of them circled down to a broad, scrub-covered plain that sat atop low cliffs overlooking the rocky shore. Zuumerzohn had a fat living here, taking walruses and other large sea creatures at the water's edge as well as the deer that occasionally came to this plateau to graze.

Andi and Zuumerzohn went through the dragon ritual of toasting each other with Holocaust, then Mondi told him of the recent crisis. "Call me if you should see any undead dragons here," he concluded, "though I doubt any will come where there are no men. If Sneyagflug is right and the larger undead dragon is a dragon priest, he's probably bent on terrorizing the human population into worshiping dragons again, reviving the dragon religion."

"Huh," Zuumerzohn said thoughtfully. He hadn't been alive all that many decades before the Uprising had taken his life, and on being resurrected he'd concluded that the whole business of dragons ruling humans had been a bad idea. "In the days when we dragons were far more numerous," he told the youngsters, "the dragon priests and their church pretended to worship us. But it seems to me that they were more interested in using us as a means to have power over their fellow humans, and over the drachen as well. They had many secret arts, and though some they could not hide from us, like their 'Reward,' I suspect there were many others. Likely this priest-turned-dragon plans to use undead dragons under his thrall as enforcers to set himself up as the ruler of Iscandia – a ruler who will never die."

"He died once, he can die again," Andi said. "Even if we have to burn his body and scatter the ashes, we can put an end to him taking physical form. And if my mom or I can be near when he dies, we can capture his soul and end him for all time. But we'll have to catch him first!"

"Well, I hope that you will succeed," the elder dragon replied. "I wish never to see the dragon priests back in power. Was this the only reason you have sought me here?" It was a long way out of the way, and the old drache often went years without seeing another sentient being.

"Indeed there is," Mondi admitted. "My father Sneyagflug suggested that we should seek council with Ehrgeizig, assuming he still lives. I think that you were once one of his followers?"

"Yes," Zuumerzohn said with an ironic edge to his tone, "old Ehrgeizig was a teacher to me for a time after the passing of

88

Tarragin. He had given instructions in the casting of dragon spells to those old men on Muuterhorn for thousands of years while he was the only dragon living, all the while anticipating Tarragin's return. But after your mother defeated Tarragin in Asengard, he tried to set himself up as the new leader of the drachen."

"You didn't stay with him and his teachings, then?" Andi asked. The dragons he knew best were his own siblings and their father, a dragon who had known Ehrgeizig of old and had not cared much for him. He had no idea in what regard the ancient drache was held by the rest of his kind.

"We drachen are too independent to cleave to a ruler who would guide us with words," Zuumerzohn explained. "Tarragin was something of a god to us, Vaterhiin made flesh. But after his defeat on Muuterhorn and later his death, some sought the leadership of Ehrgeizig because he had been on earth longer than any dragon yet remaining. He may still have a few who defer to him, but I was not the only one who tired of his pedantry. He spent too many years alone on that mountaintop, I fear."

"How long has it been since you saw him last?" Mondi asked.

"Only once since I came here to live," Zuumerzohn replied. "It was two… no, three years ago. He came through here and spoke with me for a time, trying to convince me to join him at his fastness and resume lessons in the spoken spells. I thanked him, but declined the offer."

"His fastness? Where's that?" Mondi responded.

"Oh, hadn't you heard? He set up housekeeping at Todenstor."

Andi was amazed. Todenstor, of course, was a huge ancient Norse complex unreachable except from the air. Had not Sneyagflug carried his mom and papas-to-be there on his back, they would never have been able to cross through the dragon priests' portal to Asengard and kill him there. It was an ideal place for dragons, he supposed. No men but aptrgangr, accessible only by those with the power of flight. But maybe Mom had it on her map? He certainly had no idea how to fly there.

"Mondi, do you know how to find Todenstor from the air?" he asked his brother.

"No," he replied. "Father knows, of course, but none of us kids have ever been there – and *he* must not have been there since Ehrgeizig moved in or he would have known where to look for him." To Zuumerzohn he said, "Old one, is there a chance you could escort us there?"

Amusement touched the older dragon's tone as he said, "Sorry. That's too long a flight for little purpose and I don't like to leave my territory. Suppose some upstart should move in while I was gone?"

"As I see it," Andi said to Mondi, accepting that this dragon who hardly knew them had no reason to grant them such a large favor, "We can Call your father or else fast-travel back home. Mom, Erik, and Andrion should be there by the time we get back, and she's sure to have the place on her original map."

"But that means one of them will have to take us there, right?" Mondi asked.

"Oh, good point," his brother replied. Mom and both his papas had all been to Todenstor while she was carrying the map, so it would work for any of them to go there again. That would mean they'd have to borrow one of the members of the Strike Team for a round trip that was going to take hours. "It'd probably be better to try calling," Andi told Mondi.

"Shall I do the honors?" Mondi asked, hoping his father wasn't going to be annoyed at being Called. He was out looking for the undead dragons just as were his dragon siblings, and likely wouldn't want to be interrupted. He cried "SNE-YAG-FLUG!" and they all continued to sit on the ground, waiting for the big red dragon to appear. Nothing happened.

After five minutes had gone by and Sneyagflug still had not appeared, Mondi said "Shria! We must have caught him at a bad time, I guess. I hope he's all right. He's big, but from what I hear that priest dragon is bigger still."

"Let's go home, then," Andi said. "Maybe we can get one of my parents to take us there and then come straight back. Probably Erik or Andrion, so that they'll be able to add it to their own map. And I'll be adding it to mine." With that he cast a spell and became a tall naked youth, for the time it took for him to hurry into his clothing. Zuumerzohn watched bemused.

Before the brothers left, the older dragon had one more thing to say. "So Drachmondien, how are those sisters of yours?" Though his facial features remained immobile, he seemed somehow to leer.

"Still *way* too small to breed, Zuumerzohn. Give it another twenty years, probably. That'll give you time to practice your social graces. My sisters aren't going to be making babies with just any dragon that flies in out of the wilderness." Zuumerzohn just sighed.

Chapter 18: Sneyagflug

Flying over Iscandia's north shore, high in the chill air, Sneyagflug spotted some walruses basking on the gravel beach below him. He'd been flying for hours, keeping a sharp eye out for dragons. During that time he'd spotted two of the search groups and conversed with them. Neither had seen any signs of the undead dragons they were searching for, and he'd continued on his way. Now he dived, snapping up one of the blorpy-looking pinnipeds in his massive jaws and downing it in a couple of bites. They weren't all that big compared with him, but they were rich and high in calories.

He'd spent the night roosting at a mountaintop altar, occupied only by the skeletons of creatures ranging from goats to men and even a couple of dragons. He had to admit to himself that he was drawn to such places, though after years of spending time in the company of his children he found it lonely somehow. And sad to contemplate that this, which should have been a choice territory sought after – even fought over – by any dragon in the area, should now be home only to dry bones.

Another couple of the walruses were too slow to get away, and Sneyagflug topped off his tank with them. Schunmurte might prefer to toast her meat before eating it, as did his son Drachmondien; but he and the rest of the brood were just as happy to eat it at body temperature – moments after the prey had ceased to breathe.

He waited a quarter of an hour on the strand, letting his meal digest a bit. Then he launched himself back into the air, and began flying in an easterly direction. He spotted the settlement of Norcove, little more than a fishing village though it was the seat of a march, down below him. And were those flames erupting from the harbor?

As he flew lower he spotted flying figures. He had found those he sought! But now it appeared there were *three* undead dragons. Could he take them all on? He wasn't about to Call any of the children here to face these foes, and while he could try to Call Schunmurte that would only work if she were in dragon form. She would not even hear the Call if not, and as she was planning to team with her human husbands (he still considered herself one of her husbands, still loved her as much as was possible for one such as he) she would likely be remaining human.

Well, he couldn't just hover here and watch them destroy the place, could he? He dived, coming in above a leathery-looking undead dragon far smaller than himself as it hovered over the ships in the harbor, setting one after another aflame. All dragons had the Holocaust spell, but it was used more as a greeting than a weapon among themselves. Actually other than the names of his consort and their children, Holocaust was the only spell in Sneyagflug's own arsenal. But he was big, and he had teeth and claws – and considerably more mass than the flying mummy beneath him.

As his rending front claws sank into the undead dragon's shoulders and he bent his head in an effort to bite through its withered neck, he heard his son Drachmondien Call. Sorry son, he thought, making a mental note of the young dragon's whereabouts. He'd never tried answering a Call after a long delay, and wasn't sure if the spell would still work. But he really, *really* couldn't leave just now!

The undead dragon struggled in his grasp, unable to fly or turn its head around to strike at him with its teeth. This one looked to be in pretty good condition, and had likely been dead only a few years. Sneyagflug shuddered mentally to imagine what would happen if this dragon priest and his minions started killing some of the remaining live dragons and bringing them back to life under his control. A fully-fleshed dragon was much more dangerous than a mummified one.

His powerful jaws met in the dragon zombie's neck, a few feet up from the shoulders, and using his own immensely powerful neck muscles he twisted savagely, breaking the spinal column and shredding the desiccated flesh surrounding it. The head and neck broke off from the body, which had now gone limp in his claws, and he released it from his jaws with a toss of his head that sent it spiraling down onto the deck of one of the ships that was blazing below them.

Just as Sneyagflug released the body, hoping it would burn as well (though it seemed likely that whatever this priest's magic, he could not reanimate a dragon that was in two pieces), he heard an angry roar and was hit by a blast of intense cold right between his upper set of shoulder blades. His wings went numb for a moment, unable to flap. Fortunately he could still glide, and in another few moments feeling came back and he swooped back up into the air before turning to face his attacker.

By Vaterhiin, the creature was enormous! How could it even get aloft, with such size and with wings so tattered and shredded it looked like a pile of leathery rags? "SNEYAGFLUG!" it bellowed, "I know you!" The big red dragon flinched as he felt a writhing within him. There had been magical power behind that calling of his name. He hadn't felt anything so awful since the time when lovely Schunmurte, the object of all his desires, had felled him with repeated applications of the dreaded Dragonfall spell.

If Sneyagflug was a hawk to the recently fallen dragon's crow, so this creature (who could only be the undead dragon priest in dragon form) was an eagle. Yet he could not just fly away leaving Norcove to its fate. Perhaps the undead tissues were flammable? He tried Holocaust, but the flames licked around it without seeming to touch the undead monster at all.

Hovering in mid-air with those ruined wings, it bellowed laughter at him at the futility of his attack. "You have destroyed Schlangsachflom," it then raged, "my 'first-born'! I have others now, but I need more. Are you volunteering to replace him?" Instead of replying, Sneyagflug flipped a wing and took off at full speed toward the center of town, where another of the shape-shifted priest's undead minions was perched atop the rooftree of a building beside the second of the town's two streets.

A group of guards and ordinary villagers with bows were attacking it, filling it with arrows that didn't seem to do it much harm. Likely one would need to get it on the ground and go at it with swords, in order to damage it to the point where the animating magic would be severed beyond hope of resurrection. The priest was behind him, but had nowhere near Sneyagflug's speed. He had time to do these people one more favor before he had to flee.

While the undead dragon's attention was on the townspeople below him, Sneyagflug stooped from above. He tore, not at the creature's neck, but at its left wing. If even one wing was shredded beyond usability, it would never be able to get off the ground again. Surely if the priest's resurrection magic extended to repairing damage done to dead flesh, he would have started on himself. As fast as he could, claws sunk into the dragon's back, he mauled its wing with his teeth until the leathery membranes were nothing but a thin ruffled edging along the bones. That ought to do it!

With a mammoth effort, still holding on with the claws of all four feet, Sneyagflug lifted off the roof carrying the undead dragon. It turned its head to snap at him but couldn't quite reach. He glided down from the roof tree to a spot in the street with no people standing in it and dropped the dragon to the cobblestones. It struggled to arise again, but with one wing now stripped of lifting surfaces it could no longer fly.

The human defenders now ran to attack it, many of them wielding swords and axes, and Sneyagflug flew off to leave them to it. "Cut off its head!" he warned them in Common as he took to the air. He had expected that absurdly huge undead priest/dragon to be on him by now, but it was nowhere in sight. Then he spotted it. Instead of flying after him, it had come down to land on the broad expanse of snowy hillside just south of the town.

It said something, and in a moment the dragon had vanished to be replaced with a naked, skinny, not particularly tall aptrgangr. The priest himself! And seemingly, he was suicidal and had decided to put an end to his rampage by offering himself up to Sneyagflug on a platter. One rather distasteful bite, and the undead monster would trouble Iscandia no more.

These thoughts had no sooner crossed the big red dragon's mind, however, than the priest cried out again and was now seen to be fully armored and holding a staff. Uh, oh… He pointed the staff at the incoming dragon and fired a bolt of some kind of energy. Sneyagflug had been gliding in low, and as he realized what the priest was doing he suddenly flapped down hard, lifting himself a couple of dozen feet just as the bolt sizzled through where he'd been a moment before. Behind him, there was a loud explosion as it hit the peak of the roof on the town's inn and set it ablaze.

The priest was already taking aim again when Sneyagflug realized that it was probably time to get the hell out of here and call for reinforcements. The staff's second blast hit his tail, exploding and taking off the tip of it in a burst of agony that only sent him winging away faster.

Watching his adversary disappear over the horizon, Meiskomtot let fly with a colorful burst of profanity. Down the town's easternmost street, the defenders had killed Scharfmordiir and were busy hacking him to pieces. Two of his most promising recruits, forever destroyed! While their souls still lived, their bodies were beyond repair. He made a mental note to himself to acquire some magical essence vials of the largest type, so that he could capture his minions' souls and save them for later use the next time that happened.

As fireblood, even undead and in dragon form, he would absorb those souls if he was within range at their deaths. Or in this case, at the severing of the magic that animated their undead bodies. But he would be unable to re-deposit those souls in other bodies once they were absorbed – whereas if they were in magical essence vials he had full control over them. He could put them into soulless dragon bodies, should any become available.

Another thought occurred to him, as he transformed back into dragon form once again and took to the skies. Let the men of Norcove await their destruction another day. He needed to look in on his other "children" before too many more of them fell. But he wanted Sneyagflug dead, and he wanted that magnificent body. Not for one of his minions, but for himself. He knew the spells – not only for the transfer of his soul, but the dragon spell that could transform a natural-born dragon into a man. A big tall redhead, he'd be willing to bet. If the body was not too damaged when he took possession, it might almost be like being alive again!

Chapter 19: Drakespring Farm

Riki sat alone on the veranda in the late afternoon, gazing out at the beauty of the river and the mountains beyond it, and sighed. Being the "adult" in the house and looking after her little brother hadn't been nearly as different from regular life as she'd hoped. She missed her parents, but she was certainly capable of handling the farm chores by herself, doing housework, or cooking meals. With just her and Sigi there, it was actually less work than usual.

The big issue, the one that had filled her with anxiety when Mom and Erik went off to Sylvanian leaving her and Sigi alone, had proven to be no issue at all: an hour or so later Alfmund had stopped by with three of his fellow Brave Company members, off on a quest to clean out a cave full of bandits near Coldstein. This was supposed to be a training mission, hence they'd sent more of their number than usual. He kissed and hugged her goodbye, regret clear in his gray eyes, before taking his leave. They would likely be back about the same time she was expecting her parents to return.

Her chores finished, she spent some time with her sketchbook and re-read one of her favorite romances. Real life didn't seem to be anything like the stories. Even the story of Mom and Riki's two papas seemed kind of made-up. Was it ever really like that? She knew Anja and Lars were in love, had been together for years but showed no signs of wanting to get married and settle down. Maybe when they got tired of adventuring they'd tie the knot. Riki longed to be swept off her feet, washed away in a flood of passion… and feared it at the same time. She didn't like losing control, even as she wished she could experience feelings too strong to let her head overrule her heart.

Of course Mom was nine years older than she was now when all that happened. Maybe Riki just needed to be patient and wait for true, overwhelming love to come. She sighed again. Sigi came back from playing with Joqui and swimming in the big outside pool at the Maiden, and she put a simple supper of grilled chicken with bread and veggies on the table.

It was high summer, so even after they finished the meal there was still some light in the sky. It was still warm out too, one of the warmest evenings of the season so far, so they went out onto the veranda together to watch the evening come on. Thus they were well-positioned to see Andi and Mondi return, shimmering into existence on the road below the house.

They jumped off the settee and walked down to greet them. Riki and Sigi, who was less than a year younger than Mondi, hugged the young dragon's head. "I'm starving!" he declared. "I don't suppose you happen to have a stag hanging in the cold room?" Part of the rear section of Drakespring House's basement, built entirely of stone, had been fitted out for hanging game and storing root vegetables.

"Sorry," his sister told him.

"Are Mom and the papas back yet?" Andi wanted to know.

"Not yet," Riki said with a shake of the head. "I thought they'd be here by now, but something must have delayed them. Maybe they ran into those dragons." Their parents might be old, but neither Riki nor Andi doubted for a moment that they were a match for any dragons they might need to fight – living or otherwise. Hadn't they defeated Tarragin? So they were not worried… yet.

"Well, I'm going to go hunting while there's still a little bit of light," Mondi said. "I'll come back to sleep in the farmyard tonight, and see you in the morning if not sooner." He quickly flew off, heading for the hunting grounds east of the river where he'd made his home for much of the past five years.

"He's not the only one starving," Andi said with a grin. "What is there to eat?" His sister smiled back.

"Fear not, O ravenous one! I cooked too much food for dinner, so there's plenty of cold chicken, bread, and some seasoned veggies." She'd been cooking for years and wasn't bad at it. Neither was Andi, for that matter, and Meri was learning how as well. Sigi's repertory so far only included his personal favorites.

They all returned to the house and Andi made short work of the leftovers. "Since the parents aren't back yet," he announced, "I think I'll go up to town. Maybe I can pry Fjuri loose for a little visit. We've hardly seen each other in weeks, except for that dinner the other night."

Tell me about it, Riki thought bitterly as she smiled and said, "See you later, then."

At Brightsgate Cottage Andi found the family relaxing around the firepit, though no fire had been lit and the front door was open in hopes of catching some of that breeze. He was greeted with enthusiastic warmth, his transgressions regarding luring Fjuri off for an authorized quest last year pretty much forgotten.

Edla of course wanted news of Meri, and unfortunately Andi couldn't supply any. He hadn't seen his leukalfar sister in weeks. Edla, tall now and approaching puberty, was at an age where Meri's trips around Iscandia, the projects she was involved with, seemed infinitely interesting and exciting compared with her daily round of domestic chores. She hadn't discovered boys yet, a fact for which her mother Lifa was profoundly grateful.

"So, what have you been up to recently?" Lifa asked. She loved Andi like a son, but one about whom she was a little bit uneasy. He was so much more... "out there" than her own boy. That whole fireblood thing, she supposed, and having standout parents like Bernadette and Andrion, must account for it. Andi gave her his best grin, guaranteed to melt all females above a certain age. Unfortunately, that age appeared to be about the same as his mother's. But it sure enough worked on Zira, and that was enough for him.

"Mothris and I went up to Mrzhgradfendz and collected Gylabris and Kziintke, along with that leukalfar lady who was one of the main leaders of the slave revolt in Mrzhandtham. We took them to meet Miurlion, Diane, and Georges down below Dypendwelve, and discovered another dypalfar mech like Kziintke in Miurlion's old museum. Kziintke himself activated it – and it's a her!"

A flood of questions erupted, and it was some time before Andi could move on to the more urgent news. He lowered his voice somewhat, leaning forward and urging his audience to do the same. "This isn't general knowledge, and it would be a good idea if it doesn't go outside this room yet." That certainly got everyone's attention. "It seems that one of those old undead dragon priests, like Mom and my papas have fought down at the bottom of ancient Norse ruins a few times, got out of his crypt and went dragon. He's been raising dead dragons as zombies, though they seem to have more volition than the usual zombie from what I've heard – and they've been attacking human settlements."

This announcement was met with horror and more questions, but Andi didn't have a lot of answers. He knew of only one attack, but more were expected – and he and his kin were doing what they could to deal with it. As one of only two known firebloods alive in Iscandia, Andi was going to be a key person in stopping the dragon attacks by stealing the souls of the rogue dragon priest's minions.

"We have to go to Todenstor and talk with old Ehrgeizig," he told them, "as soon as Mom, Erik, and Andrion get back. They hadn't gotten home yet when Mondi and I arrived, after talking to an old dragon Mondi knows who told us where to find him. We hope he'll have some more information that will help us fight the guy, so I'll probably be gone again sometime tomorrow."

"I want to go with you!" Fjuri declared. The young man, a few months short of his seventeenth birthday, was now close to looking Erik in the eyes and had filled out dramatically in the past year as he continued working construction. He was also now sporting a decent growth of facial hair (something Andi had yet to achieve), a neatly trimmed black chin beard and moustache that made him look years older. To all intents and purposes he was a man, but he was still tightly wrapped in the bosom of his family and had not yet seized control of his own destiny.

Lifa and Bjorn exchanged glances. Between the two of them they had enough gravitas to anchor a large dragon – or an exceptionally large and well-built young man – but they were all too aware that the time was coming when they were going to have to let their nestling fly on his own. As was often the case in their family, Lifa spoke first – though Bjorn, as Hegmar's foreman, ought rightfully to be the one deciding if employee Fjurbund Steadfast could be let off of work.

"Fjuri," she said coolly, "if you think that you can help Andi and his family with this fight you should go. I'm sure (another glance at Bjorn) Hegmar's crew can manage without you until this crisis is over." He had become so formidable physically, and they had allowed him to train with weapons since before his fifth birthday. How could they possibly deny him the chance to fulfill his obvious destiny? The conflict between her pride in the strong young warrior she and Bjorn had produced and her maternal fear of harm coming to her baby was nearly tearing her apart; but scarcely a flicker of this showed on her face.

Bjorn chimed in. "Yes, son. I see no reason why we can't arrange a leave of absence for you. We're nearly finished with that project up the road, and still waiting on materials for the development out to the west. Go, and show that undead son of a bitch what modern Norsemen are like. Oh, and be careful out there…" His frequently stony countenance cracked a little, and to the astonishment of both Andi and Fjuri a glint of humor seemed to be shining in both the Steadfast parents' eyes.

Who would have thought it? Fjuri had half expected to be chained into servitude as a construction worker for the rest of his life, eventually sliding into marriage with some wide-hipped Norse girl who would bear him six kids, with never a taste of freedom. Maybe his parents didn't have it in for him after all?

"That's great!" Andi exclaimed. "Fjuri, why don't you gear up and we'll go back to my place? We can spend the night there and be ready to leave for Todenstor as soon as Mom gets back with her map!" A white-toothed grin splitting his handsome face, Fjuri hurried up the stairs and came down a few minutes later attired in his latest set of elven armor, his daimonic longsword on his back and a few other useful items in a pack.

The goodbyes with his family almost put tears in his eyes, then he and Andi were out the door. "Wow!" Andi said, "I can't believe they cut the apron strings like that!"

"Me neither," Fjuri replied. "I've been dying to get out of Waterdon for months, but with you running all over the place there wasn't any excuse for me to leave." They could have fast-travelled, but the night was still warm and pleasant and they decided to walk.

As they approached Drakespring Farm, Andi said "What do you say we go down to the Maiden for a while? It's not bedtime yet." At the Maiden the two could eat and drink to their heart's content for free. More importantly, at the Maiden Andi was very likely to find one Rezira Bagrum, the beguiling (and sometimes infuriating) dypalfar maiden who had completely captured his heart. He really wanted to see her before they left again.

Fjuri had been hoping they'd be going right to the farm and a chance to spend some time with Riki, who had similarly captured his own heart. But he couldn't bring himself to mention this to his friend – or to put any barriers in the way of Andi being with his girl. Like pretty much everyone (possibly exception, Andi and Rezira themselves) Fjuri was aware of the problems inherent in a man-alfar love match. But how could he possibly deny his best friend on Terris, his brother almost from birth, the love that had blossomed between him and the astonishingly beautiful dypalfar girl? Any problems that the difference in lifespans might cause were decades away, in any case.

So, they walked on past Drakespring Farm and went to the Maiden. The place was jumping, torches lit around the deck in back and a small group of musicians playing in one corner of it while inn guests milled around, danced, ate, drank, and disported themselves in the large unheated pool. The common room inside was crowded too, but the elaborate Owner's Table was always kept free. And as the son of The Fireblood, Andi and anyone he brought with him were allowed to sit there.

It didn't take Rezira, who was on duty as a server this busy evening, long to spot her boyfriend when he came in through the front doors of the inn. She was over there like a shot. He'd been gone so much this past year, and she missed him so! He'd removed his armor before going into Waterdon earlier, wearing a tunic and trousers, so she was able to hug and kiss him as thoroughly as she liked.

Fjuri, sitting stiff in his armor, witnessed their reunion with a trace of bitterness. He imagined Riki greeting him like that, melting into his arms, covering his face with kisses. As if. She was all locked up with that Alfmund guy, nearly two years older than him and a man in his own right, a member of the Brave Company. He could be a member of the Brave Company if he wanted, he thought. Well, he wasn't really sure if they took people as young as sixteen. But he felt every bit as much a man as Alfmund was. He could surely lick him in a fight… Not that he really disliked him – the guy was actually quite likeable except for his obsession with Riki. Sigh.

Rezira broke away from her embrace with Andi. It was possible that his frequent absences since they had met had only strengthened her affection. "Oh, I love you!" She exclaimed, startling him. Though it was clear that they *did* love each other, the words had never actually been exchanged. "But I'm on duty and I need to get back to work! Can I get you something?"

Andi ordered a couple of ales and, as it had been a couple of hours since his late supper, some food. He and Fjuri had no trouble devouring a platter of mini-size sandwiches and a basket of Dragon Fries, and got another couple of ales afterward for good measure. "Wow," Andi said, "Look at all the women here tonight!" Fjuri eyed him askance. Was his friend's relationship with the lovely Rezira not as deep as he'd thought?

"You know," Andi went on, "you really ought to go chat some of them up. I mean, check out that redhead over there in the corner! She's looking right *at* you!" Oh, now he got it. For the most part, Fjuri was completely unaware that he was rapidly turning into the physical image of every girl's Prince Charming. In his own mind he was dull, tongue-tied, someone no girl would ever want to talk to – let alone be in a romantic relationship with.

That included Riki, the girl he could not get out of his head. He had first become aware of her as something other than Andi's pesky little sister about a year ago, and at that time he thought he had seen some signs that she might be interested in him as well. But he hadn't had the slightest idea of how to cope with those feelings, had been terrified of her. It was only after another guy had claimed her attention that he realized how much she meant to him – and now it was too late!

"I'm not really interested in meeting any girls right now," Fjuri mumbled and took another sip of his ale. "If we're going to go to Todenstor early tomorrow, hadn't we better get to bed soon?" Andi sighed slightly. He'd been madly in love with Zira for nearly a full year now, and his friend Fjuri was still single even though he was turning girls' heads all over Waterdon. What was it going to take to get him to see the potential he had for snagging female companionship, maybe even Miss Right? Well, Fjuri had a point about getting to bed. It had been a long time since he'd last slept.

"Wait right here," he told Fjuri. "I'm just going to find Zira and say goodbye." He sighed again. His love life had really been put on hold a lot these past few months, and it seemed as though he was no sooner home than it was time to head off on another mission. He looked all over the common room without seeing his beloved, then went out the back doors (which, on this warm evening, were standing open) and found her by torchlight serving drinks from a tray to a party of revelers seated at one of the tables overlooking the river.

As she began sliding sinuously through the crowd, returning to the common room, Andi intercepted her and took her by the hand. "Come with me," he murmured into her gracefully pointed ear, and led her off around the side of the building to where there were some dark corners between torches. He took her in his arms, his body pressed hard against hers, and kissed her fervently.

Rezira gasped. She had been longing for him for so many weeks, it seemed, and the reality of being in his arms triggered a flood of desire. She knew that he had been given an amulet of the type worn by the Maiden's "hospitality specialists" for his sixteenth birthday, but neither of them had felt ready to take that next step in their relationship. They were approaching adulthood, were beginning to take adult responsibilities, but they still felt in some ways like children. Oh, but she wanted him!

"I'm leaving again in the morning," Andi told her – putting a damper on her passion. He explained to her what was happening with the undead dragon priest, once again making the request not to tell anyone else. And then he kissed her again, and left. Rezira stood by herself in the dimness for a moment, feeling bereft. What if he went on one of these quests, and never came back? She couldn't bear the thought.

When Andi and Fjuri reached Drakespring Farm, Sigi had already gone to bed. But Riki was still up, reading a book and trying not to worry about why her parents had not yet returned. When the boys opened the door she bolted to her feet, half expecting it to be them. Then her eyes met Fjuri's, and a moment of half-disbelieved understanding passed between them.

Fjuri was stunned to see Riki's beautiful face light up with joy at the sight of him, and utterly flabbergasted when she rushed over to give him a hug – armor and all. "Oh, it's so good to see you," she caroled. "Why don't you ever come by anymore?" His expression a fine mixture of exultation and astonishment, Fjuri hugged her back.

Chapter 20: The Strike Team

As Bernadette had feared, fast-traveling from home to Sylvanian in the middle of the afternoon, she and Erik arrived in the middle of the night. Meri, Liamdor, and Andrion would all be sleeping at the eorl's palace, she knew, but she didn't want to cause a fuss; so they took a room at the Dancing Rabbit to wait out the night.

Besides, the Rabbit held many fond memories for Bernadette and Erik. They had stayed there often in the early days of their relationship, both before and after their trip to Asengard. As soon as light began to come in through the amber bottle-glass windows, they got up and dressed in the armor they'd been wearing when they arrived. Fairly starving by now, having eaten nothing since lunch the previous day, they bought a bag of sweet rolls and some apples from the innkeeper before setting out on foot for the eorl's palace, munching as they went.

They found Eorl Odwyna and her husband, along with their son Arnwin, having breakfast in the palace's dining hall in company with Andrion, Meri, Liamdor and various eorl's palace residents. The eorl, who had been appointed to the office by Imperial Decree after the death of her first husband, had long regarded Bernadette as a friend. She was surprised and delighted to see her and urged them to sit and join them.

"Thanks, Odwyna," she said graciously. "We wouldn't mind some tea, but we've just stuffed ourselves on sweet rolls I'm afraid." She went over to give her daughter, whom she hadn't seen in weeks, a hug and kiss. Then she took a seat next to Andrion, and Erik sat on her other side. Andrion eyed her questioningly. He could tell from her air of tension that something was amiss.

"What's up, love?" he asked softly. "Is everything all right at home?"

"The kids are fine," she replied as quietly, "but a dragon situation has come up." Andrion' brows knit in a frown. In his younger days as a member of Team Fireblood, he'd have cheerfully slaughtered every one of the scaly beasts at the side of his beloved. And when Sneyagflug had trapped her in dragon form and extorted her cooperation in producing the next generation of dragons, he had very specifically wanted to hunt down the big, scaly, red monster and tear him limb from limb.

But he had come to love Mondi as one of his own children, and knew Mondi's eighteen brothers and sisters well enough to realize that they were one and all good kids. Now he could no longer see dragons as the enemy, he found it very hard to raise his hand against one – even the occasional rogue that needed killing. So the words "dragon situation" filled him with apprehension.

Until now, Bernadette and Erik had tried to keep the problem as quiet as possible, not wanting to cause widespread panic – or worse, trigger attacks against friendly dragons by people who'd somehow gotten the idea that all dragons were enemies. Dragons were large and powerful, and if left unmolested, could live forever – but they were no more immune to being killed by force of arms or mischance than any other living creature.

But Odwyna was the eorl of a powerful march, and she deserved to know what was going on in Iscandia. Bernadette trusted her not to make the kind of public announcement that might send the populace on a dragon-killing rampage. So, her next words were addressed to all those seated at the table. "I have some distressing news to report," she said. "An undead dragon priest has escaped his tomb and is creating dragon zombies, then ordering them to attack human settlements (not that it would take much urging, she thought – most of those dragons were dead at the hands of humans, after all). He himself takes the form of a huge undead dragon, and if his zombies are killed he can resurrect them again as long as their bodies are intact enough to move."

There was a gasp around the table, and Odwyna paled. Still lovely in middle age, she put a protective arm around her well-grown son though he didn't seem particularly frightened by the news. He'd met quite a few friendly dragons and never encountered a hostile one, nor had he ever seen the undead walking in daylight. As if by an offstage cue, at this moment a panting messenger arrived and skidded to a halt before the eorl. "Drachenbruch is under attack, Mistress!" he announced. "They say it's an undead dragon, and arrows do it no harm!"

Bernadette was on her feet in an instant, tea forgotten. She and Erik were armored, and Andrion was wearing a set of Magister's robes she'd enchanted with the power of protection from harm – very nearly as good as a full set of plate while weighing a fraction as much. "Let's go!" she exhorted her husbands, "this is our chance!"

"We'll be back as soon we take care of the threat," Bernadette called back over her shoulder to Odwyna and Meri. She, Andrion, and Erik hastened from the room, stopping only long enough to pick up the magical staff he'd brought with him on this trip. It was leaning up against the wall of the sleeping quarters he'd shared with Meri and Liamdor. They dashed out the front doors into the courtyard, and in another few moments by map they were standing on the outskirts of Drachenbruch.

Little actual time had elapsed, as the village was only an hour or two's walk from the front gates of Sylvanian itself. Bernadette had hoped they might find the dragon priest himself attacking with one of his zombies, as had been the case in the hapless village of Wolf Crossing. But no: there was only one dragon here, a little ragged around the edges but showing no sign of having been dead for millennia. And from its size, little bigger than her own dragon form, it was not the priest himself.

The creature had been having a field day, flying around shooting flames. Half the structures in the village were ablaze, and three or four half-charred corpses lay motionless on the main road. Two dozen people, virtually the entire population of the village as well as some guards from Sylvanian, were firing arrows at it without much effect. It was very hard to successfully attack a dragon while it was on the wing.

As soon as they'd gotten their bearings Bernadette bellowed "FJURBLUT!" That got its attention. It circled around and came to a standstill in the air before them, preparing to incinerate them with Holocaust. "Alt-Wach-Sterb-Tot!" she then cried, blasting it with the Dragonfall spell. It backpedaled in air, lifting a little further away from them. And then it laughed!

"Ssso Fjurblut," it hissed in a voice like the echoing of dusty tombs, "do you think *I* fear death?" It laughed again, and went on "Twice before I have died, and twice arisen. And should I fall, my master Meiskomtot will bring me back again!" Meiskomtot, Bernadette thought, committing the name to memory. It was a piece of information that might come in handy. Meanwhile, she held her peace and didn't point out to this over-confident dragon zombie that if *she* was anywhere near when he fell there would be no soul to inhabit that resurrected body.

As the hovering dragon drew closer again, once again preparing to fill the air in their vicinity with flames, Andrion hit it with a medium-width beam of energy, lightning interwoven with ice. This technique for focusing and combining dual-wielded battle spells was something he had pioneered, and he was still Iscandia's foremost practitioner of the art.

The beam punched a fist-sized hole through the base of the dragon's neck, and it backed off with a roar – flying up out of range as it circled the town. This Meiskomtot must have been busy, searching throughout Iscandia for the corpses of dragons to resurrect, Bernadette realized. How many more of them were out there now? She and her people needed to act quickly!

"Help me with my armor, Erik," she said urgently. Bernadette paid the gaping villagers no mind as she stepped free of her clothing to stand naked in the road in the center of town. "It looks like Dragonfall won't work on the undead," she told her husbands, "but for a dragon this size there's more than one way to bring him down to earth." They knew what she was about, and scurried out of the way to make room for the large red dragon that appeared in the moment following her spoken spell. "Stay close!" she told them. "Once I get him down he may not stay down long. Oh, and don't shoot me!"

On that parting note she took to the sky. Though she was roughly the same length and wingspan as the dull brown-colored, mummified and eroded dragon zombie, her mass was much greater. She had all of her muscles and organs, all of her scales and bones. Not to mention razor-sharp talons and a fund of dragon spells greater than any other dragon beside her son, Ehrgeizig – and perhaps, this Meiskomtot she had yet to meet. She suspected that much magical lore had been lost to the world after the demise of the dragon worshipers. And now it was back.

The unnamed dragon zombie circled above the town at a height of about a hundred feet. It was a lot of work keeping aloft considering the tattered state of his wings, and he felt it. But it did not make him tired, nor did he get hungry from the effort. His motion was now powered by magic, the spell that had reanimated him somehow drawing what energy was needed from another plane of existence. I'd rather be alive, he thought. But this isn't bad!

He'd caught only a streak of red when the large red dragon had materialized in the road as he was on his outward loop. Distracted by the puny human defenders of this town that had the nerve to name itself after dragons, he completely missed Schunmurte's climb as she quickly flew above and then came in from behind him. She rose several hundred feet. Then, taking careful aim and calculating her trajectory with precision born of long practice, she folded her wings and plummeted.

Dragons are a lot less aerodynamic than, say, the jet fighters of another universe. But a creature that massive, legs tucked up, wings folded to reduce drag and tail out straight behind, can build up a lot of speed. Just before Schunmurte hit, she cried "Eiz-Nehm-Bild-Stalz!" As a dragon her *furml* had several times the power it did when she was human; and while it wasn't enough to turn an entire dragon the same size she was into a block of ice, it did serve to immobilize the area of the dragon zombie's shoulders and neck – completely halting the beat of the tattered wings and preventing him from changing direction.

Her weight and momentum bore the undead creature on an angle down onto the road, not far from where Erik and Andrion were waiting. As she and her adversary fell, she raked his back with her claws trying to rip out the spine, and savaged the neck. It took a lot to kill the undead, as their animation was not dependent on the normal body functions that are so easily disrupted in the living.

The dragon zombie hit the paving stones of the road with a heavy crunch, no doubt breaking his legs and flattening his rib cage. But would that be enough to kill him? At the last moment Bernadette released the grip of her talons and the bite of her jaws, flapping her wings and heading skyward as her foe plummeted to earth. Erik,

Andrion, and some of the more aggressive defenders were on him in an instant.

Erik had armed himself with his khopesh, an ugly-looking, razor-sharp single-edge blade a handspan across, with a slight curve to it and a wicked hook at the tip. It was the perfect melee weapon for a man of Erik's size and power, utterly devastating at close quarters. Before the dragon zombie had had a chance to recover from his hard landing Erik darted in from the side, completely severing one wing near where it joined the body.

The undead dragon was far more slow and clumsy than a live one would have been. Erik turned and began trying to hack through its neck at the base, though the flesh was hard and woody. Meanwhile Andrion tried a paralysis spell and found that it, too, apparently didn't work on the undead. Damn, this was a whole new class of enemy to discover! Not that he didn't welcome the challenge.

The village's defenders, who after trying to fight this monster off for hours had realized that arrows were largely ineffective, began hacking at it with whatever edged weapons were to hand. It was like chopping hardwood, and no easy task. But they were angry and now that their chance to do some damage was finally at hand, they went at it with a will.

Andrion stepped back, facing the dragon's head, and threw up a strong ward spell as it attempted to incinerate him with a burst of flame. Then, his magical energy rebounding quickly thanks to both his advanced level in magecraft and the helpful items Bernadette had enchanted for him, he took careful aim from a range of no more than twenty feet and hit it square in the face with a blast of destructive energy that essentially obliterated its skull.

Bernadette had touched down on the road where her armor lay and turned human again, hastily donning her underwear so that she was not offending public decency by walking around town in the nude. Then, triumph shining in her eyes, she approached the thrice-killed dragon and laid a hand on its withered flank.

A wordless chorus arose in her mind while the dragon's desiccated flesh vanished in moments. Only bones remained, as she took possession of its soul. For as fireblood, she was in essence a living magical essence vial – and her close presence an essence capture spell. Let Meiskomtot try to resurrect *this* dragon. There might be some spell that would let him operate the skeleton like a puppet, but there would be no volition, and no power of flight without flesh to cloak the lifting surfaces of the wings.

As the townspeople cheered, and Bernadette beamed in triumph at her husbands, they looked back at her with a surge of love. What a woman they had married! "Good job, everybody!" she cried. Erik, Andrion, and the residents of Drachenbruch had all done their part to put an end to this abomination. She had enabled them to do so thanks to the "gift" of dragon transformation – initially a curse forced on her by Sneyagflug – and had finished the job thanks to her inborn ability to capture dragon souls. She did not feel as if any of her own part in it was deserving of praise.

Nonetheless, praise came. The villagers had been fighting off this bizarre monstrosity since dawn, and after hours of effort had only been able to delay it in its intention of bringing utter destruction to their home. Then these three champions had appeared, and in only a few minutes the evil creature was brought to ruin. "Take the skeleton apart and sell the bones," Bernadette urged them. "Dragon bone brings good prices at smithies."

The stuff could be used to craft an incredible heavy armor if you had the skill (which she did), stronger than any other known to mankind but also so heavy that only a warrior the size of Erik could wear it without strain. She hoped that the townspeople, eager to recoup some of the expenses of re-roofing/rebuilding half the village, would leave nothing by which Meiskomtot could even tell what had happened, should he come to check on his minion.

Erik and Andrion helped Bernadette back into her armor, then after a brief leave-taking they fast-travelled back to the eorl's palace. The morning's events had not been what she expected, but they had not been without value. "Meiskomtot, huh?" Andrion remarked as they entered the doors and went up the stairs into the eorl's palace. Some hours had passed since they'd left and it was now afternoon. They were all feeling hungry.

"Andi and Mondi went looking for Ehrgeizig," Bernadette told Andrion. "We won't know if they found him until we can get back home, but if they haven't yet we can add that piece of information. Maybe Ehrgeizig will have known of that particular priest from the time of the Uprising. Anything we can get on him might help us to defeat him." Andrion and Erik both nodded.

They found Odwyna on her throne, conducting the daily business of the march. Meri and Liamdor were also at their day job, running the leukalfar trade outpost in Sylvanian's market district. Bernadette hoped that someone else, equally fluent in the Common tongue and with a good understanding of mainstream Iscandia culture, might be found to take over this position from her daughter. Twelve years old was far too young to be working full time.

"We successfully destroyed the undead dragon," Bernadette reported to the eorl. "There was just one, thank the gods."

"Excellent!" Odwyna exclaimed. Over the years since they'd first met, she'd come to rely on Bernadette (and those connected with her) as someone who could get things done.

Bernadette explained the details, and urged "My dragon children are at this moment spread across Iscandia in teams of two, searching for dragon zombies and the priest who animated them. Might you issue a proclamation, making it very clear that is only these undead dragons people need fear, and that live ones – especially my children – are no threat to mankind?"

A mother now herself, Odwyna understood where Bernadette was coming from. Not that she could imagine turning into a dragon and producing children by the dozen! "I will do anything possible," she assured her friend, "to make sure that everyone in the march understands it is only undead dragons that are causing these attacks. Your children should be safe."

"Thank you, Odwyna," Bernadette replied. She hoped Odwyna's efforts would be enough. That they might see all they had worked for this past decade fall to ruin because of the malice of one ancient undead priest, filled her with a sense of desolation. "We'll take our leave now, and will be found in Waterdon unless there are any more sightings of dragon zombies."

Odwyna nodded, saying "fare you well." She sincerely meant it.

The three of them walked down through Sylvanian and found Meri and Liamdor at the premises of Hidden Treasures, the shop they had opened some weeks ago. It was in a building fronting Sylvanian's market square, where small booths were set up. They offered a wide range of dypalfar and leukalfar wares, and the store (the first of its kind in Iscandia) had met with a fair amount of success.

The leukalfar, as heirs to the departed dypalfar, had many highly desirable items available to them as well as their own unique handicrafts – mostly made from mandimant products. They were already talking about renting one of the market square booths to offer hand meals of leukalfar flatbread wrapped around seasoned mandimant meat.

They shook hands with Liamdor, and made much of Meri. "Any luck finding someone to take over for Meri?" Andrion asked the chubby Mirskhrazana Chanter. Their expectation had been that their daughter would provide the entrée for a leukalfar presence in the city thanks to her family's connections with the eorl, but that she would not be expected to make this her permanent post.

"The number of leukalfar who are fluent in Common is growing," he told them, "but so far none of them has become available here. With the need for tutors throughout the tribes, most of them are going to teach others."

The three Drakespring parents looked unhappy at this news. They wanted their daughter back. "However," Liamdor went on, "if we might be willing to overlook the requirement that store personnel be leukalfar… I have had an application from a young saurion. He speaks Common as a first tongue, has no problem working with leukalfar, and he's at least as alien-looking to the human inhabitants hereabouts. I think he might work out fine…"

Almost in unison Bernadette and Andrion said "Sure, hire him! How soon can he start?" Liamdor twinkled.

"I think he might be willing to start almost immediately," he admitted. "He's been staying down at the stables, mucking out stalls in exchange for meals and a chance to sleep with the horses. Shall I fetch him?" Bernadette sighed. They were in a crisis situation, and they'd already lost the better part of the day. But she really wanted to bring Meri back with them.

"Run fast, Liamdor," she told him. "We'll help keep an eye on the store until you return". The plump little leukalfar was faster than he looked, and apparently now familiar enough to the local residents that he met no barriers as he dashed down to the stables a quarter mile beyond the city gates and returned, panting, with one Taren-Ra – a lizard-man who looked to be scarcely out of his teens. Not half an hour had passed, during which Meri had dealt with sales to several customers and had not needed any help at all.

This was wonderful! The Drakesprings, now increased by one who was delighted beyond belief to be going home, soon bid Liamdor and his new employee farewell and fast-traveled to the eorl's palace to collect Meri's belongings and thank Odwyna for her hospitality. Then they all went back to Drakespring Farm, arriving in the middle of the night.

Chapter 21: Mobilization

The Drakespring parents and their younger daughter went quietly to bed without waking anyone else in the household after their arrival. In the morning, after only a few hours of sleep, Bernadette awoke with love and happiness rising in her soul. For though they were hard-pressed and Iscandia was in peril, they had had a victory of sorts the day before. And more, for the first time in ages every single one of her children was at home –they'd spotted Mondi curled up in the back yard when they came in, and that meant Andi must be here too.

In order to spend much time with her dragon son (or any of his numerous siblings) she would have to become Schunmurte, the mother who had borne them – and that would have meant losing the ability to love and care for her human husbands and children. So though she truly loved them, she had not been with them as a mother should – and it bothered her.

As others began to stir Bernadette was already bathed, dressed, and in the kitchen making tea and some scrambled eggs and toast. With their own chicken flock, the farm family ate a *lot* of eggs. She was surprised to discover that Fjuri had spent the night – just as Sigi, Riki, and Andi were delighted to learn that their sister Meri had returned home. The crowd for breakfast was loud and raucous, with much discussion of the undead dragon situation.

"Mondi, Fjuri, and I need to go to Todenstor to talk with Ehrgeizig, Mom," Andi explained. "We need you, Andrion, or Erik to take us there using your original map."

"That should be okay," she mused, thinking the situation through. If Fjuri was to join her sons on that quest, they would need to fast-travel there as neither young dragon was large enough to carry that enormous young man on his back.

"I'll go, if you like," Erik said. "I'll just turn around and return here as soon as I drop them off, and if you get any dragon calls in the meantime you and Andrion should be able to handle it." He had a profound respect for his brother's abilities in battle magic. Bernadette fetched the map from the bedroom and gave it to him, and he tucked it into his shirt. After this trip, his own map would have Todenstor as a fast-travel point should he ever need to return there.

"By the way son," Andrion said, "if you have time, there's a really good magical staff there by the portal to Asengard. We never got the chance to pick it up because when we returned from there it was to the Hochstein, and it didn't seem worth going back to Todenstor just for the staff." Andi grinned at his father. He liked cool weapons as much as the next mage.

"If I get the chance, I'll grab it." The phrase "and don't you dare think about popping in on Asengard just to see what it's like" did not need to be spoken.

As she continued bringing food to the table, Bernadette told Andi and Fjuri, "We found out some things yesterday. The name of the undead dragon priest who's doing this is Meiskomtot. Don't know where he came from, and that might be important too. We also discovered that the Dragonfall spell doesn't work on undead dragons. I suppose the concept of mortality doesn't cause them much consternation after they've already been dead a few times."

"And the paralyze spell doesn't work on them either," Andrion added. Only he knew he had even tried that spell, as it had no visual manifestations beyond the collapse of the target. "Any spell that can be applied to an inanimate object, like most of the battle spells, works fine though." Good to know, Andi thought. Face to face with this Meiskomtot would be a bad time to find out his strategy for defeating him wasn't going to work.

He hastily finished his breakfast then stepped outside to see how Mondi was doing. He saw his brother just lifting off from the spot in the back yard where he'd spent the night. "Morning, Andi!" he called. "I'm just going to rustle myself up some breakfast, then I'll be back. Are we good to go?"

"Erik's taking us. We can leave as soon as you get back," he said and waved. He turned back toward the front door to discover Zira coming up the walk.

"Andi!" she cried, rushing to give him a hug and kiss. "I'm glad I caught you!" "We won't be leaving for about another hour," he told her as he held her close. She was nearly a foot shorter than he was and fit nicely against his chest, as he inhaled the scent of her glistening raven hair. Oh, Zira…

In moments she was all business. "I brought you something," she said. "Where's your pack?"

"Downstairs with my armor," he replied. "Do you want to come down with me and give me a hand?" In the kitchen, Fjuri found himself caught in Riki's gravitational field – though he ought to have finished his breakfast by now. She kept looking up at him with sparkling eyes, then back down at her plate with a little half-smile.

He still felt stupefied by the reception she'd given him last night. He'd utterly convinced himself that his cause was a hopeless one, that a beautiful girl like Riki could have any guy she wanted (and had one already, dancing to her tune) and would never look at him with anything beyond sisterly tolerance. He just didn't have a way with women.

It was crowded at the table, and Fjuri finally realized he'd better go down to Andi's room and get armored up for their expedition. He had to assume they'd be leaving soon, since Erik had volunteered to fast-travel them to Todenstor. And the excitement of their forthcoming quest (and the astonishing freedom granted to him by his parents) was almost enough to drive out the delighted confusion Riki was causing him.

He stood up to thank Bernadette for breakfast and go out the front door, and somehow Riki was right there with him. She put a hand on his arm as he turned to go down the stairs to the basement, and said softly, "Fjuri, wait…" He turned back and his gaze was captured as she seized his hands in her relatively tiny ones. "Be careful out there," she told him. "I couldn't bear it if anything happened to you."

With that she rose on tiptoe and planted a soft, sweet kiss on his mouth. Then as he responded to it, she kissed him harder, pressing herself against him with her eyes closed, breath coming faster, heart pounding. In a moment they broke apart, wild-eyed. What just happened? "Riki…?" he asked softly. "I thought you and Alfmund…?"

Still holding Fjuri's hands, Riki dropped her eyes. She loved the fact that he was almost seven inches taller than her, such a nice change from most of the boys. Then she looked up into his face again. "I like Alfmund," she admitted. "He's sweet, and nice, and we have fun together doing swordplay up at Ynglingar. And it's very flattering that he pays me so much attention and likes me so much. Maybe he even loves me. But I don't feel that way about him. I've never wanted to kiss *him* like I just kissed you. Do you understand?"

Fjuri took a deep breath, emotions flashing across his handsome face in a quick parade. Then he bent and pulled his hands free from Riki's so he could take her in his arms. After which he proceeded to kiss her in a way he had never kissed anybody before, a way in which she had never been kissed – right out there in the front yard of Drakespring Farm on a warm summer morning, in full view of anybody who might be passing by. It was the most wonderful experience of his life to date.

Finally he broke off the kiss, murmured "I love you, Erika Drakespring," and bolted for the basement. Riki just stood there, heart pounding still, a dreamy expression on her face as it seemed that every bird in the greater Waterdon area had suddenly begun singing its heart out at the same time. So *that* was what it was like!

In the basement, Fjuri interrupted Andi and Rezira doing much the same thing he and Riki had just been doing in the yard. Embarrassment all around, but Andi soon got back on the sidetracked project of gearing up for their expedition. After both boys had their armor on and their weapons hung about them (in addition to his longsword, Fjuri had a pair of wicked daggers with which he'd become adept, and Andi brought a short sword as well as his bow and arrows) Rezira produced the item she'd brought: a magic-block collar. "I'm not sure if it will be any help, but I thought it might possibly be useful," she told him. "Thanks, Zira!" he said, tucking it into his pack.

"And another thing, let me teach you the magic-block spell. If you're going up against magic users, it might let you get close enough to your enemies to be able to put the collar on." They practiced it on Fjuri, which was like striking a horse speechless; but Andi had seen this spell in action, had had it used on him by Zira's mom. So he trusted that it worked, and after some practice he cast it

119

on Rezira and she confirmed that, for the time being (the spell lasted about three minutes), she was utterly unable to use her magic.

"Thank you, love," he told her and gave her another kiss. Now that he was fully armored hugs were unsatisfactory, however. The three of them emerged from the basement, finding that Riki had already gone to milk the cows. Just then Mondi returned from his hunting expedition, earlier than expected. "I stumbled on an ogre before I'd gotten two miles," he crowed. "Boy, those things are buttery!" In his younger and much-smaller days, the young dragon had happily eaten the full range of human foods and loved them. But no normal family household could hope to continue feeding a largely carnivorous creature bigger than two horses put together, for long.

As the boys were about to go back in the house and bid the rest of the family goodbye, there was a rush of wind and Sneyagflug came in to land in the road below the house, hitting hard and roaring in pain. He spotted his son and pleaded, "Drachmondien! Get your mother!" Andi, Fjuri, and Rezira were horrified. She had only met the gigantic red dragon once before, but none of them had ever seen him like this!

His scales were dull and lackluster, some of his body spikes seemed to have been broken off, he looked unusually thin, and he was missing a couple of feet from the tip of his tail. It filled Andi with horror to see the dragon who was in some ways like a stepdad (or at least an uncle) to him in such a state. Mondi obviously couldn't fetch Bernadette out of the house, but he called loudly as Fjuri and Rezira hurried inside to alert her.

Meanwhile, Andi rushed to Sneyagflug's side and began applying a healing spell. He lacked the fine control with healing magic that his mother had, but she'd taught him the spells from an early age and he was pretty good at it. His huge fund of magical energy could restore major injuries before he would run out and have to rest.

"Ooooh... thank you, Guldekiind," the big red dragon groaned. "I have flown here from Norcove without food or rest, but now that my injuries are healing I will soon have the strength to go hunting."

"What happened?" Andi asked, slipping into dragon tongue without missing a beat.

"I… encountered your dragon priest," came the pained reply. "He is larger than me, larger than Ehrgeizig even – though how that is possible I cannot say. I was able to help the townspeople of Norcove destroy two smaller undead dragons who were with him burning their town, but him I could not defeat."

At this instant Bernadette burst from the house and ran to Sneyagflug's front, hugging his enormous scaly head. "Oh, Red," she said sympathetically, "are you all right?" She began delving him with her healing magic, starting the regrowth of his tail tip. The injury was now completely healed, but regrowth of the lost bit of tail and its spikes would take months or years – and until then, Sneyagflug would have to adjust his flight maneuvers to account for the change in balance.

"What's really bothering me now," he told her in what passed for soft tones among the drachen, "is that I am seriously in need of a small herd of cattle to restore my energies." Bernadette looked alarmed. A dragon the size of Sneyagflug could devastate the economy of a medium sized town, if he stayed around for a few meals. Unlike Mondi, he was not used to eating human food – and a couple of sacks of potatoes from their root cellar, as packed with calories as they might be, wasn't going to do it.

"Hang in there, Red," she told him and hurried back to the house. A couple of minutes later a medium-sized red dragon took off from Drakespring Farm's back yard and few off to the east. Another few minutes and she returned, flying heavily, with a dead cow elk clutched in her talons. She dropped it in the road in front of Sneyagflug and then flew over the house again – returning a few minutes later, in human form once again and freshly bathed and dressed.

By the time she got back Sneyagflug had devoured every scrap of the elk and his color was beginning to look better, his skin overlying his muscles with more firmness. "Thank you, dear!" he said, rearranging his drooping wings as he prepared to fly again. "I have the energy I need to hunt for myself now. I told your son some of what happened, but before I go let me add that this dragon priest has some kind of dragon spell that makes his clothing and weaponry come back to him after he changes from dragon form. I saw him go human, naked – he's just a skinny little aptrgangr, not that impressive looking – and then he spoke a spell and suddenly he was armored and carrying a staff that causes whatever it hits to explode. He had one of those metal masks, too. I was lucky to get out of there with my life, lucky you all are not having to fight *me* as a zombie." He shuddered.

As Sneyagflug took to the air and headed east, off to further thin the elk herds along the Brightwater, Bernadette and Andi exchanged a glance. *A dragon spell to bring one's clothing and possessions back from apparent nonexistence? I want it!* Now they were more eager than ever to get their hands on this Meiskomtot, even if he was a dangerous character.

"We'd better get going for Todenstor, Mom," Andi said. The entire rest of the family, plus Fjuri and Rezira, had come out to see what the commotion was about and were still standing, talking, in the front yard. Andi came by to give hugs to Meri, Sigi, Riki, and Andrion. Then one for his mom, a kiss as well for Rezira, and it appeared they were ready to leave. Erik also hugged them all. Both he and Andi were surprised when Fjuri then exchanged a kiss and hug with Riki. What had been happening, there?

Andi, Fjuri, and Erik went into the back yard where Mondi waited. They were far enough from the rest of the people that there was no danger of them being accidentally brought along. In a moment the four shimmered and disappeared from view. "Well," Bernadette said after they'd left, "I guess now we just relax until Purpurflug and Wissliiben show up here with a report. We'll need to be ready to leave at a moment's notice, but in the meantime there's no reason we can't get some things done around the place." She headed for the house, planning to change into her smithing gear. A worm of anxiety for the safety of her children and husband gnawed within her; but she shook it off.

Chapter 22: Westmarch

When the young dragons had assembled their teams and assigned search territories to each of them, they had tried to work it so that at least one of those patrolling any particular region were familiar with it. Over the several years since Sneyagflug had finished their educations and the youngsters had dispersed (in groups of two or three, enjoying each other's company), there had been frequent reshufflings so that all of them had spent time in at least two or three different areas – learning of the region's resources and meeting its people.

Schickemaad and Gotteluub had shared this area of Westmarch with their brother Uverlos for the past couple of years, and as they quartered the skies together during the daylight hours it appeared that nothing was amiss on the ground below. They hunted when they grew hungry, and curled up in the shelter of the woods when it came time to sleep.

There were many Insurgent encampments in the area. The new Eorl of Alfenstein (son of Galdur Staerlin, who had worked for years to beat them back) had made peace of a sort with the remaining Insurgents, leaving them alone to live their lives as they liked in exchange for ceasing to attack travelers. The two young dragons doubted there would be any undead dragon attacks on the Insurgents, though. They had little enough to burn, and their encampments were full of young, well-armed people and powerful magic users – not a soft target.

And as the Insurgents had little truck with the rest of Iscandia society, attacking them would not be the most useful sort of terrorist tactic. If this dragon priest's aim was to reinstitute dragon rule of the human populace through intimidation, it would make more sense to attack villages or farms whence the word could get out. On the morning of the third day since they had left Drakespring Farm with their assignment, Schickemaad (Beautiful Maiden, and she was – if you were a dragon, at least) spotted a column of smoke rising on the horizon to the north and east of where she and her brother were cruising at high altitude. "There!" she cried, "Come On!"

The two dived lower and approached rapidly but with caution. "Don't forget," Gotteluub warned, "we promised Mama we wouldn't try to fight the dragon priest."

"Do I look like I want to mix it up with an undead, shape-shifting wizard six times my size?" his sister responded flippantly as they drew nearer to the smoke. "We're just going to take a look and then Call Wissliiben so he can relay the location to the strike team."

When they had drawn close enough to the source of the smoke to see flames as well, they found a nearly intact-looking (but clearly undead) dragon far smaller than their father circling above a collection of buildings that was not quite a village, but more than a single farm. In fact it was a farm where successive generations had added barns and bunkhouses, putting more land under cultivation as the family grew. The source of the smoke was a wheat field, near to harvest but now rapidly going up in flames.

The two hovered in midair several hundred feet above the scene. "That can't be the dragon priest," Gotteluub insisted. "He's not that much bigger than *we* are!"

"I'll Call," Schickemaad responded, shouting "WISS-LII-BEN!" She and her brother then watched in anxiety as the dragon zombie directed his flames at the roof of a farmhouse. It was thatch, not shake or slate, and in a few seconds it had become a roaring inferno.

The attacker wheeled away roaring his triumph, then circled back around as a woman and her two children fled out the house's front door, cowering before the flames. Her husband, and several other adult residents of the settlement, were already outside trying to drive the undead dragon off with arrows. They had little effect.

"He's going to flame that mom and her kids!" Gotteluub cried. "We have to stop him!" One and all, the children of Schunmurte and Sneyagflug were the most tenderhearted dragons to have lived in recorded history. His sister knew he was right. Even if Wissliiben showed up in the next ten seconds and then reported back, it was going to be hours at least before the strike team could arrive. And unless they pitched in and helped, there'd be nothing here by then but smoking ruins and charred corpses.

Gotteluub dove, realizing as he got closer that the dragon zombie attacking the farm was around half again his size. Between him and his sister, they outweighed him; so they should be able to overpower him. First, though, to try a dragon spell: "Ang-Los-Scher-Flieg!" he bellowed as he approached within range, Schickemaad close behind him. The Terror dragon spell had been the turning point in the Battle of Mrzhgradfendz last year, the last straw that forced the dypalfar Great Army to throw down their arms.

Against an undead dragon, it was somewhat less effective. Todenangst was not truly a zombie, as his soul remained in his reanimated dead body and his actions were directed by his own mind in obedience to the instructions given to him by his master. He had little enough to fear, being already dead; but the Terror spell didn't need a rational reason to produce the desire to flee.

Just short of incinerating the fleeing humans Todenangst abruptly sheared off, looping back up into the sky and looking for whatever had attacked him. The two young dragons dived to either side, avoiding a mid-air collision. The human defenders, realizing that the newly-arrived living dragons were ones who had brought them game in the past – and that they were trying to drive off the undead attacker – held their fire.

As Todenangst hovered in air, trying to recover from the inexplicable wave of fear that had shot through him, Wissliiben arrived on the scene flying fast. "Where are we?" he demanded as soon as he spotted his brother and sister. He had never spent any time in this area. "It's a farmstead about twenty miles to the northeast of the sanctuary of the ancient Guardians!" Schickemaad informed him. "We have to kill this guy or drive him off, before he destroys this place!"

Wissliiben was taken aback. He probably had only a few minutes before his sister called him back. A pity he couldn't simply *go* back on his own, immediately. He supposed they could Call their father for aid, but what if he was busy? As soon as he had heard Schickemaad's Call, he'd alerted Purpurflug that he'd been called and by whom. Their plan was that, whichever of them was Called, the other would immediately fly like the wind for Drakespring Farm before calling them back. That way they'd be much closer to alerting the strike team when the information was received.

"But," he began, hovering in air as the undead dragon seemed still to be hesitating in his attack, "we promised Mama…"

"We only promised her not to try to fight the dragon priest!" Gotteluub pointed out, "We can *take* this guy if we gang up on him! Come on!" Reluctantly, Wissliiben joined his siblings as they converged on the still-shaky Todenangst.

Working as a team, the three young living dragons fell upon the larger, undead one from above and behind. Schickemaad and Wissliiben each sank their talons into the leathery membrane of a wing, one on either side, teeth attempting to bite through the woody flesh of the shoulder joint where the wing met the body. Gotteluub took the top position, talons digging into the tough and spiky hide of the back as he ripped at the equally tough, mummified neck skin.

Truly alarmed now, Todenangst struggled in a panic as he was borne down by three vigorous attackers swarming all over his upper side. Together they were nearly twice his weight, and as they stopped trying to fly he couldn't flap his own increasingly-more-tattered wings enough to stay aloft. He didn't fall like a stone, but glided down at an angle to land on the dirt road in the midst of the settlement with a thump.

"MEIS-KOM-TOT!" he cried just before he hit the ground. His master had not told him about the possibility of organized resistance by living dragons. Weren't they all supposed to be on the same side? None of the youngsters had any idea what the spoken spell intended. It was not one they knew, and didn't seem to have any effect.

Still clinging to Todenangst's back, Gotteluub spat out a mouthful of dragon jerky and yelled at the human defenders, "Quick, bring axes or swords or whatever you've got! You need to kill him before he can get back into the air!" He had no idea how long the three of them would be able to hold him down.

Gotteluub knew the Freeze dragon spell as well, and he thought that perhaps if he cast it at the undead dragon's head and neck where they rose in front of him he might prevent it from flaming the human defenders. Maybe one of them would even get lucky and snap the dragon zombie's head off his body! Wings outspread to steady himself as he reared back, he was taken utterly unaware as the gigantic undead dragon Meiskomtot swooped in from behind and dragged him aloft again, enormous fangs in powerful crushing jaws sunk deep into the flesh where his left wing joined the body.

Stunned and terrified, eyes wide, Schickemaad and Wissliiben released their grip on the fallen Todenangst and took to the sky, scattering in two directions before turning to see what had happened. By Aderos, this Meiskomtot (as they now realized must be his name) was enormous! Larger than their father by a considerable margin, though so ruinous in appearance it was a wonder he could fly. And he had their brother in his jaws! Crimson blood ran from Gotteluub's breast and fell to the ground in smoking drops as he struggled futilely in the grip of the far-larger dragon.

As they watched in horror, the gigantic Meiskomtot hovered some two hundred feet above the road. Then he shook his head vigorously from side to side. Their brother's wing and a large chunk of muscle powering its motion tore off in the larger dragon's jaws, the rest of his body falling to earth in a shower of blood. "Gotteluub, nooo!" Schickemaad roared. Wild with grief, she was nearly paralyzed and unable to imagine what to do next.

Just then Wissliiben heard Purpurflug's Call: "WISS-LII-BEN!" beckoning him to go to her at a point no more than five minutes' flight from Drakespring Farm. Retreat was the only sane course. Schickemaad had not heard it, as only the dragon Called would hear it beyond earshot. "Schickemaad!" he cried, "I'll Call you as soon as I get back! Come soon!" With that he vanished.

The human defenders, as stunned as the young dragons at this turn of events, backed away as Todenangst began struggling back up into the air. Their opportunity to hack him to pieces with edged weapons had slipped away. Meiskomtot had spat out poor Gotteluub's wing and looked around to find one of the three who had attacked his minion vanished, the other rapidly disappearing in the direction of a nearby copse of trees.

Well, he'd gotten one of them, at least. These must be the young generation of "helpful" dragons he'd heard about, children of The Fireblood and some unidentified dragon those "adventurers" had mentioned. He looked down at the pieces of dragon on the ground below and concluded there'd be little point in resurrecting it as a zombie – too small, even if the body weren't too damaged to fly again. He turned his attention to the settlement, and the humans trying to defend it.

Chapter 23: Todenstor

Somewhat to Andi's surprise, the map dropped them on the far side of a gorge across which a narrow bridge led to an enormous stone fortification. From the description in the stories, this must have been exactly where Sneyagflug had left Mom when she rode his back here, his part of the bargain by which she'd freed him after trapping him in Wyrmshalla. Andrion and Erik had stowed away on that flight, without which fact it was questionable whether Mom would have been able to fight her way through the dragons, aptrgangr, and even a dragon priest between her and Asengard.

At least they knew now why Sneyagflug had not come to their call earlier, Andi mused. He was glad the old fellow was all right. He'd been old enough to understand what was happening when Mama had been trapped in dragon form, but too young to blame the big red dragon for her plight.

Andi turned to his papa. "Thanks, Erik," he said, and gave the bigger man a squeeze. "We'd better let you get back to the Strike Team." Erik squeezed him back, and in moments had vanished again. There were still aptrgangr on the walls here, but seeing the two young warriors accompanied by a dragon they must have concluded they were not enemies. No shots were fired, and the boys walked across the ravine and up the flights of steps to the courtyard beyond while Mondi lifted into the air and flew there to rejoin them.

As they converged on the courtyard from two directions all three of them spotted an enormous, ancient-looking dragon perched on the roof of a huge building to the left. This must surely be Ehrgeizig! None of them had ever seen this eldest of living dragons before, but the young men were thrilled to be meeting him. His role in the defeat of Tarragin was a favorite part of the stories they'd read over and over again in childhood.

He spotted them as well, lifted off his perch on creaking wings, and came spiraling down to land on the stones of the courtyard just as Mondi touched down a few feet away. "What is this?" he said in dragon tongue, his voice deep and resonant. All three of the visitors were fluent in this language, so the ancient dragon found no need to translate as he went along.

"Greetings," Andi said respectfully. "Am I addressing most ancient Ehrgeizig, founder of the order of the Old Ones?" The old drache was surprised to be spoken to in his own tongue by this very young-seeming mortal. Did the boy look… familiar, somehow?

"I am Ehrgeizig," he answered shortly. "Who are you, if I may ask, and how came you here?"

Andi grinned. He figured that if this ancient creature had spent thousands of years atop The Hochstein (Muuterhorn, as the dragons called it) with nobody to talk to but humans, he might have picked up some of the nuances of facial expression that gave clues to humans' attitudes and intentions. "I am Andreas Drakespring, called Guldekiind, and I am the son of the fjurblut Bernadette who you knew in the past. My companions are my friend Fjurbund Steadfast, and my dragon brother Drachmondien."

Ehrgeizig turned his head from side to side taking in each of them in turn. He was making a low rumbling sound in his throat, perhaps the equivalent of a human saying "Hmmm…" "Young Bernadette's son!" he said at last, lost in memories of the last time he had seen that remarkable young woman. "With one of those champions who fought at her side atop Muuterhorn, I suppose?"

"That's right," Andi replied.

"I am surprised you were able to find me," the old dragon said next. "I have not seen or spoken with Bernadette since I left Muuterhorn. I had hoped then that I might assume leadership of the drachen after Tarragin was gone, and for some time there were many who came to me here to learn the furml. But most did not stay, until after only a few years I became as you see me now, alone again. But I have heard that there are some new dragons in the world, dragons that are doing as I once did and becoming friends to humankind."

"I'm one of them," Mondi spoke up. "I, too, am a son of The Fjurblut. But in her dragon form as Schunmurte, and by a different father." Ehrgeizig stared at him for a moment as if he had just sprung up out of the stones of the courtyard.

"In her dragon form…" he muttered. "She has the Reward? I don't understand."

Now it was Andi who answered him. "Zuumerzohn told us where to find you," he explained. "and he mentioned the 'Reward' as well. Can you tell us what it is or was?"

"In the days of the dragon worshipers," Ehrgeizig said as he slid into Teacher Mode, "the dragon blood was far more common in the races of mortals than it is now. Only those who were fireblood could attain the higher levels of the priesthood, because of their affinity with the drachen. And only those with the highest skills in both the furml and other magical arts could reach the top level."

Realizing that his audience was utterly rapt, and enjoying the attention, Ehrgeizig went on. "I believe that there were many secrets of the priests that were known only to those at this highest level, certainly not to any of the dragons whom their priesthood was supposed to serve. We were given whatever food we wanted to eat and free rein in whatever we wanted to do, and most were content with this life. Just as some men will happily spend all their time eating, drinking, brawling, and copulating, so many dragons of that time had no desire to seek knowledge. I was otherwise, and before the Uprising I had learned much."

"Did you teach the dragon priests the furml, as you did to the Old Ones?" Andi asked. It had not occurred to him until just this moment that there were any similarities between the living Old Ones and the ancient and long-dead dragon worshipers.

"In fact," the ancient dragon replied, "some of them taught *me*. Not all of them were as stingy with their secrets as others."

"In any case," he went on, "the Reward. The dragon priests worshipped dragons as the manifestation of our lord Vaterhiin, or Aderos as he is called by mortals, on Terris. They desired to become like us. And some genius among their kind had discovered, or perhaps developed, a potion and four furml that would grant any human fireblood – though this secret was only imparted to those who achieved the highest level of the priesthood – the power to become a dragon, then change back into human shape again."

"*Four* furml?" Andi asked, baffled. The potion and two of the dragon spells he certainly knew about already.

"As dragons have no pockets," Ehrgeizig explained, "one of the furml allowed the priest to seemingly rid him or herself of everything he or she was carrying or wearing, while still having it within easy reach. The second furml transformed the priest into a dragon, its size and coloring dependent on the age and coloring of their human form, the third would turn them back from dragon to human, and the fourth caused whatever items they had had with them before the first spell had been cast to be restored to them. All this after they had first ingested the potion in order to prepare their bodies for the change, of course. But surely you must know this, if your mother can transform into a dragon?"

"You know Sneyagflug?" Andi asked. Ehrgeizig nodded.

"He and I are not friends," he said slowly, "but we know each other. He was never one of my supporters."

"Well," the boy went on, "it's like this…" Some minutes later Mondi's existence and that of his eighteen dragon siblings had been explained, as had Andi's own ability to transform into a dragon and the campaign of improving dragon-human relations that had inadvertently led to a decline in the number of Ehrgeizig's adherents. Dragons hostile to humans had mostly been driven away or killed, while those willing to coexist were in little need of the spells.

By the time he'd finished his tale, the sun was almost down though they were far to the north and it was high summer. "I don't suppose you happen to know the dragon spells to banish clothing and summon it again?" he asked hopefully. Those would make switching back and forth between dragon and human *so* much easier! "Sorry," Ehrgeizig replied, "I do not. You will probably have to speak to a dragon priest about it, or you may find them on a Spell Wall. If you approach one in dragon form, all on it will be made known to you."

"Wow, it never even occurred to me to try that!" Andi exclaimed. He was burning with excitement to put this idea into practice. Who knew what dragon spells he might find, maybe even ones Mom didn't know? And of course once he knew them he could teach them to her as easily as speaking them aloud. But it dawned on him that this was *not* why he was here.

Fjuri had remained mostly silent, just standing there looking like a hero out of legends with his commanding size and impressive armament. But now he spoke. "Andi, I'm about half starved. And aren't we supposed to be finding out about this Meiskomtot guy?"

"Oh, sorry!" Andi exclaimed. "I suppose you're starving too, Mondi?"

"Could eat something," his brother admitted. "What do you do for food around here, Ehrgeizig?" he asked the elder dragon.

"I eat seldom," the old *drache* said. "As I seldom move at all. As well, I find that as the millennia pass I somehow need less sustenance. But there are plenty of goats in the mountains around this fortress, and many bears as well. Mondi had only recently gotten big enough to prey on bears, and he found them quite delicious. They were as buttery as ogres. "I'll just take a quick hop out and pick up some supper," he suggested. "Why don't you two eat some provisions from your packs in the meantime?"

The boys threw some bedrolls down onto the stones of the courtyard for padding and came up with bread and cheese, apples, dried meat, and a little trail bread. They'd packed well for this expedition. Ehrgeizig rested there, watching them eat, with the bemused air of a biologist observing wildlife. For such small creatures, they certainly could pack it away!

Dusk was well advanced by the time Andi and Fjuri had finished eating and Mondi had returned, flying a little heavily. "Boy, those brown bears are enormous!" he remarked cheerfully, licking his chops.

Seeing that conversation could now resume, Ehrgeizig asked, "You mentioned a Meiskomtot?"

"That's right," Andi said, and explained how the undead dragon priest had gone on a rampage across Iscandia, raising dragon zombies and attacking human settlements. "Have you heard of him?"

"The name is familiar," Ehrgeizig admitted. "It was early in the Uprising, I think. I was relatively young then, of course, and hungry for knowledge. I didn't speak with this priest, but one with whom I was on friendly terms mentioned that he had risen rapidly in the priesthood and had achieved the highest level while younger than any other in those times."

He explained further: "Among the priesthood, there were different political factions. Some were truly sincere in their worship for dragonkind and thought that bringing Iscandia under the rule of the dragons was a command of divine Aderos. Wissagleb was one such, and as interested in lore as I was. Others seemed only to see the priesthood as a way to create power for themselves, and achieve immortality. When a human starts taking dragon form, their life is extended and aging is greatly slowed. Thus those with the Reward, even of the races of men, could have lifespans to rival the alfar. And it was their plan, of course, that when age eventually overtook them they would stay in the dragon form forever after, never dying."

Andi gasped. Could this mean that he and Zira might be able to marry and grow old together? It was a riveting thought, but he wasn't sure he was ready for sex yet – never mind marriage! "Your friend, Wissagleb – what happened to him?" Andi asked.

The old dragon hesitated a moment before replying. "He died," came the answer at last. "As they all did. All of the dragons did, as well, save Tarragin who had fled to his private world and I, who stayed atop Muuterhorn awaiting his return." His voice sounded sad.

"But the aptrgangr? If the dead priests had the ability to get up and walk again, why didn't they keep fighting the war?" Andi was learning so much, he felt as if his head were about to burst. Fjuri and Mondi were as fascinated. "Eventually all of the highest level priests, those with the secret of the Reward, had fallen in the war," Ehrgeizig explained. "And with Tarragin banished and all of the dragons fallen, those who remained decided to prepare for the future. They interred the dragons with rituals that would assure their resurrection as live dragons, for it had been prophesied that Tarragin would return. The dead priests were sealed in their tombs, ready to rise again, and with many lesser aptrgangr as servants and defenders for them. Though only a god could restore them to life, their unlife would make them useful when the dragons came back."

Andi was dazed. It was so much to take in! "Thank you, Ehrgeizig," he said in awed tones. "You have taught me much." The dragon fairly preened. He had been a teacher for a long time, and having an eager and appreciative student was a joy. He wished it didn't have to end, but he knew that he couldn't delay any longer. If Meiskomtot was loose and seeking revenge (or perhaps a new era of dragon rule, with himself as Iscandia's eternal master), the boy needed to get the information he had come for.

"I had better send you on your way, young Guldekiind. Your mother named you well. You wish to speak with a dragon priest and learn more about Meiskomtot?"

"Yes, yes! I need that information as soon as possible!" The enormous dragon seemed to purr.

"You should find what you seek quite close at hand," he said. "My old friend Wissagleb is interred deep in the bowels of that building on the far side of the courtyard."

Chapter 24: Sorrow

It was early afternoon, and Bernadette was working at their outdoor forge in the warm sunshine. Erik had returned exhausted from his round-trip to Todenstor, and was now taking a nap. Riki and Sigi had split the afternoon chores, and then gone down the road to the Maiden together. Her friend Sintra worked there, daughter of Drelos and Larissa Elendion, and they would get some time to spend together while Sigi played with Joqui. Her erstwhile suitor, Alfmund, was still away on a mission with the Brave Company.

Meri was in Waterdon spending the day with her friend Edla, and Andrion was in the workroom rifling his extensive library for any mention of spells that were effective against the undead. What he really needed was something that would just drop these creatures out of the sky. But while such things had not been systematically eliminated from the lore, as had apparently been the case for the secrets of the dragon worshipers, the subject was esoteric and information about it was hard to find.

Suddenly there was a flurry of wings and three young dragons came hurtling out of the east to land clumsily in the road below the farm. There was no open space in the farmyard big enough to hold all three of them, now. Schickemaad was still in a panic and disoriented, after answering Wissliiben's Call. It seemed possible that Meiskomtot might not have bothered to pursue her even if the spell had *not* allowed her to translocate hundreds of miles in an instant, but her brother was not leaving her anywhere near that undead monster.

Wissliiben and Schickemaad had witnessed Gotteluub's death and were heartbroken, Purpurflug confused and disbelieving. Their brother, dead? "Mama! Mama!" Schickemaad called out as soon as she spotted Bernadette working. Bernadette took one look at the three and knew something was very wrong.

"Erik! Andrion!" she bellowed with the voice of power she used for *furml*, hoping they might hear. Then she set her smithing tools aside and rushed down to the road.

Dragons are physically incapable of crying, a lack that had distressed Bernadette a great deal when she had been unwillingly transformed into Schunmurte. Schickemaad and Wissliiben looked as if they might be feeling a similar distress. They showed signs of having been in a conflict, and she hastened to apply healing magic to them. But even after all of their hurts were healed, they were paler than their usual vivid red, scales raised as in alarm, eyes wild.

"What is it, Schickemaad?" she asked, trying to coax her daughter into telling her what had happened. The suspense was driving her insane. They were speaking in Common, as was their own preference when conversing with her in her human form.

"Mama, he killed Gotteluub!" the young dragon choked out. "There was just a small undead dragon, and he was going to kill a mother and her children. We couldn't just hover and watch him do it, and the people there weren't having any luck stopping him with bows! But we didn't know...!"

The young female was breathing so hard she looked ready to faint, gasping uncontrollably, and her brother took up the tale. "Schicke Called me like we arranged," Wissliiben said somewhat more calmly. "But the three of us were more than enough to stop that undead dragon. It wasn't the big one, the master. Then when we had just gotten him down he Called Meiskomtot, and suddenly this giant undead dragon flew in out of nowhere and snatched Gotteluub off the other one's back like a crow picking up a grasshopper. Then Purpe Called me back, and I Called Schicke to get her out of there. He's probably killed all the people by now."

Bernadette's eyes had gotten bigger, her skin paler as her dragon children told their story. Just as Erik and Andrion arrived, puzzled looks on their faces, she asked Wissliiben, "Meiskomtot killed Gotteluub? Are you sure?" The young dragon hung his head. Though his heart was submerged in misery, there was no doubt.

"He ripped his left wing right off his body and dropped him from a couple of hundred feet up," he acknowledged in a voice fraught with grief and anger. "Gotte didn't move at all when he hit, and there was blood everywhere."

Oh no. Bernadette could not bear it. While her dragon babies (with the exception of Mondi) had not been as close to her as her human children, she loved them all. And they were supposed to live forever, to be riding the air above Iscandia when she herself was nothing but dry bones and an old tale. Meiskomtot could not, he *would not*, kill her children!

Instead of breaking down in sobs, as a part of her wanted to do, Bernadette became all business. To her husbands, she said "Let's get changed. We're going there by map as soon as we can. Andrion and Erik were in shock. They'd been mentally prepared to drop everything and rush to stop Meiskomtot wherever he might turn up. But the news of Gotteluub's death had been a blow. They both regarded Mondi as a son, and his many brothers and sisters as one might the children of a close friend. Bernadette might have had little choice in bearing them, but she loved them – so how could *they* not?

"Wissliiben," Bernadette went on, "maybe you should go get a drink from the river while we're changing our clothes. I suppose you're not hungry?" He shook his head, a gesture employed by both humans and dragons.

"We'd eaten not long before Schicke Called me," he said. "I'll get a drink and be right back." Unlike fast-traveling by map, which appeared to take only seconds but actually used up nearly as much time as walking from place to place, the magic of the Calling dragon spell could translate a dragon (and a rider, if the dragon was capable of carrying such) across any distance in only seconds.

"Purpurflug, please look after your sister until we return," Bernadette tasked her daughter. While the loss of a sibling was something all of them would feel with heartache, the trauma of watching it happen seemed to have unhinged young Schickemaad. "Riki and Sigi are down at the Maiden, so if they come back before we return tell them what happened. All right?"

"Yes, Mama," the lithe female dragon replied solemnly.

Erik (still rubbing the sleep out of his eyes) and Andrion had already begun walking to the house to put on their armor and gather their weapons. They had packs standing ready, hoping for a call to battle. Bernadette put on her best elven armor. She was pleased that she was still able to look good wearing it though she was now past forty years of age – but at the moment, she paid such considerations no mind. Only two things occupied her thoughts – she must see the body of her son and know that he was truly dead; and she must take revenge.

Chapter 25: The Tomb of Wissagleb

"Looks like I won't be coming along on this part of the expedition," Mondi said, eyeing the doorway that led into the fortress. "I'll stay here and keep you company, Ehrgeizig, if that's all right. I'd love to hear some more of your stories about the ancient times." The old dragon felt a deep joy well up within him. This young dragon was precisely the sort of pupil he had longed for.

The dragons of the ancient world were old and set in their ways, and though some had come to him at first they had not stayed, had not been interested in learning all he had to teach. Maybe, just maybe, he hoped, when this crisis had passed young Drachmondien might stay longer – might even encourage some of his siblings to come as well. As the children of a dragon who had been born human, they would have a fresh perspective on the world.

"Aah," he said with a deep sigh. "I suppose I *might* be induced to pass the time with you." To Andi and Fjuri he added, "Beware the aptrgangr guardians inside. They lack the ability to make decisions, for the most part, only acting as the priests programmed them to do with the rituals performed at their interment. You may have to kill some of them, I'm afraid."

"Thank you, Ehrgeizig," Andi replied politely. Then he and Fjuri walked across the broad courtyard and opened the broad wooden gates at the main entrance. Soon, the two young warriors found themselves moving through a series of broad chambers interspersed with corridors far too small to pass a dragon the size of Mondi, let alone Guldekiind. Everywhere a cool light was coming from clusters of glowing crystals caught in silvery metal cages.

At first the rooms seemed to be for the purposes of the living, with kitchen facilities, barracks or dormitories, storerooms, and areas that in the past had served for chemia, enchanting, or smithing. All were deserted. A few eroded rags remained of clothing and bedding, and there were some weapons scattered around; but no living men had been here in millennia. It reminded Andi somewhat of that ancient Norse barrow where he'd gone to obtain the dragon spell to transform Mom back into human form, though that one had been neither as dry nor as cold.

Though their quest was for knowledge and the need was urgent, the two couldn't resist doing a little exploring for treasure. Andi had never forgotten the excitement of that quest with his two papas when he was five, the jewels and exotic weapons they'd found and passed over as they searched for the Spell Wall that would bring Bernadette back to them. And Fjuri, despite his superb armament and years of weapons training, even having an older sister who was an adventurer, had never been inside an ancient Norse ruin before in his life.

So, they lingered for some time exploring each room for anything useful or valuable. Fjuri pocketed some gold coins of an antique design, along with a few loose gems and a silver and sapphire necklace he intended to give to Riki. Was it really true that she loved him, that she might be his girl now? He felt little more settled about that notion than he had about the idea that his love was hopeless.

Andi, for his part (coming from a wealthy family and never having wanted for anything, within reason, that money can buy) was more interested in different sorts of loot. He took a fine elven dagger that had some kind of enchantment on it. Enchanting wasn't his forte, but he'd be willing to bet that Mom or even perhaps Riki could identify it. It felt warm in his hand, a surprise since the air in these upper rooms of the fortress was near freezing.

He also took a book he didn't recognize from a shelf in one of the craft rooms, a present for Papa Andrion, and a couple of tightly-sealed potion bottles. He recognized one as the strongest type of healing potion – which could fully restore your health, repairing any damage, in an instant. Such things were useful to have even for a mage with good healing skills, as a serious injury might leave you too weak to perform magic.

The other potion he was not certain of. The bottle looked, and no doubt was, ancient. Perhaps Lucia down at the Potent Potion in Waterdon could identify it. He tucked it into his pack, in any case. The further in they went, the less dust there was on everything. Probably when they'd opened the front doors just now, that had been the first breath of fresh air inside this place since before Andi's remotest ancestors had been born.

They passed through a large dining hall, lined with simple wooden tables on which stood plates, cups, platters, and other dinnerware. It looked as if the people who once ate here had set the tables for supper and then wandered off, never to be seen again. At least there was no food lying around – though Andi supposed that if there had been, it would have dissolved into dust long ages since.

The room had a small wooden door at the back of it, which led to a corridor descending a series of staircases to the level below. And there, the two young adventurers saw their first aptrgangr. She had not been lying in her crypt, ready to rise up and defend the tomb, but rather on duty: patrolling the corridors in a slow, stately pace with ancient Norse bow to hand.

Moving to a lower level had triggered extra caution in them, and Andi was walking very quietly a couple of paces ahead of Fjuri, bow out and an arrow nocked. The aptrgangr sentry made slight rustling noises as she walked along, her foot-coverings reduced to rags by the centuries. Andi drew and shot before she spotted him, and her chest erupted in flames for a moment before she fell to the floor, her bow clattering across the stones. Both boys froze, alert for the signs of anything aroused by the noise. But she had been alone, it seemed.

"Wow, so that's an aptrgangr," Fjuri murmured as Andi bent over the twice-dead corpse, retrieving his arrow. She had a quiver of arrows and the bow, of course, but nothing that was worth the trouble of taking with them. "How do they move around, anyhow?" Fjuri asked quietly as they proceeded on their way.

"It's all magic," Andi tried to explain, though he was far from expert on the subject. "Sometimes a killing blow will disrupt the magic enough to break its connection with the corpse, and then they'll stay dead forever or until a necromancer revives them. But it's not like with a living person or animal, where you could shoot them with an arrow and then they'd bleed out and die. Your attack either kills the undead right away or not at all."

"Hmm," Fjuri said, nodding sagely. In his slow but thorough way, he was thinking about the undead – and what he and Andi needed to do about them. More corridors, more steps, and they found themselves passing through a pair of ornately-figured iron doors into an area that was clearly a catacomb.

"Here's where it gets tricky," Andi told his friend quietly from the lofty eminence of his one prior quest in such a place. The corridors split in two directions, and Andi motioned Fjuri to take the left side as he tried the right.

Moving silently, Andi recalled what Mom and Erik had told him about aptrgangr. The ones who were primed to arise and attack intruders were usually a little livelier-looking than the corpses who were just corpses. Not every Norse servant of the dragon worshipers had been interred with the ceremony necessary to bind them to service after death.

The light down here was dim, but enough to see by. The glowing crystals had been replaced by ever-burning candles and torches, fueled by a magic perhaps similar to that powering the aptrgangr. Andi spotted a corpse lying on its back within a wall recess and thought it had a suspicious surplus of mummified flesh on its bones. His current bow was a daimonic one Mom had made for him, enchanted by her with fire damage and enhancement of his marksmanship. When his arrow struck home, there was a brief burst of flames and the corpse twitched before subsiding once more – never having left its crypt.

Phew, Andi thought. Standing here in a room full of corpses, any of which might decide to wake up and attack him, was even scarier without Fjuri at his back. As he stood there peering at the bodies on either side for any signs of incipient life, he heard a shout from ahead of him. Fjuri!

His trepidation forgotten, Andi raced forward. The left and right passageways must connect ahead, and his friend was in trouble! As he raced along the passageway, two of the occupants of the niches on either side rose from their slumber, eyes glowing blue, and put their near-skeletal feet on the floor. He was already long past them and out of sight around the bend.

Andi found Fjuri standing in a corridor that continued on, free of crypts, after the two passages had joined again. His longsword flashing, he held off two aptrgangr as a third, one of a higher type, approached from several yards down the corridor he had just left. Just as Andi arrived one of them fell, cloven from neck to breastbone by a powerful blow. Fjuri pulled hard to retrieve his blade from the corpse, as Andi put a flaming arrow into the back of the second aptrgangr's skull.

Fjuri looked up, relief showing on his face as he realized reinforcements had arrived. "Gods, I didn't think there would be so many of them!" he gasped. Andi took two strides down the passageway his friend stood in then turned, side by side with him as they faced the foes that were coming their way. Two on the left looked like more of the basic aptrgangr soldier, while the one on the right was taller, and wore a helmet surmounted with horns joined together in a circle, an amulet of some kind dangling below them. Andi recognized the uniform, from a childhood experience that would always be graven in his memory.

"An overlord!" he gasped. If not the highest level of the dragon priesthood, these guys were at least commanding officers of the aptrgangr troops, and most of them had the power to cast dragon spells. This one stalked toward them in its insectile gait, wielding an enormous sablium longsword. As it stood side-by-side with the lesser aptrgangr before them Andi cried, "Waf-Ond-Nied-Lorn!"

The longsword flew from the overlord's bony hand to clatter on the floor behind him, as did the short sword and war axe wielded by his cohorts. But a moment later the undead commander cast the same spell Andi had just delivered, sending Andi's bow and Fjuri's own longsword flying. The two lesser aptrgangr halted, unsure what to do next. Whatever limited thought processes they had, their volition did not extend to improvising when Plan A went awry.

The overlord, however… a purple glow arose on the palms of his withered hands, and he moved his arms as if he were about to cast a spell. "Andi! Use that magic-block spell on him, quick!" Fjuri yelled. Snapped from his momentary paralysis as he tried to figure out what to do next, Andi hurled the spell. But he gave it a broad focus, encompassing all three of the aptrgangr that opposed them even though only one of them seemed about to use magic. And all three of them collapsed to the floor as if they were puppets whose strings had been cut.

"Whoa!" Andi said, astonished at the result. He and Fjuri hastily retrieved their weapons, and the overlord's valuable longsword as well, then examined the three aptrgangr where they lay motionless on the stones. Fjuri stood upright, working through something in his mind. "You said that they move by magic," he said. "So the magic-block spell severs you from magic for a while. But what if magic is all that makes you alive?"

"By the gods, I think you're right!" Andi exclaimed. He was the one with all the magical education and ability, but his un-magical friend had hit the nail on the head. Why hadn't they realized that before? "But will it reconnect when the spell has run its course?" he wondered out loud.

"Here," Fjuri said, handing him the handsome sablium longsword. "You take the overlord, I'll take these two and we'll wait. Three minutes, did you say?"

Fjuri hadn't wanted to carry off the aptrgangr grunts' weapons, which were neither particularly good nor of any monetary value; but as they stood over their foes, waiting to see what would happen, he picked them up and hurled them off down the corridor. No point in taking chances! Watchful and tense, the two young men stood silent for nearly a full minute. Then, all at the same time, the aptrgangr at their feet began stirring once again.

"Drat!" Andi exclaimed as he swung the sablium longsword and took off the overlord's head before it could get upright. "I was really hoping that would be a permanent thing. Think how useful that would be against undead dragons!" Meanwhile Fjuri was busy dispatching the two lesser aptrgangr with his own longsword. Finished with that task he turned and grinned at his friend.

"It'll still be useful against undead dragons," he said. "Depending on what the range is, the fall alone might kill them. And three minutes ought to be enough to hack them up to the point where they can't fly again, at least – assuming you've got plenty of helpers with swords."

The two did a high-five, then strode on down the corridor with a new sense of confidence. With Andi's ability to adjust the scope of any spell up to an angle of nearly 180 degrees in front of him, they were (at least temporarily) safe from any undead for a span of three minutes. Plenty of time either to permanently sever their connection to their animating magic – or simply slip away leaving them to wonder what had happened, assuming they had that much awareness.

They soon came to a new section of catacombs, but this time the two stayed together and followed the labyrinthine pathways as a team. Splitting up could only lead to grief, and if they came to a dead end and had to go back together and try another path, it was no big deal. Andi continued taking the lead and hitting any suspicious corpses with flaming arrows as they went along, saving them the trouble of dealing with aptrgangr *after* they had come alive. He was able to retrieve most of his arrows, so the technique cost him little.

Even within this city of the dead they found a few rooms that had clearly been intended for the living. In the days when the surviving members of the dragon church were interring their fallen priests, providing them with defenders and helpers, there would have been need for those yet alive to eat, and sleep. And young men who had been on the go for something like the past 24 hours with only one meal and no rest had the same needs.

Andi and Fjuri ate from their packed provisions, washing them down with water, in a small chamber with an enchanting station and a dining table in it. A magical fire burned in the room's fireplace, providing a welcome warmth – though the ambient temperature had risen as they'd descended below ground level and they weren't uncomfortably cold.

Barring the room's door against any aptrgangr sentries who might come wandering, they took off their armor and curled up in their bedrolls for a much-needed rest. There was no way of telling how many hours had passed when they awoke at last, relieving themselves in a convenient urn and breakfasting on trail bread and water before donning their armor and continuing on their way.

The optimism and feeling of near-omnipotence that Andi and Fjuri had enjoyed since their discovery of the magic-block spell's effect on the undead returned, as they passed through more catacombs and traversed staircase after staircase on their way to the tomb's central chamber. None could stand against them, and any aptrgangr who escaped Andi's watchfulness and rose from their rest soon found themselves immobilized – before being returned to death.

And at last, they came to a pair of enormous double doors that looked very familiar to Andi from his trip through Gunderthal eleven years previously. Those dragon worshipers had been very traditional when it came to the architecture of their tombs and fortresses, and he didn't doubt that on the other side of these doors they would find an enormous chamber with a Spell Wall at the back of it, lined with sarcophagi full of aptrgangr defenders, and with the stone coffin containing the dragon priest Wissagleb located in a central position atop a stone stage of some kind.

He expected there would even be enormous carved stone dragons flanking the entrance; but in this case Andi did not intend to climb up and hide behind one as he watched the action unfold. He did, a bit, wish that Papa Andrion and Papa Erik were here, however. Then he brushed the thought aside. He and Fjuri were men now, lifelong friends and a match for whatever this tomb had to throw at them! Who knew, maybe they'd go on to marry the same woman. Well, since he sort-of intended to marry Zira someday and she didn't seem to find Fjuri much to her taste, perhaps not…

They stepped through the doors, and then took in the room. By the gods, it seemed bigger yet than the main burial chamber in Gunderthal – even in the memories Andi held from when he was much, much smaller! There were many similarities, though. Stone sarcophagi lined the walls on either side and rose in tiers toward the multi-layered stone stage, which held not one but several sarcophagi with one considerably-larger one taking the place of honor at the exact middle of the top tier.

Andi sagged. His original plan had been to suppress the presumed waves of aptrgangr here with the magic-block spell, then when Wissagleb popped out of his coffin, announce "Ehrgeizig sent me," and take it from there. Since the undead dragon priest would be in possession of at least some of his mental faculties, he would be swayed from attacking them by the mention of his old dragon friend and order all the aptrgangr (after they woke up, of course) to cease their attack.

But this cavernous room, and the sheer number of sarcophagi within it, made that plan ludicrous. Before they could activate, then subdue, all of these aptrgangr (and here, in the central burial chamber, every one of them would be undead versus dead-dead), there would be no time to deal with the undead dragon priest before he took action that was likely to be deleterious to their health.

After the two had stood there for a couple of minutes in the doorway, unmoving, Fjuri said "Andi? What's the plan?" Andi's quick mind was still running through the imagined results of each course of action, and finding each of them wanting from a "staying alive and unhurt" perspective.

"Still working on it," he said softly. "This is a bit more than I was expecting." His previous experience of exactly one ancient Norse tomb had not prepared him for this.

"When we got here," Fjuri said softly, "I noticed that there were aptrgangr on the walls but they didn't attack us. I think it's because Mondi was with us. So, why don't you go dragon and fly up on top of whatsisname's coffin? Maybe he'll assume you're one of his bosses." Andi's mind immediately followed *that* scenario to its conclusion, and he liked it.

"Don't ever let anyone tell you you're not a genius, Fjuri," he said in an undertone. "Help me out of my armor."

A minute or two later, the medium-sized bronze dragon Guldekiind stood where Andi had been – Fjuri busily stuffing Andi's clothing, armor, and weapons into his friend's pack. The enormous room was capacious enough even for a dragon of Guldekiind's size to take flight, though it wouldn't be more than a second or two before he would have had to circle around.

"Stay back and wait," Andi warned Fjuri. "No point in anybody getting hurt." With his powerful rear limbs he launched himself into the air, wings spread, and more jumped than flew to the top tier of the stone stage on which sat the sarcophagus he assumed belonged to the dragon priest they'd come to speak with.

He landed to one side of it, easily within trigger range from what he knew of such things. "Wissagleb, come forth!" Andi commanded forcefully. "Guldekiind would speak with you!" The heavy stone lid burst aside with a crack, and a medium-sized aptrgangr clad as a dragon priest sat up within his coffin and began making his way down to the platform on which it sat. He adjusted his ruined clothing in a way that seemed fussy somehow, then said in a cracking voice "Lord, how may I serve you?"

Chapter 26: Reconciliation

Bernadette, Erik, Andrion, and Wissliiben arrived near the sanctuary of the ancient Guardians in darkness. Cursing the map's time lags and wishing for the hundredth time that it offered travel as instantaneous as the Calling dragon spell, she led them stealthily to the north – avoiding any Insurgent sentries. While the Insurgents were no longer at war with the other human inhabitants of Iscandia, they took it amiss if strangers trespassed in their settlements. She had long wished for the chance to learn more about these people; but though they were as human as she was and spoke her own tongue, their society permitted no interlopers.

Unfortunately, though Bernadette and her husbands had undoubtedly been through the tiny settlement where the attack had occurred more than once, it was so unimportant that it had not registered on any of their maps. It might as well have been an anonymous bend in the road, though Bernadette was sure it had been an important place for its inhabitants. All now nothing but charred corpses, she imagined grimly. She was using anger to drive out desolation, and so far at least it was working.

Wissliiben soon took to the air – flying slowly no more than fifty feet above them and frequently circling around, as he waited for the oh-so-slow humans to catch up. His speed in the air was far beyond what even the fastest land-bound runner could achieve.

The smallest of the three moons was nearly full in the sky, and it provided enough light for them all to see the road as it wound its way between hills, leading north. They tried to run at first, but soon realized the pointlessness of the effort. Gotteluub was most likely dead as Wissliiben had reported, along with every human being in the little settlement – and the attacking undead dragons long since gone elsewhere.

So the three humans trudged along. Bernadette could see no point in going dragon, only to arrive at the scene of the massacre sooner – in the middle of the night. As they walked Erik threw an arm around her and kissed her cheek. There were no words that were going to make it all right, but that sweet gesture helped somehow. In another minute Andrion pulled even with her on the other side, and also squeezed her close for a moment. Then they walked on.

Four hours later they had traveled most of the twenty miles, and dawn was still some time off. Bernadette abruptly walked to the side of the road, peeled off her pack and sat on it. What were they doing? The utter futility of their frantic charge to the site of the dragon attack hit her like a club, and she sat struggling with the desire to just lower her head into her hands and sob.

In a moment Erik and Andrion were by her side, their concern and love buoying her up like a piece of driftwood thrown to a drowning woman. They embraced her from either side, just holding her as her son Wissliiben came in for a landing in the road. He approached her clumsily, neck extended to gently nuzzle her, brushing the hair out her face with the tip of his tongue. "Good idea, Mama," he said quietly. "Let's all just rest until it gets light."

They'd missed their supper in the interstices of map travel, so laid out some bedrolls and sat eating some trail bread and water as they waited for the sun. Long before it appeared over the eastern horizon the sky began to get light, pink clouds glowing here and there, and they got back onto their feet and went on. "It's right up this road," Wissliiben said. "I'll meet you there." Trying to maintain pace with people walking was much more tiring than simply flying, and he too was growing hungry.

There seemed to be no smoke rising as the three Drakesprings approached the settlement, though all of the buildings were at least partially collapsed. More to their surprise they found people there, beginning to clear away rubble. Was it possible some had survived, or were these neighbors come to look for the dead?

Off to one side of the road, curled up as if in sleep, was the torn and battered corpse of Gotteluub. The severed wing had been laid beside the body, and there were bunches of wildflowers around it. What? Even as grief tore at her and a sob rose in her throat, Bernadette wondered at this. What did it mean?

One of the men, seeing them arrive, stopped what he was doing and walked over to talk with them. Just then Wissliiben touched down, having stopped to catch and eat a goat before arriving. He, too, was dumfounded to see the body of his brother arrayed with such care. "I don't know you," the man, a worn-looking Norseman in his middle thirties, said to Wissliiben. "But you were here helping yesterday, were you not?"

Wissliiben nodded his head. "Gotteluub was my brother," he replied solemnly. That the local humans were able to distinguish among the young dragons was a sign of how closely they had interacted with them. Bernadette, kneeling beside the body of her son with silent tears running down her face, drew a hand across her eyes and rose to her feet. She looked up into the eyes of the man, whose face was painted in sorrow and sympathy.

"I am their mother," she told him, and his eyes widened in surprise.

"The Fireblood?" he asked. "We had heard, but I thought it was just so much talk… You can truly become dragon, and the young ones are yours?" She just nodded, then looked around at the ruined settlement.

"How is it that any of you are still alive?" she asked.

"All of us are alive, ma'am," he replied, "though Sigurd's burnt something bad. I don't suppose you have any healing potions to spare?" Shaken out of her grief by being needed for something, Bernadette immediately demanded to see Sigurd. The lad, perhaps a year younger than Andi, was lying on a bedroll near one of the ruined buildings and appeared to be only semi-conscious. His clothing was charred, and he had second- and third-degree burns over much of the front of his body.

Horrified at the damage and surprised he had not already died of shock, Bernadette knelt beside the boy and applied her healing spell. She took particular care with his face, easing and directing the magic so that he might heal without scars. Not one healer in a hundred had a touch so delicate. It took a long time, and without being prompted Erik held a stamina potion to her lips. She drank it without ceasing her efforts. He'd seen her work at healing until she fell into a faint in the past, unaware of what was happening in her own body as her mind inhabited the body of her patient.

Some ten minutes later young Sigurd sat up, covering himself with his hands as he realized that he was nearly naked in the presence of an attractive strange woman. "Wha… what happened?"

he stammered. He'd lost his awareness at the point when Todenangst had flamed him, early in the attack yesterday morning.

As Bernadette rose to her feet, the boy's mother (a rawboned, plain-featured Norsewoman a few years older than the man and possibly his sister) pounced on her and smothered her in a hug. "Thank you, oh thank you," she said, tears running down her face.

"I don't understand how you all have survived," Andrion said, having prepared himself emotionally for facing not only the death of his wife's dragon child but a village full of charred corpses.

The man spoke up again. "When the main house was built," he said – gesturing toward the largest of the now-collapsed structures – "they put in a full stone cellar for roots and hanging meat and so forth. After the young dragons came and drove off that undead one as it was about to fry my wife and kids, we sent them running for the cellar. Then when the big one came, we realized it was hopeless and we *all* went down there. I think the big one figured he'd gotten us after he collapsed the roof, didn't know we were safe below. After the two of them left, the fires went out and we came out through the escape tunnel."

"Escape tunnel?" Andrion asked, surprised.

"This place was homesteaded by my grandpapa," the farmer explained. "There were a lot of Insurgents back then, and they were known to raid farms sometimes. He ran a stone-lined tunnel three hundred yards down into that copse by the creek. Never thought we'd need it for a dragon attack, though."

Bernadette, who'd been released from the thankful embrace of the boy's mother, was feeling a little better now. Gotteluub was dead, and that was irrevocable. But she had saved another mother's son, and though these people's homes had been destroyed they themselves were still alive. "You moved the body of my son?" she asked. The man nodded.

"Young Gotteluub and his sister have lived in these parts for a couple of years now, and they were nice kids. Used to bring us elk sometimes, and once they took care of a family of bears that were harassing our stock. He gave his life for us, in a way, and I thought we should show some respect."

"Thank you," she said solemnly. "Since these undead dragons have appeared, I have been very afraid that people would assume my children were part of the problem. It is good to know that they've been making true friends." Looking around at the devastation she added, "Do you plan to rebuild?"

He followed her gaze. "The foundations are still fine," he admitted. "But most of the wood is beyond salvage I'm afraid. It's not easy to come by, out here. Grandpapa brought in three wagon-loads when he and Grandmama first came to build, helped by his brothers. With me and my brother and sister and their families we have enough manpower. But no materials, and those dragons killed our livestock. Didn't eat 'em, just killed 'em…"

"You could probably obtain some lumber and livestock in Sylvanian," Bernadette mused aloud. The man looked at her in confusion. Sylvanian was hundreds of miles away, and his extended family's farm had been a subsistence operation. They had no cash.

"I could fly to the moons, too, I suppose," he said somewhat bitterly. He was grateful to The Fireblood for saving his nephew, but her suggestion was remarkably unhelpful.

As they spoke, a couple of chickens turned up and began pecking around, looking for something to eat. "It looks like the dragons didn't kill *all* your livestock," Bernadette pointed out. "What about food? Do you have some food to get by for a while?" He nodded, not understanding where she was going with all this. "There's two or three months' worth of cabbages, carrots, and potatoes down in the cellar. And an elk we were hanging."

"Good!" she replied, smiling for the first time since before the news had come in. Erik and Andrion eyed her. They had some idea what she was planning. But would that work? Bernadette pulled out her map and pointed triumphantly at it. "See?" she demanded of her husbands. "Check your own and see if I'm right!"

Three maps of Agena were produced, and on each of them the arrow representing the bearer was atop a small notation that read "Creekside Farm." "That wasn't there last night, I looked!" Erik exclaimed.

"I think it finally registered as a quest marker," his wife replied. "Let me just test my theory before we run off."

152

All business once again, she set off at a firm walking pace for the grove of trees that stood around a small nearby creek. They watched her go, then vanish. Soon she was standing, not in their midst, but down the road a few dozen yards to the south. "All right!" she said, returning to where she'd been standing minutes before. "Um, what is your name?" she asked the farmer.

"Thongeld, ma'am," he replied.

"Very well, Thongeld. Andrion and Erik can stay here for a couple of days and help clean up the mess while you and I make a quick trip to Sylvanian for supplies. I'm buying."

Thongeld's eyes were wide with amazement. "Thank you, ma'am," he said softly.

"Hurricane Berni is picking up speed," Erik murmured to his marriage-mate. Andrion smiled and nodded. He knew that more than anything else she needed to be taking decisive, useful action to ward off the grief that might otherwise leave her paralyzed.

Leaving Thongeld to inform his family of her plans, Bernadette turned her attention to Wissliiben where he sat on the ground, communing sadly with the corpse of his brother. "I think that we will inter Gotteluub here, near where he lies," she told him. "I hope these people here, including Erik and Andrion, will be able to excavate a grave. When I get back from Sylvanian, we'll Call everyone for the ceremony."

What she had in mind was not the necromantic rituals the elder dragons had been buried with, but something akin to a human funeral rite: a farewell to the young dragon who had lived scarcely more than a decade but had already touched many lives. She kissed Wissliiben on the nose and then kissed and hugged each of her husbands in turn, before taking Thongeld by the arm and leading him a few paces up the road. They soon vanished from sight.

Chapter 27: Dragon Lord

"Ehrgeizig sent me," Guldekiind told the withered undead dragon priest as they stood facing each other on the flat top tier of the burial platform. The aptrgangr had remained in their tombs.

"Ehrgeizig!" Wissagleb said in a voice like the rustling of sheets of dry parchment. "He lives, then? How long have I been dead, I wonder…"

There had been a few dragons in the time of the Uprising no older or larger than Andi was now. Indeed, Ehrgeizig himself had been not a lot bigger then. But looking down at his withered undead body, Wissagleb knew it had to have been a long time. The burial rituals of the dragon worshipers had been intended to preserve the corpse for eons.

"I'm sorry to tell you it has been several thousand years, Wissagleb," Andi replied. "The Uprising ended a long time ago."

"Yet here you are, a living dragon. Did mankind reach some kind of accord with their once-masters? Or has Tarragin returned?" Wissagleb, just as Ehrgeizig had said, had a quick mind.

"Tarragin has come, and gone again," Andi reported truthfully. "And while *drachen* fly again in the skies of Agena they are now few. I am a member of the new generation."

"New… you are truly no more than twenty years old?" the undead priest wanted to know. He seemed to know dragons well enough to have some idea of how size should correlate to age. Andi nodded.

Wissagleb seemed puzzled. "How is it that you have the Reciprocation then?" he went on. "You could not have come here as a dragon." Um… Andi decided that they'd gotten off on a friendly-enough footing that he could reveal the truth. He *hoped*.

"I was born human, Wissagleb. As human as my friend Fjurbund there." Fjuri had been taking all this in from near the cavernous chamber's entrance, pleased with the way it was going while remaining alert for threats.

"Then you are…" "That's right, I'm fireblood, and I have taken the potion and learned the dragon spells to transform back and forth between dragon and human forms only. All lore concerning the Reward was lost in the mists of time, possibly even intentionally hidden by the remaining dragon worshipers before the church's ultimate destruction. I am of the same blood as you, but there are no more living dragon priests."

Wissagleb' shoulders slumped. He was clad in sablium armor and his mask, which conferred the powers of life detection and enhanced capabilities of healing, was hung from a hook on his belt. But he was not a very imposing figure. "I had hoped…" he sighed. "So you don't have the other two dragon spells? You'll find them on the wall below, if you like." He seemed a bit defeated.

"I came to meet you and gain knowledge," Andi told him, "but I have something to tell you as well. Please wait just a moment." Such a polite young dragon, the undead priest thought as he watched him lift slightly and glide down to the Spell Wall at the rear of the chamber. Landing within the wall's slight curvature, Andi was bombarded as nearly every set of runes graven into its surface blazed white. The familiar chorus rang in his ears as word after word, spell after spell, embedded itself in his draconic mind.

There! The Send Within dragon spell that would place his clothing, weapons, and other belongings in a kind of limbo where they were hidden but accessible. And its counterpart, the Return dragon spell, that would restore those belongings to the places on his person where they'd been before. Several others, some of questionable utility, came to him as well. And one that didn't seem to make complete sense, Go Human. Return to Human, the dragon spell he'd obtained in Gunderthal, was what he used to resume his human form when he was a dragon. And here was another, Return to Dragon.

The process complete, his mind bubbling like a cauldron from the magic that had infused it (even as his innards bubbled with the formation of the stones needed to power those spells), Andi spread his wings and hopped back up to where Wissagleb still stood. "Wow," he said, revealing his age as much as did his relatively small size. "Thank you, Wissagleb. Tell me, what is this 'Reciprocation' of which you speak?"

Wissagleb shared with his old friend Ehrgeizig an urge to teach, and he responded to the pull of Andi's curiosity with an outpouring of information. "Not many of the *drachen* took advantage of it," he said. "It was something developed by the greatest minds among the priesthood, the same who developed the Reward or so it was said. It was intended as a gift from us to the dragons we worshipped, a chance to walk in our shoes and see the world from another perspective. Not to mention take advantage of facilities like this one, and have the use of hands with opposable thumbs," he added wryly.

"So, it enables a natural-born dragon to transform into a human and back again?" Andi asked.

"That's right," his teacher went on. "As with the Reward, a potion was required to prepare the body for the action of the magic. Once that was ingested, the dragon could transform back and forth at will. Those who opted to do this usually learned the two auxiliary dragon spells of the Reward as well, to make dealing with the accoutrements of humanity easier. And because they were dragon at least some of the time – most of the time, usually – their lifespans and aging process were not harmed by taking the form of mortal men."

"This potion, what was it?" Andi asked eagerly. He'd been longing for his brother Mondi to be able to turn human so that he could continue to live with the family, ever since the young dragon had outgrown the house.

"Oh, a concoction of many things," Wissagleb replied vaguely. "Similar to the potion for Dragon Transformation, but with different ingredients. And in much larger quantity, of course. A dragon would need to ingest a quantity as much larger as it itself was, relative to a human being. Perhaps gallons, though most who accepted the Reciprocation were younger and smaller. Curiosity seems to be a trait mainly of the young."

"Why are you interested?" the dragon priest asked.

"When I said I was a member of the new generation, I wasn't kidding," Andi explained. "I'm the only child in my human family who's fireblood, but my mom has nineteen dragon children that she produced while in dragon form. Long story, but I know they would all be very interested in trying out human existence."

"Aah, remarkable!" the cheerful aptrgangr said. "I believe I have a quantity here somewhere, if you would like to take some with you." He strode in the somewhat stiff gait of the undead down off the platform and headed toward a small antechamber off to one side of the Spell Wall.

"If you don't mind, I'm just going to change back to human now," Andi called to him.

He returned to where Fjuri was standing, a look of amazement on his handsome features. "Wow, I think we hit the jackpot!" he said. He, Andi, and Mondi together had been the best of buddies when they were all kids together, but he'd seen little of him in the years since. It occurred to him that Mondi's human form would be that of an eleven-year-old boy, but his mind should be the same as it was now – at a stage of development similar to his own.

Andi quickly went back to his human form and donned his underwear, armor, and pack with its weapons slung on it. Then he cried "Weit-Stos-Zet-Blik!" and stood naked again. A huge grin spread over his face as his friend gaped at him. Lifting a hand, he rapped on his chest. His armor was somehow there, but not there. He couldn't grab a weapon or get something out of his pack, but everything he was actually wearing still existed in some way. Excellent!

He now cried "Yetz-Dies-Ruk-Shao!" and everything reappeared. Gleefully, Andi went into a little jig. "This is awesome!" he crowed. "I can't wait to tell Mom!" Wissagleb returned from the anteroom lugging a large sack, and made his way over to them moving as if under a great burden.

"Hmm, you weren't kidding when you said you were under twenty, either – were you? Galise, are you?" Andi was surprised. There couldn't have been that many visitors to Iscandia from Auverne all those thousands of years ago.

"How'd you guess?" he asked.

"Oh, I visited most places in Agena when I young," the dragon priest replied somewhat smugly. "Your people have a powerful affinity for magic, the strongest of the races of men. And I'm attuned to such things." He had set the sack down on the floor between them, and now opened it to lift out some items. There were two large jugs made of something like elvengild, from which elven armor was crafted. "These contain the Human Transformation potion for dragons," he said. Then he produced an ancient-looking tome that seemed to be in a remarkable state of preservation. "And here's a book with the formulae for that and some other potions. It's in Common, which should help. Though I couldn't begin to tell you where to get all the ingredients."

"Thank you!" Andi exclaimed sincerely. This was like a dream come true! "My mom is a really good chemiast, and has been studying and crafting potions since long before I was born. If anybody alive today can figure out how to make more, it's her.

"She's welcome to it," Wissagleb replied. "It's certainly doing no one any good down here in this... tomb." He spoke the last word with a trace of disgust.

"I can hardly wait to embrace my dragon brother for the first time as a human," Andi said, "but this is not really what we came to talk about. A fellow priest of yours, a guy named Meiskomtot, has emerged from his tomb. And as an undead dragon, he is flying around reanimating the dragons who were restored to life by Tarragin only to be killed again. Those my mother killed can't be brought back except as the crudest sort of zombies, but there are a lot that still have their souls intact. He and they are attacking human settlements and killing people."

"Him!" Wissagleb snarled. "That bastard always was a mean one. Deeper into the necromantic arts than any other in the priesthood, I'll wager. And it was probably the shock of his life... er, unlife, when he came to and found out he was a desiccated corpse! He was firmly convinced he was going to live forever. Well, we all were, really..."

"You didn't seem surprised when I called you forth just now," Andi remarked.

"I was killed near the end of the war," the undead priest explained. "I saw my death coming, and had not the strength to heal myself nor to take dragon form. Had I done so, I likely would have died anyway. You say all of the dragons from those times were killed?"

"All but Ehrgeizig," Andi admitted. "He had hidden himself away atop the Hochstein, and founded the Order of the Old Ones to continue teaching humans how to cast dragon spells. He gave my mom a lot of information she needed, and helped her find Tarragin where he had gone after she and my papas nearly defeated him. All three of them went to Asengard and killed Tarragin there with help from the three heroes from antiquity who'd originally banished him to another dimension. But before he was killed, he'd already brought a lot of the dragons the priests had interred back to life."

Did the boy say he had two fathers? Odd. Wissagleb pushed the thought aside for the time being. The domestic arrangements of The Fireblood were of less importance than some other things. "I wonder," he said out loud though half to himself, "whether old Meiskomtot is merely seeking revenge on the descendants of those who destroyed our church? Or if he plans to reestablish the church and the rule of the *drachen*?"

"I don't see how he could reestablish the church," Andi said. "My mom and I are the only two humans in Iscandia with the dragon blood, so far as I know – and neither one of us is interested in becoming a dragon priest. Up until recently, we've been living a nice quiet life on our farm near Waterdon."

"Waterdon," the undead priest echoed him. "A little jewel of a city, built out from the mead hall of the Brave Company and with that marvelous palace at the top where the eorl used to keep a captive dragon?"

"That's the place," Andi smiled. "But it's grown quite a bit just during *my* lifetime. Things have gotten relatively settled in Iscandia, and without a lot of wars people have time to build and grow and prosper. But anyhow… the other reason that it's unlikely Meiskomtot could resurrect the dragon worshipers is there are probably fewer than two hundred dragons living in the entirety of Agena. And about ten percent of those are my siblings, who were raised to regard humans as partners and allies – not worshippers."

"Ah, but Meiskomtot is a necromancer of amazing skill!" Wissagleb pointed out. "What need has he of living dragons, or a living priesthood, when he can call on armies of the undead?" That was a chilling thought, but it seemed wrong somehow. Andi exchanged glances with Fjuri, and saw that his friend's brows, too, were knit in concentration. Then Fjuri spoke, his first contribution to the conversation since the undead priest had arisen from his tomb.

"What do you want, Wissagleb?" he asked rhetorically. "Do you hunger, or thirst? Would you like to enjoy a woman, or perhaps a hot bath?" Wissagleb stood stock still for a minute, communing silently with himself. This was his first bout of consciousness since his death, and he had so far had little time for introspection.

"Nothing…" he breathed finally. "I want nothing, though I admit that I am enjoying conversing with you young fellows and learning about the world in which you live. But though I move and breathe, speak and think, I am dead. And the dead have no need or desire for the pleasures of the flesh."

"So Meiskomtot cannot lust for power in the way he probably did when he was alive. He must want it for the mental satisfaction it brings, or perhaps it truly is revenge that he wants. Maybe he's just furious because he got cheated out of the immortality he'd been promised, and he wants to strike out at the whole living world. But whatever he wants, I think it's something he can't have. And we need to stop him before he hurts any more people trying to find it." Andi gazed at his friend in wonder. Fjuri was indeed the strong, silent type – and the foregoing speech practically qualified as oratory.

"Wait," Wissagleb said, "Fjurbund, is it? There's no magic in you, so how come you by a dragon-tongue name? Eh, never mind. I wish to tell you that I have just realized what it is I want." The boys looked at him, eager to learn the answer. Had you told them last week that they would soon be standing near the bottom of an ancient Norse tomb having a friendly chat with the animated corpse of a dragon priest from thousands of years ago, they would have laughed. Yet here they were.

Wissagleb drew himself up. He had probably once been of average height for a Norseman, but being dead for a few millennia has a way of shrinking a man. He now stood far shorter than either Andi or Fjuri. "What I want," the undead priest declared, "is to help you defeat Meiskomtot and his undead minions, and send their souls to hell."

Chapter 28: The Home Front

Alfmund walked down the road from Waterdon toward Drakespring Farm with a spring in his step, head held high as he inhaled the delightful air of a mostly-clear summer morning. The mission to clean out the bandits' nest had been a rousing success, every single one of the buggers wiped out and only minor injuries to the party of Brave Company members who had gone after them.

Their chief had proven to be a tough customer, but Alfmund had defeated him – and won the chief's useful and valuable steel plate armor as a prize in addition to the money he'd received from Szaras. He was having it fitted to his measurements at the Godsforge, where the latest in a long line of Snowhair smiths plied the legendary forge on the behalf of the eorl and the Brave Company.

At the moment he was dressed in ordinary clothing, a reasonably nice tunic and a pair of well-fitted trousers above leather boots. He had tried to look his best, for he was going calling on his lady-love. Ah, Riki! The last time he had seen her, when he stopped by the farm to say goodbye before leaving for the bandits' lair, he thought she had said something about a crisis – a dragon attack that had sent her parents on a quest of some kind, leaving her stuck at home taking care of the place and looking after her younger brother. Not only was she as beautiful as a spring morning and as lithe as a young smilodon, she was skillful and responsible as well. How he loved her!

At his age Alfmund had not yet acquired any great fund of patience, and he was already re-thinking his earlier resolve to hang in there for another two years until Riki had reached an age at which it was more common for Norse maidens to wed. Fourteen was not unheard-of, after all. "Old enough to bleed, old enough to breed" was a crude aphorism he'd heard repeated more than once. And Erika Drakespring was clearly a woman, no little girl.

Riki had returned from the Maiden with Sigi yesterday afternoon to find two upset young female dragons in the yard, and her parents gone. Purpurflug, her dragon sister whom she knew but slightly, explained that their brother Gotteluub had been killed fighting the undead dragon priest Meiskomtot and that Bernadette, Andrion, Erik and Wissliiben had gone to investigate.

She'd been stunned. She'd known her brother Gotteluub no better than she knew Purpurflug. Andi, able as he was to become a dragon, had spent vastly more time with their scaly half-siblings than had she or any of the other Drakespring children. Only Mondi really seemed like a brother to her, and she missed him as they all did. Awhile later Meri had returned from her visit with Edla, and the news had had to be repeated again.

So without warning, Riki once again found herself mistress of Drakespring House – this time with two younger siblings to watch over as well as *all* of the farm chores and *all* of the housework. She was upset about Gotteluub, worried about Andi, Fjuri, and Mondi, and wished bitterly that Mom, Erik, and Andrion were here. But what could she do but carry on?

By midmorning the next day Riki was starting to feel better about things. Meri, who after all was only a couple of years younger than she was and a smart kid to boot, had suggested that she return to Brightsgate Cottage and see if the Steadfast family could put her up for a few days. She'd had sleepovers there with Edla in the past, and could be a help to Lifa with the household chores.

Could be a help to *me*, Riki thought, but stifled it. Better for Meri to get some more time to spend with her best friend, before she was dragged off to whatever assignment the Leukalfar Initiative had in store for her next. The poor girl's life was scarcely her own, just because she was the only leukalfar girl in Iscandia who'd been raised as part of a "normal" family.

That left Riki with only Sigi to look after again, and she could probably have farmed him off to stay with Remy and Hildi at the Maiden, had she wanted to. He was at an age where formal schooling was mostly behind him and serious work had not yet claimed his days – that golden age of childhood where your time was your own, and your imagination was the only limit to your travels. She sighed. But she didn't want to be left completely alone at home, and besides he could still help with the chickens, harvesting of crops, and the weeding. It was only chores like the milking and the cleaning out of paddocks that really required an adult's strength.

Sigi was harvesting tomatoes and Riki was in the kitchen, putting away the last of the clean dishes and cutlery from the drain rack, when Alfmund came in through the gate at the bottom of the path. Quite a few years ago Erik had installed a hip-high ornamental iron fence that completely encircled the property, delineating its boundaries. Andrion had contributed a spell that warded off rust, so that nearly a decade later the fence looked untouched by time.

He spotted Sigi in the tomato patch and called to him. "Halloo, Sigi! How goes it?" Sigi set down his basket, which was getting heavier with each ripe fruit, and gave Alfmund a big smile. He liked the young Norseman, though he sensed that his overwhelming love for Riki was not returned in kind and that probably meant Alfmund would not be coming around much longer. Oh well.

Alfmund knocked lightly at the front door, but didn't wait for a response before trying the knob and finding it (as he'd expected) unlocked. He opened it and peered inside, spotting the object of his affections standing on tiptoe to deposit some plates on an upper shelf even as she turned to see who was knocking.

"Alfmund!" she said, half guiltily. She'd been enjoying his attention so much, and she really did like him as a friend. But she knew that he wanted something from her she did not have to give. And now that the ice had been broken with Fjuri, she felt as if she couldn't lead Alfmund on any longer. It was Fjuri she loved, Fjuri she wanted – and it was not fair to Alfmund to let him think there was any hope she would ever be his.

"Erika, my love!" the young man called heartily. "Is it just you and the boy, then?" Riki finished what she was doing and turned to face him. She could see the happiness shining in his open, boyish face, and quailed at the thought of bursting his balloon. Maybe a bit of seriousness to take the edge off first…

"All went well with the bandits, then?" she asked.

"Obliterated them utterly, we did!" he crowed. "And how are you?" He stepped close to embrace her, which she allowed. But as he leaned in for a deep kiss she wriggled away from him.

"There's been some more bad news," Riki told him. "Will you sit?" she gestured at the table. His face showing chagrin, Alfmund took a chair and she sat across from him.

"Do you recall I said an undead dragon priest, transformed into an undead dragon, had raised other undead dragons and had attacked a human village?" Alfmund nodded, his face a mask of serious concern. He hadn't truly paid that much attention to what she'd said earlier, caught up in the excitement of the Brave Company quest. "They've attacked at least twice more that we know of," Riki went on. "While you were killing your bandits my mom and Papa Erik went up to Sylvanian to get Papa Andrion, and while they were there an undead dragon attacked a nearby village."

"By the gods!" Alfmund exclaimed, "What happened?"

"Oh, they killed it of course," Riki replied. The idea that any reasonably manageable peril could defeat the likes of her mom and papas was something she'd never even considered. "Then they came home," she continued, "but yesterday we learned that another undead dragon had attacked a small farm out in Westmarch. And one of my dragon brothers got killed when the undead dragon priest showed up. So Mom and my papas are out there now, and meanwhile Andi, Fjuri, and my dragon brother Mondi are off trying to find some really ancient dragon to get more information."

Alfmund sat stunned. This lovely young creature, a paragon of Norse womanhood to all seeming, kept reminding him that her background was *not* the usual. She'd mentioned her dragon siblings, the full story of her life and family situation gradually emerging. But what had seemed like a fantastic story was now solidifying into reality before his eyes. And he was having a hard time taking it in.

After digesting this all for a minute or two he said somewhat feebly, "Riki! I'm so sorry! Are you all right?"

Her eyes downcast, she replied "I suppose. I don't really know most of my dragon siblings all that well. I can't turn into a dragon and go flying with them like Andi can, and I usually only see any of them once or twice a year. Even Mondi, who grew up with us when we were little, hasn't been living here for a long time."

"But this undead dragon priest, he's a threat to all of Iscandia!" Alfmund went on. He was coming to realize that the personal aspects of this crisis were just the tip of the iceberg.

"Yes," she said, meeting his gaze. "But apparently my job is just to keep milking the cows and taking care of my younger brother and sister, at least for now." He detected a note of resentment in her voice.

"Sister?" Alfmund asked. He thought he'd met the whole family. Had there been a mention of a sister who was not there at the time?

"Meri," Riki said, puzzled. "I thought I told you about her?"

"I don't think so," he replied in all innocence. She raised her lovely eyebrows, as red-gold as the hair on her head but a shade darker.

"Sorry, I guess I've been distracted. Meri, Merelle I mean, was adopted into our family as a baby when I was about two. She's been working up in Sylvanian since before I met you."

"Younger than you, but working out of town?" Alfmund was having a hard time processing this new information.

"Yes," Riki said, beginning to see a way in which she might fend him off without hurting his feelings. "Did I mention that my family is deeply involved with the effort to integrate the leukalfar into mainstream Iscandia society? No? Oh, my goodness! There's so *much* we haven't talked about! Yes, the reason we're involved with the leukalfar is that my sister Merelle *is* leukalfar. My mom found her while she and Papa Andrion were questing below a dypalfar ruin."

Alfmund sat in stunned silence for a while. He had believed that he and Riki were intimates. He had met her family, and he had certainly told her much about his own family back in Eisenstag. They had spent so much time together, but what had they really talked about? There'd been swordplay, and kissing, hand-holding, a bit of groping... but no really deep conversations about anything. Was his love for her based entirely on her beauty, and the fact that she was kind?

"I had thought," he said finally, "before I met those two that were here the first time I came, that the leukalfar were a degenerate race of elves who lived like animals below the ruins of abandoned dypalfar cities. After meeting them, I had assumed that they were somehow different from the rest of their race."

"Gods, no!" Riki exclaimed, beginning to sense victory. "They might be 'degenerate' in appearance because of the way they were poisoned by the dypalfar thousands of years ago. And they are certainly very tribal and unfriendly to strangers. But all the leukalfar, not just the ones who've learned to speak Common, are as human as you and I are. They have their own language, culture, crafts… And after Meri and Andi got to learn their language and meet a tribe of them last year, we've discovered a lot more about them."

Alfmund had come here with the intention of pressing his suit all the harder, asking Riki to marry him, perhaps (with the parents and elder brother gone) even getting into her bed. But he realized now that he did not know her as well as he thought he did. She still blazed in his mind like a beacon of desirability, he still wanted her desperately; but he had suddenly decided that he needed more time. He reached across the table and took her by the hand. "Please," he said, looking into those bottomless blue eyes, "tell me more."

Chapter 29: The Dead

"So," Andi said to the undead dragon priest, "what can you tell us about Meiskomtot?" The macabre figure stood pondering for a moment before speaking.

"He was much older than me," Wissagleb said. "He was already at the highest level of the priesthood and had received the Reward by the time I went through the Testing at age twelve and joined as an acolyte. We met a couple of times, but I doubt whether I made any impression on him. A very ambitious, very ruthless man. He cared not what harm he caused, as long as he achieved his ends. He was already dead and in his tomb, awaiting reanimation, by the time I was elevated and received the Reward."

"I doubt I would even have ascended as high in the priesthood as I did," Wissagleb went on, "were it not that we were losing the war and so many had already fallen. Most of my fellow priests, especially the powerful ones, didn't think I had what it took. I was always more interested in sharing knowledge than in subjugating those we ruled…"

"I see you have one of those masks," Andi remarked.

"This? Oh yes," Wissagleb replied deprecatingly. "Our names, in the dragon tongue as you know, came to us with our dragon forms at the ceremony during which we received the Reward. Along with that each priest of the highest level was given a mask, named for him. Mine enables me to see living things within the range of sight glowing, and greatly enhances my powers of healing. I can't quite restore life to the dead, but if there's a tiny spark of life left in your body I can restore you to full health in a minute – if I'm wearing the mask."

Andi, though deeply versed in magic for one so young, had never encountered the regular spell for detecting life – though he had just gotten the Finder dragon spell, which did much the same thing, off of that wall behind them. "Will it let you detect the undead as well?" he asked.

"As long as they are animate, connected with the magic that enables them to move," the dragon priest explained.

"And what about Meiskomtot's mask? What does that do?" Andi asked.

"Hmm, let me think… he'd been gone for decades before I died, but it was somewhat famous. I recall it now! Wearing the mask completely shielded him from magical attacks – fire, frost, lightning – any hostile magic, including dragon spells, would just wash right over him while he had it on. And it gave him a dragon's power to cast the same spell repeatedly with scarcely any waiting time in between. It was his *Drachansstab* that was really dangerous, though."

"His what?" Andi asked.

"A magical staff," Wissagleb explained. "Every priest of the highest level had one, another badge of office."

Wissagleb gestured with the magical staff he was holding in his withered claw of a hand. "Mine produces ice storms, that will spread out and momentarily freeze all of my foes within a radius of around fifty feet. It robs them of their stamina as well as harming them. Meiskomtot's was much more powerful. Whatever he hit with a burst of its energy would explode. He could turn a man into a red paste in an instant, or knock down city walls. I'm halfway surprised he ended up killed like the rest of us, with such resources at his disposal."

"What got him, then?" Andi asked, feeling as if he might be homing in something that might help them.

"Heh," Wissagleb chuckled, recalling something that, had his face not been so stiff, would have made him smile. "It was an accident!" he crowed. "Mister 'I'm-going-to-live-forever-and-rule-you-all' was crushed to death in a rockslide! It was in the middle of a battle, and there was a lot going on, so I'm not sure whether the rockslide was caused by an earth tremor or by something done by one side of the other. But it took them days to dig him out after the battle was over, and the body was a bit… deteriorated by then. I don't look so great," he continued, gesturing with his wasted limbs, "but Meiskomtot must look completely ghastly by now. Funny how things work out."

"Wow," Andi said, then gathered himself. "We really need to get back to my dragon brother outside and then hook up with my parents for a strategy session. Is there a back door here?" In every quest through an ancient Norse ruin Andy had ever heard about, there was a secret back door that could save you hours of travel.

"It's right over there," Wissagleb gestured to the opposite side of the Spell Wall from the room where the potions had lain. "But I think we'd better go back the way you came in."

"Why's that?" Andi asked, puzzled.

"For one thing it leads to a narrow ledge overlooking the canyon, and I don't think your friend Fjurbund can fly," Wissagleb explained. "But mostly, we need to gather our troops. I hope you didn't kill too many of them on your way in, though I can fix that if need be." Andi and Fjuri were speechless as the undead dragon priest made his way around the room, speaking some kind of invocation. As he passed them, fifty stone sarcophagi flew open and fifty aptrgangr, men and women, climbed from inside them and fell into formation behind Wissagleb.

Under the control of their superior, the undead guardians ignored the two living young men who walked just behind Wissagleb as they retraced their path through the labyrinthine catacombs. Where aptrgangr had arisen only to fall again, the dragon priest paused to reanimate them. It wasn't exactly necromancy, he explained, but more a renewal of the magical connection that had been established millennia before between him, the ranking priest interred here, and the aptrgangr who had been dedicated to his service.

Andi and Fjuri, beginning to feel weak from hunger, took advantage of these pauses to eat from their packs, drink from their water skins, and relieve themselves in corners before the ever-growing party marched on. Not every waiting aptrgangr had been activated by their presence on the inward journey, it seemed, for far more than they had killed were now marching with them, taking their places at the end of the procession.

At last they trooped through the wooden entry doors and down the broad staircase to the plaza, as early morning sunshine was peeking through herds of fluffy clouds. Across the plaza Andi and Fjuri saw that Ehrgeizig was still resting where they'd left him. If he was able to go without eating much, he must also remain motionless a lot. But where was Mondi?

He's probably gone hunting, Andi realized. He knew well what it was like to be a young dragon. It was pretty much like being a teenage boy, only on a larger and more bloodthirsty scale. The ancient dragon watched them with interest as they approached, Andi and Fjuri now flanking Wissagleb as an army of nearly a hundred aptrgangr strode in a rough formation behind them. "Ehrgeizig, my old friend!" Wissagleb called as they approached. "It saddens me to see you looking so much the worse for wear!" The tattered old dragon snorted in amusement.

"I might say the same about you, old friend. It has been long indeed since last we met. And if you are changed, yet I am glad to see you once again."

Then, to the astonishment of Andi and Fjuri, the old *drache* lowered his head and the creaking undead priest stepped forward and hugged his snout. After which he stepped back and began pacing back toward the center of the plaza, waving his troops to a halt. "Stand back," he said, "I don't know how big I'm going to be." With that he cried "Weit-Stos-Zet-Blik!" and stood naked. Another dragon spell, another instant, and an enormous undead dragon stood before them.

His long neck snaking around to examine his body and wings, Wissagleb looked up and remarked, "Bigger than I expected. I guess the growth equation works even when you're undead. How odd. And I'm not in all *that* much worse shape than you are, Ehrgeizig!" Indeed, when the undead priest's armor had vanished they had seen that, though thin and desiccated, his body was not particularly moth-eaten. And as a dragon, he was thin and mummified-looking but largely intact – whereas his old friend had weathered millennia of damage from wind, weather, and miscellaneous small attacks.

Dragon Wissagleb launched himself into the air and circled the plaza for a full minute, swooping up and looping around in a way that reminded Andi of the first time he'd taken flight. Flying was *fun*! Finally he fluttered back down to earth and approached Ehrgeizig in human form once again, belongings restored. "Ah, that was wonderful!" he declared. Then more quietly, he added "Shall I fix that for you, old friend?"

"Fix… ?" the ancient dragon got out, before the sablium-clad aptrgangr laid hands on him. As Andi and Fjuri watched in wondering delight, Ehrgeizig began to glow as if lit by an inner light. The tatters in his wings healed, missing scales grew back, and his color changed from dull gray to a glossy, almost silvery hue. There was a new sparkle in his eyes as he roared, "I am young again!"

With that Ehrgeizig, bigger still than Wissagleb in his dragon form, took to the sky and went through a series of loops and rolls before darting off down the mountainside like an enormous arrow. They all watched him go, then Andi asked the dragon priest "That wasn't just an ordinary healing spell, was it?"

Puffed up a bit at the reaction to his efforts, Wissagleb said "Oh, no. My mask is what makes it possible, of course, but that's a spell of my own devising I call 'Renew.' It only works on the living, of course."

"Only on living dragons? Or does it work on people, too?" Ideas were already forming in Andi's head, though he hadn't thought out all the implications.

"Yes," Wissagleb explained – always delighted to have an eager audience. "It can rejuvenate humans as well, or any living creature that has been harmed by injury or age. I performed it on some of my fellow dragon priests prior to their initiation into the top rank, so that their aging might be stopped or slowed at a point when they were younger, less ravaged by time. Toward the end we were elevating almost anyone, hoping that the enhanced powers they received would help us turn the tide. We were too late, of course."

The vibrant Ehrgeizig soon returned, blood on his mouth and an enormous dead bear clutched in his talons. "What have you *done* to me, Wissagleb?" he roared as if objecting to being restored to his youthful vigor. "I am absolutely *ravenous*!" He set to work on the bear and had soon reduced it to a few scraps of bloody fur. "By Aderos! I haven't felt like this since around the time Tarragin first disappeared!"

"This is great, Ehrgeizig," Andi said. "But please don't eat any people or their cattle, huh?" The young-seeming old drache cast a red eye on him.

"I will attempt to restrain myself," he said reluctantly. "Actually, I was thinking of a little dragon jerky. Like our friend Meiskomtot, perhaps?"

"Excellent idea!" the youth responded. "Say, where's my brother?"

"Oh," Ehrgeizig said, "I beg your pardon. I was rather distracted by the arrival of my old friend, not to mention the return of my youth. Your brother was Called by your mother last night, or so he informed me before he flew off and vanished. I think it possible she might have tried Calling you as well, but you won't have heard it as a human of course. Some family emergency, perhaps?"

Uh oh, Andi thought. He and Fjuri had been on this quest for a few days now, and who knew what was happening out there with Meiskomtot and his minions flying around? He'd just been supposed to talk with Ehrgeizig, but the opportunity to speak with someone who actually *knew* about Meiskomtot had been too good to pass up.

"We need to get back home," he said urgently. "Uh, Wissagleb? Do you want to bring your 'troops' back to Waterdon? That's where we've been mobilizing our team of people who are trying to bring Meiskomtot down."

"You have a magic map, I assume?" the undead priest said, once again revealing the insightfulness of his mind.

"Yes," Andi replied. "It's how we got here, since neither my brother or I are big enough dragons to carry my friend."

"A rather large young man, yes. Well, the maps' power to bring along companions is really only limited by your strength of mind – though inborn magical ability helps. Are you very good at magic?"

"Um, pretty good at battle magic," Andi admitted. "And I thought I was good at healing magic, until I saw *you* do it. But my magical energy level is pretty high, anyhow. I've been doing magic since I was five."

"Remarkable!" Wissagleb exclaimed. "That certainly ought to be enough to do it. Should we arrive in daylight, though, we may provoke some unfavorable reactions. Is there somewhere my people can get under cover in a hurry?"

Andi pictured the basement at Drakespring House in his mind. Beyond the subterranean workings for the bathing pool, and the bedrooms that had been built for him and Riki, the entire northern half of the basement was one big room except for the cold room where they stored root veggies and hung meats. The aptrgangr were standing tightly packed, and it appeared that the entire group could fit handily in that space as long as they stayed upright.

"Can they remain standing?" Andi asked.

"Certainly," Wissagleb replied. "The magic that animates them can hold them in any position with little additional expenditure of energy. And they will remain as I command them to, until I give a different command."

"All right then," Andi said. "Gather around, folks, and let's be off. What about you, Ehrgeizig? We're going to my home east of Waterdon, between the city walls and the road, if you need to find us."

"I think I will go flying," he replied. "I have your name and that of your brother, so I should be able to Call one or the other of you to report should I find your undead dragons. I feel as if I could rip them to shreds right now. You who have never been old cannot imagine what a feeling it is to be suddenly young again! Until later…" with that, Ehrgeizig took to the air. Moments later, concentrating harder than he ever had in his life, Andi embraced everyone standing in the plaza with his mind and wished them all to Drakespring Farm.

Chapter 30: Sendoff

Bernadette and Thongeld shimmered into existence on the road to the south of Creekside Farm. Or what once had been, and would be again, Creekside Farm. They were driving an enormous wagon, behind which another was in tow, pulled by a pair of oxen. Each wagon was stacked high with lumber, foodstuffs, animal fodder, and other items needed for the rebuilding of all that the undead dragons had destroyed.

Though what Meiskomtot had done was none of her responsibility, Bernadette had more than enough money to pay for the rebuilding – and being able to do so helped her to drive off the wrenching grief and guilt (that she had hardly known the son who had died, had scarcely shared her life with him at all) that threatened to overwhelm her and leave her unable to do what she must.

No doubt undead dragons are attacking someplace else in Iscandia now, and did already twice while we were gone, she thought morosely. But the catastrophe of their first attempt at stopping the attacks had pointed up how flawed her scheme had been. Unless the force that spotted Meiskomtot at his murderous business was strong enough to stop him by themselves, there was no point in the alert system. The dragons could be Called and appear within minutes, but she, Erik, and Andrion – likely the most effective warriors they had available – would be hours in getting there by map. Too late to do any good, and meanwhile putting the watchers at risk.

She and Thongeld had put up in a couple of rooms at the Dancing Rabbit overnight while their order of goods was being assembled, But she still felt exhausted by the two long fast-traveling trips in as many days. Or perhaps it was more an emotional exhaustion. Gotteluub was dead, her plan to track down the undead dragons and stop them was a failure, and she had no idea what to try next. Meanwhile, homes were being destroyed and people killed.

Erik and Andrion had kept busy while she was gone. While Andrion's superb magical abilities were of less use in this situation, he was able to call demons from the planes of the Netherworld to provide extra strength for a short time where heavy loads needed to be moved. And he had kept in shape. For a man of fifty, he still had immense strength. Not as much as Erik, though. Years of work at the forge as well as many other activities around the farm had kept him as agile and muscular as ever. Even Wissliiben had his uses, able to grasp ropes and lift away fallen beams or quickly start fires. He also hunted for himself and the humans, bringing in game to supplement the food in the root cellar.

So when Thongeld returned to the homeplace where he'd been born, he found all of the destroyed buildings razed to the foundations, space around them cleared. What wood and other materials that were salvageable had been neatly stacked, while timbers too shattered for further use had been converted to a good supply of firewood for cooking.

A deep pit had been dug some 20 paces from the road in which to inter Gotteluub, and a wooden platform built on which the body rested in state. Andrion had been using frost spells to preserve the body, necessary as it was now the middle of summer. When he and Erik saw Bernadette arrive, their eyes widened at the sight of the wagons. That was a *lot* of stuff to haul, but it would be needed. Over the generations of Thongeld's family the farm had expanded to three residences and half a dozen outbuildings.

But what claimed their attention more than the wagons was the sight of Berni, and the emotions that were playing over her face as she sagged on the driver's seat of the lead cart and whipped the oxen forward. They rushed over, setting aside what they'd been doing, and helped her down off the seat before smothering her in a group hug.

After taking a nap atop a bedroll and having a meal, Bernadette was feeling better. She had to be strong, no matter how discouraged she was feeling. And experience had shown her that often when things look the darkest, a solution to your problems was just around the corner. After all, wasn't she The Fireblood, the woman who had saved Terris from extinction and been rewarded with luck and love manifold? Right.

While Bernadette slept the men had unloaded the wagons, and were already building a pen in which to house the oxen. As she washed her food down with a sip of water, she rose to her feet and called her husbands and son to her. "I think it's time to bring everyone together, while there's still plenty of daylight," she told them. "Wissliiben, will you help me with the Calling?"

They Called alternately, Shouting the names of each of the children of Schunmurte and Sneyagflug. Only eighteen of them now, but Guldekiind made it nineteen again. He did not respond, however, and Bernadette sighed. He was going to be more crushed than any of her other human children to learn of the loss of his brother, having spent far more time with him. He'd seen more of his dragon siblings, and for longer periods of time, than she had herself in the years while they were growing up. The Call would only reach him if he were in dragon form, and likely he had remained human on that trip to find Ehrgeizig. *What I need is a Call Human dragon spell,* she thought with a trace of lightness.

Bernadette had feared that she would be breaking the sad tidings to all of them except Purpurflug and Schickemaad; but as it turned out Purpurflug had been spreading the news. She had Called one of her siblings from each of the groups, telling them of the death of Gotteluub and asking them to pass it on. One and all now knew that their brother had fallen, and had been awaiting her Call.

Purpurflug had not reached Mondi though, and when he came to his mother's Call he was devastated at the news. One other (not counting Andi, who Mondi reported was down at the bottom of an ancient Norse ruin seeking the counsel of an undead dragon priest) had not yet heard. He had been recovering from his injuries when they left, but he was in the fullness of his strength when he came to Bernadette's Call.

Sneyagflug was surprised to find himself north of Westmarch, flying toward a fleabite settlement in the middle of the countryside with young dragons in the air as thick as gnats. What was this? The magic of the Calling dragon spell only told you who was calling and opened a pathway for you to go to them, if you chose. It didn't tell you what their situation was, or what they wanted.

His sharp dragon sight went first to Schunmurte, standing there beside the road in her human form as Bernadette. He'd learned to call her that over the years, at least when she was human. Though forever in his heart she would be his Schunmurte, the first person he had ever loved. Now he had nineteen other people he loved, and he was rather fond of her fireblood son Guldekiind as well. He had become civilized.

Then he saw what she was standing beside, and the reason for the gathering of dragons became clear. His heart sank, turning cold as ice, even as his mind blazed with hot anger. Meiskomtot! You will pay for this! Sneyagflug came down in the middle of the road, where there was room for his bulk. Bernadette turned to him, her eyes swimming with tears. While she had loved her dragon children organically, the inescapable love of a mother for the children she has borne, their father had nurtured them – spent all of his time with them, known them as she had not. How much more wrenching must be his grief?

"Schunmurte!" he choked. "Gotteluub?"

"I am so sorry, Sneyagflug," she said tremulously. She'd been fliply and affectionately calling him "Red" for years, but the gravity of the situation had made her more formal. "If I hadn't sent them out looking for that monster, this never would have happened," she went on. He bent his head toward her. Nuzzling her would have knocked her over, but he breathed softly on her like a caress.

"It's not your fault, dear," he told her. He'd never abandoned the human terms of endearment he'd begun using after they had mated and begun their family.

Her sense of guilt threatened to engulf her, but Bernadette turned it aside. Regret might haunt her for the rest of her days, but now was not the time to be swept under by the first setback. Her son was dead; but he might just as easily have died in infancy, like the majority of dragonlings did in ancient times with only their mothers to protect and feed them. That the brood she and Sneyagflug had brought forth had all lived to independence, and had survived nearly to their eleventh birthdays, was something of a miracle.

Pulling herself together, Bernadette said "We're here to send Gotteluub off, and put him into the ground," she said shortly. "I'll go change." For this ritual, the mother of dragons must be a dragon herself. Andrion and Erik provided her with a privacy screen, as she stripped and quickly transformed. Now Schunmurte, Sneyagflug, and their eighteen remaining children circled above the bier as Andrion, Erik, Thongeld, and three other members of his family gripped its handles and carried it to the grave.

They lowered Gotteluub by ropes down into the deep hole. Dragons are not as massive as they seem, else flight would be impossible; and though the young dragon had been as long as three men laid end to end, they were able to lift him. The humans on the ground said their own words over the corpse in Common, asking the gods to look kindly on this young person and take him into their hearts – as above the dragons circled, each in turn calling out a benediction in the dragon tongue.

Schickemaad had recovered from her ordeal, and was the first to speak. "Goodbye, my brother. You were ever a true companion, and you had a technique for hunting bears that was better than any I have ever seen."

Another spoke, gliding above the open grave as he shared his remembrance of Gotteluub: "Goodbye, my brother. When first we learned to fly it was you who discovered how to pluck salmon from the river below Og Vulanz."

And so it went. After each of Gotteluub's brothers and sisters had contributed a memory and said their farewells, their mother spoke. This was easier, somehow, in dragon form. Had she been human saying goodbye to one of her human children, she would have been too devastated to speak. "Goodbye, my son," she said. Her dragon voice was an octave below her human one, but still mellow. "I wish that I had spent more time with you, that I had known you as these others did. But, Gods Praise (the meaning of Gotteluub in dragon tongue), know that I loved you. And I will always love you."

The humans below were not following the dragons' speech. Erik and Andrion had picked up a few words of the dragon tongue over the years, but they were not fluent. Yet when Bernadette spoke they could tell from the way her voice resonated that she was in a lot of emotional pain. There was nothing they could do but send her silent thoughts of love and support.

Sneyagflug, the father who had worked so hard to bring about these young dragons' birth and raised them single-handed through the first few years of their lives, was the last to speak. Like Bernadette he was filled with roiling emotions, and while he was deeply sad at the loss of his son the feeling that was seizing the upper hand now was anger. Deep, blinding anger that he struggled to contain.

He had gone up against Meiskomtot once, and he knew that he was not a match for the dragon priest alone. That undead monster had all the advantages of being a dragon along with all the advantages of being a human mage – and being undead gave him advantages, as well. Had he but known that Meiskomtot was eager to have Sneyagflug's corpse in the best possible condition, he might have been less reluctant to engage him again.

Schunmurte and her children backed off and hovered in the air as Sneyagflug, far larger than any of them, flew in tight circles above the grave. "Goodbye, my son," he said. "You and your siblings have been my path to love and joy, and the pride of my life. From your clumsiest attempts at flight to your first solo kill, I have watched you all with delight. The kindness you showed to these humans has helped to forge a bond between our species that will last for generations. Your life will always be remembered with honor."

Even his children, who had known Sneyagflug closely throughout their lives, were stunned at this touching speech from their father. He could be a bit extreme at times, and had never expressed his feelings for them so frankly. Then he finished his elegy with, "And I will not rest until that undead monster who put you in this grave has been utterly destroyed!" With that, he flew straight up, his powerful wings beating furiously until he was nothing but a red dot in the afternoon sky. Then he set off in an easterly direction, flying fast.

The dragons remaining all touched down and stood around the grave as the humans began shoveling dirt over the corpse of Gotteluub. When the grave had been filled, Thongeld and his people began laying stone over the top of it. "We'll erect a plinth here, saying what happened," he promised Bernadette. She had returned to human form and put on her clothing once again.

"Thank you," she said in a subdued tone. The ceremony had been cathartic, but she was feeling tired again and was anxious to go home. She spoke up, so that all of her remaining children could hear her. "We're all going back by map to Waterdon," she said. "Does anyone want to come with us?" The area couldn't really support more than three or four dragons, even these relatively small ones, for long.

"I want to come, Mama," Mondi said.

"I'll come too," Purpurflug put in. "That's where Wissliiben and I have been hunting lately. I think we should all go back to the hunting grounds we were in before, except maybe Schickhimseel and Tapferverd, since they were all the way down in Remus. We'll keep an eye out, but if anybody sees any undead dragons we'll fly to a safe distance before Calling."

"I'll come back with you, Purpe," Wissliiben said. He'd enjoyed his time in Remus with Schickhimseel and Tapferverd, and he hoped that the Bendari family was surviving all right in their absence. But he also liked his sister Purpurflug for her sharp mind and no-nonsense attitude – and he wanted to stay close to the action.

"All right," Bernadette said, feeling more in control of her emotions than she had since she and Thongeld had arrived here this morning, "Mondi, Purpurflug, and Wissliiben with me. The rest of you, go find someplace where you can eat. Approach people with caution – I'm still not sure some lunatic won't decide you guys are the same as Meiskomtot and his minions. And if you see anything we need to know about, get to a safe place before you Call one of the dragons who are near home base. I'll Call you if there are any developments. All right?"

"Got it, Mama!" came the chorus, and in twos and threes the fifteen young dragons who would not be going with them to Waterdon dispersed and flew off. Bernadette turned to Thongeld, who was lingering nearby. If he lived to be a hundred, he thought, he would never forget this time. What stories they would have to tell their great-grandchildren! "I hope that you will have enough materials to rebuild, Thongeld." She slipped him a pouch of gold. "Just in case," she said with a wink. He recoiled.

"No, Fireblood, I can't take anything more. We're already deeply in your debt. It's not as if those undead dragons had anything to do with *you*."

Seeing that she'd pushed it too far, and wanting to leave this sturdy farmer (a man who truly lived the life she and her family only dabbled at, so close to the city and with nearly infinite cash resources at their disposal should their cattle die or their crops fail) his pride, she withdrew the purse. "I wish you well, then," she said with a smile. Then, stepping a few paces away and with her three dragon children and her two husbands gathered close, she transported them all home.

Chapter 31: Revelations

It had been fairly late in the afternoon when Bernadette had touched Drakespring Farm on the map, and dawn was just breaking as they arrived – seemingly a few seconds later. Bernadette felt bone-weary, nearly as tired as she'd been after her round-trip to the Eparchy last year – where she'd learned for sure that Andi, Fjuri, and Meri had gone off the reservation. It was more than physical tiredness, she knew. She was emotionally drained, and at this moment she didn't have a clue as to what their next move was going to be.

The young dragons were ravenous. "We're going to go hunting," Mondi informed her as soon as they had arrived. "I'll be back later, though. I want to stay close to home as much as I can until things settle down." His mother smiled weakly at him and waved goodbye as he and his sister and brother took to the air and flew off toward the rising sun.

Erik and Andrion were tired as well. They were no longer young men, despite their fit condition, and they had been working at hard physical labor the past couple of days. Though young Gotteluub's death had not been as devastating for them as it was for their wife and her dragon children, it had still filled them with sorrow. As they walked slowly and stiffly up the walk, Erik suggested "Hot bath, then bed?" Bernadette turned and gazed up at him with that look of deep love that had nearly knocked him off his feet when he first saw it some eighteen years previously.

They went quietly into the house and sat soaking away their aches and sorrows in the blissfully hot water of the house's bathing pool. Then, wrapped in towels, they went across the hall to the master bedroom and fell into bed. A few hours later Bernadette awoke feeling considerably rejuvenated. The bath and nap (perhaps four hours) had worked wonders for her outlook and she now realized she was starving.

When sleeping with both her husbands she habitually slept between them, though this frequently created a problem in the morning – since she almost always woke first. Erik was usually alert not long after being awakened, but Andrion had always had trouble achieving consciousness with anything like speed. So she always tried to crawl out of bed past *him* – and usually failed to do so without waking him.

Screw it, she thought. We're completely out of synch with local time and we all ought to be up and moving. Recovered from her despondency and indecision of the day before, Bernadette was ready to tackle her problems head on – just as soon as she'd eaten breakfast. Andrion woke only briefly as she slipped past him and threw on some clothing, but Erik began stirring and was already out of bed as she gave him a quick kiss and hug and headed out the bedroom door, down the hall toward the kitchen.

Bernadette was surprised to see Riki in the kitchen, in the midst of cooking breakfast. "Mom!" she cried, not having realized that her parents had come home during the night. "You're back!"

"Please tell me the cows have already been milked," Bernadette said, before stepping forward to embrace her daughter.

"Oh, hours ago," Riki assured her –hugging her back. She was so glad to see her. With Mom and Erik and Andrion here, everything would be all right! She hoped…

Bernadette grabbed a fresh bread roll from a plate and took a big bite off the end. "My stomach thinks my throat has been cut!" she exclaimed, then took a closer look. It appeared that Riki was preparing breakfast for more than herself, but less than herself plus Meri and Sigi. "Are Meri and Sigi all right?" she asked between bites. Erik came in at that point and snagged another bread roll. Riki hugged him, then began digging in the cold chest for more food. It appeared she was going to have to revise her cooking plans.

"They're fine. Meri's up at the Steadfasts' on an extended sleepover with Edla," Riki explained, hands flying as she dug more food out and arrayed it on the counter. "Fjuri was here with Andi, but he went home right away so his folks wouldn't worry about him. I fed Sigi a couple of hours ago, after I finished with the milking. He took care of the chickens, and now he's down at the Maiden with Joqui." She began breaking eggs into a bowl. "I assume Papa Andrion is here, too?" Riki asked.

"Well, you know him…" Bernadette replied. He might often not be up and moving until the rest of the household had finished eating. He was almost as bad as a teenager in that respect, though he certainly had redeeming qualities. Riki decided against adding another two eggs.

"When Andi and Fjuri came back late yesterday," she went on, "they brought some… people with them. But I don't need to feed *them…*"

Bernadette grabbed an apple from a bowl on the table, and ate four bites of it before she spoke again. "Did Andi have a lot to report?" she asked casually. Riki poured the bowl of beaten, seasoned eggs into the buttered frypan and began stirring it with a steel spatula, sprinkling in some shredded cheese and keeping a close eye on the pan lest the mixture stick and burn.

"He and Fjuri and Mondi found Ehrgeizig all right at Todenstor," she said distractedly.

"Yes, Mondi mentioned that," her mother replied. "He said Andi and Fjuri went down into that fortress on the opposite side of Todenstor from where Andrion, Erik and I went to find Tarragin's portal into Asengard. Looking for some undead dragon priest who'd been a friend of Ehrgeizig during the Uprising."

"That's right," Riki said, as she pulled the pan off the fire and scraped its contents out onto a platter. "Andi ought to be here any second now – I checked to make sure he was up before I started cooking. You should let *him* tell it." Riki put the platter of fluffy eggs on the table along with plates, cutlery, and the platter with the remaining bread rolls. Not exactly a feast, but she hoped it would do.

As if he'd been waiting for food to hit the table, Andi suddenly appeared through the front door. He looked as if he'd dressed hastily in whatever clothes he could find that smelled clean, and was still rubbing his eyes as he came in. "Mom! Erik!" he exclaimed. Then to his sister, "Thank you Riki, I love you!" She gave him a patient smile.

Andi seated himself at the table and began scooping quantities of eggs onto his plate as Riki joined them. She had had a bit to eat when she'd first gotten up hours ago, but after all she'd done she was ready for a snack. Bernadette eyed her son. She supposed that for a teenage boy, food on the table took precedence over a hug for Mom. But he seemed awfully cheerful.

"Riki," she said quietly, "you didn't tell him…?" Riki's eyes went wide and her face took on a guilty look.

She was sitting beside her mother, and said even more quietly, "About Gotteluub? I didn't mention it. I thought maybe you ought to…" She trailed off. She was only fourteen, Bernadette realized. She couldn't be expected to take the burdens of the world on her shoulders, or make the kind of hard decisions that seemed to be falling on them like raindrops lately.

"We'll discuss it after eating," she said, and tucked back into her plate of eggs.

Andi, so wrapped up in his hunger and the food, had completely missed their exchange. After they had all eaten, he came around the table and Bernadette stood for a hug. Then Erik engulfed his son, still smaller than him if not by a hell of a lot, in a bear hug that would have crushed a smaller man. He knew what was coming, and his love and sympathy flowed out as he embraced the young man who, if not technically related to him, had been his son since birth.

"So, why did you call Mondi away?" Andi asked. He'd been bursting with eagerness to give his brother the potion and the dragon spells, and see him as a human being. Not that he didn't have a thousand other things to do, of course… "Did they find those undead dragons?" Then he looked closely at his mother's face, at the look of sorrow in her blue-gray eyes, and he knew he wasn't going to like the answer.

"What happened?" he demanded. Though logistics had made it impossible for him to know any sooner, he still felt resentful that something momentous had happened and he had not been informed.

"Your brother Gotteluub is dead," Bernadette stated simply. "Meiskomtot killed him while he and Wissliiben and Schickemaad were trying to defend a farm settlement, and yesterday we held his funeral." Her lip quivered, even as she watched her son's face go white with shock. "I'm sorry!" she wailed, then took him in her arms.

His brother, dead! Andi could hardly believe it. His dragon siblings were only eleven, and they were supposed to live forever! He hadn't known Gotteluub as well as some of the others, as they were constantly moving around and forming new groups. But he loved all of them, so much like him yet so different. They had been supposed to take care, not to attack Meiskomtot but only to call for help. How could this have happened?

As his mother held him and he held her, Andi realized that she was sobbing into his chest. It shook him out of his childlike need for comfort in the face of tragedy, as he realized Gotteluub's death had hit her just as hard. He somehow intuited the guilt she had always felt, forsaking her many dragon children in order to cling to the human ones. Tears welling unheeded from his eyes he squeezed her tight, murmuring "there, there" even as Erik embraced them both from one side and Riki from the other.

Some time and some cups of hot tea later, they had all recovered enough to begin talking about the news that Andi had brought from his expedition to consult with Ehrgeizig. Though a deep sadness still lingered around his heart, Andi's youthful resilience had reasserted itself. That Gotteluub had died was a tragedy, but there was nothing to be done about it. On the other hand, he was fairly bursting to tell his family of all that had happened, all he'd learned.

Luckily Andrion made an appearance at about this juncture, rubbing sleep from his eyes and looking around for breakfast. He'd long become used to the idea that if he stayed in bed as long as he liked everyone else would have eaten – so he was content with a couple of bread rolls and an apple. He squeezed in between Bernadette and Erik, facing Andi and Riki across the table. She'd already dealt with the breakfast dishes.

"So when Mondi and I got to Todenstor we found Ehrgeizig right away," Andi began his tale. Andi was not a bad storyteller, and they all settled in to listen. "He was pretty friendly, and surprised to learn that Mom had found out how to turn into a dragon. Apparently the potion and dragon spells that Sneyagflug led us to were only part of a set of spells that the dragon priests called the 'Reward.'"

He couldn't resist standing up and demonstrating the other two dragon spells that comprised the full set. It wasn't as if they hadn't all seen him naked before. The family had been bathing together since the kids were old enough to be trusted without a diaper. There were gasps of amazement from Riki, Andrion, and Erik – and a crow of elation from Mom.

Her sorrow seemed to have evaporated in the sun-rays of delight at this discovery. "Bless you, Andi!" she exclaimed. "That alone was worth the trip, even if we don't manage to scotch Meiskomtot with what you've learned! I'll need to go dragon to make the stones, though, I guess."

Andi nodded. "I found out that if you go to a Spell Wall in dragon form you can get everything on the wall in one go, though it takes a little while for the stones to form," he explained. "It's quite a rush."

Bernadette sat back down, now leaning over the table with eagerness. Andi was grinning, his sorrow driven out by the wonders he'd found as hers had been. He'd brought his pack upstairs with him. "Is Mondi here?" he asked hopefully. He hadn't seen his dragon brother when he came up the stairs and then in through the front door.

"He went hunting with Purpurflug and Wissliiben right after we got back around sunup," his mother told him. "He ought to be back by now."

Andi got back on his feet, and the entire family stood and followed him out the door as he went looking for his dragon brother. He found him curled in a ball not far from the western side of the house, probably trying to shelter from the sun while he napped. "Mondi!" he cried, and the young dragon awoke and sat up immediately.

"So you finally made it home, brother! I suppose you've now heard the sad news?"

Andi nodded soberly, though his anticipation of what he was about to reveal was bubbling up within him and he could hardly contain himself. "Our brother will be sorely missed, but revenge will be ours," he promised.

Never one to linger in sadness if there was joy or hope to be found, Mondi shrugged off his grief and asked, "What great things did you find inside the tomb, then? Did you meet Ehrgeizig's dragon priest?"

"Him, and more," Andi admitted, the smile growing ever broader on his face. "Mondi," he said then, growing more serious. He did not intend to spring this on his brother as Mondi's father had

187

done on the mother they shared. "I have long wished that you could take human form as I can become dragon. Have you wished the same?"

Bernadette, Erik, Riki, and Andrion were staring rapt, wondering what Andi was getting at. It had been a dearly-held fantasy of all of them that the dragon child who had stolen their hearts some eleven years ago could stay with them always. Mondi flushed a deeper red, a sign of emotion. Dragons could not widen their eyes, or smile, but their feelings – and the state of their health – were often reflected in the color of their scales.

Haltingly, he said "I have wished it since the first time that I came here and met my human family. I love being a dragon, but I don't think I will ever be complete unless I can also be human." All of his carefully planned showmanship left Andi, as he blurted out with glee, "Mondi, I found it! A potion and two dragon spells, and you can change back and forth just like I can!"

He rummaged in his pack and produced one of the jugs of potion Wissagleb had provided. That the undead priest might deviously seek to provide him with poison, never crossed Andi's mind. What earthly reason could he have for such an act of treachery? Mondi, trusting his beloved big brother, eagerly lapped up the potion as Andi slowly poured it into his mouth.

After the first swallow Mondi remarked, "It tastes cool! Not like a mountain stream or anything but as if it would be cool even if you boiled it."

"Other than that, how's the flavor?" Andi asked, as he tipped the container for another swig.

"Hardly tastes like anything, really," his brother replied. Within a minute he had downed the entire jug of potion.

"How do you feel?" Andi asked anxiously. He was suddenly having second thoughts. Mondi seemed transfixed, deep in introspection.

"Cool," he replied after a moment. "Calm, clear, strong… all right."

Andi smiled. "Here they are, then. The Go Human spell is Drache-Mon-Zur-Einz, and the Return to Dragon spell is Mon-Yetz-Drache-Ruch. There are also a couple of dragon spells that let you manage clothing and weapons, which you'll only need if the other two work. Are you ready to try it?"

"Wait a second…" Mondi said, feeling the stones forming within him. Then he nodded.

All five humans seemed to be holding their breaths, spellbound, as Mondi drew air into his lungs and cried "Drache-Mon-Zur-Einz!" As those who loved him watched avidly, he shrank before their eyes. Where the twenty-two-foot red dragon had rested, a skinny preadolescent boy now stood. He was tall for eleven, but lean and wiry. He had flaming red hair that stood up all over his head in two-inch spikes, and he looked a bit like Bernadette around the eyes and cheekbones.

But where she had the typical redhead's pale, freckled complexion, Mondi-as-human's skin was a medium reddish tan. And instead of blue-gray, his eyes were a reddish brown. Those eyes were as wide as saucers, and his hands with their long, graceful fingers were roaming over his body in disbelief. "By the gods!" he squeaked, his newly-formed human larynx in the midst of the adolescent change even if dragons never went through such a stage.

Mondi lunged forward and threw his arms around his big brother. They'd been aligned with each other mentally since Mama had first brought Mondi home, but the five-year-difference in their ages made a huge difference in their heights at this stage of their lives. "Thank you, brother! I can scarcely believe it!" Andi hugged him back, hard.

Next the boy stepped hurriedly to enfold his mother in a firm embrace. He was nearly her height, and she was rocked by the power in his thin-looking arms. "Mama, I've wanted to do this all my life," he said softly. As they stood there hugging one another, Mondi said "My eyes! What's wrong with my eyes?" Bernadette released him to look into his face with concern. Then she smiled.

"The same thing that's wrong with mine," she told him wonderingly. Tears of joy blurred her vision.

Chapter 32: Reinforcements

Mondi wanted to do everything he had never been able to do before, and he wanted to do it all at once. They found a set of Sigi's clothing that would fit him, nearly – Sigi, too, was tall for his age. That, Mondi found, he did not like as much as being naked. But he could see the reasons for it, especially in other seasons. Humans had neither the internal fires nor the mass-to-surface-area ratio of a dragon to keep them warm.

He had to sit at the table and eat with a knife and fork, which he managed not badly considering it was his first time. And he used their flush toilet for the first time ever, finding the process of urination and that little tube through which he did so both fascinating. Andi, Andrion, and Erik were all proud of him, while Riki and Bernadette rolled their eyes.

When all the excitement had died down Andi realized that his most important piece of news was still to come. By now it was around noon; but since most of them had eaten only a couple of hours before, lunch could wait. "Why don't you all sit on the veranda," Andi suggested. "There's someone I want you to meet." Riki knew what was going on, but the rest of them were mystified. Bernadette recalled she had mentioned something about "not having to feed them" while she was getting breakfast ready.

The five of them snuggled up together on the settee, Riki between her two papas and Bernadette beside Erik, with Mondi on the far end. They watched as Andi trotted down the stairs to the basement. He returned a couple of minutes later, accompanied by a figure armored in sablium. Its limbs were stick-like, and it moved stiffly. Gods preserve us, it was an aptrgangr!

Andi led the undead dragon priest up the steps to stand before his siblings and parents. Andi, Fjuri, Riki, and Wissagleb as well had all thought it a good idea for the undead army and its commander to get down into the basement and out of sight as soon as they'd arrived yesterday evening. It wasn't as if they needed to eat, drink, or sleep.

"This is my mother Bernadette Drakespring, The Fireblood," Andi said, making formal introductions. "My papa Erik Drakespring, my sister Erika Drakespring, my other papa Andrion Drakespring, and my brother Drachmondien Drakespring. Mondi is usually a dragon, but he's just become human thanks to your help." By Aderos, the undead priest thought, he wasn't kidding about having three parents either. "Everyone," Andi went on, "this is Wissagleb, a top-level priest of the dragon church. He has heard about his former colleague Meiskomtot, and has volunteered to help us stop him."

"I am pleased to meet you all, though of course I met Erika last night," Wissagleb said politely. There were a couple of beats of stunned silence, then Bernadette responded. More than most in Iscandia, she had always been willing to take people at face value. Despite having killed dozens of bandits, renegade mages, aptrgangr, leukalfar, and attacking dragons, her motto was usually "can't we all just get along?"

She rose to her feet and extended a hand, which surprised Wissagleb. "I am so very glad to meet you, and delighted to welcome you to our home! Is there anything I can get you?" Wissagleb thought about it, and asked "Might I trouble you for a chair? It feels awkward to be standing." Bernadette ducked back inside through the master bedroom's veranda door and shortly returned with a couple of the chairs that usually sat at a small table on the eastern side of the room.

The undead priest seated himself with a creak. He had his mask hung on his belt, so that they could see his face. It was thin, mummified, but not horribly deteriorated and as they spoke with him they soon learned to see past his appearance. He was cheerful, courtly, and quite knowledgeable. Andrion soon recognized a kindred spirit. Had he been born with the dragon blood in that long-ago age, he supposed, he too might have joined the dragon church.

They sat on the veranda talking for hours, as the sun moved further to the west. Riki returned to the kitchen and brought a platter of sandwiches and some potato chips and ale, with milk for herself and Mondi, and they continued the discussion as the living members of the group ate their late lunch. Sigi came back from his visit with Joqui at the Maiden, and stunned his entire family by walking up and saying "Mondi! You turned human!" How had he recognized him, knowing no more about the Reciprocation than any of them had before Andi's trip to Todenstor?

He joined them as the discussions went on, Wissagleb imparting all he knew about Meiskomtot and his powers to a new audience. "We don't know how many dead dragons he has reanimated," Andrion said. "If we succeed in killing him, will that break the spell?" If you killed a conjurer, any daimon he or she had called forth from the planes of the Netherworld would vanish on the spot.

"I'm afraid not," Wissagleb replied. "I fear Meiskomtot may have been the most powerful necromancer of our times, but though I never practiced it as he did I do know that with the spells he would have used, his death would only break his mastery. Until you could break the connection with the animating magic, as with a death-blow, the undead dragon would be operating entirely under its own volition. I doubt if any of them would have a benign attitude toward mankind."

"Oh!" Andi spoke up. There had been so much information to absorb, it had been driven out of his head. "Papa Andrion, Zira taught me the magic-block spell her mom used on us when we were delaying them in front of the portal last year. I used it broad-band on a trio of aptrgangr, and they all just fell over. It severs their connection with the magic that animates them, but when the spell wears off it seems to reconnect on its own. If there's not too many of them, it gives you a few minutes to make it so they can't rise again"

Andrion was electrified. "Andi, that's great news! You'll have to teach me that spell. The one I know only blocks your opponent for less than a minute. But with this, especially if two of us can cast it at the same time, we can knock the undead dragons out of the sky and then hack them up with edged weapons."

"What is this 'magic-block' spell?" Wissagleb asked. There'd been nothing like it when he was alive.

"It's a defense against magic users," Andi explained. "It severs their connection from magic for a period of time, and since the aptrgangr are animated by magic it temporarily renders them fully dead."

"It likely won't work on Meiskomtot, as he will surely be wearing his mask," the dragon priest pointed out. They'd already discussed the powers of their enemy's mask and staff, as well as his abilities in necromancy.

192

Andi had another thought. "Wissagleb was too modest to mention it," he told his gathered family members, "but he has the most amazing restoration spell I have ever seen. I'm hoping he can teach it to me and Mom." Bernadette sat up, looking interested.

"It's something I developed myself, and I never had it published in spellbooks," the undead priest said deprecatingly. "If you can learn by watching, I may be able to teach it."

"I promise, you will not recognize Ehrgeizig the next time you see him," Andi went on. "He and Wissagleb were friends back during the Uprising, when both of them were young. But Ehrgeizig has been alive and growing all this time while Wissagleb was sleeping in his tomb. Anyhow, he did that spell on him and it's like Ehrgeizig is a new dragon now! It completely changed his attitude, and he flew off looking to kick Meiskomtot's tail for him."

Wissagleb sat musing. "I hope that if those two should meet, that will be the outcome. But Meiskomtot has powerful magic at his disposal, and is immune to both battle spells and dragon spells directed at him. Ehrgeizig as he is now would be very tempting, I think. Should Meiskomtot manage to kill him without damaging the body too much, he could capture his soul in an essence vial and then transfer his own soul to Ehrgeizig's body."

"He can do that?" Andrion asked sharply, worried. He was imagining them thinking they confronted a friendly dragon, never guessing that it was the evil dragon priest in disguise.

"Yes, that is in his power. He would need to obtain some magical essence vials of the largest type in order to trap my old friend's soul without incorporating it into his own, however, and that might not be easy. I am guessing they are no more common in this age than they were in my own era?"

"I have a couple of empty ones in my collection," Bernadette admitted. "But I have never found an essence capture enchantment powerful enough to trap the soul of a dragon." After a moment's thought she added, "Of course, being fireblood, I haven't needed one. I will automatically capture the soul of any dragon who dies in my vicinity. Hum… if a shape-shifting dragon like you or me or my son here dies, does the soul get captured as if they were a regular dragon?"

"Your dragon blood has given you a soul that is a blend of human and dragon," Wissagleb explained. "And the potion that you took to enable the transformation made it more draconic than before. If you are killed in dragon form, your soul can be absorbed by any fireblood within range, destroying your flesh as it takes its leave of your body. If you are human, of course, your soul can as easily be taken if the essence capture spell is in effect and there is a sufficient magical essence vial within range."

Ugh, Bernadette did *not* like the idea of her soul, or that of any of her loved ones, being captured in a magical essence vial instead of being allowed to travel to Asengard. Or worse, going to feed the essence of a creature like Meiskomtot. "Remind me just not to get killed, then," she remarked facetiously.

"If you are not, you have long to live," the undead priest remarked. "Did your son tell you that the dragon transformation slows the aging process?"

Bernadette's face went white. She had thought, and several people had remarked, that she was wearing her age well. She looked closer to thirty than to forty. So that was it? She was going to stay thirty forever, or maybe for another few decades – while her children grew up and aged, her beloved Erik and Andrion became creaking old men and died? What might have seemed like a dream of heaven to some vain women sounded like a pronouncement of doom to her. But there didn't seem to be any point in discussing it further right now.

Getting back to an earlier subject, Bernadette asked Wissagleb, "What about this restoration spell? Can you demonstrate it?" The undead priest looked around, searching for a subject. Everyone here appeared to be in excellent health, and not particularly aged. He spotted the cattle in the pen, visible in the yard to the north. They stood companionably close, dozing as they chewed their cud. One was clearly nearing the end of her productive life as a milker.

"How about that old cow there?" he suggested, stepping down from the veranda and moving in his stiff gait toward the paddock.

"Freydis?" Bernadette asked. "She's nearly sixteen. We've been thinking about putting her out to pasture next year." She, Andi,

194

Andrion, and Mondi trailed Wissagleb across the yard, leaving only Erik, Riki, and Sigi left sitting on the veranda.

The undead priest removed his mask from the hanger on his belt and put it on his face. Then, seemingly at home around farm animals, he climbed the rail fence and went over to stand beside Freydis. She ignored him. He placed his bony hands on her flank, and that same glow arose – encompassing the old cow in an aura. She jerked her head up, startled as the sensations ran through her body, lowing and rolling her eyes. Yet she seemed rooted to the spot.

After only a little more than a minute Wissagleb stood back and admired his work. The somewhat moth-eaten hide was now glossy, firm muscles rippling beneath it. Freydis' liquid brown eyes were bright and clear, her joints no longer swollen and aching, her udder pink and smooth-looking. She swished her tail and veered away from the unfamiliar figure in her pen, and the undead priest hastily stepped back out of the way.

As he climbed back over the fence, he surveyed his audience. "Yes!" Bernadette said. "Amazing, but I don't know where I would get the magical energy required to perform the spell. That was like a torrent!"

"It's the mask," he admitted. "Without it I doubt I myself would have the ability to cast it for the length of time that's usually required. The larger or more injured or infirm the subject is, the greater the continual application of the spell is needed to effect complete renewal. But if, as your son says, you are a healer of some power, you should be able to do it long enough to restore small or slightly-injured creatures."

Bernadette looked around the yard and spotted some butterflies flitting around over the cabbage patch. Pretty, but most likely they were laying eggs from which voracious larvae would hatch. There were chemial poisons one could apply, but those would poison people as well as caterpillars – so they usually waited until the critters were big enough to see and then hand-plucked and squashed them.

Sure enough, when she looked close she spotted some telltale raddling of a cabbage leaf. On its underside, she found a fat green caterpillar a couple of inches in length. Inured to ickiness after years of farm life, she pinched its rear end with her fingers, and some green guts squirted out. Then, giving it everything she had, she hit the little creature with a blast of the Renew spell as she had learned it from watching Wissagleb cast it on their cow.

The spell kept operating until her magical energy was exhausted, then winked out. And the injured caterpillar in her hand very quickly regrew the damaged gut. But then something very unexpected happened: it began to shrink. As she and the others stared in fascination, the caterpillar grew steadily smaller until it was no thicker than a cloak pin, then seemed to fold in on itself. In another second, a tiny white egg sat on her palm. Bernadette looked up at Wissagleb with wide eyes. "What just happened?"

"Oh dear," he said, "I hadn't realized that could occur. I've only ever used it on people or creatures that were suffering from advanced age. The spell does not just repair the body's tissues to the state that they were in when the subject was younger. It actually regresses their age. The amount of force you were able to put into the spell unaided was enough to send that caterpillar three weeks back, to when it was an egg. I recommend using some *other* healing spell on young people."

Bernadette stared at the tiny egg in her hand again, then tossed it to the wind. If it hatched and came back to eat her cabbages in the future, so be it. Maybe life as an unaging, shape-shifting dragon didn't offer as bleak a prospect as she'd feared. They all went down into the basement then, to inspect the "troops." Wissagleb's century of aptrgangr, ranging in rank from common soldiers who would fight like automatons to overlords who could think for themselves, stood motionless – nearly filling the available space. A corridor had been left through to the cold room, though no one was eager to go in there through a forest of the undead.

"If you don't mind," Wissagleb said while they were down there, "I think I would like to rest here with my troops for some time. While my magically reanimated body doesn't seem to need food, drink, or sleep, my mind needs time to process what I have seen. I hope I may come up with a stratagem that will let us come upon Meiskomtot in our strength."

They left him there, chattering about the events and revelations of the day among themselves as they returned upstairs. Sigi was set to weeding the cabbage patch, with an admonishment from his mother to keep a sharp eye out for caterpillars as he worked. Mondi, eager to perform a task that required delicate use of these new and marvelous hands, happily volunteered to help. His slightly-younger brother had some trouble convincing him that it was better to squash the caterpillars rather than popping them gleefully into his mouth.

Andi and his parents were all map-lagged, though he'd had more time to recover from it. Bernadette, Erik, and Andrion shut themselves into their bedroom to take another nap, with a request to Riki to wake them before suppertime. They planned to go down to the Maiden for supper, sparing them all any cooking or cleanup tasks – and introducing the Maiden staff to the new incarnation of the son they'd first brought home eleven years before. Mondi took a bath after the weeding, another first, and then went into the nursery to take a nap as well. This being in a new shape was surprisingly tiring!

Riki and Andi were sharing the settee on the veranda, she drawing in her sketchbook and he lazily just gazing out at the view, when Fjuri came up the path from the road and walked over to join them. "Did your folks make it back OK?" he asked Andi. "Yeah, they were already here when I got up this morning. It turned out one of my dragon brothers got killed."

Fjuri looked woeful. "I'm so sorry! How's your mom doing about that?"

"I think she feels guilty because Mondi's the only one of her dragon brood that she was ever really a mother to," Andi replied thoughtfully. "But she seems to be getting over it. The fact that we successfully turned Mondi into a human being this morning seems to help."

Fjuri's face had gone from sad and sympathetic to elated. "It worked, then?"

"Like a charm," Andi said with a trace of smugness. To have returned from one simple, fairly easy quest with such riches made him feel like a man who finds a cache of gold while taking out the night soil.

"I can't wait to see him," Fjuri replied. "But that's not why I'm here."

"No?" his friend eyed him. Fjuri turned to Riki and took her hands.

"I came here to see my girl," he said. Then he folded her in his arms, right in front of her brother, and kissed her.

Chapter 33: Ehrgeizig Hunts

Ehrgeizig wheeled higher and higher, savoring the icy air far above Iscandia as well as the feeling of power as his rejuvenated, intact wings lifted him to heights he had not traversed in centuries. Father Vaterhiin be praised, what an astonishing thing! In some ways he felt as if the service he had given to mankind, teaching the use of spoken spells, had been repaid at last.

He had assisted that young fireblood woman, Bernadette, in achieving her destiny by defeating Tarragin. Now, just a few years later, here comes her nearly-grown son (how quickly these *sterbliim* grew up!) with a request that led to his old friend Wissagleb being reanimated – and providing Ehrgeizig with a new lease on life.

From this altitude he could see for many miles in every direction, as he wheeled in the air about the central plains. Spotting a lone mammoth below he stooped on it, plucking it off its feet with his now-razor-sharp talons. Though many another dragon had been hatched long before Ehrgeizig had, only he of all the dragons now living had been alive and growing through all the millennia following the Uprising. With Tarragin gone, he was the largest living dragon in Iscandia.

He dropped the mammoth from thirty feet up, plenty high enough to break its bones and kill it almost immediately. It had been away from its herd and the humanoid giants that usually protected them, so he fed heartily on it where it lay before taking to the air again. He cruised on the thermals with little need to flap his wings, as he digested his meal and searched the ground below.

Ehrgeizig had been only a few decades out of the egg when the Uprising had begun in earnest, one of the smaller dragons around. Dragons he had known then, older and larger dragons like that red brute Sneyagflug, were alive once more – and they would cower before his majesty now he'd been restored to his full strength and energy.

But before he started laying down the law to the dragons remaining in Iscandia (and he felt sure he'd be able to gain the support of young Drachmondien and his brood-mates – perhaps even mate with one of the youngster's sisters when they were of age) he planned to see to it that Meiskomtot's campaign of raising undead dragons and attacking human settlements was stopped.

Humans, even in a sparsely-populated province like Iscandia, outnumbered dragons by a factor of hundreds to one – and with the way they bred, they always would. That meant it was a poor survival strategy to attack them. He hadn't cared much for Drachmondien's father Sneyagflug when they'd known each other before the war – the older dragon hadn't thought much of the scholarly, pedantic young Ehrgeizig and hadn't been shy about mentioning it – but he had to admit that he'd had the right idea in bringing up his children. Far better to stay away from humans, or else learn to get along with them.

Ehrgeizig doubted he would be able to spot any undead dragons from up here. The undead, whether human or *drache*, tended to be a mottled gray in color – which, with atmospheric perspective, was a good match for the ground. What he had his keen eyes (keener now, thanks to Wissagleb!) alert for was rising columns of smoke in areas away from major cities.

And before the sun had gone too far down into the west, he spotted one. He was cruising now to the south of Muuterhorn, his home for so many years, and spotted a thin trace of dark gray smoke rising from among the trees of Lakemarch, south of the river there. There were only a few scattered farmsteads and the odd ruin or two in that stretch of hardwood forest between Bohrsstead and Lakedon. It could possibly be a forest fire, ignited by a bolt of lightning; but the weather was mostly clear, and Ehrgeizig glided down for a closer look.

No forest fire, though one might be started at any moment. The shake roof of a large farmhouse was ablaze, and as Ehrgeizig halted in the air a couple of hundred feet above it, wings flapping heavily to maintain position, he spotted a smallish (compared to him) undead dragon sweeping past below him and shooting flames at the barn. He'd found what he sought, or at least one of the undead dragon priest's minions.

The people living on the farm were running around like ants whose anthill has been trodden on by a cow. Some of them were attempting to fend the dragon off with arrows, while a woman with a baby was fleeing into the forest. If the dragon didn't catch her (pretty likely, actually, since outside this clearing the trees grew too closely together for a dragon to move among them) she and her infant would probably be killed by a bear. This area was full of them.

Ehrgeizig had been using his voice, the voice trained for speaking dragon spells, for thousands of years. Even when only speaking, without the words of power employed in dragon spells, it was a force to be reckoned with. He dropped a little closer to the action, still hovering, and called loudly, "WHAT DO YOU?"

The undead dragon below him broke off its flaming of the barn to hover in the air and gaze up. The sight of a dragon, and a live one, nearly as big as its master gave it pause; but having died and then risen a couple of times has a way of insulating one from fear.

"I do my master's bidding," the flying corpse replied. "What business is it of yours?"

"I am Ehrgeizig, now eldest of dragons, and I say that this shall not be!" he declared in ringing tones. No time like the present to establish his dominance! The smaller dragon seemed insufficiently impressed.

"You're looking better than I expected, Ehrgeizig," he responded. "I am Rustungtier, and I knew you of old. You have grown a bit since then, yet I do not fear you!"

Rustungtier! Older than him by some decades, more heavily armored than most though that also made him slower in the air. Ehrgeizig realized that the fear of death was not something likely to sway any being who had already experienced it, the more so if they'd been brought back multiple times. That didn't mean he couldn't crush this upstart like a bug, however.

"Kraf-Luft-Struung-Wund!" he cried, and the smaller dragon was hurled through the air to tangle in the trees on the far side of the clearing. Ehrgeizig could hear a rattling sound as bones broke and brittle, mummified flesh cracked and fell apart. Rustungtier slid in a series of jerky movements, catching on branches that broke under his weight, until he landed on the ground.

He lifted his head and said, "Curse you, Ehrgeizig! It's lucky I can't feel any pain!"

Still hovering, the bigger dragon considered this information. It was another advantage of the undead, he realized – pain was intended to protect a living creature from harm, by making you cease activities that were harmful to the body. An animated corpse, on the other hand, could keep using that body unto utter destruction – or until a killing blow severed its connection from the magic that animated it.

Rustungtier was no longer able to fly, the long bones of the wings on both sides snapped in multiple places. Yet he limped forward on his four feet dragging the wings behind, snapping at the braver human defenders as he came. One of them was foolish enough to give him the opportunity to seize her in his jaws, rending her flesh with his teeth before tossing her away.

This had to stop! Ehrgeizig roared out in Common "Get out of the way, you people! Run for the woods!" before stooping on Rustungtier standing helpless below. As he landed atop the smaller dragon, claws digging into the leathery tissues of his back, Rustungtier cried "MEIS-KOM-TOT!" Then Ehrgeizig had the dragon zombie's neck in his enormous jaws, and began pulling hard, ripping at the hardened flesh and tugging with a twisting motion. With a crack and a sound like tearing parchment, he pulled Rustungtier's head (and several feet of his neck, as well) off of the body and flung it to one side. Feh, it tasted awful!

So, the minion had Called his master – as Ehrgeizig had hoped. Now, he was going to get to talk to somebody who was in charge. Still on the ground in the middle of the clearing with his claws sunk into the mummified flesh of the dead-again dragon's back, he looked to right and left. Terrified but determined human defenders stood scattered around at the verge of the woods, staring at him. He'd killed their attacker –but was it just so he could take over destroying their home himself?

"Run for it!" he urged them. "Another undead dragon is coming!" Somehow his command of the Common tongue seemed sharper now that he had been rejuvenated, and he no longer found himself searching for a translation. Ehrgeizig pulled his claws out of his victim and launched himself into the sky again. It definitely took more effort to fly when you were this size, though correspondingly you had more strength, more muscle.

Meiskomtot was beginning to get annoyed. Could these reanimated minions of his perform even the simplest of tasks without constant supervision? He had instructed Rustungtier, who ought to have been heavily armored enough to withstand anything these homesteaders could throw at him, to find isolated settlements and destroy them – with maximum casualties, but always leaving one alive to tell the tale. He wanted the human populace of Iscandia terrified – and if they lashed out at those "helpful" young dragons like the one he'd killed a few days ago, so much the better.

The spell had dropped him a quarter of a mile away from the settlement, and facing it. He saw the smoke immediately, then an enormous draconic figure that rose from the clearing and flapped heavily up into the air to confront him. It gleamed silvery gray in the afternoon light. Alive, definitely a living dragon – but what dragon could be so enormous, yet so glowing with health? Though dragons did not age in the way that humans did, their organs failing over years of use until they could no longer live, they did suffer a certain amount of surface deterioration over millennia of life.

There was not so much as a ragged wing membrane on this creature as it rose up and hovered in the air before him, blocking his path. It was a little smaller than him, but not by a whole lot. Magnificent! With this body, Meiskomtot realized, if he could only manage to capture it without doing too much damage, he could dominate every living dragon in Iscandia.

Meiskomtot's midnight raid on a fortress occupied by necromancers, coming on them in his undead human form, had yielded a couple of the special magical essence vials needed to contain the souls of sentient beings. With those, he could siphon off the soul inhabiting a likely body, preventing it from destroying the flesh (as would have been the case with his fireblood powers otherwise) and then place his own within it – leaving this tattered, mummified ruin to lie forever where it fell. But as he sized up his adversary, he suddenly had a thought.

After occupying a natural-born dragon body he would no longer be able to turn human. He had expected that he'd be able to obtain the potion and use the dragon spells of the Reciprocation, which he knew quite well, to assume a human form – one also undead, but freshly dead and much more powerful physically than the human body he now possessed. Dragons, and the human forms they took with the Reciprocation, had an inborn affinity for magic similar to that of the alfar races – so that his knowledge of spells and dragon spells should transfer easily to a new body.

But he had already learned that he was unable to consume food or drink while undead. Suppose he was unable to consume the potion, even in a fully fleshed and freshly killed body – or, if able to drink it, suppose it would not work? Curses! He decided to play it by ear. "Who are you, who dares to defy me?" he bellowed.

"I doubt you would remember me, Meiskomtot," Ehrgeizig replied. "I was yet young when you were interred in your tomb, and I don't believe we ever met. I am Ehrgeizig, master of the furml and longest-lived dragon in Iscandia now that great Tarragin is gone!"

The name didn't ring a bell for Meiskomtot. If, as the magnificent dragon before him claimed, he had been young when the dragon priest had died, he must have been alive all the time since the Uprising in order to have attained such size. He glanced down and saw the body of Rustungtier lying in two pieces in the clearing below. Another one gone. Seemingly, it was nearly impossible to get good help.

As Meiskomtot hovered, considering his options, Ehrgeizig hit him with the Mana Drain dragon spell. Delivered in such force by an enormous and ancient dragon, it should have severed him from the powerful magic that animated his undead form – perhaps permanently. But the mask Meiskomtot, which protected him unseen, deflected the attack.

Ehrgeizig fluttered his wings and rose a few dozen yards. That was one of the most devastating of the offensive dragon spells, and it should certainly have worked against an undead opponent. It affected health (probably not an issue with an animated corpse) but also magical energy – without which the corpse should cease to be animated. He suddenly wished he had consulted with Wissagleb for a few more minutes before flying off on this mission – his friend knew this undead priest as he did not.

Meiskomtot felt a surge of satisfaction. This Ehrgeizig was clearly a master of the furml; but attack by either dragon spell or ordinary spell could find no purchase while he wore the mask. "Hah!" he roared. "You think to attack me with your spells? I am Meiskomtot, and I am immune to all magic! Come and meet your doom!" He rose up, firing a stream of ice before him.

Ehrgeizig dodged. Since his rejuvenation he felt so much more supple, his reactions quicker. To think he'd been prepared to stay old forever! He looped up and then came down on his larger opponent in the air, trying to rake him with his claws as his jaws with their enormous, sharp teeth sought to rip out Meiskomtot's spine.

The flesh was as hard as oak! He recalled now that this particular dragon priest had been killed in an accident that had prevented the timely retrieval of his body for the rituals and procedures that would preserve the flesh. It was a wonder he was able to fly, seeming like an animate block of wood. What in all the hells was he supposed to do to defeat this Meiskomtot, then – if he was immune to dragon spells and magical attacks, too big to bear to the ground, and too hard to bite through? Ehrgeizig's confidence wavered as he considered for the first time that he might literally have bitten off more than he could chew. He released his grip and flew off a few dozen yards.

Meanwhile, Meiskomtot was having problems of his own. He wanted this magnificent, oversized body as a new home for his much-abused soul – wanted it so *much*! But unless this Ehrgeizig had already taken the Reciprocation he could not risk trapping himself within it. He had been born human, and as much as he enjoyed the power of the dragon form it was not enough by itself. He needed to find out, somehow, whether his adversary could be used in this way before finishing him off. It would certainly be a lot easier to kill him if preserving the condition of the body were not a consideration.

Flapping those stiff, tattered wings to gain some altitude, Meiskomtot rose above his antagonist before hovering again. "You cannot defeat me in my dragon form," he taunted. "Why not go human, and we will fight it out man to man?"

"I know not how to become human," Ehrgeizig replied. His friend Wissagleb had apparently not told him everything! "It would have been much easier to find students for my training in the furml, had that been a possibility."

"Hah!" Meiskomtot crowed. "Oldest of all the dragons in Iscandia, yet so ignorant? None told you of the Reciprocation?" Cursing silently, scarcely believing that such a critical piece of information should have escaped him for the last few thousand years (dragons can take *human form??!*), Ehrgeizig backed off a pace, flew higher and then resumed hovering in midair. He was having second thoughts about that dragon jerky.

"Why are you doing this, Meiskomtot? What is it that you want?" Ehrgeizig called to him. He was beginning to suspect he was not going to be the winner in this contest, but maybe he could come away from it with some useful information.

"Why am I raising dead dragons? Why am I attacking these pathetic mortals? What do I *want*?" Meiskomtot snarled, still hovering. "I'll tell you what I want – I want to *live*! Is that too much to ask? It is only what you have, what I was promised by right of my dragon blood. Find a way to restore me to true life, and I'll happily go about my business (of enslaving you all, he didn't add). But until then, someone must *pay*!"

Meiskomtot's magical skills were strongest in necromancy, and that was not likely to be useful in bringing this enormous and vibrantly healthy dragon down. But Ehrgeizig was clearly a threat to his minions, who lacked his immunity to attacks by magic or dragon spell – and he needed to die. Resurrected as a zombie, he would make a valuable addition to the team. The human defenders of the settlement, heeding Ehrgeizig's urging, had left their homes to burn and fled into the forest. So not fearing attack from behind, he gently lowered himself to the ground and returned to human form.

Another spoken spell, and he was wielding the Staff of Rending. Ehrgeizig's unease turned to sharp alarm as he saw the staff, and to panic as Meiskomtot shot a bolt from it. The big dragon was dodging even as the bolt came, and it hit the treetops behind him – causing an area fifty feet across to erupt in flames. Shards and splinters of burning hardwood pierced his newly intact wing membranes, causing pain both physical and psychic. For just a short time, Ehrgeizig had been perfect.

Mind ablaze with anger tempered by fear for his life, he lifted a hundred feet in an instant before streaking off to the northwest. He had not visited his old haunt atop Muuterhorn since Tarragin's fall, and flew there now to lick his wounds. Meiskomtot could not have gone dragon again quickly enough to follow him as he flew above the clouds. The cold soothed his hurts, and Ehrgeizig pondered his recent experience.

I had better tell the young fireblood about this, he realized. The information Ehrgeizig had gathered during the brief battle was something he'd better know. He tried calling him, but got no response. Not surprising, if the boy was usually human. Nor did calling Drachmondien work, which *was* a surprise. The youngster had been friendly, polite and respectful during their long conversation while the fireblood boy and his friend had gone into the tomb looking for Wissagleb. Surely he would not refuse a Call?

Wait, the boy had told him where they were going – east of the walls of Waterdon and west of the Brightwater. That was just down the hill from here, Ehrgeizig realized, and likely easy enough to spot from the air. Besides, Wissagleb had gone with him – and he was eager to discuss this "turning human" business with him. Were his injuries to be healed as well, all the better.

Meiskomtot stood in the clearing beside the ruined body of Rustungtier, cursing quietly. Escaped again! He was out of practice aiming the Staff, it seemed, and he took out some of his anger by blasting chunks from the burning buildings. Soon flying, burning debris had set fire to the woods in a wide circle around the clearing, and things were getting uncomfortably hot. Best he not incinerate himself out of anger over losing his quarry!

As he took to the air in dragon form once again, Meiskomtot wondered that Ehrgeizig had not known of the Reciprocation. He had boasted of being the eldest living dragon of this age, and he had the size to prove it. Had he actually been alive for all the millennia since the Uprising? Perhaps there had been no dragon priests left to offer him the potion and the dragon spells, then. Was it possible that the lore might still exist that would let them be recreated? If he could just talk Ehrgeizig, or possibly Sneyagflug, into taking the potion, he would have the next best thing to being alive – a beautiful, intact body to inhabit as he ruled Iscandia for all eternity.

Chapter 34: Sneyagflug Returns

The enormous red dragon touched down in the road below Drakespring Farm. Grief for his lost son and frustration at his inability to find (or fight) the undead dragon priest who had killed him filled his mind with swirling misery. He sought solace from some of his remaining children, and he knew that here at least he would find the one of the brood he had known the least: Drachmondien.

Up the hill a human stripling was scattering feed for the chickens, but it was not Bernadette's son Sigi – a child whose existence he himself had had a hand in. This boy was of a similar size, perhaps a little taller and thinner – but he had flaming red hair rather than Sigi's dark auburn. Sneyagflug was sure he had seen him before, but couldn't recall when or where. And what was he doing here? Bernadette and her family would hardly be likely to hire an underage farm hand, when they had their own home-grown crop of them.

But why did the boy look so familiar? As the lad finished dispensing the cracked grain, he looked up and spotted the red dragon in the road. Then his face lit in delight and he ran down to the road, crying "Father!" in the dragon tongue. What…? The boy threw himself against Sneyagflug's flank, and said "It's me! Drachmondien!" With that he stepped back and cried "Weit-Stos-Zet-Blik!" His clothing disappeared, leaving him standing naked. Another dragon spell and the familiar form of Sneyagflug's human-raised son appeared where the boy had stood.

All of the negative emotions roiling in Sneyagflug's head were swept away with wonder and delight. How many times since being resurrected had he fantasized about being able to turn human? He had cared little for the priests of the dragon worshipers in the earlier years of his life, acting as most dragons had and simply enjoying a life spent doing whatever he'd pleased. Nor had he much enjoyed the company of his fellow dragons. Had some of them known of this, while he had never learned?

"Drachmondien, how is this possible?" Sneyagflug demanded of his son. The young dragon returned to human, and a second spell found him clothed once again. He reverted to the Common tongue as he said enthusiastically, "Andi got it for me! Something I've wanted since I first saw Mama transform back when we were babies!" His enthusiastic babbling sounded more appropriate to the preadolescent he seemed to be, rather than the young adult he was mentally.

"It's a potion and a couple of dragon spells, just like for fireblood humans to turn dragon!" Mondi explained. "Plus there's those other two I just showed you, that make it easier to deal with clothing and so forth – humans are always carrying stuff around. I got to hug Mama and my papas, Riki and Sigi and Meri, oh and Andi first thing of course… I've been eating with a fork, sitting and eating at the table with the family instead of having to fly off and catch myself a whole elk. And I can write, make potions, take a hot bath whenever I want…" He paused, grinning from ear to ear, to catch his breath. "It's *wonderful*!" he concluded.

Affection and joy glowed in Sneyagflug's breast. This boy, of all his children with Schunmurte, was the one closest to human. That he'd been able to fulfill that dream made his father proud and happy. "You've got me convinced, son," he said in Common. "Where do I sign up?"

"You want to be able to turn human, too, Father? That's great! I can hardly wait to hug you!"

Mondi turned as if about to run into the house, then called back over his shoulder, "We have the book with the formula for the potion, so when Mama gets the time and we can find the ingredients we can *all* get this ability. But there's one more jug of potion made up, that we got from our new friend Wissagleb. Be right back!"

As he watched his human son scurry off, Sneyagflug thought Wissagleb? Wasn't he a dragon priest? Andi had not been at Gotteluub's leave-taking, and he knew that Bernadette's fireblood son was if anything closer with his dragon siblings than she had been as their mother. He must have been out of reach… perhaps down in an ancient Norse barrow asking questions of the dead?

Though the threat of undead dragon attacks was still upon them, Team Fireblood had not yet come up with a viable plan to deal with it. And in the meantime, life must go on. So at this hour of the morning Bernadette, Erik, and Andrion had gone to town to carry a consignment of arms and armor to Valkyrie and then consult with Eorl Ormund about the results of their efforts so far.

They'd taken Meri with them. Riki, Andi, and Sigi had walked down to the Maiden, each of them with a friend to visit. They would swim in the big outdoor pool and stay for lunch. Mondi had been planning to join them there after he'd finished a few of the chores Sigi usually did. The novelty of being able to perform these tasks was still strong enough that he delighted in them, though his human-born siblings had long since lost their enthusiasm.

So, the recent dragonling was alone in the place and there was no one to ask whether it was okay to deliver their only remaining jug of the dragon-to-human potion to his father. And why should they object? It wasn't as if they couldn't make more, and Sneyagflug was certainly as worthy of receiving this gift as any dragon they knew. Though maybe old Ehrgeizig would like it too, if he didn't already have it. The subject hadn't come up during their long talk.

Mondi found the jug of potion on a shelf in the chemia corner of the craft room. Bernadette was a skilled chemiast with decades of experience, and she kept everything in her work area neatly organized and carefully labeled. Ughn, it was heavy! Mondi had a wiry strength, but there must have been a couple of gallons of the potion in the metal jar.

He hefted it back down the hallway and out the front door, but found that holding the jug at arm's length and high enough that the fluid could be poured into his father's cavernous mouth was beyond his strength. "I can deal with it," Sneyagflug said with a barely-perceptible hint of impatience. His eagerness for this new experience had him as excited as he'd been when he first beheld Schunmurte.

The lid having been removed, Sneyagflug carefully put his head down over the jug so that it was captured in his jaws. Then he lifted his head, jug and all, and let its contents run down his neck in a couple of long swallows. Next he set the jug down again, examining the sensations that were coursing through him from nose to tail. "Don't say the spell yet!" Mondi suddenly said, and dashed off again. He returned in a moment with one of the household's bathrobes draped over one arm. They had some quite large ones, needed for bathers the size of Erik.

The road was really the only place near the farm with room for
Sneyagflug to stand, but fortunately there was nobody in view at the
moment. "Okay, the coast is clear," Mondi said. "Go ahead and say
the spell now." The small delay had been enough for him to form the
stones needed to power the spells – though they had not begun
forming until the potion had done its work. In a moment, where the
gigantic red dragon had been, a most unusual-looking naked man
stood in the road. Mondi hastily helped him into the robe.

Sneyagflug was in shock. It was impossibly strange, to be so
small – yet he suspected he was bigger than most humans. In fact he
was around six feet six inches tall, lean and muscular, with skin
coloring similar to that of Mondi's human form but hair of a darker
auburn closer to Andi's and eyes of a deep, amber-flecked green. He
had a full beard a little redder than the hair of his head, and chiseled
features that were handsome in a somewhat cold-looking fashion.

As with Mondi, his first act as a human was to use his newly
acquired arms for hugging someone he loved. Oh, what an advantage
humans had over the drachen when it came to the expression of love!
No wonder it had taken him centuries of life to realize what that
feeling could be. After a whole day of being human Mondi was eager
to initiate his father into all of the new experiences that awaited him,
and he led him by the hand up to the house.

He took a chilled bottle of ale out of the cold chest and gave it to
him, saying "Try this. I find I prefer water or milk, but you might
like it." Sneyagflug did. The taste was deep and rich despite the chill,
tiny bubbles breaking on his tongue as he sucked down the ale. In
almost no time the bottle was empty. "I want to see myself!" the new
man declared, and his son led him down the hall and into the master
bedroom. One of the built-in closets, Bernadette's, had a full-length
mirror mounted on the door.

Sneyagflug had never seen such a thing, but what it showed him
was stranger still. He took off the robe and tossed it onto the huge
bed before standing, turning this way and that, to behold what he had
become. He had little hair on his body, but there were bushy growths
of it, the same color as his beard, in the armpits and above the crotch.
The dangling genitalia concerned him a bit. They seemed so...

unprotected, so sensitive. Perhaps this was one of the reasons humans usually wore clothing.

Sneyagflug had had many more dealings with human beings in the past decade than in his entire earlier life, and he had come to have some understanding of what they thought was attractive in a member of their species. He'd always considered himself to be a handsome specimen of dragonkind, certainly a worthy consort for Schunmurte. And after studying himself in the mirror for some time, he concluded that his human form would do. Bernadette would surely desire him as he had desired her for all these years.

Sneyagflug retrieved the robe from the bed and put it back on. "This bed, this is where your mother and her husbands sleep?" he asked his son.

"Most nights," Mondi replied, "though when the kids were younger there were often a lot of little ones in here with them. I even slept here a few times! But Papa Erik and Papa Andrion each have their own bed, in the rooms on either side of this one. Sometimes Mama might sleep with just one of them for, uh, romance. I guess. I don't really know that much about how humans do it. I suppose I can find out now, though!" he added, having only just had this happy thought. His human body wasn't yet sending him urgent demands to get busy, but that time wasn't many years away.

"I wonder," Sneyagflug mused, "if this is how we got fireblood humans in the first place." Mondi seemed struck dumb for a moment, considering the idea. It didn't seem right, somehow.

"Andi and Fjuri and I went to see Ehrgeizig right after you came in, injured from tangling with Meiskomtot. He's been hanging out at Todenstor. Anyhow, he knew a dragon priest named Wissagleb back during the Uprising, who happened to be interred right there in that big fortress thing on one side of the courtyard."

So, it *was* a dragon priest. "Andi and Fjuri went down in the tomb to see if they could find the guy and pump him for information about Meiskomtot. I couldn't go, obviously, since I was too big to fit through the corridors. So I stayed and talked with Ehrgeizig for hours. Then Mama Called me for what turned out to be Gotteluub's farewell gathering, and I didn't find out what happened until after we all got back from that."

"Say, do you think there are any clothes here that will fit me?" Sneyagflug asked. He would probably have preferred to be naked, but really wanted some protection in his crotch area. Besides, he had the idea that the robe might not be considered adequate clothing for going out in public.

"Hmm, you're a lot taller than Andrion but not nearly as wide as Erik. I don't think anything's going to be a good fit, but maybe you can borrow some of Andrion' underdrawers and one of his mage robes. Those are kind of one-size-fits-most."

As he was rummaging in Andrion's closet for some clothing to borrow Mondi continued his tale. "I was trying to explain about the dragon to human transformation. From what Wissagleb said it was something that had been developed by the dragon worshipers a long time before he was born, by the same person or maybe people that developed the transformation of fireblood humans into dragons. If that's true, dragon blood couldn't have gotten into the human population in the first place by dragons turned human, because the dragon priests were already fireblood. The potion and dragon spells you found to turn Mama into a dragon were part of something the church called the Reward, which was given to priests when they achieved the highest level of the priesthood – along with a magical mask and a staff of some kind."

Mondi had to help his father put on the clothing. He had only owned the body parts it was intended to cover for less than an hour, and it was not immediately obvious how the garments were supposed to go. No sooner had he had become clothed, though, than Sneyagflug felt a curious sensation of pressure in the area south of that odd indentation Mondi told him was the navel, a scar left over where the human baby had been attached to the inside of its mother. Since neither this human body nor the one Mondi wore had been born of woman, it was odd that they had this mark – but if neither of them looked like a run-of-the-mill Norse or Galise, they were fully and perfectly human. That ale had gone through quickly.

After he'd explained his problem Sneyagflug got another lesson in human accommodations, one he found particularly odd. So much more of this body was accessible to itself, with its flexibility and these hands. He could touch every square inch of his smooth, soft skin – so vulnerable, no wonder they usually wore armor. Though he had enjoyed being a dragon for thousands of years, the experience of living in a human body was endlessly fascinating.

"Are you feeling hungry, Father?" Mondi asked after their trip to the bathroom.

"Yes, I believe I am. Some feelings are the same no matter what shape you are in!" With that Sneyagflug laughed, something that seemed to just come to him naturally, and felt the corners of his mouth turning up spontaneously. A smile!

"Come on, then," his son said, leading him out through the front door and locking it behind them. "We're meeting the rest of the kids except Meri at the Maiden for lunch. I think you'll be amazed." The insides of buildings less cavernous than the broad space atop Wyrmshalla were something few dragons got to see, though of course Mondi had been scarcely bigger than an eagle when he first came to live at Drakespring Farm and had been inside the Maiden many times.

Just the act of walking a quarter mile down the road with this curiously efficient bipedal gate, not galumphing along on four clawed feet, was amazing. Sneyagflug started at a walk, then tried a trot, and before they had reached the building he was going at a full run – Mondi whooping beside him.

They found Andi, Riki, and Sigi sharing the Owner's Table with their guests: Maiden residents Rezira, her foster sister Sintra, and the head innkeeper's son Joqui. Rezira and Sintra would ordinarily have been waiting tables during the lunch rush, but Bernadette had asked Drelos to let them off for today. She knew that things might be coming to a head soon, and she wanted her children to enjoy some special time with their friends before the next crisis hit.

Mondi was quickly spotted and welcomed over. Rezira and Joqui had already met him in his human form, but Sintra was astonished to see that it was true. Every one of them was still more astonished to learn that the tall man in mage robes accompanying Mondi was his father Sneyagflug. Andi stifled the urge to come down on his brother for appropriating their last jug of the potion without asking permission. He was never going to be Sneyagflug's biggest fan, but he could certainly see how the loving and warm-hearted Mondi would long for the chance to have his father share the experience of being human with him.

Sneyagflug was clumsy at the table, not knowing what to order or even what plates and utensils were for – let alone how to use them. But he was good-natured enough about it, and they eventually dealt with the problem by having Hildi bring them an enormous platter with an assortment of hot and cold sandwiches, Dragon Fries, and other finger foods. Sneyagflug had to try everything, of course, and ate with an appetite that was just this side of draconic.

This was amazing! He'd spent a long time acquiring a taste for slightly toasted fresh-killed deer and similar animals, eaten whole including the intestines, bones, and hide. But Sneyagflug's human mouth seemed to have the ability to detect nuances of flavor and texture that made everything seem delicious. Of course, perhaps the food here just *was* delicious. So Mondi had said.

The three young women at the table were beautiful, something Sneyagflug knew instinctively as he felt his body react to their presence. Yet they were scarcely more than children, the eldest of them only a year older than young Andi. They didn't appeal to his mind as much as they appealed to his eyes. There was another human woman who had claimed his heart years ago, and as much as he was enjoying this experience he was anxious for their first meeting.

The leisurely meal concluded at last, Andi, Riki, and Sigi took their leave of their friends and accompanied Mondi and Sneyagflug back up the road to Drakespring Farm. "I think you ought to meet Wissagleb, Father," Mondi was saying. "You and he need to compare notes. We're still trying to think of a way to get a sufficiently strong fighting force to the site of one of Meiskomtot's attacks, so we can stop him for good."

It was not an undead dragon priest, whatever fascinating information he might have to impart, that was on Sneyagflug's mind as they approached the house. He could see that the senior Drakesprings and their younger daughter had returned while he and Mondi were eating lunch. Erik was setting up to work in the forge, while Bernadette and Andrion sat talking quietly with Meri on the veranda. They lived a lot of their lives outdoors, when the weather was nice.

Bernadette was having a fairly serious discussion with her husband and daughter when she spied the party coming from the direction of the Maiden. Looking at Mondi as a human boy still gave her a little thrill. But who was that tall man walking with them, dressed in a mage robe that seemed a little too short for him? He towered above Andi, who was now around the same height as his father. She was quite sure that she had never seen him before, yet somehow she felt she knew him.

Excusing herself, she left the settee and went down the steps toward the gate. The tall man broke away from the group of kids, who were looking at her questioningly, and stepped toward her somewhat hesitantly – as if he'd lost his nerve after that first impulse to run to meet her. Their eyes were locked together, hers growing wide as she saw what was in his. Love, excitement, passion… fear? When they stood no more than two feet apart he looked down at her, a full foot shorter. "Bernadette!" he said, almost a moan. Then he seized her in his arms and planted a hard, inexpert kiss on her mouth.

Chapter 35: Battle Plans

Andrion did not, quite, have to be physically restrained from blasting the transformed red dragon with battle magic until there was nothing left but a smoking crater in the ground. But it was a close thing. Now he, Erik, Mondi, and Andi were in the craft room with Wissagleb, preparing for a strategy session while Bernadette handled Sneyagflug.

They were sitting side by side on the settee, and he was holding her hand. Touch was so much more important in this form, he realized. "But Bernadette, I love you! You're the mother of my children!" Not by my choice, she thought, but kept it to herself. She had long since reconciled herself to what had passed between them all those years ago, and truly loved her dragon children even if she had borne them under duress.

"Sneyagflug," she said calmly, squeezing his hand and looking up into those curious green eyes, "I will always treasure you as a friend, and I can't deny that there is a bond between us. But your being human isn't going to change anything. Erik and Andrion are the loves of my life, and always will be. I am not leaving them for you, and I am not hopping into bed with you for old times' sake. If you want to experience human sex, you will have to look elsewhere."

He looked so heartbroken it was breaking her own heart to let him down, but though he might only have been human for a few hours Sneyagflug was a big boy. He was just going to have to get over it. Releasing her hand then, he stood and said. "I understand. I'll just return to dragon and fly away out of your life, then."

She rose as well. "Don't be ridiculous," she said. "The children we have together are a link between us that can never be broken. Mondi is as much a part of my family as any of my human children, and he is yours. Besides, we need your help dealing with Meiskomtot. Come on in the house and join the conference. Don't be such a baby, Red."

Sneyagflug turned, willing to be her friend if he could not be her lover. Besides, the dragon transformation would extend her life far beyond that of her human husbands. If he was third choice, perhaps someday his chance would come. Dragons could be very patient. As they were about to go into the house through the door to the master bedroom, there was a swirl of wind and a thump as an enormous, silvery-gray dragon landed in the road below the house.

Both of them turned to stare. Though he had never stood beside himself in dragon form, Sneyagflug had the sense that this dragon was bigger than he was. But other than some recent minor damage, he looked untouched by the wear and tear you would expect from the millennia of living it would take to reach such a size. Who could it be? Bernadette was pretty sure she knew, after hearing the tale of Wissagleb's Renew spell and witnessing its effects on their old cow. She strode toward the dragon in the road, calling "Ehrgeizig?"

"Fireblood, well met!" he rumbled in dragon tongue. "May I assume that the language of the drachen is now yours?"

She answered him in kind. "It came to me from the moment that I first sprouted wings," she acknowledged. Then after examining him more closely and seeing that he was bleeding from a hundred little cuts in his leathery wings, she said "It appears you've been in a battle. May I heal you?"

"Ah, yessss, thank you!" the gigantic and ancient drache said, as she began using her healing spell. Ehrgeizig's injuries were many but slight, and she saw no reason to try anything fancier on him. In a minute or so all of the little wounds had closed and the blood was drying, flaking away in the light breeze.

"I have met Wissagleb, and he told me of what he did for you," Bernadette remarked. "But hearing about it and seeing it are two different things. You are magnificent!" The great silver dragon seemed to purr. Now that he was no longer in pain and bleeding, the pride and joy of his recent transformation had returned.

"I went out looking for Meiskomtot," Ehrgeizig volunteered, "and I found him. To my regret, I fear. It turns out that he is somehow immune to attacks by any kind of spell."

"Yes, Wissagleb told us that was likely the case. I'm sorry he did not warn you before you flew off."

"My own fault," he replied. "My blood was hot after the renewal, and I was so eager to be off that I didn't stay to listen to counsel. Is Wissagleb here, then? We need to consult."

"He and my team are inside, where we were about to discuss strategies for defeating Meiskomtot," Bernadette told him, "but I think you need to be included in our plans." She looked around. There was no spot on the farm free of obstructions or crops that was big enough for several humans and an enormous dragon to stand and confer, and they certainly didn't want to block the main road north. Passersby might become alarmed, to say the least.

"Why don't we convene right over there," she suggested, pointing due east to where the Brightwater sparkled at the bottom of a gentle slope. There were several hours of daylight left. "You can fly down there, and I'll go fetch the rest of the crew."

"That will be fine, Fireblood," Ehrgeizig replied. "Thank you again for healing me." He made to get airborne and Sneyagflug said, "Wait, I'll join you in flying there." He stepped a few dozen yards further down the road, and then after two dragon spells the big red dragon stood where the man had been before.

"Sneyagflug!" Ehrgeizig said in amazement. "So, it was true!"

"The dragon-to-human transformation, you mean?" Sneyagflug replied. "The 'Reciprocation,' as the dragon priests called it? Obviously, it's true." Ehrgeizig had been a scholarly kid scarcely worthy of notice when the two of them had been alive all those thousands of years ago. After his resurrection in the modern era, the red dragon's opinion of Ehrgeizig had not improved much. But now, he realized, they were truly on the same side and it was time for him to set aside his dislike. Yet he couldn't resist twitting the larger dragon about something he knew and Ehrgeizig did not.

As Bernadette went back into the house to fetch the rest of the war council, the two dragons lifted off and flew the short distance down to the river. "Did you have it before, then?" Ehrgeizig wanted to know. He was smarting with a sense of betrayal that his friend Wissagleb had never revealed this power, this opportunity to him. It would have made his life over the intervening millennia so much easier!

Sneyagflug relented. "I just found out about it earlier today, in fact," he admitted. "My son Drachmondien, who you met recently, partook of this gift – which Bernadette's son Andi obtained for him from Wissagleb. Or, the potion from Wissagleb and the dragon spells from a Spell Wall within your friend's tomb. I must assume that the dragon worshipers only intended the knowledge of those spells to be passed by humans to dragons, at their own discretion. And certainly dragons cannot concoct potions."

This still left Ehrgeizig wondering why Wissagleb had not mentioned it to him, but he set that aside. There were other things to consider. "So," he said, "you and The Fireblood, eh?" Sneyagflug preened.

"I'm surprised you hadn't heard the whole story long since," he said. "The kids are eleven now, and they've been roaming all over Iscandia and beyond for the past five years or so, working to improve the attitudes of the human population toward dragons. That's involved the 'removal' of quite a few dragons who wouldn't go along with the program."

Ehrgeizig was still a little miffed. If she was going to turn dragon and mate she could have had *me*, he thought. Then he realized that up until a day or so ago he had not been anything a young female dragon would want to mate with. *Now*, however... "I had begun to hear rumors of young dragons in the world," he admitted. "But of course I had not met any of them, and didn't know who their parents were. I was by myself at Todenstor for the past several years."

The two spotted a party of humans walking purposefully toward them, and halted their conversation at their approach. Bernadette had come with Andrion, Erik, Andi, Mondi, and Wissagleb – who was completely swaddled in a hooded cloak to help disguise the fact that he was an aptrgangr. The undead don't feel the heat of summer, fortunately. They'd left Riki at home watching Sigi and Meri, as none of these family members were expected to be included in what they hoped would be the final takedown of Meiskomtot.

As the humans gathered near the two large dragons Sneyagflug spelled himself back into human form. Instead of immediately reclaiming his clothing from the dimension where it hid, he caught Bernadette's eye and stood there grinning at her for a moment, naked, before spelling a second time. She glared at him, but inside she felt relief that he seemed to be getting over his personal tragedy and finding a sense of humor. She was thankful that neither of her husbands had noticed, as well – though she doubted Erik would have been bothered by it.

As the senior fireblood, Bernadette seemed to have assumed the role of Mistress of Ceremonies. "All right, people," she said, "we're here to hammer out a strategy for our next attack on Meiskomtot, something that will stop that bastard once and for all. Ehrgeizig here is the last person to actually see him, so I'd like him to speak first. Can you tell us what happened, please?"

Ehrgeizig inclined his head, and spoke. He knew that most present had the dragon tongue, but thought it likely that the Fireblood's two husbands (her battle companions, he remembered well from the time when they had arrived at Muuterhorn with that potion-laced goat) did not. So he spoke in Common. He was quite fluent in the tongue, having conversed in it over thousands of years with humans when he and they were the only sentients living after the Uprising had ended.

"I found an undead minion of Meiskomtot's attacking an isolated settlement in Lakemarch," he began. "He was of no great size, nor did he have many defenses. I came down on him from above, but just before I ripped his head from his body he Called his master – as I had hoped and intended." Ehrgeizig paused for a moment, letting the suspense build. He found it hard to resist an audience.

"Meiskomtot arrived, and he was truly enormous. Possibly the most preposterously ruinous creature I have ever seen aloft, though perhaps it is magic that allows him to fly. I soon discovered that my *furml* had no effect on him." He glanced at Wissagleb, and his friend cringed a little.

"My apologies, Ehrgeizig," he said in his dry voice. "After performing the Renewal on you I found that things moved too fast, and it did not occur to me to warn you of his mask. In his dragon form his armor and mask still protect him, and the power of the Meiskomtot mask is to ward him from all magical harm."

Ehrgeizig dipped his head for a moment in acknowledgement of his friend's apology. The reminder of the vast service Wissagleb had done him had not gone unnoticed. He continued his tale. "It seemed that he was heavily protected from my spells, and his immense size meant that there was little I could do to bring him down using a normal physical attack. Then he suggested that I should turn human and fight him, as he put it, 'man to man.'" Another look at Wissagleb.

"You were never offered the Reciprocation, Ehrgeizig?" the undead priest asked.

"I never even *heard* of it!" his friend of old replied in wounded tones. "Do you not think you might have mentioned it?" Wissagleb stood as if rooted to the ground for the better part of a minute, searching his dust-laden memories.

"Is it true," he asked finally, "that we never saw each other again after I had reached the top level of the priesthood?"

Ehrgeizig considered. It had been a time of intense turmoil, there near the end. His friendship with Wissagleb had flourished when both of them were quite young, but then the escalating Uprising had shattered normal life. He had learned of his friend's elevation, and later of his death and interment, but he did not remember ever seeing him in dragon form. "I think not," he said sadly. "You never came to see me as a dragon, as I can recall."

Wissagleb hung his head. "I greatly regretted the loss of the times we once spent together," he said. "But after I was elevated, there was no longer any time for relaxation, for friendship, for anything but the war. I knew not of the Reciprocation before my elevation, though of course there were rumors of the Reward among the lower ranks of the priesthood. That was hardly the kind of thing you could hide. All was revealed at my initiation, and then all was swept away. I am sorry."

So, his friend had not played him false! A pity he had had no *other* friends among the dragon worshipers, but most of them were ambitious men (and rarely, women) whose quest for power and immortality overrode every other consideration. The world was better without them, and he had gladly taken the part of the Norse heroes who were fighting them. "All is forgiven, my old friend," Ehrgeizig said after a few moments. "The service you have done me recently pays for any omissions, thrice over. Let me continue my tale."

"At the point where Meiskomtot realized I could not defeat him as a dragon, and I told him that I could not turn human, he seemed...

disappointed. I don't know why, unless turning human would have put me at a great disadvantage and he was anxious to finish me."

Wissagleb seemed riveted by this last remark, then crowed "He needed you able to turn human!" The other people there turned to look at him. "It's the potion!" Wissagleb explained. "Meiskomtot is dissatisfied to find his soul residing in a body that, human and dragon both, is heavily deteriorated. He has the ability to capture the essence of a freshly killed dragon – or human – and place his own soul within that nearly-intact body. But he needs a body that has already been prepared, either by the Dragon Transformation potion or the Human Transformation one, to transform between the two shapes using the dragon spells of the Reward or the Reciprocation! Without that he will lose the ability to change forms, as dead bodies cannot be acted on by the potion."

"I believe you are right!" Ehrgeizig said. "I asked him why he was doing this, what it was he wanted, and he screamed that he wanted to live. What he wants above all else, it seems, is the immortality that was promised to him by his church. Evidently an eternity undead does not suit him, but I don't doubt he would covet a body such as mine as a second choice to true life."

The group fell into conversation, absorbing and discussing Ehrgeizig's information. It seemed that their adversary was powerful indeed, but the tale that they had just listened to suggested he had a weakness. After some minutes it was Andrion who asked, "Ehrgeizig, you said that Meiskomtot came when Called by his minion?"

"That is so," the enormous dragon acknowledged.

"And Berni, didn't Wissliiben say that he also came to the Call of the minion that he and his siblings were attacking out in Westmarch?" Bernadette nodded, her eyes wide as her agile mind began following his train of thought.

"I think," Andrion said as he addressed them all, "that Meiskomtot is hungry enough for a freshly killed, transformation-capable body that he would find a challenge almost irresistible if it came from the right person. Why don't you, Sneyagflug, Call him in your human form from some appropriate location where we can marshal our forces? From what Berni and Andi have told me, he'll be able to tell who you are and what state you're in, and how to go to you – but no details beyond that. Am I right?"

Some men, confronted with a suggestion from the jealous husband of the woman they desired that they place themselves in danger, might have flinched. Not Sneyagflug. He had been a man for less than a full day, and a dragon for many years. He thought it was a marvelous idea. "Perfect!" he said. "We can assemble an army in hiding, ready to attack him when he comes within range. When he realizes he's been trapped he'll call his minions, and then we can take them down all at once! If we're lucky, we'll have the opportunity to kill all of the undead dragons within range of The Fireblood, so they can never rise again. If Meiskomtot's not in dragon form you'll need an essence capture spell to put *him* permanently out of action, but that shouldn't be too hard to come by. Let's *do* this!"

Andrion had to admit, he was kind of impressed with Sneyagflug as a man. He still wanted to kill him, and was only restrained from doing so because Berni wouldn't hear of it. As much as he resented and preferred to ignore it, the once-dragon was the father of the lion's share of her children. Including Mondi, a boy he truly loved as a son. Sigh.

The group broke down into discussions of logistics. Where should they stage the ambush, who would comprise the force, and when would Sneyagflug make his call? They eventually decided they would use the dragon altar at Osteon Rise, some miles south of Coldstein, as the location for the ambush. The area was the site of an outdoor Spell Wall, the terrain a broad flat hilltop surrounded by rocky prominences that would help to contain the conflict. It was also not all that far from Waterdon.

The issue of timing depended on whom they wanted to invite to the party. Too many seemed like a better choice than too few, as once they had sprung this trap they would be unlikely to get the chance to spring another. "We have to have Fjuri with us," Andi insisted. Their recent quest had convinced him that his friend was as commanding a warrior as you could possibly want at your side.

"You're right," Erik said. "What about his parents, as well?" The senior Steadfasts had been busy making a living and raising children for the past couple of decades, but they were still a force to be reckoned with. "Bjorn will have to get some time off work," Andrion pointed out, "and I guess Edla will have to come stay at Drakespring Farm. I'm sure Meri will like that, but I don't know how Riki will feel."

"She'll do it," Bernadette promised. She had come to have a lot more confidence in her daughter and her abilities since the crisis had begun. Riki was bright, strong, level-headed, and responsible.

"Hey, how about Kziintke?" was Andi's next thought. He'd left the tri-lingual, highly-accomplished dypalfar mech working with his master Gylabris at Dypendwelve in Alfenstein a little while before the undead dragon situation had arisen. But he'd been a valiant fighter and a big help to them when they'd been trying to beat back the Great Army of Mrzhandtham as they sought to free that dypalfar city's slaves last year.

"Good idea," Andrion said, "Kziintke, or any automaton, is immune to most dragon spells if not to lightning spells. Maybe you could bring along a small herd of bugs or some rollers, too?"

"I'll have to fast-travel to Alfenstein and see what's available," Andi said.

"And then there's Wissagleb's aptrgangr troops," Bernadette reminded them all. Nearly a hundred strong, they might be limited in their ability to react to changing situations in battle. But they had all once been formidable warriors – and if they were not completely destroyed, Wissagleb could resurrect them when they fell.

"That ought to about do it," Erik said. "If dozens of aptrgangr troops, four Norse warriors, a couple of top-level mages, a dypalfar mech or two, a dragon priest and our very own Fireblood can't handle Meiskomtot and his zombies, it might be time to move to Zahar."

"And the timing?" Wissagleb asked. Bernadette ran over their plans in her mind.

"Maybe I should take you and your aptrgangr up there right away," she suggested to the undead priest. "You can get them all into position and then just sit there waiting for the rest of us to arrive."

"That sounds appropriate," he said. "What about the rest of you?"

"We can bring Sneyagflug with us when we come with the rest of the group," she replied. "I'm guessing that will be four days from now – to allow Andi time to get to Alfenstein and back, and have some rest. Meanwhile we'll arrange things with the Steadfasts, and have them with us when we travel to Osteon Rise."

"Ehrgeizig, I assume you want to join us when the time comes?"

"Of course I do," he replied. He was smarting from his ignominious defeat and anxious to get some back – if not from Meiskomtot himself, then from his minions at least. "Just Call me when the time comes, before Sneyagflug Calls Meiskomtot, and I will be there with you."

Bernadette turned to Sneyagflug. "Will you stay human and enjoy our hospitality at Drakespring Farm until it is time to go to the ambush site?" The tall man gave her a somewhat haunted look, then turned to meet the gazes of her husbands, each in turn. They were looking at him as the farmyard dogs might regard an intruding fox.

"Thank you, my dear," he said urbanely, "but I think I will return to dragon form for the time being. Just Call me when all is in readiness, and I will come. As I always will come, for you," he added. Even Erik glared at him, then. Nervy bastard!

Chapter 36: The Calm Before the Storm

After the two dragons had flown off, the five members of the Drakespring family and one shrouded dragon priest walked back to the house. "I don't think you should come on this trip, Mondi," Bernadette told her transformed son. He was essentially an adult, though a young and small one – but in his human form he looked so much like a vulnerable child that she could not bear the thought of putting him in danger. Besides, look what had happened to Gotteluub.

Of all her children, only Andi seemed grown-up and formidable enough to be fit for battle. She quailed at the thought of putting him in peril as well, but steeled herself. It was time to let her eldest seize his own destiny. "I'm all right with staying behind, Mama," Mondi assured her. "I can help Riki look after the younger kids." Though he was less than a year older than Sigi and younger than Riki, Edla, and Meri, he was older than any of them in his mental development.

When they had reached the house and gone inside, Erik asked "Are we going to take the aptrgangr to Osteon Rise immediately?" Afternoon was wearing on, and suppertime wasn't that far off. Whoever fast-travelled to deliver Wissagleb and his troops to the ambush site would be exhausted and starving by the time they got back.

Bernadette considered. "I think we'd better wait and go tomorrow morning after breakfast," she said.

"I want to come along on this trip, Mom," Andi said. "I should have it on my map so I can get there on my own or with reinforcements, if I need to."

"That's a good idea," his mother replied. "Probably Erik and Andrion should come along too. That way we'll all have it. Then maybe you can head right for Alfenstein from there, Andi, and bunk with the Baudin family while you're gathering up your reinforcements."

Riki wasn't exactly thrilled to learn that it had been decided she would be in charge of the farm and four youngsters while her parents, the Steadfast parents, Fjuri and Andi all went off to ambush the evil dragon priest. But she accepted the situation without complaint. They were knuckling down to their responsibilities, as she should do with hers. And at least hers weren't likely to get her killed or horribly maimed.

Mondi was eager to acquire all the skills of a human being, including enchanting and chemia. Before suppertime he and Bernadette looked over the chemia book Andi had brought back from Todenstor, studying the formula for the dragon-to-human transformation. Like the one both Bernadette and Andi had taken to enable them to become dragons, this one had a long list of exotic ingredients.

Bernadette had travelled widely around Agena in the years since her first ingredient-hunting expedition on Sneyagflug's back, and she thought she knew where to find most of these. But that would have to wait until after they had stopped Meiskomtot. It might well take weeks to gather all of the plant and animal reagents in quantities enough to provide the potion to Mondi's seventeen remaining dragon siblings – and Ehrgeizig as well. She suspected *he* might need a double-size dose of the stuff.

She guided her son through the preparation of some simple health potions, then gave him the formula for a poison that would drain your enemy's magical energy for a period of three minutes after being struck by a weapon it had been applied to. Mondi picked it up well, and made several bottles of the stuff.

This was fun for both of them, but Mondi happily set the chemia aside as suppertime approached. Erik was cooking tonight, and he had a joyful kitchen helper in his second-youngest son. The sheer delight the boy took in working with his newly-acquired hands was a kick to watch, and the rest of the family shared his pleasure. They were already getting used to him being a human boy, instead of an enormous scaly creature too big to fit inside the house.

After supper with the family Andi walked down to the Maiden for the second time on this seemingly endless day. What a lot had happened! He wondered about Sneyagflug and his seeming belief that Mom would just fall into his arms if only he could become human. They had spent nearly three months living together as a mated dragon pair back when Andi was little, and had seen each other a few times a year since then – yet he knew her so little?

He had never seen married people so deeply in love, and so committed to each other, as his parents were. Even the brotherly bond his papas shared was far stronger than any normal friendship. Well, he hoped for Mondi's sake that Sneyagflug would put that notion out of his mind. Either Erik or Andrion could break that guy in two, no matter how tall he was – and might not hesitate to do so, if he kept pressing his suit. Yet the man *was* his brother's biological father, and it would make Mondi very sad if violence erupted between him and his other fathers.

As he reached the Maiden and stepped up on the porch, Andi's concerns about Sneyagflug and his disruption of their family were swept away by anticipation of seeing the girl he loved. He spotted her almost as soon as he walked in, leaning against the bar and talking with her foster father Drelos. He was manning the bar and both Rezira and Sintra were on duty as wait staff while Larissa and others worked in the kitchen.

At the moment business at the Maiden was on the quiet side, with relatively few travelers staying here and the local dinner crowd already gone for the evening. There would be more coming in later, mostly for drinks and snacks, enjoying the convivial atmosphere with dancing, singing, and music. The Maiden's original inside bathing pool, where Andi's own parents had first met, was still a popular place for young singles to strike up acquaintances.

"Mind if I steal Zira from you for an hour or so?" Andi asked Drelos. Though the elf's appearance had not noticeably changed during Andi's lifetime, he had been friends with Erik and Andrion, and later Bernadette, since long before the boy had been born. He grinned sardonically and said "That'll be all right. But don't go too far. I'll need her when the late rush gets started."

"Thanks, Drelos," Rezira said as Andi took her by the hand and led her out the back doors to the Maiden's rear deck. Though she'd been living with the Elendions as part of their family for nearly a year, and had come to regard Sintra as a younger sister, she was old enough that she was never going to start thinking of Drelos and Larissa as "Father" and "Mother."

Rezira was still far short of the age of majority, which among her people was twenty-five; but in her own mind she was an adult.

She still thought about her parents sometimes, trapped now forever in their dypalfar paradise. She missed her younger brother, and wondered how Mother had weathered the storms that were sure to have descended on her after she had nearly lost the entire Great Army under her command – and failed to prevent the loss of all of Mrzhandtham's slaves.

Andi led her to a bench that lay against one of the deck rails, off in a dark corner behind the guardhouse. "Twice in one, day Andi!" Rezira said mischievously. "To what do I owe this great honor?" He drew her to him in a passionate embrace, locking his lips on hers as she melted into him.

After around a minute he broke away, panting slightly. "Gods, woman! Don't you think I would be with you every minute of the day if I didn't have so much else going on?"

She smiled at him to let him know she'd been teasing. It was not just him; both of them had many things to occupy their time. Even when she'd been working with his papa Andrion and the old leukalfar, Gylabris, on technological projects, he'd often as not been out of town working on what his family called "The Leukalfar Initiative." Well, maybe separation helped to keep her interest strong. From what Andi said, Andrion had often been away throughout the time he'd been married to Andi's mother – and those two seemed to still have the spark even after so many years together.

Andi had his hands on her shoulders now, and a serious expression on his handsome face. She loved those brown eyes of his, so warm and loving as he gazed into hers. "We came up with a war plan today," he told her. "A way we think we can trap old Meiskomtot and stop him once and for all. If it works, we'll kill off all of the undead dragons he's raised and stop him from ever raising another one. Then life can get back to normal." Her blue-violet eyes registered surprise and a little fear.

"Where are you going to fight him?" she asked, hoping it was not anywhere around here.

He grinned at her, sensing her concern. "Way over on the other side of the mountains, at a dragon altar called Osteon Rise," he assured her. "My parents and I are going there tomorrow with Wissagleb and his aptrgangr army, and they're going to get into hiding around the place. Then I'm going to Alfenstein and see if I can get some dypalfar mechs to join our forces. We should be able to get Kziintke at least, and maybe his 'girlfriend' can help too. We're getting Fjuri and his parents to join us, and since we can temporarily stop the undead with the magic-block spell you taught me, it should just be a matter of hacking up the dragon zombies once they hit the ground."

"So you're not fighting him right away?" Rezira asked, still looking worried.

"Not for another four days or so, not until we've assembled all our team," he said.

"And how are you going to bring dragons down without having them land on your head?" she asked. Her worry seemed to be growing deeper as her imagination painted all the things that could go wrong with their plan.

Andi seized her in his arms and kissed her some more, murmuring "Don't worry, Zira love. Everything's going to be all right." She clung to him, tears escaping from her closed eyes and moistening her cheeks.

"I can't bear to lose you," she murmured back. "Promise me you will think this all through in the time you have left and be very, very careful that you're safe."

They heard the bard starting his first song of the evening, the tinkling notes of the lute wafting out through the open rear doors. The night was warm, and the doors had been left open to catch the breeze off the river. "Come on," Andi said, grabbing Rezira by the hand and leading her back inside. "Let's dance!"

The Maiden had a continual parade of bards and musicians coming through, some who played limited engagements during a brief stopover and others who became regular employees of the inn and performed nightly for months. The current bard, a young sylvalfar graduate of the Academy in Sylvanian, was skilled with lute and flute, and favored lively tunes over soulful ballads.

"Play it, Gylffen!" Andi called cheerfully as he led his lady onto the dance floor. Gylffen grinned back and laid into the tune with a will, a fast and cheerful song of his own composition:

Dance, as the evening's falling,

Dance, for the spirit's calling,
Dance, send your feet a flying,
Dance, leave the ladies sighing,
Dance, round the circle spinning,
Dance, life is just beginning...

The song went on for many verses, with an instrumental break, and ended at last with *"Dance, though the dawn is breaking, Dance, though your feet are aching..."* Andi and Rezira had been joined on the dance floor by another young couple, and two unattached women who were not exactly dancing with each other but just leaping and pirouetting for joy, letting the music lift their souls. As the song ended they all stood panting for breath, eyes sparkling and cheeks glowing.

When Andi got back home, somewhat later than intended, he found his parents and Wissagleb arraying the silent army of aptrgangr in the area behind the house. "It's about time you got back," his mother said. "We thought it would be a good idea to get everyone in position and ready to leave first thing in the morning. They can spend the night out here standing in the yard as easily as down in that room in the basement, and this way we're not escorting aptrgangr up the front stairs in daylight."

"Ooh, I hadn't thought of that," Andi admitted. "Good idea. I assume we're leaving early, then?"

"Right," she replied. "I'll be giving you a pre-dawn wakeup call, we'll all grab some breakfast, and I hope be out of here before it gets light enough to see. I shudder to think what the reaction would be if anyone glances over and notices we have an army of walking corpses in our back yard."

Chapter 37: Details

Riki stood near the front door, watching as the entire enormous party of undead together with her parents and older brother shimmered and vanished. There was barely enough light to see them by. She'd been tasked not only with watching over the children and making sure the farm chores got done, but going into town later today and requesting that the Steadfast family join the forces that were massing at Osteon Rise for the ambush they all hoped would put an end to the undead dragon attacks once and for all.

Walking back inside the house, she sighed. She was very much looking forward to seeing Fjuri again. His forthright declaration, in front of Andi, that she was "his girl" had thrilled her to the core. But with everything that was going on, they'd barely had any time to spend together. She had known him her whole life, but both of them had become different people in the past couple of years. She really wanted to know that commandingly tall and powerful, incredibly handsome man who had claimed her for his own. Maybe when all this was over, there would be time for them to discover one another all over again.

At the moment, though, she'd already been up for hours and half wished she could go back to bed – but there was work to be done. There'd seemed no reason for the younger kids to get up at the crack of dawn, so she'd let them sleep. Later she'd have to feed them all breakfast and probably eat a little more herself, after the cows had been milked. Just in the last day Freydis had started giving more milk – which required more effort on Riki's part. At least she was as sedate and sweet as ever, even if she *did* look like a new cow.

Hours later, doors locked behind them, the young Drakesprings set off along the road to Waterdon. The party less resembled a mother hen leading her chicks than a sober young adventuress who had somehow attracted a herd of underage maniacs. Riki had decided to go with her leather armor and a few weapons, liking the way it made her look.

Meri had only been home for a few days after weeks away, and a lot of that time had been spent staying with the Steadfasts. Sigi, who'd been feeling a little lonely in the nursery, now had both his older sister and his dragon brother to play with – the latter human for the first time, and a huge novelty.

Though Mondi was a little old mentally to be playing childish games, and Meri too was maturing rapidly with all the responsibility that had fallen on her shoulders, for the moment they were young and gleeful. The serious situation that had sent their elders away didn't seem to bother them in the least. They were whooping and running about, playing a game of tag that sent them racing around their sister (struggling both to maintain her dignity and keep a grin off of her face) and covering three times the distance she did as they burned off some of their youthful energy.

Mondi had always been a happy kid, and now despite the threat from Meiskomtot he felt ecstatic. He could take to the air and fly whenever he felt like doing so, or enjoy the company of his beloved family members and other humans, inside their dwellings. And if it hadn't been for Meiskomtot and his attacks, Andi would never have discovered this! In the midst of a grave peril to every person in Iscandia, most especially some of his loved ones, he yet felt more joyful than he ever had before in his life.

They approached the guards at the gates of Waterdon with the usual banter. It was Rolf and Jurgen on duty again, but they were taken aback to see that the familiar Drakesprings were accompanied by an unfamiliar, rather odd-looking boy with bright red hair and tanned skin. Rolf swallowed as he took in Miss Riki in that skin-tight fitted leather armor. He often seemed to have nearly lost the power of speech when she showed up dressed like that. But this kid was another matter. "Who's your friend, Sigi?" he asked, assuming the boy must be with the youngest of the Drakespring clan.

"Rolf, don't you recognize me?" Mondi asked with a grin. This was such fun! "It's me, Mondi!" Rolf's city guard helmet hid his features, but his seeming paralysis suggested he was having a hard time processing that statement. The voice was familiar, but higher in register.

"Dragon Mondi? Drachmondien? You're human!" he finally got out, stating the obvious.

"It's a new spell I got, Rolf. Do you and Jurgen want to see me change back to dragon? I warn you, I'd have to get naked first…"

The four were admitted through the gates and all of them, Riki included, cracked up after they'd closed behind them. "Mondi, you are such an *imp!*" Riki exclaimed. "Bad boy!" He just smiled. The hour was now a bit past nine and Alessia was out working at her forge. She had Julia with her, training her in the technique for producing verdalfar armor. The stuff was valuable, though not to the taste of everyone. But learning how to make it was something every smith must do on the journey toward mastery.

Riki couldn't resist leading her siblings down to say hello. It had been a hoot blowing Rolf and Jurgen's minds with Mondi's transformation, and here they were in Waterdon with all sorts of people who had known him as a dragon and had yet to meet him as a human boy. They approached quietly, not wanting to disrupt the lesson. Julia looked up and smiled at her friend. "Hi Riki! Good to see you. Just let me finish this…"

In recent months Julia, who'd originally approached learning the trade of smithing as a punishment, had begun to get caught up in the joy of it as her skills improved. Riki knew that both her mom and Papa Erik got a lot of pleasure from smithing, making beautiful and useful items with their own hands. And their efforts formed a significant part of the Drakespring clan's income, as well. She hoped Julia would get into it more and take it up as a career, instead of just marrying some guy and raising children. She could see where raising children wasn't without its rewards, but eventually they grew up and got lives of their own – and then where were you, if that was all you'd ever done in life?

When Alessia and her daughter were free to take a break, Riki introduced her brother. Both women had been eyeing him surreptitiously. There *was* a family resemblance, though it was slight. "Alessia, Julia, I'm sure you remember my brother Drachmondien. He's been away for a few years but he's back living with us now." She drew blank stares. What?

"I've discovered how to take human form, just as Andi can become a dragon!" Mondi explained. "What do you think?" He turned from side to side as if demonstrating a new product.

Alessia had initially been a bit taken aback to be introduced to her friend and business partner Bernadette's dragon son. Julia had actually spent some time in his company over the early years before he'd become too large to live at Drakespring Farm, and she'd liked him. Her not-quite-pretty face broke into a big smile, and she swept him up (she overtopped him by several inches) in a hug. "Mondi! It's so good to meet you in this form! Haven't you always kind of wanted to be human?"

"I'll admit it," he said after she'd released him. "This is something I've always dreamed about. But I still like flying!"

They went next door and found Lifa and Edla at home. Bjorn was supervising a small construction project in the upper city, the remodeling of a house that had recently changed hands when its owner had died. Fjuri was working with them, Lifa said. She and her husband had decided to let their son have free rein, and as his quest with Andi was concluded he'd decided to rejoin the construction crew. It was a steady source of income for him, and something he was becoming good at. He wasn't sure he wanted the life of an adventurer, the life his big sister Anja had chosen. At least not at this point in his life. He wouldn't be seventeen for another couple of months.

After Lifa and Edla had gotten over the surprise of meeting Mondi in his human form, Riki broached the subject she'd been sent to relay: "That quest Fjuri went on with Andi? It was all part of our trying to stop this undead dragon priest Meiskomtot. He's been calling up dragon zombies all over Iscandia and siccing them on isolated human settlements, killing everyone and burning their houses. He killed one of my dragon brothers, Gotteluub. Did Fjuri tell you about Wissagleb?"

"Yes," Lifa said patiently. "Fjuri's told us about the whole situation. They came back with a small army of aptrgangr, right?"

"That's right," Riki said. "My folks and Wissagleb went with Andi to take the aptrgangr to Osteon Rise over east of the mountains this morning. They're mounting an ambush, and after we get all of our forces in position Mondi's father, Sneyagflug, is going to Call Meiskomtot. They think he won't be able to resist coming because he wants a better dead body to inhabit than the one he's got now."

"So, you want Fjuri to join this team to ambush the dragon priest?" Lifa asked. As long as Riki had known her, which was her entire life, Lifa had been a wife and mother – and somebody you did *not* want to cross. Supposedly she had been a warrior woman back before Mom had married her papas, and you could still sort of see that in her. Last year, she'd been part of the team that went searching for Andi and Fjuri when they'd vanished with Meri and gone through that dypalfar portal.

"Not just Fjuri," Riki told her. "We're hoping that you and Bjorn can come along, too." Lifa's eyes lit, then a frown crossed her face.

"I can't just leave Edla by herself," she said. Edla was twelve now, and Riki was pretty sure she'd have been capable of managing without supervision for the short time that this ambush was supposed to take. But that was beside the point.

"I'm looking after Meri, Mondi, and Sigi while the mission is going on," she said. "We can have Edla stay with us."

Lifa agreed, conditional on Bjorn being able to get some time off from his job. In Iscandia, the concept of an annual several weeks' paid vacation had not yet been invented – and as the sole breadwinner for his family, the doughty former warrior labored year in and year out. Riki and her troop left Brightsgate Cottage, heading for the construction site. It would be a couple of days before the Steadfasts would need to meet at Drakespring Farm.

The door of the house was standing open, and a trail of small debris told where its former walls had been broken up and carried away. Some of Hegmar's crew, moving around the front of the project, greeted Riki with friendliness. They'd seen the beautiful Drakespring lass hanging around construction sites many a time. Usually, though, she was accompanied by her cute friends – not a pack of kids including that odd-looking leukalfar girl. And that stripling boy with her was scarcely less odd-looking, with his curious coloring.

She barged right in through the front door, looking for her quarry, as the kids followed behind her. They looked around with interest, having rarely had the chance to see the builders' art in action. "Bjorn?" Riki called out.

"Yo!" came the muffled answer from down the hallway. The tall, broad man, now in his late 40s, poked his head out of a room to see who was calling him. He came down the hall, a questioning expression on his scarred face. "Riki? What brings *you* here? Everything all right?"

She smiled to reassure him. "Not exactly all right, but under control I hope. How would you feel about putting down your ruler and picking up a sword?"

Chapter 38: The Automatons

Andi found himself standing just inside the gates of Alfenstein as darkness surrounded him. From the lack of activity on the streets, he guessed that it must be hours before dawn. He and his parents, with Wissagleb and the aptrgangr, had arrived at Osteon Rise in early afternoon after leaving home at dawn. He hadn't stayed to see to the disposition of the troops, who with their undead commander were to remain in position, hidden, until the trap was sprung.

Instead, after checking that the place now showed on his map, he'd immediately left again. But Alfenstein was such a long, long, way away – almost all the way to the far western edge of the continent. Now it had been perhaps half an hour of subjective time since breakfast, and Andi felt as if his stomach was attempting to work its way up his throat and digest his head.

Fortunately he'd had the forethought to bring along plenty of water and rations with him. He grabbed a big slab of densely nutritious trail bread out of his pack and began gnawing it as he ascended the steps leading up to Eastview. This handsome residence, which had been in his family since before he was born, was kept by the Drakesprings as a sort of vacation home, a place where they could always stay whenever they happened to be in Alfenstein. He'd stayed with Georges and Diane instead when he was last here, enjoying spending time with a family – but Eastview would do well enough for him to get a few hours' rest before morning.

Andi's personal sense of time had been thoroughly disrupted, and he overslept. The morning was well advanced when he finally came to in one of the smaller beds the house (really more like a townhouse or apartment, as it was of a piece with the surrounding structures) offered. He awoke feeling both hungry and groggy, and dressed hastily. Then he had more trail bread for breakfast, wondering how long it was going to be before he had another *real* meal, and set off for Dypendwelve.

The guards recognized him, and in a couple of minutes Andi found himself walking in through the front doors of Miurlion's dypalfar museum. The place had gone from being a secret known only to a few, to one of Alfenstein's foremost attractions. Visitors to the Elven City would count their visit incomplete unless they had been able come here and spend a couple of hours, at least, looking at the amazing collection of dypalfar artifacts on display. His beloved, Rezira, had contributed more than a little to the knowledge those visitors would now have available.

As he stepped through the doors Andi flinched back as a small mech on multiple jointed legs ran up to him. It reminded him of Gylabris' first successful attempt to reprogram a dypalfar automaton, a bug the leukalfar tinkerer had called Insko. Had Gylabris activated another such, then? The little device, which barely came up to his knees, was constructed somewhat differently from Insko, however. There was a prominent swivel-mounted lens atop its dome-shaped head, with a blue light shining from within it.

As the mech stood there in front of him its lens scanned him, lingering on the face and then moving down his body. It paused for a few seconds, then a mechanical voice intoned, "Andreas Drakespring. Welcome back to the dypalfar museum. How may I guide you on this visit?" Andi was so flabbergasted he was unable to formulate a reply, as the little mech stood there patiently – evidently awaiting a response. To the best of his knowledge, no dypalfar bug had ever spoken, let alone recognized an individual and expressed a willingness to accept that person's commands.

Finally he stammered out, "Uh, I would like to speak with Gylabris." The little mech seemed to take a moment to process his request. Then the mechanical voice said "If you will follow me, I will lead you to Gylabris." It set off, its pointed dypalfar metal legs ticking on the stone floors, and led Andi in a circuitous route that eventually took him to the workshop where the museum's exhibits were prepared.

Along the way he was astounded to see that many of the museum's exhibits were now animate. For as long as Miurlion had been operating the museum the many examples of dypalfar technology had been as still as statues. But now they were moving around, speaking and being spoken to – what astonishing breakthrough had Gylabris and Kziintke made in the short time he'd been gone?

He found Gylabris at the workbench with Kziintke on one side and Jerzha on the other. "There," she was telling the little leukalfar in her mechanical but mellifluous voice, "Hold it still while I insert the cog." Andi held back, not wanting to interrupt them in the middle of a delicate operation. Jerzha bent over the back of a roller that was laid out horizontally on the bench, and inserted something too small for Andi to see into a panel in its front. "You can let go now," she told Gylabris in a moment, and he stepped back.

Jerzha did something else around that panel, then closed it with a click. Lights glowed. Then she commanded it in Common, "Execute program 37B." The Roller coiled itself up into its hemispheric base, assuming the form of a large dypalfar metal ball, and then rolled down off the workbench onto the floor as the three who'd been working on it stepped back out of the way. It hit the stones with a clang, but neither the floor nor the mech seemed to have been harmed by the impact.

The automaton kept rolling, and as Jerzha, Gylabris, and Kziintke turned to follow its progress toward the door they spotted Andi watching them open-mouthed. "Andi, you're back!" the leukalfar tinkerer said in Common. "Just here for a visit? Mothris and Umina are doing quite well in their work with the Elskhrazana."

"Elskhrazana?" Andi asked.

"The tribe who inhabit the depths below this keep," Gylabris explained. "We have already begun training volunteers in Common, and the plan is for their trade mission to be set up within one of the chambers of the museum. This place brings in a lot of traffic, and we think that the Alfensteinians will find it easier to accept leukalfar among them if they see and speak with them here first, before they start opening stalls in the marketplace."

The "beautiful people" tribe, Andi thought. Well, he supposed that leukalfar had their own standards of beauty – and certainly his near-brother Mothris had been captivated by Elsila. She was one of those forceful young women who, confident of the power she held over men, saw what she wanted – and took it. Come to think of it, that was sort of the way his relationship with Zira had started out. But it had deepened considerably in the last year.

"That sounds great, Gylabris! I'm glad things are going so well, though I hope we'll be able to break Mothris loose for other duties soon. But I'm afraid I'm not just here for a visit. Is there somewhere we can sit to talk?"

"Jerzha and I have no need to sit, Andi, and we have work to do. Perhaps you and Gylabris could go to the private quarters while we continue our projects?" Kziintke suggested in perfectly fluent but mechanical Common.

Andi considered. "Any chance of some real food?" he asked. It was probably closer to lunchtime than breakfast here, thanks to his failure to arise when he should have. Gylabris grinned at him.

"I'll have one of the rollers bring us a tray from the kitchens," he said. We can take it in my rooms." Though the little leukalfar was supposed to be part of the mission here to contact the leukalfar living below the city and bring them into contact with mainstream Iscandia society, he had been so entranced by the opportunity to tinker with dozens of intact dypalfar automatons – not to mention the discovery of Jerzha – that he'd left the diplomatic efforts to Mothris and Umina while he moved into the museum so he could spend all his time here.

A section of the museum hidden behind locked gates had been configured as living quarters. Miurlion had his own quarters on another level, but this small suite offered a bedroom and a living area with a dining table – though no cooking facilities. It would appear that since the last time Andi was here Gylabris and his cohorts (including Diane, Georges, and the two robons) had managed not only to activate some more of the mechs but to configure them as household servants.

They'd passed a roller on their way to the rooms, which recognized Gylabris and asked if it could assist him. The little leukalfar placed their lunch order, to be delivered to his rooms, and it whizzed off as Gylabris and his much-taller companion continued on their way. They sat at the table and Andi was offered a bottle of ale, which he was surprised to find was quite cold. "How did you get it cold, Gylabris?" he asked as he took a refreshing swig. At home they had a cold chest that required periodic doses of a frost spell to maintain a cold temperature.

The little leukalfar walked over to the medium-sized, dypalfar metal-clad box from which he'd gotten that ale and opened its lid, gesturing grandly as a cloud of fog arose from inside it. "It's something Jerzha put us onto," he explained with delight. Nothing thrilled him more than associating with people who were enthusiastic about technology. "It's driven by a robon power cell, which according to her obtains its power through a link to another plane of existence. She had not lost nearly as many memories as Kziintke had, and I think that she was intended as something more than a translator as well. You would not believe the things we've discovered just in the last couple of weeks!"

Andi was dazzled. "Wow," he said, "with that people all over Agena could keep their food from spoiling. It would do a lot to eliminate hunger." Gylabris nodded.

"And it's great for chilled beverages, too!" he pointed out with glee. "The issue is that we still don't know exactly how the dypalfar created the power cells, and I'm afraid Rezira wasn't able to help us there. Once the ones the dypalfar left behind are exhausted, there will be no more – unless someone re-invents the technology."

"Papa Andrion would be the one for that," Andi replied. He'd gotten sidetracked from his urgent mission by hunger, thirst, and his fascination with what Gylabris was engaged in here. "Maybe you and he, and possibly Zira, could form a team here or up at the Academy for a research project."

"I've enjoyed working with your father – and your lovely lass – in the past. I hope we might get the chance to do that. But I don't think that's why you're here...?"

Just then the roller appeared, entering nearly silently with a laden tray balanced on its metal arms. Those arms had been designed for combat, but this one seemed to have been modified with some additional fittings bolted on to improve its ability to carry burdens without dropping them. "Your lunch, Master," it said in a somewhat tinny mechanical voice, carefully setting the tray down on the table. On it were two plates, each laden with some kind of roasted meat, roasted potatoes with gravy, and an assortment of grilled vegetables.

"Thank you, Baledon," Gylabris said. "You may return to the main museum floor." In a moment it had glided away. Andi was transfixed by the sight and smell of the food on his plate, and it was a couple of minutes before his mouth was free for speaking again. After using a napkin that had come on the tray with the plates, he said at last, "By the gods, how have you gotten all these lesser mechs taking orders in Common – and talking back? I thought it was only robons of Kziintke's class that had the ability?"

Gylabris took another bite of his potatoes. The food here in Dypendwelve was quite different to what he'd become used to during his long life in Mrzhgradfendz, but he'd acquired a taste for it. "Jerzha again," he replied after swallowing. "It turns out that most of the mechs left behind required only minor alterations to restore them to the state they'd been designed for. The dypalfar had intentionally disabled their ability to interact verbally, as they had been programmed to attack anyone moving within the abandoned cities, and they didn't want them to be deactivated with spoken commands. They were sort of like a final 'screw you' to those they guessed would come down into their cities seeking them after their departure. Not a nice bunch of people…" He glanced up, realizing his faux pas. "Rezira excepted, of course! Delightful girl…"

Andi grinned at him around a bite of the savory meat… venison, he thought. Rezira herself would be the first to tell you her people had a lot of flaws. None of which resided within *her*, of course. "Amazing," he said when he'd swallowed. "I really regret that I haven't been able to be here for all these discoveries you're making. But a very serious situation has come up. Have you perhaps heard about attacks on human settlements by undead dragons?"

Gylabris' face twitched slightly, the leukalfar equivalent of a blink, and then he nodded. "Yes! Just yesterday Miurlion mentioned a report that some isolated farmstead in Westmarch had been attacked and burned. But no one killed, apparently?"

Just one person," Andi replied soberly, "my brother Gotteluub."

"One of the dragons?" the little leukalfar asked. He'd stayed with the Drakesprings at their home and knew all the human children. Andi nodded.

Despite his air that left you thinking Gylabris was not all there, he had a sharp and incisive mind. "This was not the only attack by undead dragons, then?" he asked, his jocularity dropping away to be replaced with seriousness.

"At least five that we know of, and I'm guessing a lot more," Andi said. "One of those old priests from the dragon worshipers, who was locked up in his tomb 6,000 years ago awaiting the return of Tarragin, missed his deadline. He came out of stasis in response to what I would guess was somebody in there looking for treasure, and then he went outside and discovered that Tarragin had already come and gone, that the dragon worshipers were not going to rule the world again, and that he personally had gotten gypped out of the immortality he'd been promised. He didn't take it very well."

Lacking eyes, the old leukalfar still somehow contrived to goggle at him. "That is very bad news indeed," he said. "So this undead priest is able to turn into a dragon, as you can?"

"An undead one," Andi confirmed. "And he's a necromancer, so he's able to find other dragons that were raised by Tarragin as live dragons and later killed again by somebody other than my mom." Andi had never killed a living dragon or a living human, and was just fine with that. His ties to both species were far too close.

Gylabris hesitated, his meal forgotten. "Because… your mother is fireblood, and if she killed them she would have absorbed their souls… preventing them from being reanimated?" Andi nodded again, impressed at Gylabris' knowledge. Clearly his interests went beyond dypalfar technology, and he actively sought to expand that knowledge. This attitude put him in the same camp with Papa Andrion, Ehrgeizig, Wissagleb, and to some extent, Mom and Andi himself.

"Bodies from which the souls have departed can still be animated using necromancy," Andi explained. "But they are just zombies, incapable of independent thought. You can tell them 'kill my enemies' and they will fight on your side until the spell is ended, or until the magic that animates them has been severed. Just like with a human, a killing blow will bring down a zombie. Or one of these undead dragons that still have their souls. Unfortunately a killing blow on a dragon isn't that easy, and they don't really take incremental damage like a live opponent would."

It was Gylabris' turn to be impressed. He had never been a warrior, indeed very few people of his tribe had taken up weapons against a foe in thousands of years – until last year. But he sensed that Andi spoke from experience. "So this is a growing problem, a crisis?" he asked.

Andi (who had somehow, as if by magic, caused all of the food on his plate to disappear while they'd been speaking) replied, "Yes. From what we've learned, this undead dragon priest Meiskomtot doesn't intend to stop. He's raising undead dragons all over Iscandia and sending them to cause as much damage as they can. But my parents have come up with a plan."

The cleaned plates had been returned to the tray and set to one side, ready for whichever mech next came here to take them away. After Andi had explained the battle plan, Gylabris said, "I think you need to speak with your friend Mothris. There have been some discoveries and developments down below, and I believe you can obtain the reinforcements you need. You'll need to bring Kziintke or Jerzha with you, of course…"

Chapter 39: Triangle

Riki put her feet up on the footstool with a sigh, looking out across the Brightwater to the mountains beyond. The view never failed to instill a sense of calm happiness in her, but in this instance it had a hard fight. Whuff, a whole day of riding herd on Sigi, Meri, and Mondi. Mondi was theoretically older than *she* was, mentally (or so it had been explained to her by Mom years ago) – but his transformation to human seemed to have regressed him or something.

He'd gotten completely tuned in to Sigi's level of fun, fun, fun – and keeping the two of them, along with Meri (who certainly might have been acting a bit more ladylike) under control was exhausting. Here she was only two years older, and *she* had to be the mature one, the responsible one, the one who was holding it all together.

At least her parents were back now. They'd returned late last night, Andi off to Alfenstein from Osteon Rise and not expected for another day or so. But it had been Riki that had had to get up early, cook breakfast, and settle the younger kids down before Mom, Erik, and Andrion got up. They'd evidently been map-lagged after the round trip from the ambush site and had decided to sleep late.

After that Riki had milked the cows. They really couldn't wait, no matter how tired you were. Letting a cow go without milking when she needed it would be as cruel as deliberately torturing a helpless animal with a hot poker, or something. You just didn't do that. But now, she had a chance for some blissful rest and contemplation. She was worried about Meiskomtot, worried about Fjuri and her family members who'd be joining the battle, worried about surviving what might prove to be another couple of days of minding the kids. The fact that she was but two years older than Meri and Edla did *not* help. It was as if she lacked the authority to order them around, though she'd certainly done her best.

She tried to shake off her funk. The new relationship with Fjuri held such promise, though now that it had actually been achieved she was beginning to realize that she wasn't sure where it was going to go. She was far too young to marry, and he was not much more than two years older. Besides, didn't she want to *do* something with her life before she settled down to marriage and babies? Mom certainly had. Riki wished she knew exactly what that was supposed to be. She didn't think she wanted to join cousin Anja as a tomb raider, though she enjoyed listening to the tales of her exciting adventures.

Annoyed with herself for bringing up still more unsettling questions, Riki made a conscious effort to relax – and spotted Alfmund swinging up the walk from the road. He looked cheerful and confident. Uh oh. She had really had some hopes that after their long talk the other day he would have just decided to give up, judging her background too strange for him to get mixed up in. She liked him a lot, and wished they could just be friends – but his ardent pursuit of her as a lady-love seemed to rule that out.

He spotted her, and cut across the front yard to climb the steps with a big grin lighting his face. "Riki!" he said, eyes glowing with delight at seeing her. "You look lovely! Mind if I join you?" Lovely? Her long red-gold hair was tied in a knot to keep it out of her way, she was wearing loose trousers and an old frayed blouse, and her farm boots were caked with mud and manure. It must be love. Riki gestured for him to sit beside her.

"I haven't seen you since our talk the other day," she remarked casually. He smiled.

"Sorry, I'd be here every day if I could. But the Brave Company doesn't pay me just to sit around Ynglingar and eat. I have some free time now, though, and I was hoping we could get in some arms practice and then have lunch. What do you say?" The stunned reaction he'd shown after their discussion seemed to have faded away to nothing.

Riki considered. Mom and Erik, if not Andrion as well, should be putting in an appearance soon. And a little practice swordplay would be fun and good exercise. But she was supposed to be letting Alfmund down, not leading him on – now that she and Fjuri were "together." Whatever that meant, for two teenage kids living with their parents.

"I'm kind of busy, Alfmund," she said. "In a few days my folks and Andi, along with Fjuri and his parents, are going to Osteon Rise to try to ambush and destroy that undead dragon priest that's been causing trouble all over Iscandia. And I'm going to have to be here taking care of everything and looking after four kids as well."

Alfmund pierced her with a questioning look. "*Four* kids?" he asked. Was she about to hit him with another chapter in the ongoing saga of how bizarre her family was, with another few extra siblings to back up the claim?

She ticked them off on her fingers, smiling slightly at him with an air of mischief. She had sensed his thought. "Sigi, Meri, Fjuri's little sister Edla Steadfast, and my brother Mondi."

"I thought your brother Mondi was a largish dragon and didn't live here anymore," Alfmund said with a wounded air.

"Oh, he is," she assured him. "When he wants to be. But when Fjuri and Andi came back from their trip to talk to that ancient dragon I mentioned, they brought with them the long-lost potion and dragon spells needed for a natural-born dragon to turn himself into a human being. So now Mondi's human. He's really enjoying it, and we love having him back home. He was more or less just one of the kids, living with us, until I was about eight years old."

Alfmund was having some trouble processing all this. Riki was an amazing, beautiful woman; but he was beginning to think he could do with just a bit less of the amazing part. "Are there any other family members you've omitted to mention?" he asked, with just a touch of asperity.

Her blue eyes lit as if she'd just remembered something. "Did I tell you about my six uncles who are giants?" she asked innocently. Then, seeing his expression, she broke into a grin and gave him a sisterly shove on the shoulder.

"No, you dolt!" she cried. "That's it. Mom, Erik, Andrion, Andi, me, Meri, Mondi, Sigi, Mondi's seventeen remaining dragon siblings, and that's it!" After another moment she added, "Oh. I forgot to mention Mondi's father Sneyagflug. He got turned into a human, too."

"Is he also married to your mom?" Alfmund asked nervously.

Riki laughed. "Far from it! When he had just learned how to become human he tried to get all lovey with Mom and Papa Andrion just about brained him! I think she cares for him as a friend, and they do have all those kids together – but maybe he thought they had something more." Get the hint, Alfmund, she said silently.

After digesting all this for a while, Alfmund seemed to shake off whatever was troubling him. His cheerful expression returned, and he said "Well, if you can't come up to Ynglingar, how about some weapons practice right here? It looks like you're set up for it." Riki relented. She really would like to have some fun, before the grim battle commenced. She jumped to her feet.

"Wait right there," she told Alfmund. "I'll just go get changed and fetch us some practice swords."

"Sure," he said, beaming at her as she left.

When Bernadette made her way toward the kitchen for a cup of tea, yawning after not enough sleep, she heard Meri and Sigi chattering in the nursery down the hall, and wondered where Mondi had gotten off to. As she put some water on the fire for a fresh pot, she heard clattering and shouts outside, and stuck her head out the door.

Riki, clad in her fitted leather armor, was leaping and dancing with wooden sword and an elven shield, practicing her swordplay with Alfmund. That was a bit of a surprise. She had gotten the idea that her daughter had something going on with Fjuri, a match she had secretly hoped for since the kids were little. What more perfect guy for her girl than the son of their longtime friends, binding the families together by marriage? On the other hand Riki was only fourteen, and though she might be madly in love with Fjuri this week she could well be on to someone else before long.

The two stopped their battle as she appeared, and Riki dipped her sword toward the ground, looking at her questioningly. "Have you seen Mondi?" Bernadette asked. Her daughter grinned, and gestured off beyond the house.

"He's weeding again," she said. She and Sigi were both delighted at their newly-human brother's interest in performing such chores.

"Thanks. I'll leave you to it, then," Bernadette said and returned inside the house.

The two young warriors went back to their practice bout. Alfmund had a lot more weight and upper body strength, and some reach on her as well. But Riki was both tall and strong for a girl, and lightning quick. She wasn't as overmatched as all that. They'd only been at it for another five minutes, though, when Fjuri came walking up from the road.

He'd been given the morning off from the construction crew, and had made the excuse of wanting to discuss logistics for the forthcoming ambush with the Drakesprings. After all, he and his parents had been drafted onto the strike force without having participated in the war council. They needed to know all the details, what equipment to bring, and when to arrive. So it was a valid excuse, but an excuse nonetheless. Fjuri just wanted to spend some time with Riki.

She watched his handsome face cloud up as he approached and saw her with Alfmund, the deep blue eyes getting darker and the wing-like black brows lowered. She'd told him that she didn't feel about Alfmund as she did about him, but she hadn't said she was never going to see the young Brave Company member again. Yet clearly he had assumed that was the case. Oh, things were just getting too complicated!

Riki sheathed her practice sword and came toward him, saying "Fjuri! What a surprise! Alfmund and I were just doing some sword practice. Do you want to join in?" He seized her fiercely and drew her in for a deep kiss, which Alfmund witnessed with a sinking heart.

As Fjuri released her, he looked up at Alfmund and grinned. "Sure," he said. "Why not?"

Fjuri was dressed in town clothes, not armor, but they were able to cobble up some protection for him out of the spares stashed in the forge building. He had his own practice sword that he kept here, as there was no space available around his home for such activities. It was a match in weight, balance, and length to the daimonic longsword Bernadette had gifted him with for his sixteenth birthday last year.

The two tall young Norsemen stood sizing each other up, waiting for the bout to begin. Though he was beginning to sense what way the wind was blowing with Fjuri and Riki, and he didn't like it at all, Alfmund's inborn friendliness and cheerful good nature reasserted itself and he asked, "Been practicing long?" The grin Fjuri gave him in return had little of cheer or friendliness to it.

"Let's see," he said, as he got into his stance. "I'll be seventeen in a couple of months and I've been practicing with swords since I was four. So what's that, thirteen years?"

Alfmund's eyes widened. He hadn't been allowed to put a hand on a sword of any kind until his tenth birthday, yet had thought himself something of an expert. "Uh, ever killed anyone?" he had to ask next. Fjuri's nasty grin widened.

"Just a walrus and the odd troll, and some aptrgangr," he said casually. "Oh, and there was that one dypalfar guard I broke into a thousand pieces after Andi froze him with a dragon spell…" At the time he'd been utterly horrified and had puked his guts out, but now it made a good story.

"Well, let's get started then," Alfmund said. He had a sinking feeling, which soon proved to be justified. In under a minute Fjuri's highly skilled and powerful two-handed attack had whacked him hard twice and then sent his own wooden sword flying. Riki was watching this with mixed feelings. She loved Fjuri, and thought his strength and skill with the blade were thrilling. But at the same time she liked Alfmund and didn't enjoy seeing him getting his tail kicked all over the farmyard. From what she'd seen of swordsmanship he wasn't too bad – just overmatched.

"I think you need more of a challenge, Fjuri," she called. "Come on and fight us both!" Alfmund was buoyed by her support. For some time he'd been getting the feeling that though she hadn't turned away his advances he hadn't exactly been sweeping her off her feet. Then when this enormous… boy, he wanted to think, but since the "kid" was bigger and taller than him and less than two years younger, that didn't seem appropriate… When *Fjuri* had walked up and kissed Riki like that, and she'd melted into his embrace, he'd realized for the first time that he had a serious rival. But wasn't he a family friend, somebody who should have been like a brother to her? Whatever was going on here, Alfmund appreciated that she had come to his side and had her sword out, facing off their adversary.

Fjuri's eyes sparkled. This was part of what he loved about Riki. It wasn't just that she was beautiful, she had an inner fire and strength that was not often unleashed. He wanted to fight at her side, as his parents had not ever done together – though they were about to, and soon! But in the meantime he'd settle for sparring against her and this "boyfriend" of hers. He could even spare a moment of pity for Alfmund, now that he had defeated him at arms as well as in the quest for Riki's affections. The young Norseman wasn't such a bad guy, really. His grin was genuine this time, as he lowered his sword and went on the attack.

Fighting two opponents at once was very different from one-on-one, and not something that Fjuri had ever had much chance to do before. The Drakesprings all practiced at arms for sport and exercise, not because they had any desperate need to be good at fighting, and most of the training he'd gotten in his life had been here. So Riki and Alfmund combined, darting in from either side, provided him with more of a workout than he'd expected. Hey, this was fun! He realized that swordplay had gotten stagnant for him, almost always with Andi as an opponent. The two had trained together since childhood, but Fjuri's superior size and strength had begun to tell. If he wanted to keep doing this, he needed more challenges.

It was a hard and furious fight, and before it was over both Alfmund and Riki had gotten in touches. Neither would have been fatal had they been using real swords, though, and the bout continued. Eventually he succeeded in disarming Alfmund, then whirling and tripping up Riki as she lunged in to stab him from behind. As she fell to the ground his wooden sword point went to her breast in a symbolic touch. Then he threw the sword aside, gave her a hand up and kissed her briefly but passionately.

Riki was glowing, eyes alight, red-gold hair popping out of her braid to form a halo around her face. "Whoo!" she said, gasping for breath. "That was *fun*! Anybody besides me hungry?" They hung up their practice swords and went inside, to find Riki's parents gathered at the dining table having a meal that might have been breakfast or lunch. Noon was approaching, and after all the exercise she'd gotten Riki was quite ready to eat. "Mom, can we feed Alfmund and Fjuri?" she asked.

Bernadette gave her a fond smile and said, "The makings are still out on the counter. Help yourselves."

After lunch Fjuri broached the subject of the ambush, and details were hammered out. The Steadfast contingent should all be armed with the biggest, sharpest swords they could handle, as it was expected that they would mostly be kept busy disabling undead dragons that would be felled by magic-block spells cast by Andrion or his son. As soon as any of these dragon aptrgangr expired, either Bernadette or Andi would be absorbing their souls and they'd be out of commission permanently, nothing but bare bones.

Bernadette and Erik warned Fjuri that they'd all need to keep a sharp eye out above, as they expected an unknown number of undead dragons in additional to their master. All of them could breathe fire, and when they fell out of the sky it was not going to be a good idea to be standing underneath them. "We'd better all have pretty good armor, then," Fjuri said.

Bernadette and Erik eyed each other. "Do you think you could get your parents down here for a fitting?" Bernadette asked. "I'm guessing they may not have had a new set of armor in a long time, and that steel stuff Lifa had last year is okay but some dypalfar plate might be better." "I'll see if I can get them here later today," Fjuri promised.

"Oh, why don't you all come for dinner?" she said. "I can take measurements and then we'll all go eat at the Maiden, and tomorrow Erik and I can get the armor made. From the look of you, you can handle dypalfar plate too. And I can get your measurements right now, before you go home." "Yeah," Fjuri said, "I wore some last year while we were sneaking around in that dypalfar city. It's heavier than I'm used to, but not that bad."

Alfmund had stayed and was taking this all in. Finally he spoke. "Mistress Drakespring? I'd like to join your forces when you go to ambush the dragon priest." Bernadette looked him over. She liked the boy, and if he'd failed to capture her daughter's heart he hadn't committed any offenses like treating her unkindly or trying to get into her pants. And he certainly appeared to be a likely lad.

"If you want, Alfmund, you are welcome to join us. We plan to leave for Osteon Rise in the morning day after tomorrow. We'll be gathering our forces then, and traveling by magic map. You already heard what you'll be expected to do when we get there, so dress and arm yourself appropriately. That steel plate armor you're wearing should be fine."

Alfmund sensed he had just been dismissed. Unlike his rival for Riki's affections, he was not the son of the family's long-time friends. But this fight against the undead dragon priest seemed like an important one, a worthy cause – and maybe, his valor in helping to defeat that menace to Iscandia would make Riki see him as a worthy suitor. He certainly couldn't shirk the task if Fjuri was going to be there. He approached Riki, who was relaxing at the table, and squeezed her hands. "See you in a couple of days," he said, and she smiled and said "Thanks, Alfmund. We appreciate your help." Well *that* was all right, though a kiss would have been nice.

Chapter 40: Drumroll

Bernadette and Erik were working in the forge creating dypalfar plate armor for Lifa, Bjorn, and Fjuri. They hadn't often done this as a team, in the years since Erik had built this forge with his own hands – with some help from Andrion and Bjorn. Usually one or the other of them would be working here, as the space wasn't all that big. But they were enjoying this time together.

"At this rate," Bernadette said as she worked on a breastplate, "Fjuri will be able to swap with Bjorn in another year. At least, if he keeps up with the construction work."

"Hells, he'll be able to swap with *me* if he keeps up the construction work," Erik replied. He stood six feet, five inches tall, and now in his early forties had maintained a muscular two hundred-fifty pounds. "That boy is destined to be a titan."

"Oh!" Bernadette said suddenly, as she flipped the breastplate over to hammer it out on the other side, "I completely forgot about Andi! Shouldn't he have something heavier than his elven plate?"

"Is what he's wearing enchanted?" Erik responded.

"No," she replied, "I hadn't been sure what if anything it needed."

She had never enchanted either Andi's or Fjuri's armor over the many sets she'd made them as they were growing up. But at their age, they might be close to completing their growth. Perhaps it was time to start adding some enchantments. The largest size magical essence vials filled with the souls of non-sentient creatures the size of mammoths were not easy to come by, and it hadn't been worth the expense when today's armor would be melted down and remade in another few months.

"Then why don't you just enchant the armor he's got now with some more protection?" Erik suggested, tapping lightly as he formed a set of bracers.

"Good idea, love," his wife replied. "That'll take a lot less time than making new armor." They'd be busy most of today with what they were working on now. Erik happened to be glancing down toward the road when he saw a familiar shimmer in the air. Someone was coming in by map, and surely it could only be…

"Andi!" he cried, downing his tools and making for the path down toward the road. Bernadette did the same and followed him. As they joined their son, they were both a bit surprised and disappointed to see he was alone. Where were the hoped-for reinforcements?

After he'd been embraced and kissed by his parents, the questions began. "You're here alone?" his mom asked, giving him a lead to explain why. He grinned.

"Help is coming," he promised, "and Mothris is bringing it here just as soon as they can make a few modifications. Hey, I'm starving! What is there to eat?" Andi never managed to fast-travel for more than a couple of hours' worth of time offset without developing a powerful appetite – and Alfenstein was a long way off.

"We'd probably better get back to work," Bernadette told her son, "but there's plenty of food in the kitchen. Help yourself, and don't forget to check in with Andrion and the rest of the family. Later today we can all get the details."

"Thanks, Mom!" Andi replied, moving toward the house.

The house was a hive of activity, and it wasn't until dinnertime that they were finally able to sit down together and discuss what each of them had been doing. "I gave Mondi some archery lessons today," Sigi said proudly. His brother smiled appreciatively at him.

"It's harder than it looks," he admitted.

"That's just one of the reasons you're going to stay here and help Riki with the other kids," Bernadette said. Mondi looked a little crestfallen. He wanted revenge against the undead dragon priest for the death of his brother. But he knew he didn't stand a chance against even the smaller undead dragons, let alone a magic-proof monstrosity with spellcraft at his command.

"I've been trying to find out what works and what doesn't on the undead," Andrion said. "And doing some work with necromancy. It's not my favorite subject, but I was able to practice on a dead chicken, then revive it. The spell Meiskomtot is using is one that apparently only works on sentient beings, since it gives the reanimated corpse the ability to use its own mind and make its own decisions within the constraints of its master's commands. We ought to have held onto one of Wissagleb's upper level aptrgangr for some experiments, but I didn't think of it."

"But anything that works on a zombie chicken might work on an undead dragon," Andi said, "Right?"

"I think so," his father replied. "The magic-block spell definitely severs the animating magic for a period of time. Paralysis, and spells like health drain or stamina drain, don't work. But the physical damage caused by battle spells using fire and lightning work as well on the undead as they do on anything else – like a steel plate or the side of a barn. Oh, and spells or potions that drain magical energy can weaken the animating force or knock it completely out, if they're strong enough."

"What about Rain of Death?" Andi asked. This particularly deadly battle spell, the dragon-spell version of which the late Tarragin had used against his parents when they'd fought him before Andi was born, was one Andrion had rediscovered and taught to his battle students at the Academy.

"I'm sure it would work fine on the dragons," Andrion replied, "would probably work on Meiskomtot even – since it's a physical object hitting him rather than a direct magical attack. But don't forget we're going to be standing on the ground below the dragons, and anything coming out of the sky is as likely to hit us as it is to hit them."

"Good point," his son murmured.

"I crafted up some health and stamina potions to bring along," Andi contributed. "And some anti-magic poisons, though I'm betting Mom could make some stronger ones."

"Good idea, Andi," she said. "I'll do that this evening. We're supposed to be marshalling our forces and leaving in the morning, then calling Ehrgeizig and Sneyagflug after everyone's assembled. But where are Mothris and those reinforcements you mentioned?"

"I thought they would be here by now," Andi admitted. "I'm not sure what's keeping them. Kziintke said that he would definitely come along, but you would not *believe* what they've been doing out there with all those mechs in the dypalfar museum. It's seems that female translator mech he reactivated when I was there a few weeks ago is *not* just a translator. She was sort of like the principal assistant to one of the dypalfar artisans, and her memory is packed with technical information about her fellow mechs. She has turned out to have way more knowledge about such things than Zira does. They have half the mechs in the place running around talking to people and taking orders in Common, and more getting activated every day."

"Wow," Andrion said. He'd happily have gone to Alfenstein and spent his time making dypalfar discoveries with old Gylabris, if he didn't have so much else on his plate. "So Mothris is bringing us some of these mechs?"

"I thought it would be hard for me to break him loose from what he's doing with the newly-contacted leukalfar tribe beneath the city," Andi said. "But he was pretty excited when I explained to him what we need."

He went on. "Part of our deal with the leukalfar, of course, since we couldn't just hand the city over to them, was that they have exclusive rights to the lower city and its contents. That means they own the mechs, including Jerzha. But they've agreed to lease her to Gylabris long-term, and he will share in the proceeds from any of the mechs that they activate and sell or rent out. The mechs that come with Mothris, Kziintke aside, will be on loan to us just for the ambush and then they're supposed to go back home. And I think they'll probably expect something in trade. But Mothris promised he'd get us some useful ones. They're going to refit them for battle against flying monsters."

There was a moment of silence at the table, as people chewed their food. Then Bernadette said, "Well, I certainly hope they get here soon! I don't much like the idea of going into battle with troops that show up five minutes before the first shot is fired."

"It's too bad they can't just go straight to Osteon Rise," Andi replied, "but here is the closest Mothris could bring them with his map."

"Is Mothris planning to join us at the ambush?" Erik asked, looking a little concerned. Andy smiled wryly.

"I don't think so," he said. "Mothris is more of a lover than a fighter. Just ask Elsila."

That evening Andi went down to the Maiden again, and once again stole Rezira away from her duties as a server. He was glad that his family, while owners of the inn, didn't work the business themselves. He'd done his share of heavy farm chores before Riki got big and strong enough to take them over, but here he'd probably be stuck washing pots and tending bar until he was in his twenties unless he managed to come up with a career move that would let him escape.

Rezira seemed to be under a cloud. When he got her alone in a dark corner she kissed him passionately, then just stood gazing up at him in the dim light as if trying to memorize his face. "What's the matter, Zira?" he asked softly. Here he was going into a fight that might well see him or somebody he loved killed or severely injured, yet it didn't seem to bother him as much as it did her. Being sixteen and therefore immortal, Andi looked on the forthcoming battle as more of a grand adventure than something to be worried about.

She stood on tiptoe and kissed him again. "I don't like you going off to fight Maker knows how many undead dragons," she told him. "I wish you had the Joining, so we could always stay in touch when we're apart. The worry is driving me crazy!" He squeezed her tight.

"Mom's enchanted my armor with resistance to fire and enhancement of health, stamina, and magical energy regeneration," he told her, speaking into the top of her head. She was nearly a foot shorter than him. "I'll be very nearly immune to all harm, so there's nothing to worry about."

"I don't care," she said, a tear leaking out of one violet eye and running down her smooth, pale cheek. "I want to spend more time with you before you go, but I have to work tonight. Can I come down to your house after midnight?" He looked at her in surprise.

"I don't know," he told her. "Mothris is late bringing the mechs that are supposed to be part of our forces. And if he's there when I get back, we might be kind of busy getting them set up and ready to go. We're supposed to be gathering early tomorrow with the rest of our fighters, to go to the ambush site, and that probably means an early bedtime." Tears forgotten, she gave him a look that sent a thrill through him. "That's all right," she said, eyes luminous. "Leave the basement door unlocked, will you?"

Mothris had not come, and though everyone was getting concerned they had hopes he would arrive in the night. It was a long trip from Alfenstein, after all. And meanwhile, they all needed a good night's rest. When Bernadette, Andrion, and Erik turned in, after Meri, Sigi, and Mondi had gone to bed, Andi and Riki locked the front door behind them as they headed down the stairs to the basement and their own rooms.

Where he'd been relaxed before, Andi now found himself nearly vibrating with tension. He waited until there were no sounds from across the hall, then crept back to the basement door and unlocked it. Though they had excellent locks on Drakespring House, the reputation of its inhabitants was such that they'd never been troubled by burglars.

Midnight was still more than an hour away, and dawn (when, he had no doubt, Mom would be rattling his door and telling him to get up) only a few hours after that. Andi decided he'd better try to get some sleep, so he undressed and got into bed. He left a lone candle burning on the nightstand beside the other single bed in the room.

The soft click of the door closing woke him, and Andi opened bleary eyes to see a small, cloaked and hooded figure before him, dimly visible in the last rays of the guttering candle. "Ssshh," she said softly, and came over to sit on the bed. He sat up to pull the hood down and look into her face, what little he could see of it in the dim light.

"You came," he breathed in wonder. She was so beautiful!

"Are you wearing your amulet?" Rezira asked. Andi's heart began pounding. Though he'd had it for months without any reason to need it, he'd been wearing it day and night since Mom had given it to him and told him what it was for. He usually kept it hidden away, tucked down inside his clothing.

"Yes," he murmured. "I… you…" he sputtered to a halt, not sure how to articulate his feelings. His body was already on full alert and aching for her.

She gave him a sweet, satisfied little smile. She might be as virgin as he, but she sensed that she had complete control of the situation. "I want to be with you, Andi," she said simply. "Completely, because I love you. And this might be our only chance."

"If that's what you want, Zira, I want it too. I've wanted you since the moment I first saw you, but I… we… I didn't think it was the right time."

"The time is now," she pronounced, rising to her feet. She took off her hooded cloak, dropping it to the floor. She wasn't wearing anything underneath it.

Chapter 41: Marshaling the Forces

Hours later Andi and Rezira were sleeping, wrapped tightly together in his narrow bed. The first time had been a little bit painful, embarrassingly awkward, and far too brief. By the third time, they both felt like they were getting the hang of it. A rap came at the door, and Bernadette's muffled voice could be heard calling "Andi! Up and at 'em! Breakfast is on the table."

They had both awakened. Andi gave Rezira a squeeze then slipped out of bed and, by feel, applied his fire spell to a fresh candle. They didn't keep the ever-burning dypalfar lamps in the bedrooms, and these basement rooms had no windows. That was better! In a trice he was back in bed and wrapped in the warm, smooth arms of his beloved.

Oh, Zira! Mom may have mentioned something once about how making love could add a whole new dimension to your relationship, but he'd paid it no attention at the time. Now that he knew this wonderful joy, he wanted to stay right here in bed with this unbelievably sweet, beautiful girl and practice until he got it perfect. Except – he needed to put on his armor and eat breakfast, because he had to go fight undead dragons today. It just didn't seem fair!

Rezira squeezed up a little closer to him and ran her hand down his chest as she gazed into his eyes. She, too, was utterly intoxicated with the experience of making love with someone she had already adored for ages. "I never dreamed it could be like this!" she said softly. "Dypalfar people are kind of constrained about it. I mean, they still do it… just look at my mom, with two kids! But they don't display affection in public and they don't ever talk about lovemaking."

"Norsemen aren't that much different," he assured her. "The goings-on at the Maiden might give you the wrong idea about Iscandia people. Our inn is considered something of a den of iniquity by the more upright matrons of Waterdon."

She giggled into his chest. "True!" she said. "When I've been up in town and mentioned that I work there, I've gotten some dirty looks. And the other kind of look from some of the young adventurers. I assume they mistook me for a hospitality specialist."

He kissed her hair. "I hope you'll only be providing 'hospitality' to me," he said seriously.

She gave him a shocked look. Did he think she was going to hop into bed with just anyone? He grinned at her reaction. "I would really like to make love with you again before getting out of bed," he sighed.

"I can tell!" she interjected mischievously, her hand dipping lower.

"But Mom is going to be down here again soon if I don't show up for breakfast, so I think we'd better get moving," he concluded.

She stuck out her lower lip, and rolled over on top of him. Oof! Then she continued on her way out of the bed and picked up her cloak, slipping into the light shoes she'd worn on the walk over here. Andi hopped out of bed, his readiness evident, and she stood watching with a mixture of amusement and regret as he squeezed into some underwear and then the newly-enchanted armor that was supposed to make him invincible on the battlefield. She sighed. Now that they had taken their love to the next step, she was *less* willing to let him go into danger, not more.

"Are you going to sneak back down to the Maiden?" Andi asked her. Rezira gave him a Look.

"Why should I sneak anywhere?" she replied. "I'm a grown woman, and your mom didn't give you that amulet just because you look so cute in jewelry. She was expecting that you and I would get together before too long, and that suggests that she approves. From what I've heard, she and your papas were having a lot of fun together before *they* got married."

Andi smiled and kissed her. "You're right, as usual," he said sweetly. "Let's go eat."

Lifa, Bjorn, and Fjuri had arrived, well laden with supplies, and had been fitted with their new dypalfar armor. They looked like a trio of dypalfar robons, one considerably shorter than the other two. There seemed to be no difference in height between Bjorn and his son, though Fjuri was not yet as wide. All three of them were armed with long, heavy, razor-sharp blades – the ideal weapon for the butcher-work they expected to be doing today.

Alfmund had come too, attired in his gleaming steel plate and wielding a verdalfar longsword. The ugly-looking blade should serve well, and he seemed fired-up and determined to outdo anybody else on the field of battle. Riki, watching the proceedings with a certain amount of anxiety, shook her head as she saw him and Fjuri posturing at each other. Men!

Bernadette had greeted Rezira cheerfully at the breakfast table. Now that she knew Andi's dragon transformations would likely grant him a lifespan the equal of any elf's, her reservations about their relationship had evaporated. The girl was smart, beautiful, and accomplished in many areas. If she turned out to be The One for her son, that was fine with her. But she was a little taken aback when, after eating her serving of eggs, sausage, bread, and fruit, Rezira had asked if she had any armor that might fit her.

"Armor, Rezira? What for?" she asked. Andi was looking at his lover with apprehension. "I want to come along on the ambush, of course," the dypalfar girl replied calmly. "You don't know how many undead dragons there will be, and I'm as good or better at the magic-block spell than Andi or your husband is. I have lots of other battle spells as well, plus I can heal anybody who gets hurt. And I'm pretty good with a bow…"

All young citizens of Mrzhandtham had trained with weapons, eventually being called on for service in the Great Army in their late teens and early twenties. Rezira wondered what they were doing now, as the Army's main function had been to make an impression at the annual Games and keep the slaves down. With no more slaves, perhaps they'd been put to other jobs. Or, horrible thought, used to attack another city and steal some of *their* slaves. The work they'd done last year had freed thousands of leukalfar, but many thousands more still lived in bondage in the now-inaccessible dypalfar "paradise."

Andi had turned white. "Rezira, no! It's too dangerous!" She turned hotly to him.

"If it's not too dangerous for you, why is it too dangerous for me?" He was now beginning to understand the wrenching anxiety that she had been feeling since he announced that he was going into battle.

"I'm a skilled warrior," he protested. "And… I'm a man." *That* set her off.

"Like your mother? Or Lifa?"

"But they've been warriors in the past, Zira! You never fought in any battles…"

Tears were glinting in her eyes now. "I may not have fought in any battles, but I have the skills, Andi! I'm nearly as good a mage as you are, and I'm stronger than I look. I need to be there with you, fighting at your side – not sitting here biting my nails down to the elbows worrying about whether I'll ever see you again! Can't you understand?"

Andi looked stricken, but he straightened and a look of resolve came over his features. He stepped nearer and hugged her carefully – since he was in armor and she was wearing nothing but a cloak. "*Do we have some armor that will fit, Mom?*" he asked. Bernadette, her face a study as emotions passed over it one after another, nodded.

With a grim smile, she said "Come back to the craft room with me, Rezira, and let's see what we can do for you."

Now it was hours later and the party was nearly ready to leave. But where was Mothris? They were all milling around in the yard in the area just east of the veranda, when at last there came a shimmering and suddenly the rays of the morning sun were glaring blindingly off an array of polished dypalfar metal in the road. A *big* array.

Andi and his parents all hurried down to the road. "Mothris! What took you so long?" Andi demanded. He'd thought when they'd parted that his friend would be following by only a few hours.

Mothris, looking tired, said "We had some trouble with the refitting, and had to fabricate parts. But I think you'll really appreciate having these guys." He looked around. "Who's going to be in command? I need to pass their command to somebody."

Everyone looked at Bernadette. "All right," she said – not entirely displeased. "I guess it's me. Can I designate a successor in case I'm knocked out?" Her being knocked out during their rescue effort last year had led to the entire Great Army of Mrzhandtham coming through the portal after their escaping slaves, and nearly to disaster.

Mothris nodded. "Sure, you can even specify a chain of succession, if you want. They're pretty bright."

Bernadette gazed up at the three dypalfar mechs the leukalfar boy had brought with him. One of them was Kziintke, an old friend. In place of the general-purpose appendages he usually wore on his arms, the seven-foot robon was now sporting something that looked like twin longsword blades with a gap between them on each side. He returned her gaze and saluted with a slight clang.

"You need their names, too," Mothris explained. "Kziintke you know. The tall one is Dengaal, and the shorter one is Saarok." He turned to each of the mechs in turn, and pronounced a formula starting with its name, then "This is Bernadette. I transfer my authority to her. You will obey her commands until they are superseded." In her turn, Bernadette introduced them to her family members. Using the same formula starting with the mech's name, she said "If I should fall and be unable to issue commands, you will continue doing as commanded previously. But you will then obey commands from Andrion. If he is not available, obey commands from Erik. And if all three of us are not available, obey commands from Andi."

Each of the mechs acknowledged the commands they'd been given, in voices that ranged in pitch from deep to basso. They all spoke flawless Common with the same mechanical intonation, though. Amazing. Mothris grinned, a look of relief on his face now he'd completed his mission. "Is there anything to eat?" he asked hopefully. "I'm starved!"

"Go ask Riki," Bernadette said, "I'm sure she can whip something up for you. Are you staying long?"

"I thought I'd wait until you get back, maybe help Riki with the kids," the youth replied. Riki, hearing this, came over and gave Mothris a hug.

"Thank you, brother!" she said. There was a round of goodbyes as the younger Drakespring children and Edla said farewell to their parents. They were all young enough to assume that nothing could possibly defeat Mom and Dad(s), so instead of being worried they were looking forward to their time under the supervision of Riki as a chance to cut loose and have some fun.

Fjuri and Alfmund were in conflict again as they both made to bid Riki farewell, and to stave off any bad feelings she gave each of them a squeeze of the hand and a kiss on the cheek. But the look in her eyes as she saw Fjuri off should have banished any doubt.

As the party of human warriors filed down to the road to join forces with the automatons, Riki was saying to Mothris, "I'd like you to meet my brother Mondi again. He's changed a bit since the last time you saw him…"

"All right everyone," Bernadette said as her "troops" milled around her and she pulled out her map. "Here we go."

Chapter 42: Osteon Rise

The party found themselves clustered near the summit of the broad, unpaved path that led up from the flatlands below. Osteon Rise was a sort of natural arena, or perhaps it had been smoothed and carved by the ancient Norsemen. It was one of the relatively few outdoor Spell Walls, where dragons who had not taken the Reciprocation could learn dragon spells.

Tall stone pillars with stylized dragon heads carved on them flanked the path, and the area was littered with the bones of mammoths and other creatures – including some of men and of dragons. Bernadette herself had killed a dragon here and taken its soul, in the months following the death of Tarragin when she'd been questing for fun and profit.

The area was deserted. As the number of hostile dragons had declined, choice roosts like this one were going unclaimed more and more often. The dozens of aptrgangr troops, under the command of Wissagleb, had been arrayed around the edges of the flat space – among the rocks, hidden under the bones, lying down as if dead. They would arise when their enemies appeared on the scene.

The undead dragon priest himself stood beside the Spell Wall awaiting them. He became alert as they approached, stunned at the sight of the automatons walking among them. "All is well?" Bernadette asked him briefly.

"There has been no sign of anything living atop this rise since we arrived," Wissagleb assured her.

Bernadette considered the sun. From its height, they were well into the afternoon. They needed to get started now, though she doubted the battle would be a long one. She was still not sure whether they would be able to defeat Meiskomtot. But at the very least they should be able to permanently destroy most of his cadre of dragon zombies, and that would put a halt to the destruction – for a while.

"We'd better get to it, then," she said briskly and Called "EHR-GEI-ZIG!" followed a moment later by "SNE-YAG-FLUG!" In less than two minutes the great red dragon and the silver had arrived, Ehrgeizig perching atop the Spell Wall. Sneyagflug came down before it, then quickly spelled himself into human form and restored the mage robes he'd been wearing to himself. Andrion finally recognized the garment as one of his own, and felt a surge of resentment that he quickly stifled. This was no time to be picking fights with the man/dragon who had volunteered to help them.

Sneyagflug surveyed the war party and his eyes widened. "It may be a little hard for *those* to hide," he pointed out. "What if Meiskomtot gets the wind up and instead of calling his minions, he just runs for it?" Bernadette's brow furrowed.

"Can't you and Ehrgeizig fly faster than him?" she asked.

"Yes, I suppose we can," he replied. "But if he realizes too soon what a force we've brought against him the best we'd be able to do is chase him and harass him from the air. And that would likely be happening miles from where our troops are arrayed."

"I've got a solution," Andrion said. "Have the automatons stand over there against the far wall and I'll cast a glamor on them so that they look just like parts of the wall. Since the spell is on them, rather than on Meiskomtot, it should get past his magic protection."

"That would work," Bernadette said. "Can you do it to Ehrgeizig, too? Meiskomtot will be winging in from some distance, coming for Sneyagflug, and initially Red should be the only thing he sees here. After Calling, Sneyagflug can go dragon and perch on the Spell Wall. Then after Meiskomtot engages him, Ehrgeizig can get above them and attack, which should have him calling for reinforcements."

"That sounds workable," Sneyagflug agreed. "Once the minions begin to arrive, we should start shooting arrows at them so it looks like a misguided and inadequate attack. We can hope he'll want to Call in all his reinforcements to wipe out the opposition. He'll still be thinking he can get my body for himself." He shuddered a little internally at the thought. He liked this body – he'd been living in it for a long time, and now that he could turn human, he was even more loath to part with it.

They consulted with Wissagleb so he could relay the right orders to his troops. About a third of them were armed with bows, as were Bernadette, Andi, and Rezira. Both Bernadette and Andi also had swords suitable for hacking up downed dragon zombies. Bernadette directed Kziintke and his fellows over toward the side of the crest furthest from the Spell Wall, with instructions to join the attack as soon as she gave the command.

Ehrgeizig lifted from the Spell Wall and perched atop a rock wall above the robons. Then Andrion cast Blend over the four enormous combatants, so that to the eye of the beholder they appeared to be the same as whatever was behind them – in the dragon's case, the sky. There was a faint shimmering in the air that betrayed them if you looked hard, which would be more noticeable when they started moving – but for five minutes they would be essentially invisible.

"Quick!" Bernadette called to Sneyagflug. "Go ahead and Call him!" The transformed red dragon stood tall and proud in his comically too-short mage robe and bellowed "MEIS-KOM-TOT!" Then, with considerably less volume, he spelled away his clothing and became once again the second-largest living dragon in Iscandia. He lifted to the air and perched atop the Spell Wall, wings spread slightly to keep his balance as he watched the skies. Surely the undead dragon priest would be unable to resist?

They waited no more than a minute to see the gigantic, ruinous, dull-gray dragon winging toward them. Only Ehrgeizig and Sneyagflug among them had actually set eyes on him, and the humans in the party were horrified at his size. Shielded against magic, how could this behemoth be brought down? Sneyagflug was playing his part, nor was much acting required. He hated this foul thing, and in his dragon form his anger swiftly rose to a pitch that left him uncaring whether he lived or died.

"You killed my son, you monster! You will die forever and become dust!" he roared in a fury. Meiskomtot smiled inside. Killing that annoying young dragon had been a matter of expediency, rescuing his minion from its attack. But how perfectly his actions had furthered his objectives! He hadn't realized that the red dragon whose body he coveted was the father of that brood. Maybe he should have killed a few more of them!

"It is you will die, little one!" he roared in defiance. "But take comfort – once I have taken your soul, your body will rise again." He came in at an angle, aiming to strike Sneyagflug, and the red dragon took to the air.

"Archers! Now!" Bernadette called, and they began shooting at Meiskomtot as he circled low, looking for an advantage.

He was far larger than the red dragon, but he wanted that body as undamaged as possible. He cast Essence Capture, a spell that would call his opponent's soul to one of the vials hidden within that dimension where his mask and other possessions resided, if the red dragon should die in the next five minutes. But how was he to keep him from simply fleeing?

"TOD-EN-ANGST!" he cried. His minion was smaller than Sneyagflug, but could fly interference and hem him in. It was at this point he realized that arrows were being shot at him. Many of them bounced off harmlessly, but a few stuck in his armored, mummified flesh or flew right through his wing membranes – making them still more ragged. There were humans down there – was this supposed to be a trap?

Hah, that had to be the fireblood he'd heard of, the mother of the young dragons. It looked like she and her consort had gotten together a little assault force and lured Meiskomtot here, hoping to take revenge on him for the death of their child. Wonderful! She was the one person in this time who could rob him of the souls of his minions, and now he had the opportunity to kill her and her friends – as well as capture the body he wanted so badly!

Might as well let some of his minions deal with the people on the ground while he and Todenangst, who was now flying in from the south, trapped Sneyagflug. Running through the list of those still active in his mind (and regretting with annoyance the several that had been killed or left unable to fly), Meiskomtot cried "KALT-GRAU-SAM! SWARZ-FLUCH-TOT! VO-KUL-DAAN! FAAS-NU-ZII! SHARF-EN-WAF!" With reinforcements on the way, he could now turn his attention to Sneyagflug, who hovered above him waiting for him to make his move. The red dragon didn't seem to have noticed Todenangst as yet. Meiskomtot hoped that Sneyagflug's anger would be hot enough for him to ignore his peril until it was too late.

As soon as the last of the Calling spells had died away, Bernadette turned in the direction of the shimmering scenery behind her and yelled, "Now, Ehrgeizig! Get above them!" Dust flew and the air blurred as Ehrgeizig, still essentially invisible, rose from his perch and flew in the direction of the confrontation between Meiskomtot and Sneyagflug. The time for the automatons was not yet, but soon.

As the Called undead dragons began winging in from all directions, like a grisly parody of the bright swarm that had filled the skies above the Battle of Mrzhgradfendz last year, Bernadette shouted to her troops. Her years of practice with the voice used for dragon spells had given her the ability to be heard even from a goodly distance away. "Andrion, Andi, Rezira! Get ready to start bringing them down, but not on our heads if you can manage it! The rest of you, swords out! As soon as they hit, start cutting off heads or wings!"

Focused on the red dragon he lusted after, Meiskomtot hadn't noticed any of this. He called to his minions, "All of you except Todenangst, kill everyone on the ground!" Then he turned his attention to Sneyagflug. Todenangst was hovering above him, pinning him between them. Meiskomtot cried "Eiz-Nehm-Bild-Stalz!" sending a blast of freezing to engulf him.

This dragon spell could freeze a smaller opponent solid, and would probably have done so on a dragon the size of those youngsters who had attacked Todenangst. On Sneyagflug, it encased him in ice but did not penetrate deeply enough into his tissues to disable him. The big red dragon flicked his wings with an effort, sending glistening shards of ice flying an all directions, and darted off to one side before hovering again.

Todenangst moved to block him from any further flight, then suddenly pivoted in air – flying in a wide arc as if seized by an unseen force. "Master!" he called in a desperate croak. Meiskomtot, considering his next attack, was dumfounded as a shimmering in the air above formed into an enormous dragon.

It was that Ehrgeizig, whom he'd chased off just a few days ago! By the wings of Aderos, how had he simply materialized above them? He had Todenangst's neck in his powerful jaws; and even as Meiskomtot hovered, stunned, the undead dragon's head – with a couple of feet of the neck attached – began dropping from the sky.

The body soon followed it, and both Sneyagflug and Meiskomtot had to duck out of the way.

"Another of your minions gone, dragon priest!" Ehrgeizig roared tauntingly. "And look what befalls the rest!" Meiskomtot left his hover and flew in a circle, so that he could see what was happening on the ground below. With The Fireblood and her companions using bows, which were very nearly useless against a flying undead dragon, he had expected that his minions would make short work of them.

No! This could not be! Two of the five were down on the stones of the rise, being swarmed over by attackers with swords and rapidly hacked to pieces. As he hovered, watching, another that was cruising above the melee and flaming those below dropped suddenly out of the sky as if it had been struck dead. It crashed to the ground, and the attackers turned from the now headless and wingless corpses to this fresh one. Some of the attackers were clearly armored humans – well-armored, at that – but some were… aptrgangr? Why were aptrgangr aiding living men against a dragon priest?

He called to them in a voice of command: "Cease attacking my dragons. Kill the human intruders!" The aptrgangr ignored him. Then a figure stepped out from the edge of the conflict, wearing a metal mask and bearing a staff. "They obey only *my* commands, Meiskomtot!" it shouted up at him. "You shall not have them!" Another dragon priest? He did not recognize the mask, or the figure in its sablium armor for that matter – though death did have a way of changing people.

"What is your name?" He demanded.

"My name is not important," came the reply, "and I doubt you ever noticed my existence. Though I watched them inter you!"

On the ground, chaos reigned. The remaining undead dragon minions were swarming above the small battlefield, shooting flames or ice on those below. In the confusion it was hard for the three mages to aim their magic-block spells at exactly the right time, so that the fallen dragon zombies' forward momentum did not drop them onto those waiting below. Andrion, Andi, and Rezira had each gotten one, and with each fallen body it became harder to maneuver.

They needed to drop the disabled undead dragons onto spots where they could reach them.

As Erik hacked at the corpse Rezira had just dropped, taking off its head with blows of his khopesh as if he were chopping down a tree, one of the ones they had already hacked up began stirring. Though it had no head and would never fly again, the magic-block spell had prevented what would have been death blows from permanently severing the magic that had animated it. Now that magic had returned, and it was lurching to its taloned feet – spiked tail lashing.

Yeow! Andrion punched a fist-sized smoking hole through its chest with a close-range bolt of entwined fire and lightning. *That* did it. "Andi!" he called frantically, gesturing at the downed body, "Get its soul!" That required a fireblood within no more than a couple of feet from the corpse. Andi picked his way around the body of the undead dragon Zira had just brought down, and clapped his hands onto the side of the dead-again, mutilated creature.

He had been fireblood his entire life, but Andi had never before been present at the death of a dragon. He was transported as the leathery flesh vanished, a vivid light filled his vision, and the familiar chorus that only fireblood could hear momentarily blotted out the sounds of the battle around him. When it was over, he stood gasping for a moment, overwhelmed by the experience.

"Heads up, son!" Andrion shouted, as Andi stood entranced and one of the remaining undead dragons came in for a strafing run, belching flame at those below. Andi blinked and threw himself to the ground. Meanwhile, the magic-block spell on the second dragon they'd brought down had expired, and it too was beginning to move. Bernadette spotted it and walked up to within a few paces of it, then put a daimonic arrow between the ribs – clearly visible where the left wing had been severed. It collapsed with a sigh and almost immediately its flesh crisped away with a roar. She scarcely paid any attention, this experience being so familiar to her now.

The Blend spell on the automatons had long since expired, but they had remained standing silently near the rock wall that formed one side of the crest. Bernadette thought it was about time for them to come into play, though. She scurried amid the confusion until she was close enough to be heard. "Get down there and hack up any intact undead dragons you see," she told them. "And if any are flying low enough, try to knock them out of the air. Especially, try to damage them so they can't fly. And watch out for our own forces, too!"

The three surged into motion with a clanking as their dypalfar metal feet rang on the stone flooring the arena. Picking their way around the obstacles and avoiding mowing down the aptrgangr and human defenders was more of a problem for them than using their wickedly sharp weapons and machine strength on the dead dragons.

Meiskomtot was in a fury. They were destroying his "children"! And stealing their souls, which was worse. He still had not figured out what spell it was that was bringing them down, but somehow they were not dead when they landed. He'd seen the destroyed corpses reanimating of their own accord, only to be captured by a fireblood. He had thought The Fireblood was a woman, but the first soul had been taken by an armored figure too tall, surely, to be female. Her son, perhaps?

Had he not been so enraged Meiskomtot might have fled, saving this fight for another day. But in any case his escape was blocked by Ehrgeizig and Sneyagflug, corralling him in the small circle of air above the battlefield and launching harassing attacks on him from above.

There, a tall mage was taking aim on one of his two remaining minions. Meiskomtot stooped, crying "Kraf-Luft-Struung-Wund!" and sending the figure flying. His target's sablium helmet was knocked off, and he circled in the air for another pass, shooting flames down on the figure from only twenty feet in the air. One down, two more to go! He circled higher, looking for another target.

Bernadette was sprinting back to the battlefield, arriving ahead of the robons despite their longer strides. The third undead dragon they'd downed was being hacked up by Erik, Lifa, Bjorn, Alfmund, and Fjuri while a party of aptrgangr stood guarding them against threats from the air. She needed to hover close, ready to get this one's soul when it reanimated. She looked around to find her mages, hoping to see one of the two remaining minions come down – and was just in time to see Andrion fall. Her mind exploded.

"Andrion!" it was a raw shriek. "Erik! Help me!" she was gripping his arm, hauling him away from the dragon. The rest of the team needed no help to finish the job. Erik saw his brother lying crumpled on the stones and dashed with his wife to where Andrion lay. His armor had protected his body from damage, but his head had been blackened by the blast – hair singed away, flesh melted, eyes gone.

Bernadette bent to him immediately, tears blurring her vision, and felt for a pulse. He lived! But oh, his face was a ruin. And he was already going into shock. She poured on her healing at full force, the spell she'd once used to bring Andrion's father back from a decade as a near-vegetable after a crippling stroke. The charred skin fell away and new pink skin took its place. Andrion's breathing and pulse steadied, though he remained unconscious.

In the midst of desperate battle, she didn't have the time for the careful healing job she'd done on that boy in Westmarch. "Carry him away, Erik! We have to get him out of the battle!" Erik, face grim and eyes blazing, lifted Andrion – who weighed around two hundred-sixty pounds in his armor – as gently and easily as if he were one of their children. Near the entrance to the bowl, by the trail where they had come in, a jumble of mammoth and dragon bones offered a little bit of shelter. He laid his stricken brother down in a hollow amid them.

Bernadette had her pack off and was digging out a potion – not of healing, but of sleep. Andrion needed to be kept out of the battle, and he was blind. When he awoke he would be frantic, without anyone to watch over him. Much better he should sleep for the next hour. After getting him to swallow it she pulled a fur bedroll from the pack and laid it over him, squeezing her eyes shut as she tried to fight back her tears. Now is not the time to be falling apart, woman! Her eyes met Erik's, then they turned and ran back to the battle.

Despite Meiskomtot's best efforts one of the two remaining mages had used whatever spell it was they had (magic-block had been developed thousands of years after the dragon priest's death) to knock another of his minions to the ground, senseless. Screaming his rage, he swooped and dived on the defenders, hoping to keep them at bay until Kaltgrausam would regain his senses.

Kziintke and Saarok broke off from where they were helping Dengaal to dismantle the third of the undead dragons downed by magic-block. Having witnessed and understood that these zombies were only temporarily stilled and would rise again, they were doing a much more thorough job – hacking the tail into several sections, severing the four limbs as well as the wings – as if the temporarily immobile corpse were a stewing hen enroute to the pot. Now they hastened to the most recently fallen, to begin work on it.

In the confusion of the battle, beset from above while his minions were dying below, Meiskomtot had not noticed the mechs until just now – and he was horrified. He had seen such things from time to time during his life. The dypalfar were fond of their toys. But by all that was holy, these things were enormous! And they appeared to be quite immune to flames or dragon spells.

The smallest one, far larger than a man, had enormous double swords where hands and forearms should have been. They opened like scissors, snapping together with a sound like escaping steam and a dull "chunk." Kaltgrausam's right wing parted from the body partway down the first long bone, held only by the attached leathery skin. The undead dragon would not fly again.

Damn! As the smallest of the dypalfar robons finished cutting away the wing a larger one, which Meiskomtot estimated must be twelve feet high, looked up at him where he circled in the air – still keeping the less-impervious of the attackers at bay. It raised its bladed arms as if to salute him. Then, the blades on the ends of the arms, apparently hinged on the outer sides, snapped back to lie along the upper arms. Two black holes appeared – those arms were hollow! And suddenly Meiskomtot, sweeping low to try knocking the mech off its feet, was hit by twin streams of fire!

Augh, the pain! Not physical but psychic, as he sensed the damage that was being done to his undead flesh. This was not a magical attack, but some infernal chemical fire of the Dwelves' devising. It shot in spectacular streams thirty feet in the air, right into Meiskomtot's face, and he veered off – turning tail and hastily climbing to avoid the flames. Whatever substance it was that created the flames, it clung to his leathery armored hide and continued burning for minutes until the fuel was exhausted. Fortunately he was naturally fire-resistant, and doubly so with the hidden protection of the dragon scale armor he wore in his human form. But his eyes were scorched, and it was hard to see. Curse them all!

The third of the fallen dragons now resembled a pile of unidentifiable dusty chunks. When it reanimated, it would take little to finish it off. The strike team moved quickly to where Kziintke and Saarok stood beside the body of the fourth one. Meiskomtot had not bothered to reanimate the body of Todenangst, who had died when Ehrgeizig ripped his head off. Andi, straying close in the confusion, received a second soul as the body gave off its flesh.

He hadn't seen his father fall, and when his mother and Erik returned to the fray he hadn't noticed anything amiss. Though this limited battle of a handful of humans, a few mechs, and a century of aptrgangr against a much smaller group of undead dragons was as nothing to the chaos of a battlefield where thousands of humans contended against one another, it was more confusion than *he* had ever dealt with in his young life.

Wissagleb stood to one side, watching the battle with a growing sense of triumph. He might have had to wait until thousands of years after his own death, but he was finally accomplishing some good in the world. He had become a dragon priest because he was fireblood, and because a life in the priesthood was many times better than the life of a weaver's son.

He'd been taught to read and write, but his passion for learning had been looked upon as an aberration in his small village. Without the chance spark that had appeared (and no one in his family could recall any others in their lineage with the dragon blood), he would have been doomed to a life of dull servitude. Instead, he'd been given the chance to become one of the rulers, a man who could guide his own destiny. And he'd taken it.

Their plan had worked! Only one more minion remained to Meiskomtot, and then they could focus all of their energies on destroying the master! As he watched with glee the gleaming dypalfar automatons, accompanied by his own forces and the ones who had come to Bernadette's call, his attention was diverted from their enemy. Silently, with only a slight rustle of leathery wings that was lost in the noise of the battlefield, Meiskomtot stooped and snatched Wissagleb in his claws, hoisting him in an instant high above the battlefield. His vision was blurred by the fire damage to his eyes, but he could see well enough for this task.

Wissagleb had gone dragon only once since emerging from his tomb after eons of undeath. In his utter panic at suddenly being lifted off his feet, he did not immediately spell himself into dragon form; and that was his undoing. "Now I have you!" Meiskomtot crowed. Aware that dropping this traitor priest from a height was only going to result in him going dragon and flying away, he quickly lowered his head.

He would bite through the midsection, a killing blow; then reanimate the twice-dead priest under his own command – thus gaining control of that dwindling but still-large aptrgangr army. They should be more than enough to kill off the human attackers – especially those damned mages – and he could continue his campaign. The red dragon still rode above, and once Meiskomtot had rid himself of these puny foes below, that prize might still be his!

Meiskomtot's enormous teeth met in Wissagleb's midsection, and he gave a groan of agony. Then, in a second or two, the Staff of Ice Storms fell. It clattered to the stones below, as did the mask Wissagleb. Meiskomtot released his bite, and the sablium armor also fell away.

Dust! There was nothing but dust! Had not the red dragon said that he, Meiskomtot, would be dust? No dragon priest who had died during the Uprising and been preserved with the rituals intended to let them rise again at Tarragin's return had ever been killed again during Meiskomtot's time. The aptrgangr could be reanimated over and over – how was he to have realized?

Below him, the aptrgangr under the (very) late Wissagleb's command had all ceased moving. They came to attention and stood rigid, as if awaiting further instructions. Meiskomtot tried to give them some, demanding they attack the humans, but as before they ignored him. Thrice-cursed! At least they were no longer helping to attack him or trying to exterminate his remaining minion, and at this point Meiskomtot was willing to accept any blessings he could find. If he could not command them, at least they would not be fighting against him.

Andi, looking around and trying to orient himself, was in time to see Meiskomtot take Wissagleb. Oh, crap! He thought, as their undead ally went to dust and his possessions fell to the ground. He scooped up the mask and the staff, thinking they might be useful. Where was Zira? He spotted her on the far side of the arena, shooting arrows at Meiskomtot as he dropped Wissagleb's sablium armor and circled above them again.

Only one of the minions to go! Above, Bosehdam circled anxiously. Given the slightest choice in the matter, he'd have been over the eastern mountains by now and moving fast. Undead he might be, but still he had a sense of self-preservation. Yet Meiskomtot's last command, to kill those below, still ruled him – thanks to the spell that had been cast on him after he'd been raised from the dead. He swooped in again, flame on, heading for a tall armored figure he knew to be one of the mages that had brought down his fellows.

Rezira had been tracking the last undead minion for several minutes in growing frustration. The area before the Spell Wall was now so littered with corpses and parts of corpses that there was almost no area free (and unoccupied by her allies) in which to drop this creature. To her surprise, she had found that instead of terrifying her and making her want to go home and hide under the bed, this perilous situation had made her feel more alive. Only her constant concern for Andi took her out of the battle frenzy that might otherwise have led her into getting killed, too caught up to look to her own safety.

That last undead dragon had looped around, and he was coming down in a shallow glide with flame on full – straight for Andi! Thank the Maker (or Andi's mom) for that armor of his. "Andi!" she screamed from fifty feet away, "Duck!" He obligingly hit the ground, avoiding the gout of flame as it shot past where his head had been a moment before; and Rezira hit the incoming minion with the magic-block spell. Its animating magic had been cut off, and it ceased breathing fire – but its wings were still held out at the side of the body and it continued its progress through the air, losing altitude gradually, until it crashed into the rock wall bordering the far side of the crest.

Andi was on his feet in a moment, waving "thanks" to Zira. That was the last of them! The one the Steadfasts, Alfmund, and the two automatons had been working over had nearly been sliced into serving portions, and Andi charged toward it. This one should be reanimating soon, and he was ready to absorb its soul. The experience was almost orgasmic, certainly rapturous. Bernadette, Erik, Alfmund, and the Steadfasts ran toward the newly fallen dead dragon, blades out. Hey, where was Andrion?

Meiskomtot wheeled, desperate to save his last minion from the fate the others had met. He had yet one in reserve, but he would not call him. He deeply regretted having called these, back when he had thought that the red dragon would be easy meat, his allies an annoyance to be brushed aside. Curse these people!

Bernadette realized that the aptrgangr had stopped moving. They had not fallen, but they were no longer assisting. And where was Wissagleb? Lying among the debris of the fallen that littered the bowl of the rise? She saw Andi near the pieces of the undead dragon they had just dismantled, and knew he was waiting to kill it again and claim its soul. That left her, Erik, Alfmund, Rezira, and the Steadfasts, plus the three mechs – more than enough to do the job on this last fallen minion.

"Fend off Meiskomtot!" she called to Kziintke and his fellows, as the party of humans descended on the dragon zombie where it lay crumpled, its head twisted to one side where it had collided with the rocks ringing the crest. Meiskomtot came down, landing atop the corpse, and shot flame in their direction. They were forced to dive and scatter, and both Bernadette and Rezira pulled their bows and began shooting arrows at him. With the power of his hidden dragon scale armor beneath the dilapidated scales of his dragon body, Meiskomtot held his ground – shooting gouts of flame followed by storms of ice. Then the mechs arrived.

Vaterhiin have mercy, the one in the middle was huge! He had not realized it from his perspective as he flew around looking down, but the thing must be nearly twenty feet tall. It utterly dwarfed the other two. The one with the flamethrowers seemed to have exhausted its supply of fuel, and was once again using its arms as swords. And the swords on the largest one were more than six feet in length. With the machine strength in those arms, it would be able to thrust a razor-sharp sword right through him, scale armor or no – and he would be so much dust like that colleague he'd recently killed. No!

Meiskomtot lifted his ponderous bulk into the sky again, continuing to shoot flames and ice at the party who were trying to get to his last minion and destroy it. He was getting desperate. The central part of the body of the one Andi was watching began to stir, and he used his father's unique flame and lightning weave to go in through the rib cage, striking a death blow as the heart and a large section of the lungs were vaporized. As the rush of the soul-taking swept through him, he tried to ignore it and concentrate on what was happening around him.

Meiskomtot was circling in the air again, harassing his parents and friends as the three mechs guarded the corpse to prevent him from taking control of it. He was flying no more than forty feet off the ground, almost within the reach of Dengaal's swords. An idea came to Andi and he ran to where Bernadette stood, shooting her bow in an effort to keep the undead dragon priest at bay. "Mom!" he said urgently in a tone that would not be overheard by their enemy, "I have a plan!"

Moments later she called her troops together. "Dengaal! To me! Everybody, stay close around Dengaal!" The towering mech was like a tree that they could shelter beneath, his sweeping sword arms keeping their attacker at a distance. "Now, Dengaal, begin walking slowly toward the undead dragon – keep out of the way of his feet, people!" The somewhat shielded group began moving toward their objective as Kziintke and Saarok stood guard.

Meiskomtot was infuriated. The gigantic monstrosity was preventing him from getting close enough for his flames to do any good! Soon they would be upon Bosehdam, and there would be nothing left for him to do but flee. He rose a little higher, mind racing as he tried to figure out what to do.

In the voice he'd honed through the use of dragon spells, Andi called "Sneyagflug! Ehrgeizig! Attack him now! Drive him down!" They mean to push me into that thing's blades, Meiskomtot realized. The two large dragons, together more massive than he was, dove on him and pressed him toward the ground. He struggled, twisting and turning in the air and snapping at them with his jaws. Then he cried "Kraf-Luft-Struung-Wund!" sending the red dragon tumbling in mid-air some distance away. That left only Ehrgeizig, but the silver dragon was enormous.

On the ground, Bernadette and Andi were watching as the dragons, two living and one undead, came closer. As Sneyagflug was hurled aside Bernadette realized that their quarry was about to escape. "Strike NOW, Dengaal!" she commanded. The gleaming robon thrust one arm upward, stretching toward Meiskomtot as the undead dragon's downward momentum carried him almost within reach.

The sight of the automaton's thrust caused Ehrgeizig to pull back, giving the hurtling undead dragon a little room in which to maneuver. He spread his wings out full to stop his fall, his tail and lower body swinging down for a moment and then up again as he clawed at the air to fly away. He was going to make it, the sword blade missing him by inches!

With the sound of a steam piston, the sword on Dengaal's arm telescoped out another six feet in an instant. It sliced through the membrane of Meiskomtot's left wing, tearing it away – and sent the damaged dragon priest careening through the air, flying lopsided and barely able to stay aloft. "We almost got him, Mom!" Andi crowed excitedly. He didn't think Meiskomtot was going to be doing much more flying, and it was only a matter of time before they put an end to him for good.

Meiskomtot landed hard atop the skeleton of one of his minions in the middle of the arena, and immediately transformed into his human form. For the first time, he was really afraid. The unlife he had denigrated as a poor substitute for the immortality he'd been promised might be traded for eternal death, instead. Curse these meddling fools! Didn't they understand that man was meant to serve the dragons, under the leadership of the dragon priesthood? Yet even one of his own fellow dragon priests had betrayed the cause.

Near the rock wall on the far side of the flat space those humans and their dypalfar mechs were now hacking Bosehdam to pieces, destroying his usefulness as a minion even if they should not manage to capture his soul. His only hope remained in obtaining the body of the red dragon in which to make his escape – or barring that, the silver one would do, even if it meant he was never able to become human again.

But first, time to get rid of these interfering idiots! He fired the Staff of Rending directly at the group around Bosehdam. The corpse exploded, and armored warriors and mechs were scattered on the ground. Dead, Meiskomtot hoped. Now for the dragons! Hitting a moving target was much harder, but he managed to get off a couple of shots that nearly hit them and the two flew off to a safer distance, watching him for signs that he would shoot again. He could bide his time.

Andi hadn't joined the group, watching to see what Meiskomtot would do next. When the explosion ripped through the corpse they'd been cutting up, he was in shock. Rezira! Mom! Erik! Fjuri! So many he loved now lay scattered around the remains of the undead dragon; but he knew that if he ran to their aid the dragon priest would spot him and he'd be the next one hit. Surely their armor would have protected them, and they would just be stunned?

Andi moved slowly so as not to catch Meiskomtot's eye, while the dragon priest's attention was on the dragons above them. He pulled a vial of magical energy poison from a side pocket of his pack and dipped the head of a daimonic arrow into it. While the magic-block spell was a magical attack that cut off magical energy, this poison affected it but was not in itself magic. He hoped that it would work where a poison affecting health or stamina (two factors that seemed irrelevant to the undead) would not.

He drew carefully, aiming for the dragon priest's right arm. His enemy had that devastating staff held with his right hand, taking aim at Sneyagflug as he circled above. Smack! The arrow struck true, a little above the elbow, and went straight through the woody flesh to lodge in the dragon scale armoring the chest. As soon as he saw it hit, Andi scurried to a nearby pile of dragon bones and ducked down behind them, hoping he hadn't been spotted.

Meiskomtot dropped the staff, but scooped it up again in his left hand the next moment. That had hurt! His footing was a little unsteady atop the spine of one of his late cohorts, his undead body less than agile in any case. He felt so weak, so dizzy! What… Any blow that was not enough to completely sever his animating magic should have had little or no effect. Yet he barely had the strength to remain upright. He hesitated, searching the area for his attacker. He thought he had knocked them all out with the blast that had destroyed the corpse of Bosehdam.

No one seemed to be stirring, and as he stood there dithering the red dragon and the silver were emboldened to swoop closer, probably hoping to catch him as he had done to Wissagleb. While his armor provided some protection, his mask would do nothing to prevent him from being bitten through by those enormous jaws! Turning his attention to the skies again, he shot a blast from the staff that exploded on Ehrgeizig's left hind foot, ripping away two of the clawed toes. Howling in pain and trailing blood, the silver dragon fled the scene.

Wonderful! Meiskomtot thought. Just go fly off and bleed to death, won't you? If he couldn't capture the red dragon for his new dwelling place (absolutely required now that his own dragon form was too damaged to fly), he could have the big silver one as a backup. Andi crouched, watching this from between the ribs where he huddled, and cursed silently as he saw Ehrgeizig routed. It didn't seem like that much of an injury for a big ancient dragon, but he had the idea that the old fellow was awfully fond of his renewed body.

Suddenly he sensed he was not alone, and whirled to see Fjuri beside him. His helmet was of the open type, not the standard full-face dypalfar design, and he was smudged with dirt and sporting bruises and cuts. Andi stifled the urge to hug his friend, instead whispering "Fjuri! Thank the gods! Are you all right?"

"This armor your Mom made us is heavy, but it's pretty good stuff. I think I've got about a million bruises, but I'll live." Andi put a bare hand to his friend's cheek and ran a little healing magic into him.

"Whew, thanks!" Fjuri murmured. "That's a lot better."

"What about everyone else?" Andi asked quietly.

"Everyone's alive," he replied. "I heard them all moaning and groaning. But I think they'll be fine after some of what you just gave *me*." After a moment he added, "At least Meiskomtot saved us the trouble of cutting up that dragon…"

Andi gave him a grim smile. "Have you seen Andrion?" He'd been so eager to impart his plan to Mom that he'd forgotten to ask her.

"I lost track of him a while ago," Fjuri admitted. "Things were pretty hectic, and I wasn't paying attention. But I haven't stumbled over his corpse, at least. I'm sure he's fine."

The two of them turned their attention to Meiskomtot, who seemed to have recovered from the temporary weakening of magical energy that the poison had caused. But it clearly had affected him. Once again the undead priest was scanning the skies, as Sneyagflug circled far enough away that he could take evasive action whenever his foe let loose with a blast from that staff of his. They seemed to be at an impasse.

"I weakened him with an arrow dipped in magical energy poison a little while ago," Andi whispered to his friend. "I think I should try it again, and if he falters maybe we can rush him." Fjuri furrowed his brow, thinking the idea through.

"Why don't I sneak over there," he beckoned to another jumble of bones some thirty feet distant. "I'll do it while he's trying to take down Sneyagflug, then when I get into position I'll signal you and you can shoot him again. Once he sways, we rush him from two sides. All right?"

"Sounds good," Andi replied. Fjuri could be so quiet, it was often hard to remember just how bright he was. He would make a wonderful general, he thought – though what need Iscandia had for generals, when there hadn't been a real war here in more than a generation, he didn't know. Not only bright, but quick and agile for such a big man. Keeping low, one eye on Meiskomtot, Fjuri timed his dashes for when the undead priest was taking aim with the staff.

Meiskomtot was now trying to lead his quarry as the red dragon swept in circles high above him. But the bolts from the staff moved no more quickly than arrows, and were much easier to see coming – a brilliant streak of light like a miniature comet, until they connected with a target and exploded. Sneyagflug was avoiding them with ease at this distance.

Three attempts later Fjuri was crouched behind the stack of bones he'd indicated, and gave Andi a wave. Andi dipped another arrow in the poison, making sure to soak it well. He'd had a thought and had ripped a small strip of cloth from a pair of spare underdrawers in his pack while Fjuri was sneaking away, tying it tight behind the arrowhead. The absorbent cloth soaked up three times as much of the poison as the arrowhead itself would take.

Now, careful not to drip any of the poison on himself, Andi nocked the arrow to the bow and took careful aim. Above, Sneyagflug had a bird's eye view and had noted what the young men were doing. He decided to help them out a little, and abruptly dipped lower, putting himself into tantalizingly closer range for Meiskomtot and his staff. For added effect he shot flames, as if he were planning to strafe the dragon priest.

Excitement rose in Meiskomtot as he saw the red dragon dropping toward him. The fool! Did he think this dragon priest any less resistant to dragon fire in his puny human form? The mask should have been a tipoff, but no matter – this was his chance. His right arm damaged but still usable, he held the staff up and out, trying to take careful aim. Being unable to sight along the length of the staff made it a frustratingly inaccurate weapon for long-range attacks.

Suddenly psychic agony bloomed in him and all of his strength faded away, as an arrow buried itself in the oak-hard, mummified flesh of his right armpit! The arrow had been shot from below, and had gone up through the opening in his armor between the breastplate and the bracer, to lodge in the collarbone as he had lifted his arm to make the shot! The staff clattered down the pile of bones to the stone floor of the arena, and he swayed on his feet.

"Now!" Andi shouted, rising to his feet and dashing toward the dragon priest with his short sword out as Fjuri came in from the other side, longsword swinging. "You! No!" Meiskomtot cried, anger and panic warring within him. His staff! What had become of his staff? Well, he still had his dragon spells.

"Kraf-Luft-Struung-Wund!" and Andi was flung back, tumbling end over end to fetch up on the near side of the pile of bones behind which he'd been hiding earlier. He was stunned for a couple of seconds before he could pull himself together. Meanwhile the dragon priest had turned toward Fjuri, who had nearly reached him but had to climb the loose pile of bones before he could get at him. "Kraf-Luft-Struung-Wund!" again, and now Fjuri went flying. He was much more massive than Andi, especially in that heavy dypalfar armor, and did not fly as far.

Sneyagflug had veered away before he got too close, but circling back he saw what was going on below. "The staff, Andi!" he roared, as he dived again. "Get the staff!" Andi pulled himself to his feet, and spotted the staff lying on the stones at the bottom of the pile of dragon bones on which Meiskomtot still stood. Damn, but there must be a ton of magic animating that wasted corpse! A triple dose of poison, and he seemed to be shaking it off again.

The red dragon dived, intent on putting an end to this monstrous creature who had so callously killed one of his precious children. The sons and daughters he and Schunmurte had made together were the most important, the most significant undertaking of his long life, and that any should be taken from him filled him with rage. Let Meiskomtot use his dragon spells, he didn't care. The impact of several tons of falling dragon hitting that frail human figure should be enough to drive away the magic that animated it.

Meiskomtot saw his death coming for him, and it riveted him to the spot for a second. The two young warriors he'd temporarily disposed of forgotten, he stood his ground and cried out as the red dragon came within range. "Kraf-Luft-Struung-Wund!" As Sneyagflug's forward motion ceased and he tumbled backward head over tail with wings flailing, Andi seized the staff. He took a few quick steps back, then fired it – not at the dragon priest with his mask of invincibility, but at the top of the stack of bones on which he stood.

With a roar, the pile of bones exploded outward in all directions. Andi and Fjuri as well – he'd just gotten back onto his feet – hit the ground as the air became full of sharp fragments and larger chunks of dragon bone. Those things were big, heavy, and hard. Meiskomtot was thrown through the air, pelted by bones, and landed heavily against the rock wall behind him - then fell to the stones flooring the arena and lay still. His mask had been knocked away, exposing his withered and ghastly face.

Andi was the first on his feet and made a dash to where the dragon priest lay. He couldn't be dead, or he'd be nothing but a pile of dust. But why wasn't he moving? Fjuri joined him, holding the Meiskomtot mask in his hands. "I found this over there," he said, pointing. "I guess that means he's not invulnerable any more, huh?"

The two stood over him a short distance away – weapons at the ready, waiting for a sign of movement. He could still presumably cast dragon spells at them or use other magic, and they wanted to be ready to stop him. On the far side of the arena, Erik had been first on his feet after Fjuri and had downed a health potion, then given one to Bernadette. While the boys and Sneyagflug had fought the dragon priest, she had been healing them all.

Now freed of bruises, broken bones, and ruptured eardrums, they gathered around near Andi and Fjuri and stared at their fallen foe. Any of them could have ended him in heartbeat – but while it was one thing to kill someone in the heat of battle, it was another to execute your enemy as he lay helpless; and none would make the move.

Sneyagflug came in for a landing over near the Spell Wall, where there was a reasonably large clear space, and went human. In another minute, clothed, he joined the rest of the party where they gathered around Meiskomtot. The undead dragon priest was beginning to stir. The grip of the animating magic in this one was strong!

"Bernadette," Sneyagflug said in his deep human voice. "This… *thing* took Gotteluub from us. I think that you and I should be the ones to rid the world of him once and for all." She looked up at him, face pale and tears shining in her eyes. She'd removed her helmet and her long, light auburn hair streamed behind her in the wayward breeze that blew in fitful circles amid the rock walls surrounding the crest.

"Yes," she replied with a hard gleam in her eyes, face stern. She drew the short sword at her side, and handed it to Sneyagflug before producing a long sablium dagger from a leg sheath. "What about you, Andi?" He nodded solemnly. Gotteluub had been his brother, and if he hadn't known him as well as he knew Mondi and some of the others, he had been dear to him.

Meiskomtot rose to a sitting position, leaning on his right arm. One of his feet had been broken off by a flying bone in the blast. He looked around at them blearily, his vision hazed even in his human form by the damage caused by that flame-shooting mech. Without his mask, he was done. He could cast a dragon spell once, but before he could do so again the rest of them would be on him.

Andi drew his own short sword. As he, Bernadette, and Sneyagflug stepped closer to their fallen foe, he asked "Meiskomtot, what did you think you were doing? Did you truly believe that a few dozen undead dragons were going to rule Iscandia and bring back the dragon worshipers? I don't understand."

The ruined face gazed at him miserably, all hope gone. "Payback!" he rasped. "It's not fair that I should be *this* while all of our dragons lie dead and forgotten, while people go about their lives without knowing or caring about the glory that was once ours. I was promised immortality, not this... this unlife! I wanted to *live*!" His left hand was clenched in a fist.

Andi lowered his head, feeling a stab of pity. Evil Meiskomtot might be, but at the root of it, back there thousands of years ago in another time, he had once been only a man. "I'm sorry Meiskomtot," he said almost gently. "We cannot help you to live. We can only help you to die. Go now, and find peace if you can."

With that he stepped forward and thrust his sword into the dragon priest's throat, above the breastplate. At the same time Bernadette pierced his neck from the other side with her dagger and Sneyagflug, with more power behind his blow, ran his short sword through the dragon scale armor and deep into the chest. As they watched, Meiskomtot dissolved into a pile of dust.

Chapter 43: Aftermath

Bernadette sighed, wiping the dust from her sablium dagger before returning it to its sheath. Sneyagflug returned her short sword to her, his curious-looking deep green eyes catching hers with a look of triumph, and hunger. She looked aside. She was happy for the father of her dragon children that he had realized his dream of experiencing the human form, and she was sure that it would be opening up new worlds for him; but at the moment his persistent belief that she was in some way "his" was only causing problems.

Her heart stopped in the next moment as she remembered what one of those problems was. Oh gods, Andrion. Fresh tears came to her eyes as she remembered his ruined face, the eyes burned away. "Wissagleb!" she cried, "Where is Wissagleb? We need him for Andrion!" Andi looked at her wide-eyed.

"Andrion is hurt?" he asked, horrified that he was only learning of this now.

Now tears were flowing freely from her eyes. "Yes! Meiskomtot knocked his helmet off and then nearly incinerated him!" she said bitterly. "I've gotten him stabilized, but his face is destroyed. He needs Wissagleb to cast the Renew spell on him."

Andi looked stricken, then brightened. "Mom, I saw Meiskomtot kill Wissagleb. He carried him up into the sky and bit into him. I don't know if he knew what would happen, but Wissagleb turned into dust." Bernadette looked wide-eyed, horrified. "It's all right, Mom," he continued, rummaging in his pack, "I have his mask!"

His mother seized the mask from him, then threw her arms around him (she only came up to around his shoulder) and hugged him fiercely. "Thank you, thank you, son!" she said – then bolted in the direction of the path leading up from the plain below, in an area of the crest that had not been disturbed by the battle. Erik and Andi were right behind her, trailed by the rest of their party.

Andrion still slept. The entire battle had lasted scarcely an hour, though it seemed like years. Erik helped Bernadette get him into a sitting position and remove the upper part of his armor, so that she had more skin on which to apply the spell. It was actually possible to heal people without touching them, but her approach worked best with full contact.

Donning the mask, Bernadette applied her hands to Andrion' chest. Below the neck he was the same man he had always been, light tan skin still reasonably smooth. He'd become a little leaner with age, though still muscular and strong, and the hairs on his chest, once a reddish brown, had begun to come in silver – along with the hair on his head. There was no hair on that head, now – it was a blob of reddened, shiny proud flesh with eyelids grown together over missing eyes, nose partially melted.

Erik stood by with a stamina potion, ready to force it down his wife's throat if she showed signs of exhausting herself. She began applying the Renew spell, as she had done to that squashed caterpillar… was it only a few days ago? The flood of magical energy at her command was amazing, seemingly limitless! It was like drinking from a waterfall instead of sipping from a bottle. "Come back to me, my love, come back…" she murmured as she let the spell flow into her husband.

They all stood around watching in awe as the spell took its effect. The reddened skin on the face smoothed and resumed a normal color, the features became those they were all familiar with. Bernadette's eyes were wide as she watched the effects continue to develop. Hair sprouted, eyebrows growing back and long, dark brown lashes on lids that, one could see, hid eyes once again. The muscles of the chest and arms expanded slightly, becoming fuller, and the skin there took on the velvety sheen of supple youth. The hair on the head was now more than an inch long, and was coming in light brown with streaks of dark blond.

Erik grasped Bernadette's shoulder firmly but gently. "Berni, Berni!" he said, getting her attention. "I think you'd better stop before he no longer needs to shave…" She removed her hands from Andrion's chest and ripped the mask off her face. Its powers were amazing, but it certainly restricted visibility! Then she just knelt, hands at her sides, gazing at the beautiful face that had captivated her from the moment she had first seen Andrion, relaxing in the hot bathing pool at the Bathing Maiden, nearly eighteen years before. He had been thirty-two to her twenty-two then, but still gorgeous. Now he looked like he might be thirty, just as she did. Her heart soared with joy.

Those long eyelashes fluttered, and Andrion opened his melting brown eyes to gaze up at his wife as she knelt there scuffed and dirty and radiant with happiness. "Berni?" he murmured hoarsely. Then he cleared his throat and sat up. "What?" He looked around at everyone standing there watching him, smiles of delight on their faces. "Meiskomtot?" he said next. "Did we get him?"

Bernadette, still kneeling, threw her arms around his neck and kissed him, hard. Then she got to her feet. "We got him, and we got all his minions, too. Ehrgeizig got hurt, and Wissagleb is gone. All of his aptrgangr stopped working when he went. Oh, and the mechs seem to have been knocked out. I suppose Gylabris will be able to repair them though."

Andrion, too, climbed to his feet, then looked down at himself in astonishment. "Why am I not wearing anything above the waist?" he asked in puzzlement. "I remember getting knocked over, I think my helmet came off, and then... nothing." He ran his hand over his head, and looked still more flummoxed. "And I got a haircut?" He'd been wearing his hair a little longer than shoulder length for years, tied back with a leather thong to keep it out of his face.

Everyone around him burst into laughter, grinning fondly at his confusion. Andi stepped up and threw his arms around his father, squeezing him gently lest his armor bruise him. Bernadette felt her heart skip a beat as she saw how much alike they were – of a height, and with matching profiles. Now that Andrion was young again, they looked more like brothers than father and son. "Do you feel all right, Papa?" Andi asked, love and joy surging through him at the transformation.

Andrion's usual half-smile became a full broad grin. "I feel absolutely wonderful!" he declared.

Andrion got back into his armor and the group walked over to where the mechs lay motionless in a circle around the remains of the fallen undead dragon. Some of the larger bits of the corpse were twitching, and Erik hacked into the torso with his khopesh. Then Bernadette stepped close and received the creature's soul, the flesh vanishing.

As Andi moved toward Kziintke he suddenly realized that all around them, the aptrgangr were moving again. And they were converging on him! "Fjuri!" he squawked, readying a broad-band magic-block spell. But he didn't cast it. Their weapons were sheathed, bows hung behind them, and they moved slowly and silently as if in a funeral procession. A tall overlord, their commanding officer, came forward and astounded Andi – kneeling before him and saying, "Master, what is your command?"

"Master? Who says I'm your master?" Andi said.

"Our master Wissagleb," the aptrgangr replied. "He commanded us that should he fall, we would take our commands from you. When he was destroyed by the lord Meiskomtot, we ceased our actions awaiting your command. But none came. I believe Wissagleb feared that his enemy might steal us from him."

Unbelievable, Andi thought. For a moment he had a vision of marching his own little private army of aptrgangr around, righting wrongs and winning treasure, then storing them in the basement with the potatoes in between runs. But no, it was not right. These valiant Norse warriors deserved better than an eternity of servitude to one master after another. They had been dead for over six thousand years – why should they not now be feasting in Asengard?

"What is your name, Overlord?" Andi asked. The aptrgangr returned to a standing position, overtopping him by several inches.

"In life I was Ranulf Stormreach," he replied in his dry, creaking voice.

"Ranulf," Andi went on, "you and your troops have given the service that you pledged and I think it is time that your souls were freed to go to their reward. Would you like that?"

The overlord bowed his head, then looked up with blue-blazing eyes. "Yes," he said, "very much. You have only to command us to be free and we can leave these withered bodies and go to Asengard. But what of our fallen comrades?" He gestured around him. Nearly half of the troop had fallen to attacks by Meiskomtot and his minions.

"They are not truly dead, then?" Andi asked. He knew little of necromancy, indeed no necromancer living knew half the secrets the ancients had possessed.

"They but sleep, severed from the magic that animated them," Ranulf explained. "The one who has their command can raise them again, as Wissagleb did with those you and your companion had stopped when we were at Todenstor. And they must be animate in order to receive the command to be free. Do you not know the spell?"

Andi was a natural mage, his ability to pick up a spell and use it almost immediately something that had thrilled his father when he had first begun teaching him eleven years ago. But while he had watched Wissagleb perform the spell to reanimate his pledged aptrgangr several times during their return to the plaza where Ehrgeizig had awaited them, he had not actually been *taught* the spell. Supposedly it was not really necromancy, a discipline he had avoided. Could he remember how it was done, for this good cause?

"I'll try," he told Ranulf, and strode to the nearest inanimate corpse. It had been hit by a blast of dragon fire, and the right arm was burned away; but it was intact enough that it should be able to rise – if he could figure out how to do it.

Meanwhile, Andrion had managed to get Kziintke activated by simply commanding him, "Kziintke, activate." Seemingly the previous command structure had been disrupted by the blast, and while his workings had received no permanent damage he was now responding to Andrion as his "master" – since that was who had activated him.

Andi searched his mind for the spell he had seen Wissagleb perform. It reached in like *this*, and then there was *this*, followed by a simultaneous push and pull… The fallen aptrgangr twitched, then rolled over onto its stomach and, with difficulty, got back to its feet. It then stood silent, eyes glowing, awaiting orders. Andi grinned at Ranulf, delighted. "I did it!" One down, around forty-five to go…

By the time Andi had resurrected all the rest of the fallen aptrgangr, even one who was forced to hold her severed head under one arm, Ehrgeizig had flown in and learned the sad news that his old friend was no more. Then Bernadette had donned the Wissagleb mask again. Afraid she might regress him too far, she tried working only on the injured foot – and found, that with the same concentration she had developed for ordinary healing spells, she was able to simply regrow the missing toes without changing the rest of him. He flew off again, saying that he would be found at Muuterhorn waiting for her Call. He wanted the Reciprocation as soon as she found time to gather ingredients and prepare the gallons of potion that would be needed. He had already learned the spells.

Finally it was time, and Andi marshalled his troops. He still felt half-regretful to be parting with them. "Everyone, gather around!" he commanded – and the undead warriors, male and female, shuffled into a tight group of just under one hundred. He couldn't resist a little speech to turn this into something of a ceremony. "Loyal Norsemen of ancient times," he addressed them, "you have given valiant service to your masters beyond any reasonable expectation. Even death was not enough to free you from your vows, and again and again you have risen to battle their foes – as you pledged in life. Now is the time for you to join the other Norse heroes in Asengard. Your obligation is at an end, and you are free!"

A speech to a different group of soldiers might have resulted in rousing cheers. When Andi spoke that last word, "free," all of them sagged and toppled to the ground – eyes no longer glowing. Experimentally, he tried the reanimation spell on the nearest one – a spell he'd gotten quite good at after all his recent practice. Nothing. There were spells, he knew, that would reanimate a soulless body to fight beside you as a mindless puppet for a time – but this was not one of them. These aptrgangr were truly free at last.

Andi turned from his "troops," a tear in his eye. He felt happy and proud that he had been able to send them on to the afterlife they deserved, yet sad at their passing. He found both Kziintke and Saarok on their feet. Evidently the shock of the explosion had shut them off somehow, yet had not damaged them permanently. They, and the rest of the group, were gathered around Dengaal where he lay, his twenty feet spread across the ground.

"I think that one of his power cells may have shattered," Kziintke was saying. "The centripetal force in the area of his head would have been far greater, because of his height. I have never really understood why our creators wished to make these outsized models. There are so many places they cannot go!"

"Without his extra height, and those telescoping sword arms, Meiskomtot might have gotten away from us," Andi pointed out as he joined the group. "Why don't we bring him home, and then

Mothris can take him back to Alfenstein for repairs. I wonder how they got him out of Dypendwelve, in the first place?"

"Oh," Kziintke replied, "he crawled. He can go through most normal-sized doors if he stretches out and drags himself along. Hardly any use for fighting in that position, of course."

"I'm exhausted," Andi said aloud, realizing it for the first time. Though the battle had not lasted all that long, it had taken a lot out of all of them.

"I'll second that!" Alfmund said. The only person not feeling tired was Andrion, who'd just had twenty years lopped off his age and felt like going out and wrestling a few smilodons just for fun. They restrained him.

Even Sneyagflug was feeling as though a long nap would be a good idea. "Bernadette," he said, "I know that all of our children will want to join Drachmondien and me in the experience of being human, as soon as enough of the potion becomes available. Will you Call me when it does? I must be there with them to experience their amazement." She smiled at him tiredly. There had been much joy and much sorrow today, though joy had triumphed – and she felt utterly wrung out.

"Are you leaving, then?" she asked.

"Yes," he replied solemnly. "There are some things I need to do, including check in with the rest of the kids and spread the word about the Reciprocation and what we've done here today. They need to know that their brother has been avenged."

"I will Call you," she promised, stepping forward with a smile to take his hands. He enfolded her in a light hug and kissed her on the cheek, then left before Andrion could build up enough outrage to create a problem. Soon the great red dragon was winging off over the horizon.

Andi stood with his arm around Rezira, squeezing her as close as he could through the armor they both wore. It had been a hell of a day, and he had often feared for her life. But she'd come through it all perfectly fine, only a little knocked about when Meiskomtot had unleashed his explosion. What a woman she was, and how he loved her!

Bernadette pulled her map from inside her breastplate, still the commander of the expedition though Andi, Andrion, or Erik could just as easily have carried them back to Drakespring Farm. "Andi," she said, looking at the piled-up aptrgangr, "surely you don't mean for the remains of your aptrgangr to just join the bones of Osteon Rise?"

"No, Mom," he replied. "We need to fast-travel them all back to Todenstor, I think, and inter the bodies within the catacombs where they had been while awaiting their call to action. It'll really be a city of the dead, now. But we're going to need to hire a good-sized crew to do that, and it's probably going to take hours even so. I promise, I'll get on the project tomorrow."

"Very well," she said, seeing the tiredness in her son and feeling it in her own bones. "Let's go home."

Chapter 44: Meanwhile, Back at the Ranch

Flamangstdrach, searching for a likely target in accordance with his master's orders, felt the spell break like a snapping in his mind. He was free! He spun in the air, cavorting in glee. The oppressive weight of Meiskomtot's mastery over him, laid on him after the spell that had allowed him to rise and fly again, had vanished like the mists of morning. Now, he could do whatever he wanted to.

Flamangstdrach flew on, scanning the territory below from the height of several hundred feet in the air. It was a pleasant afternoon, and he could feel the heat of the sun warming his undead flesh. But that was the crux of it: he was a flying corpse. All of the things he had enjoyed in his life, the flood of hot blood in his mouth as he killed prey, the allure of a female (not that he, with his relatively small size, had had much success *there*), even the joy of flight itself, were gone from him now or so muted by his undead senses that little savor remained.

So what was he supposed to do? What, exactly, was the point of this lifeless existence? He *had* enjoyed destroying that hamlet up north, he mused. The terrified screams of the inhabitants as he chased them down and killed them, the roar of the flames as their pathetic little houses were consumed by the fires *he* had caused, had filled him with excitement and a sense of grim satisfaction. This undead existence might offer few enough pleasures, but that was certainly one of them. Why not just continue with his departed master's directive?

At least he was no longer limited to habitations that were isolated, far from the areas where men clustered together in force. He gazed below him, where he was following a road that ran beside a river. A large structure stood on one side of the road, and what looked like a farm on the other. Then, a little further down the road, another farm – but this one standing alone below the walls of a large city. Perhaps they would all look down from those walls in awe, as he burned this place to the ground.

Flamangstdrach dived in low, and spotted a couple of well-grown calves in a pen. Oh, cattle! How he had loved to eat them, so meaty and delicious! In the days of his life when dragons ruled Iscandia, the dragon worshipers had provided him with as much beef as he cared to eat. Yet he had fallen in the war, and when he had been reborn at Tarragin's command he had found that the Norsemen of this day were disinclined to part with their cattle without a fight. He had died in a hail of arrows as he'd been ripping the succulent hindquarters from somebody's milk cow.

And now, he could not eat anything. Nor drink. In a fury, Flamangstdrach landed with his claws sunk into the back of one of the animals, bearing it to the ground and breaking its neck. Its companion bawled and tried to climb the rails of the pen in sheer terror as he tore a hunk of flesh from his victim's flank and then flung it aside. He could barely taste the blood, and certainly could not swallow the meat!

Riki, worried about what was happening all those miles away at Osteon Rise, had been preoccupied as she picked tomatoes. It was high summer, and the fruit was coming on like a storm. She'd be peeling and cutting them for sauce for hours, later on – though probably Meri and Edla (who, at the moment, were trying on outfits in the nursery) would be willing to help her with the task. Sigi and Mondi were in the back weeding the wheat field, a tricky operation.

Overall, she was surprised at how genuinely helpful and cooperative the kids had been. She hadn't needed to ask Mothris to pitch in with the farm chores, and he was in the craft room reading some of Papa Andrion's vast collection of books. The runes of the leukalfar might be long lost, but it had not been that hard for the young leukalfar boy to learn to read and write in Common – a skill that was now being taught in leukalfar tribes all over Iscandia. Riki hoped the return to literacy wouldn't end up destroying the leukalfar's amazing system of oral history.

When the undead dragon flew in near the northern edge of the farm and attacked their calves, her shock and paralysis lasted for no more than a second or two. Had Meiskomtot somehow figured out where his enemies' home base was? Riki couldn't imagine how that could be possible, yet here was an undead dragon attacking their farm. She dashed for the forge, where a good collection of weapons was usually to be found. Her own bow was hanging from the wall in her bedroom in the basement, but she didn't have time to go get it.

A serviceable elven bow and a sack of bowstrings was hanging in the forge building, and she had it strung in a trice. Hadn't there been some talk about the undead dragons being resistant to arrows? Better bring a sword, too. There was a breastplate hanging from the wall, and Riki slipped it over her shoulders and put a helmet on her head. It was better than no protection at all.

Slinging a quiver over her back with the bow, holding the sword in her hand, Riki ran back outside. She found the second of their calves dead and Mondi, in dragon form, harrying the undead monster as it attempted to set the house alight. The bulk of Drakespring House had been built as an addition to the original tiny farmhouse, some seventeen years ago when the place had been known as Coldburn Farm. It had a sturdy stone foundation and a slate roof, but the walls between the two were built of wood and vulnerable to fire.

Praying that Meri and Edla would have the sense to get out of the house, as the nursery was located in the end of the house that the dragon was trying to ignite, Riki set the sword down for a moment and pulled out her bow. Mondi was doing what he could. Spelling up an ice storm to quell the flames each time the undead dragon succeeded in starting a little blaze, he was frustrating its attempts to burn the house down. And every time it turned to snap at him, he darted out of reach. It was far from the largest dragon Riki had ever seen, but still quite a bit larger than her brother.

Riki drew back the bow, which had around a fifty-pound pull, and began firing arrows into the undead dragon. As the part of the house that was vulnerable to its flames was between four and fourteen feet off the ground, it had remained on the ground near the flattened remains of the calf pen. Riki spared a moment of sadness for the poor calves, which hadn't stood a chance. But they'd been due for slaughter in another couple of months anyway, and perhaps the meat might still be usable. Farm life had inured her to the realities of life and death.

At this range, and with the powerful daimonic arrows she was using, Riki's shots were felt. The flesh of an undead dragon was nearly as hard as wood, far harder than that of the living; and a killing blow with an arrow would be hard to achieve unless she was standing about a foot away along its flank near the shoulder just behind the front leg. She had participated in the butchering of enough animals to understand anatomy, and she knew that the structure of dragons was essentially the same as the structure of a man – or a mouse, except for the wings. Just a lot bigger and stronger.

Sigi had run into the house to warn Edla and Meri, and now here was Meri in her armor beside her, bow in hand. Atta girl! "Sigi!" Riki called, "get Edla to safety! Run up the road to Waterdon and see if you can get some guards down here!" With her makeshift armor, Riki didn't see how she was going to get close enough to this beast to attack it with her sword and not get fried in the process.

"Okay," Sigi said reluctantly. He was rising eleven, and it seemed to him that he should be doing more to defend their home. But Edla was a guest, and definitely not up for a fight with a dragon. "Come on, Edla, let's go!" The two of them fled to the city wall and then ran along it, cutting the better part of a mile out of the trip to the main gates of the city.

As they ran, Riki felt both relief and a sinking feeling as if she'd just become more alone. Then Mothris emerged from the house, wearing some armor that didn't fit him very well and also armed with a bow. The leukalfar boy had grown a lot in the year that they'd known him, but he was still shorter than Riki by a couple of inches. Like all Drakesprings, all leukalfar learned archery. And he was stepping up to the challenge. All right! Now she very nearly had her own army. Eat daimonic death, undead fiend!

"Meri, Mothris, spread out!" Riki ordered. She had the eerie sense that she was somehow channeling her mom. There was a sense of power to this, as she asserted her authority and the people around her acknowledged it and did as she asked. She liked it! Wishing she was wearing her leather armor instead of this mishmash of ill-fitted pieces, she directed Meri to stay on this side, shooting from a safe distance, while she led Mothris around, down near the fence line and behind the dragon.

It still rested on the ground, trying to set the house ablaze as Mondi flew in tight circles above it, spelling its fires away with ice each time. Flamangstdrach was confused, and he was frustrated. Where the hell had this little dragon come from, and why did it seem to know more dragon spells than he did? He was one of the majority of his kind from the age of the dragon worshipers, who had happily accepted his superiority and the benefits it entailed without ever giving much thought to the possibility it might all end someday. Even among his peers, he had not been the sharpest knife in the dragon drawer – nor had death and reanimation improved his wit.

Riki directed Mothris to stand near the northern end of the house, still a few yards away from the dragon but within its line of sight if it turned its head from the task it had been pointlessly trying to accomplish since she came out here. She had Meri standing a bit behind it – firing into the spot behind the wing joint. She didn't have as much power in her shots as Riki did, but the accumulation of arrows there ought at least to be an annoyance and a distraction.

"Shoot into its chest!" Riki urged, "Right where the leg joins the body. Keep it up!" In a household where the crafting of arms and armor was a major part of the family income, they had arrows enough for an army. The undead dragon was thrashing now, beset from three sides, unable to rise because of the dragonling above it and unable to back away from the house with ease because the ruins of the calf pen and the bodies of the animals it had killed blocked its path in that direction.

"Now, Mondi!" Riki called, seeing victory at hand. "Grab him by the back of the neck and hold his head up!" Mondi, understanding what his sister needed, landed for a moment on the undead monster's back – claws digging into the hard, mummified flesh. He stood tall, twisting his head to sink his long, sharp teeth into his adversary's neck just behind the head. Then he pulled hard, flapping his wings for additional leverage, dragging the creature's neck back so that its head was pointed at the roof of the house.

"Keep shooting!" Riki called to Meri and Mothris as she slung her bow behind her and gripped the sword in two hands. It was an elven longsword, light for its size, and razor sharp. She prayed it would be heavy enough, and she strong enough, to power through that hardened, undead flesh. As the dragon struggled, wings thrashing, Riki leapt up and onto its back near the base of the tail. It was like standing on a bucking horse! The ribs were clearly visible, withered flesh sunken in on either side, and she followed them forward.

She had to duck to avoid Mondi's tail, taloned hind legs, and wings as he rose into the air to make room for her, maintaining a death-grip on the undead dragon's neck. He climbed higher, letting her stand, and she picked a spot on the left side, as far down as she could reach. Holding the sword aloft with both hands, she plunged it down between the ribs, into the chest cavity, and pierced the undead dragon's wooden heart.

Flamangstdrach gave a roar of agony as the magic was severed and he collapsed, dead once more. Only another dragon priest with the ancient knowledge would be able to bring him back. Using the hilt of the deeply-embedded sword as a handhold, Riki sprang off of his back onto the ground near where Meri had been shooting. She'd stopped firing when Riki had climbed up, afraid of accidentally hitting her sister.

"You got him, Riki!" Meri crowed. Mondi released the dragon's neck as it slumped lifeless, and in another moment had fluttered to the ground – swiftly returning to human form. On the dragon's far side, Mothris still held his bow. "Nice work, Riki!" he congratulated his foster sister.

As a surge of relief and triumph flooded over her, Riki's first thought was oddly "How the hell are we going to get several tons of mummified dragon carcass out of the garden?" The four of them hung up their weapons, Riki returning the armor she'd worn to the forge, and they all retired to the farmhouse's front room for some refreshments.

When Sigi and Edla returned with a contingent of Waterdon guards, Riki put them to work hacking the dead dragon into smaller pieces and carrying them around to the compost heap up near the western edge of the property. Smiling winsomely at the big, strong, men, she even got them to hang the carcasses of the calves so they could be bled and gutted. By the time the war party returned, in the middle of the night, the younger children were in bed and the only signs of a disturbance were a few scorched siding boards and the empty calf pen – its broken sides lying flat on the ground.

Epilogue

The Sungold sun shone out of a clear blue sky onto the deck at the Bathing Maiden, which was aswarm with people. The Maiden hadn't seen a party of this magnitude since the wedding celebration of the Drakesprings, nearly eighteen years before. Andi leaned up against the rail with the river behind him, Rezira snuggled under his arm. She had her arm around his waist, and sighed with pleasure.

"I can't believe how quickly they're picking things up!" Rezira exclaimed, as she watched the horde of red-headed pre-adolescents milling around. They were eating, drinking, striking up conversations with some of the other guests, and acting like kids their age anywhere – though mentally, they were a few years older. A dozen of them were whooping and splashing in the swimming pool.

Andi squeezed his lover a little tighter, and smiled down at her. "Well, they *have* had the crash course," he said. "They've all been human for a couple of weeks now, and Mom's been working hard with them. Just finding clothes for them all was a challenge, let alone teaching them the basics – like how to eat with a knife and fork, how to use the bathroom, and so forth. But they're bright, and Mondi's been a huge help. Hey, check out old Ehrgeizig!"

On the far side of the crowd an enormously tall, slim, and impeccably dressed silver-haired gentleman was holding forth to a group of Waterdon citizens, including several business owners. They seemed to be hanging on his words. Though his silver hair gave him an air of maturity, his face with its aquiline features was unlined. He might have been anywhere from thirty to fifty, they thought.

This was the coming-out party for the children of Sneyagflug and Schunmurte, their introduction to the human society of Waterdon, and so far the kids were a hit. People found them charming, with their energy and enthusiasm – coupled with agile minds that seemed so at odds with their apparent age.

Bernadette and her husbands had taken a break from chatting with their friends and acquaintances from town, and were also leaning up against a rail on the south side of the deck. It was astonishing to her how alike her children were, yet how different. Taking human form seemed to have accentuated their personalities, making visible the internal differences that had been largely hidden when they were dragons.

For one thing, humans could display their personal traits with choices of clothing, and dragons could not. Schickemaad, with fiery hair like Mondi's but green eyes like her father's, had proven to be very feminine and requested a frilly dress to wear for this party. Her sister Zuunenwalt wore snug-fitting, dark green trousers and a brown leather jerkin that set off her dark, reddish brown hair and brown eyes.

Andrion squeezed her around the waist and murmured in her ear, "Would you look at Sneyagflug?" The tall red-headed man was leaning up against a post on the far side of the building, deep in conversation with a young woman who seemed taken by his striking looks and forceful personality. From the way she was looking at him, the fact that he was a large red dragon in his everyday life was not going to be a barrier to their blossoming relationship.

"The dog," Bernadette murmured back. She felt the tiniest twinge of jealousy. Though she had never truly loved Sneyagflug in the way that she loved Erik and Andrion, some part of her had felt flattered by his desire for her and his refusal to abandon hope that she would someday be his and his alone. Now that she had the power to keep her beloved husbands as young as she was indefinitely, he must have decided it was time to expand his horizons. She and their daughters were the only female dragons in Agena, but there were plenty of human women he could hook up with.

Elderly but still hale, Eorl Ormund came up to Ehrgeizig on the arm of Miralis, his nachtalfar body servant. "I've been wanting to shake your hand, sir," he said, and did so. "What's this I hear about Eberburg?" He was a tall man, but found he had to crane his neck far up to look the transformed dragon in the eyes.

"Yes," Ehrgeizig said with an urbane smile. His efforts to rule dragonkind had failed, but now he had a whole new species (and one both more cooperative and more numerous) on which to exert his influence.

"You should have seen the faces on the Old Ones when I showed up at the front door of the monastery and announced that I was taking it over and resuming classes. None of them had seen me as a dragon in time out of mind, nor at all as a human – I had to take them all out into the courtyard in order to prove my identity! Then, of course, they had to listen to me. I *am* the ancient founder of their order, after all."

"So you will be accepting new students, ones who want to learn the dragon spells?" Ormund asked. "Yes," the tall man replied. "Any who wish to learn are welcome to apply, though of course space is limited. I have promised Warden Bernadette that six places at the school will be for her children. They will stay for a while, learning what I have to teach, then move on to make way for another six. Within six years I should have trained them all, and those places will then be available for others. It takes much less time to teach dragons, of course…"

In the warm pool, Fjuri and Riki sat soaking and chatting with Sintra, Julia, and Giscard Caron, the elder son of the Maiden's innkeeper and his wife. For this party the Maiden's "clothing optional" policy had been revoked, and they were wearing underwear. Both of the young men were relieved about this, as bathing nude with three attractive young women might have been embarrassing.

"I saw Alfmund the other day," Riki remarked casually. Fjuri, who had his arm around her, glanced down at her questioningly. "He was having lunch at the Flying Horseman with one of his fellow Brave Company members, that young woman who always dresses in fur armor, and they were sitting *very* close together!"

She rolled her eyes, as Sintra and Julia squealed in unison, "OOOoooh!" Fjuri gave her a squeeze. He and the young Norseman had come to an understanding, and part of that understanding was that he, Fjuri, was not going to look favorably on any more attempts on Alfmund's part to court *his* girl. It was a relief to hear he had moved on.

Mondi and Sigi, stuffed with party food, had stepped away from the noisy crowds and were hanging around on the Maiden's broad front porch, gazing idly out at Stormstrife Farm across the road and having a belching contest. "You know," Sigi said, after a particularly satisfying eructation, "Papa Erik told me once that we nearly had that farm there instead of Drakespring Farm. He and Papa Andrion were going to try to buy it, because they were all living here and it was so close."

"I like Drakespring Farm better," Mondi said with chauvinistic pride. "Being right across from the Maiden would be noisy."

"You're probably right," Sigi replied. After a moment's thought he added, "I'm sure glad you can live there with us now."

"Me too," Mondi grinned. Though he still returned to his dragon form almost daily just for the pleasure of flying, he felt that he had "come home" to being human. Almost as if he were a fireblood human with the power of dragon transformation instead of a dragon who could become human.

"You know, Sigi," Mondi said to his brother after another minute's thought, "I sure wish you were fireblood so you could go dragon and come flying with us." The nursery at Drakespring Farm was now packed with beds for the transformed children, as was the space in the basement where lately the aptrgangr troops had stayed. Things were livelier at home than they had been in years, and would stay that way until all the dragon kids had learned the skills of humanity.

Sigi sighed. "Yeah, I wish I were too. Andi found out he was fireblood when he was just a little kid, and Mom says that it's only the firstborn child of a fireblood that gets the dragon blood."

"But firebloods used to be a lot more common back before the Uprising," Mondi pointed out. "Father told me that all of the higher members of the dragon priesthood were fireblood. It stands to reason it wasn't just one child in every fireblood's lineage, or there wouldn't have been so many."

Sigi shrugged. He had Erik's outlook on life, a tendency to cheerfully accept whatever it offered and find joy in any situation he happened to be in. "Have you ever tried to perform a dragon spell?" Mondi asked him. Sigi grew thoughtful.

"No, can't say as I have. I haven't really ever been around anybody spelling until recently, and I'm too big now to do it for play."

"And you never came into contact with any spell stones?" Mondi asked. Sigi grinned.

Fire Scion II: The Flying Dead

"Andi told me that after he got into Mama's stash when he was little, she hid them away. So far as I know, I've never even *seen* a spell stone. What do they look like?"

Mondi looked around. They were alone on the porch, and nobody was around on this side of the building. He stepped out into the road and spelled away his clothing, then became a twenty-two-foot red dragon. Sigi watched with interest as he went through a series of convulsions like a cat coughing up a hairball, depositing a tiny, glittering blue gem on the ground.

Moments later, Mondi was back in human form and clothed once again. He scooped the rapidly-cooling gem up off the dusty stones of the road, polishing it on his sleeve. Then he returned to the porch, grinning hopefully, and solemnly handed it over to his brother. Eyes wide, Sigi held out his right hand. As the stone touched his palm, it melted into his skin!

Eyes as big as saucers, with a grin that seemed about to split his face in two, he looked at his brother – who was wearing the same expression. "That's... I *know* that spell!" he said, astonished. Absorbing the stone had somehow made him aware of a spell he had heard but never realized he had learned.

Mondi nodded sagely. "Go ahead," he urged.

Smiling, Sigi cried "Kraf-Luft-Struung-Wund!" and blew him off the porch.

The End (for now)

Fire Scion II: The Flying Dead

"Andi told me that after he got into Mama's stash when he was little, she hid them away. So far as I know, I've never even *seen* a spell stone. What do they look like?"

Mondi looked around. They were alone on the porch, and nobody was around on this side of the building. He stepped out into the road and spelled away his clothing, then became a twenty-two-foot red dragon. Sigi watched with interest as he went through a series of convulsions like a cat coughing up a hairball, depositing a tiny, glittering blue gem on the ground.

Moments later, Mondi was back in human form and clothed once again. He scooped the rapidly-cooling gem up off the dusty stones of the road, polishing it on his sleeve. Then he returned to the porch, grinning hopefully, and solemnly handed it over to his brother. Eyes wide, Sigi held out his right hand. As the stone touched his palm, it melted into his skin!

Eyes as big as saucers, with a grin that seemed about to split his face in two, he looked at his brother – who was wearing the same expression. "That's... I *know* that spell!" he said, astonished. Absorbing the stone had somehow made him aware of a spell he had heard but never realized he had learned.

Mondi nodded sagely. "Go ahead," he urged.

Smiling, Sigi cried "Kraf-Luft-Struung-Wund!" and blew him off the porch.

The End (for now)

"Andi told me that after he got into Mama's stash when he was little, she hid them away. So far as I know, I've never even *seen* a spell stone. What do they look like?"

Mondi looked around. They were alone on the porch, and nobody was around on this side of the building. He stepped out into the road and spelled away his clothing, then became a twenty-two-foot red dragon. Sigi watched with interest as he went through a series of convulsions like a cat coughing up a hairball, depositing a tiny, glittering blue gem on the ground.

Moments later, Mondi was back in human form and clothed once again. He scooped the rapidly-cooling gem up off the dusty stones of the road, polishing it on his sleeve. Then he returned to the porch, grinning hopefully, and solemnly handed it over to his brother. Eyes wide, Sigi held out his right hand. As the stone touched his palm, it melted into his skin!

Eyes as big as saucers, with a grin that seemed about to split his face in two, he looked at his brother – who was wearing the same expression. "That's... I *know* that spell!" he said, astonished. Absorbing the stone had somehow made him aware of a spell he had heard but never realized he had learned.

Mondi nodded sagely. "Go ahead," he urged.

Smiling, Sigi cried "Kraf-Luft-Struung-Wund!" and blew him off the porch.

The End (for now)

www.ingramcontent.com/pod-product-compliance
Lightning Source LLC
Chambersburg PA
CBHW071249170626
46809CB00001B/142

* 9 7 8 0 8 9 6 2 0 0 2 8 9 *